PRAISE FOR CHRISTINE STARK

"...These brilliantly written pieces stimulated the board into a lively discussion of language, point of view, and politics, and resulted in a resounding 'yes' from everyone on the importance of using these two pieces together, as point-counterpoint on the themes of violence against women and the nuanced and challenging process of surviving that violence."

—Minnie Bruce Pratt
Creative Writing Editor for the *Feminist Studies Editorial Board*

"The judging panel believes Christine Stark's work is both art and metaphor. She creates story and mood using a stream of consciousness style. The writing is rhythmic, and lyrical with conscious and authoritative use of various techniques such as repetition. In Christine's story, the perpetrator behaves as if his act, an assault, is one of mundane evil. This story alludes to the reality of society's marginalized—vulnerable to everyday evils—mundane for some, not so for others. The panel applauds Christine's writing talents, her willingness to take a risk by composing a raw, provocative piece designed to invite us to consider the nature of mundane evil from several unexpected points of view."

—Sandra Lloyd, *The Pearls Writing Group*

"Take a dark journey with Christine Stark, deep into the dungeon that is incest. Follow crazy girl as she fights for her dignity and sense of self-worth. Then cheer when she finally finds the strength to say: 'I know my name now and you do not frighten me.'"

—Julian Sher, author of *Somebody's Daughter: The Hidden Story of America's Prostituted Children and the Battle to Save Them*

"In *Nickels*, Christine Stark powerfully portrays the story of abuse and its impact on our lives. This beautifully written and compelling story leaves you wanting more. It's riveting; a book that will capture you from the beginning and carry you through the end. Everyone should read this book."

—Olga Trujillo, author of *The Sum of My Parts*

"To be taken into the mind of a child can be an enchanting adventure, but to be taken into the mind of a child who is abused, confused, and taken for granted is a lingering, livid journey. Stark's poised yet cerebral writing style stays with you long after you have delved into the first chapter and regrettably finished the last. She has vividly exposed a world that unfortunately exists for many. I applaud her fortitude to bring an olden—too long ignored—truth out of the darkness with blazing, innovative light."

— MariJo Moore, author of *The Diamond Doorknob*

"Christine Stark has crafted a language and a diction commensurate with the shredding of consciousness that is a consequence of childhood sexual abuse. She brings us a wholly original voice in a riveting novel of desperation and love. *Nickels* is narrated by Miss So And So, as her mother names her, from the ages of 4 to 26, a character so compelling I never wanted to stop hearing from her. She names herself crazy girl, but the reader sees a different truth: there's humor and cunning and ferocious love alive in those who survive. Stark enables the reader to inhabit the intricacy and chaos of this potent inner landscape, and we have not seen this before. Every sentence vibrates with a terrible beauty. Every sentence brings the news."

—Patricia Weaver Francisco,
author of *Telling: A Memoir of Rape and Recovery*

"Stark has done something in *Nickels* that deserves our attention. She has not only remembered, but she has resisted the impulse to editorialize. Instead, she has given us the pure voice of the survivor, and in doing that, she compels her readers to experience the worldfragmented, distorted, with fragile islands of comfort and familiaritythrough the eyes and limited context of the child. And then she enables us to grow up along with that survivor, collecting and integrating the fragments of self along with her protagonist. Thank you, Ms. Stark, for what must have been a descent into some kind of personal hell to recover this fictional Eurydice , this survivor with no name, whom you have led back up into the light of publicationan indictment and a torchbearer."

—Carolyn Gage, author of
The Second Coming of Joan of Arc and Selected Plays

"Christine Stark's novel *Nickels: A Tale of Dissociation* is, in a word, stunning. It's a tough read on many levels, not for the squeamish or lazy reader. But for the reader who is willing to work a bit, reading the novel is an amazing experience. ...It is a singular book that merits every reader it can get, not only because of the subject of the book worthwhile in itself but because of Stark's artistry in writing it. When readers put the finished book down, they'll never look at nickels again in quite the same way."

—Michael Northen, Editor-in-Chief,
Wordgathering: A Journal of Disability Poetry

"Stark's writing achieves something altogether new. It allows us a glimpse into the perceptive, multidimensional, and startlingly rich dissociative mind, in which the past can suddenly seem more real than the present and even the smallest detail can trigger overpowering memories, so that the impossibly hopeful conclusion feels all the more earned and satisfying."

—Katie Hae Leo, playwright of *Four Destinies*

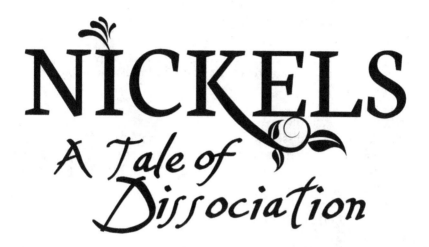

NICKELS
A Tale of
Dissociation

by **Christine Stark**

with an Introduction by Anya Achtenberg

Reflections of America Series

Modern History Press

Cover artwork "River of Life" by Jane Evershed. Used with permission.
Cover layout by D.E. West, Book Image Designs
2nd Printing: November 2011

Library of Congress Cataloging-in-Publication Data

Stark, Christine, 1968-
  Nickels : a tale of dissociation / by Christine Stark.
    p. cm. -- (Reflections of America series)
  ISBN 978-1-61599-050-4 (pbk. : alk. paper) -- ISBN 978-1-61599-085-
6 (hardcover : alk. paper)
    1. Multiple personality--Patients--Fiction. I. Title.
  PS3619.T3734N53 2011
  813'.6--dc22
                                                    2011012559

Published by
Modern History Press
5145 Pontiac Trail
Ann Arbor, MI 48105

Tollfree USA/CAN: 888-761-6268

www.ModernHistoryPress.com
info@ModernHistoryPress.com

Distributed by Ingram Book Group (USA/CAN), Bertram's Books (UK),
Hachette Livre (FR).

Visit the author at www.ChristineStark.com

Modern History Press is an imprint of Loving Healing Press

For Millie and Virginia, my grandmothers, who loved despite it all

"I'm just saying the truth. Like oatmeal."
—Tim O'Brien

"We do not know our own souls, let alone the souls of others."
—Virginia Woolf

"Dissociation splits affect and cognition, observer and experiencer, mind and body, self and self into parts, leading to fantastic permeatations and schisms in ownership/disownership, knowing/not knowing, responsibility/irresponsibility…"
—Harvey L. Schwartz

Contents

Acknowledgments

First and foremost I want to thank Anya Achtenberg for her support, brilliance, and encouragement. I'd also like to thank Victor Volkman and the rest at Modern History Press for taking on *Nickels*, and for Victor's supreme patience in dealing with my editing process. I would be remiss if I did not thank the McKnight Awards through Five Wings Arts Council for a grant to help me complete *Nickels*.

Others I'd like to thank for their support and friendship include Melinda Masi, Alison Bergblom Johnson, Trish Campbell, Cyndi Carlson, Sherri Dougherty, Johanna Morrigan, Fred Amram, Sherry Quan Lee, Eileen Hudon, Deb Blake , Skip and Babette Sandman, Karissa Stotts, Rene Simon, Donna Wegscheid, the women at *Rain and Thunder*, Fred Ho, and the Minnesota State University at Mankato English Department. I'd like to honor the support I received from Andrea Dworkin, who told me when I was twenty-two that I was a terrific writer and gave me hope my life could be something different. And lastly, a heartfelt thanks to April Posner for the love, laughter, and home we share.

Excerpts of *Nickels* first appeared in:

Dust & Fire, Rain and Thunder, Trivia: Voices of Feminism, WHLR, Feminist Studies, Kaleidoscope, The Sylvan Echo, Blue Earth Review, The Hiss Quarterly, Said It, On the Outskirts: Poems on Disability, Red Weather Literary Magazine, Primavera, Ramblings, Poetry Motel, ache, Pearls

Awards for excerpts of *Nickels*:

- Recipient of McKnight Award through Five Wings Arts Council to finish *Nickels*, June, 2008
- Second Prize for 2007 Soul-Making Literary Contest for Novel Excerpt, National League of American Pen Women, Nob Hill, 2007
- Winner of Jonis Agee Award in Fiction, *Dust & Fire*, 2007, 2004, and 2003
- First Prize for 2006 Soul-Making Literary Contest for Flash Fiction, National League of American Pen Women, Nob Hill, 2006
- Pearls Short Fiction Contest, First place, Summer 2006
- Inglis House Poetry Contest, Second place, Summer 2006
- Placed third (prose poem) Soul-Making Literary Competition, National League of American Pen Women, Nob Hill, 2003

Introduction

This is not just a great book; it is something of a miracle.

So, why an introduction? Shouldn't a great book speak for itself? Yes, and it does. But it speaks a language somewhat different from mainstream English.

So then is this "different" language an aesthetic choice? In part, I think, yes, but the real choice precedes the crafting of the work. The author, who is indeed very well trained in mainstream English, has chosen to write *Nickels* in its true language, in the language that her early and continuing severe trauma from extreme sexual and physical violence has created. This is a language that cracks open the world to allow people to see the truth. This is a language that takes as its task a highly pressurized work upon itself, the work of cracking open language that seals in the world at times, making it impermeable to truth. Stark's language is in a sense less mediated, yet fully developed in its art.

Does this sound mysterious, to read something in a new language?

Don't worry. The book itself, the reading itself, will teach you. And it begins with a language all of us who were children first spoke; it gives voice to a child's voice and a child's world, so we are beckoned in with recognition and tenderness.

The other somewhat disturbing fact, but in a sense a relief to admit, is that many of us, so many of us for so many reasons, speak the language of trauma and dissociation. We are, in a cruel sense, native speakers; in a necessary and loving sense, a community.

We know from depictions of trauma in literature, and we understand from experience, that some situations stretch time, kick us out of our bodies. Ambrose Bierce, in "An Occurrence at Owl Creek Bridge," gave us Confederate gentleman and saboteur Peyton Farquhar, who in the moment between falling through the bridge, and the Union noose breaking his neck, lived, with superhuman strength and magical sensory abilities, a lifetime of escape and return to his beloved, to die then in her arms; but in "normal" reality, he died alone under the bridge, hanged.

We know from car accidents the stretching of time, the adrenalin that slows it all down so we react or we watch, through each degree of the 360 as the car rolls over and our lives turn around us.

But the language of trauma here in *Nickels* is not the language of a moment, a single event we relive and tell about, perhaps a bit compulsively, until it loses its powerful flare up of terror. This is the language of continuing and repeated trauma, and it cracks open the world to reveal something we must know, the grit that makes the pearl, the truth of the world that challenges hypocrisy. I am one of those who believe that what we do not face, kills us. What we do not admit of the ugliness of the world, takes us down, and deforms that beauty that most assuredly dances around the earth. But like Farquhar, as he is being hung, the narrator of this story indeed watches, using her "waiting eyes" to "store it in [her] brain", and I suggest that it is this ability, these eyes, which have led to the gifted vision we see the character develop later in the book as a visual artist.

There are other books, and there will be many more, that treat the subject of the terrible violences against children which make the backdrop of our daily lives; which say that no matter how lovely it may look on one street, we have work to do.

But this book?

This is the motherboard; this, the hidden circuitry we dress up to attempt to tell a story and be understood. There are other books, fine books, which are indicators; they point to the hidden circuitry. They point to this book.

This is enough reason to read this beautiful and brutal work. But there is more.

This book reopens the world of childhood. Beauty is here. Unbearable innocence. Hope is here. Maneuvering around ogres. The sheer terror of childhood, here.

In this land between breakfast and nightmare, with its "imaginary" companions, and a cast of characters only the child could name—oatmeal lady, suit man, spider leg lady, mad dad—stories unfold of how Little Miss So And So maneuvers through and survives, how crazy girl encounters her first friend, and how she finds ways to see beauty, experience it, and create it. These are stories I would not miss.

Need more reasons to read this book? Stark brings us back to the transformative blossoming of first love, the love of our narrator for another young girl. She also writes of the girl athlete crazy girl, in a magical way I have never before seen. "I am pure speed," Stark's narrator says as she makes a moment-by-moment opening into the basketball game, into this saving power within this girl, who does, "float like a butterfly; sting like a bee." It is perhaps that slowing and stretching of time, that floating away from the body in that limitless time that stretches before the neck of the moment is broken, that brings this young woman also to have an artist's eye and gift, which Stark describes hypnotically as the character is compelled into making art.

And Stark accomplishes something in *Nickels* which presents a great and often opaque challenge to writers struggling with using a narrative voice that must show development over many years in stories beginning with childhood.

This exile from straight[forward] time is somehow an expert in it, not only showing a different kind of time or showing time in a new way, but also quite capably showing the shifts in "actual" time, informing the reader of these shifts through subtleties in the development of the narrative voice. She crafts or discovers the very distinct voices of her narrator over time, over the span of the narrator's telling; at the same time there is a necessary blurring as one moment comes back to be present in another, both crucial tasks for this narrator.

It is perhaps Stark's defeat of straight time, along with the powerful bringing forward of symbols, which eventually brings this story from the dramatic realm into the mythical, as well. Her arrival at the merging of the character's experience into the mythical realm, into her understanding of the beginning of the world with its ancient taboos and the horrific consequences of their violation, is stunning. The section including the story, "The Girl Who Dragged Her Entrails Through Life Behind Her on The Ground," is prominent among the many sections of this book which must turn up anthologized.

Crazy girl lives tethered to the extreme pole of injustice, being made the last, the one who most knows the edge of the world, whose knowledge is central, and most repressed. Her knowledge remains something that society works most energetically to make invisible, to keep hidden behind the opaque social wall.

So, we need this book. It brings forth in the reader such a powerful wave of love and tenderness, such a deep desire to care for the children, the daughters, unable to be argued with. This is a great work to do in the world.

Stark says, "the body remembers the emotions recall what the mind cannot hold the mind is a sieve the mind is an imperfect entity alone however in cooperation with the body and the emotions operating with a perfect genius." I have come to think that Stark operates in this book with a perfect genius that makes the impossible in expression, possible; the unknowable in experience, knowable.

So, prepare yourself, although, really, you cannot, for a tidal wave of brilliance, an arrival at a language both intimate and mythical for what we call the "unspeakable", and for irreplaceable gifts that make their way forward, convincing me that anything I want to save, can be saved; anything I want to make as beauty with its inextricable link to truth, can be created.

Anya Achtenberg
Minneapolis, 2011

Age 4 (Prologue)

Trip trap

> *trip trap went the bridge Who's that roared the troll who lived under the bridge his eyes as big as saucers and nose as long as a poker It's me said baby billy goat gruff Well I'm going to gobble you up as a midmorning snack Oh no wait for the next billy goat gruff he's much bigger*

> *trip trap trip trap went the bridge Who's that roared the troll licking his lips It's me said the second billy goat gruff who hadn't such a small voice I'm going to gobble you up for lunch roared the troll Oh no the second billy goat gruff said wait for the biggest billy goat gruff of us all!*

> *trip trap trip trap went the bridge Who's that roared the troll It is I the biggest billy goat gruff Well then I am going to gobble you up the troll said Well come along I've got two spears and I'll poke your eyeballs out at your ears I've got besides two curling stones and I'll crush you to bits body and bones and so he did and so he did*

> *snip snap snout this tale's told out*

> *If you sit still and be quiet when your dad gets home I'll read you one more story* mom says I say nothing stare at mom's hand a shiny ring on the green three billy goat gruff book *Okay* she says I nod nod nod *Okay* she says I nod nod nod touch the book it is shiny

> *Once upon a time there were five Chinese brothers and they all looked exactly alike the first Chinese brother could swallow the sea the second Chinese brother had an iron neck the third Chinese brother could stretch and stretch his legs the fourth Chinese brother could not be burned the fifth Chinese brother could hold his breath indefinitely*

> *Swallow the sea!* my eyes big as saucers *swallow the sea!*

> *See how slanty their eyes are* mom points at the drawing *slanty sneaky little eyes*

> *The first Chinese brother fished everyday and whatever the weather he would come back to the village with a rare fish one day a little boy stopped him and asked to go fishing he begged and begged until the first Chinese brother consented but only if the boy obeyed him promptly Yes yes the little*

boy promised the next morning they went fishing the first Chinese brother swallowed the sea

He swallowed the sea! I think inside my head but say nothing mom's shiny ring

All the fish were left high and dry at the bottom of the sea the little boy was delighted he ran here and there stuffing his pockets with strange pebbles Strange pebbles! I think *extraordinary shells* Shells! I think *and fantastic algae* Algae! I think but don't know what it is *The first Chinese brother gathered some fish while he kept holding the sea in his mouth presently he grew tired it is very hard to hold the sea he told the little boy to come back but he paid no attention the first Chinese brother felt the sea swelling inside him the first Chinese brother held the sea until he thought he was going to burst all of a sudden the sea forced its way out of his mouth went back to its bed and the little boy disappeared*

The little boy disappeared! I think the little boy disappeared! *Why!* I say *He drowned* mom says

Clomp clomp tromp tromp *Oh! Your father is home* mom says closes the book the tips of her fingers still inside *be quiet be still* clomp clomp tromp tromp *He killed that boy he is a bad man* I say *a bad man! Shh* mom says her hand on my mouth clomp clomp tromp tromp dad walks up the stairs

Age Five (1973)

School

nurse touches my back got crooked like a old lady is how I look the school nurse asks if I'm okay with her finger it crawls up my spine like a spider is how it feels

bend over so I do hands together so I do the school lady checks my back every Friday before lunch when the other kids do art shirt off the spider crawls up my back follows my spine until it reaches my head knock knock

my back's getting worse because my head's too heavy from thinking the school lady says *Why is your back getting worse you're too young* I don't tell her about my heavy head from the thinking

school nurse says: are you okay
I say: yes

now I look just like a old lady crooked and bent I get a cane and hobble to school with it not really but I could from being so crooked other kids make art a spider crawls up my back my back is a s stands for snake ssssnake like the big one in my bed crawls up lives where my spine used to be

school nurse calls me in special on a Monday to talk with a school man the school man and the school nurse say take your shirt off so I do hands together so I do the school nurse says *See one two three* she counts up my back with her spider leg fingers until she gets to a spot then her spider leg crawls over my rib under my arm

Where did you get this the school nurse says with her spider leg finger on the new spot I shrug my shoulders to tell her I don't know but my hands are pressed together it's hard to move *Do you have any more* the school man says I stand up straight like a arrow pull my pants down

the school nurse and the school man say *Oh* so I pull my pants up they call in my mom and another school lady and a policeman who takes pictures of my crooked back with my pants down my mom says she doesn't know anything maybe it was the babysitter they ask me I shrug my shoulders bent over like a old lady from thinking too much

> *Knock knock*
> *Who's there*
> *The head board*
> *Whose head board*

    the policeman and the new school lady take me into custody until matters are resolved I don't know what matters are and when I ask the school nurse what does matters are resolved mean she says *Oh you are just like a little parrot* I don't ask no more questions I wonder if the school nurse is going to walk up my crooked back anymore with her spider leg fingers

    I sleep in a new house with some people I don't know I eat oatmeal in the morning the policeman and the new school lady bring me in for questioning ask about the crooked back the s snake the spots on my butt I shrug my shoulders that's all shrug shoulders bend over one two three they find the spots on my back and my butt

    I get released for a lack of evidence back to my house I go I eat at my house and sleep at my house and go to school every morning the school nurse walks up my back the other kids do art Christmas comes and goes and I forget about how I ate oatmeal at some other house I did not know the name of

    What does lack of evidence mean I say to mom she grabs my arm and says *Stop repeating grown up words no one likes a smarty pants five year old*

    one day the school nurse crawls up my back with her spider legs while the other kids make Valentine hearts knock knock she taps on my head *Do you get headaches No* is what I say but her spider legs keep crawling to the top *What's this* the school nurse feels a spot on the top of my head bumped up like a little rock she pulls apart my hair with her busy fingers finds a spot like the ones under my pants *Good lord did someone hit you* is what she says I shrug two more school ladies come in one says *We can't keep ignoring this*

    a meeting is scheduled between me mom and the school ladies but not dad the school nurse has to check me everyday for spots which is what she said to mom one more spot and I go into custody again I worry about more spots showing up where the school nurse can find them my head gets so heavy from all the thinking one more custody means I go to oatmeal's again lack of evidence means I'm bad all the thinking my head's so heavy might break my back

> *Crack the back the headboard spat*

    me mom the school ladies talk in a official meeting about well being the school nurse with the spider fingers says we have concerns about the bruises on the back head rear how is this so mom says *I don't know* shrugs her shoulders *she's always been a clumsy girl* the school ladies look at each other one says *Missus So And So your daughter's back is degenerating alarming rate* when we leave the ladies say *We got nowhere with them* mom takes me for ice cream

an alarming degenerating rate is what my sssnake spine does no one knows it's from my heavy head thinking so many thoughts mom says nothing pretends like we never had a official meeting one two three the school nurse walks up my back looking for spots

school nurse says: are you okay
I say: shrug my shoulders

the next night snake crawls in bed with me to go up my back lay down so I do be quiet so I do hands over your stomach so I do the snake goes inside me up my back I lay with my hands together in a coffin dead the snake breathes hard one two three until my head cracks on the headboard the snake pushes my head into the headboard my board head cracked

Knock knock
Who's there
The head board
What head board

I get up go to school the school nurse checks me for spots takes me into custody for breaking the rules no more mom and dad I eat oatmeal with the people I don't know the school ladies run tests it's proven the headboard cracked my back

I still don't sleep at night I am a pile of rocks from the river waiting on my bed broken the snake will be back to crawl through the cracks

The trial

is set for the middle of November after Halloween so mom can't dress me in a mask no candy this year the oatmeal lady says stay inside play games eat fresh caramel apples baked in the oven all drippy

nothing is what I say I liked mom to dress me in a mask send me outside to get sweet tarts in the dark *No more of that young lady it's dangerous to be outside needles n poison n sugar rots your teeth* nuh huh is what I think but I don't say anything to the oatmeal lady the sugar makes the bad taste go out of my mouth and I save the masks keep them under my bed tucked in tight with the dust so snake man can't see my face if he can't see my face he can't kill me mom's mask helps me live I don't explain that or nothing else to oatmeal lady

the trial is set the date is in stone I can't move it the kids in school think I'm creepy to be on trial the school lady crawls up my back she is sick the day we make Halloween masks I make my own red n black bat mask I tie it on with string wear it everywhere no one can see me we all get deposed me the school lady the school man and oatmeal the suit man says I have to say yes or no can't shrug shoulders he says *Do you understand* looking me in the face I say yes behind my red n black bat mask

suit man says: yes what
I say: yes your honor

the trial approaches wind blowing my hair I see a child psychologist who points her fingers at me *Do you love your mother Yes Do you love your father* look at shoes *Little Miss So And So show me on the doll where the touching occurred* point one two three slide creepy crawly fingers to the spot stick it in the child psychologist blinks behind her big glasses says she will be at the trial to help cope I look at her blank n case she tries to creepy crawly her way in through the eye holes

The child is non responsive she says the next visit behind a closed door non responsive is what she says because she can't get in behind my red n black bat mask my head gets heavier than a boulder thinking about the trial is all I do

one day the trial comes creepy crawly spider up my back bone to visit me *Hello trial* I say to it n eat my oatmeal n get ready to go to the courthouse with oatmeal lady oatmeal colored hair lady dresses me up in new clothes a dancy girl with ribbons I pull out

oatmeal lady says: leave in hair
I say: rip them out throw them down

Oh oatmeal lady says I step on the ribbons under my shoe no more pretty ribbons for the honor to judge I decide not to like oatmeal lady set my mask on so tight my nose can't barely breathe through the holes makes a whish whish breathing sound

> *Whish whish*
> *Who did it*
> *The head board did it*

judge so and so presiding bam bam bam get down on your knees to pray all rise all sit I'm in the front row keep my skirt tucked tight so judge honorable won't see down it

judge says: young lady what is your name
I say: my name is Little Miss So And So

Repeat that for the court I sit stare is what I do to make people think retard the judge says *Contempt* n suit man runs over says *So And So say your full name* so I do *My name is Little Miss So And So* mom says nothing sitting in her chair in the audience

the lady who points her fingers is next to her like they are friends I am a bad girl so I won't talk no more be quiet like dad says I shake my head yes no the judge permisses it suit man is happy pulls me off the stand takes me out for ice cream then back to oatmeal get sleep don't be tired for second day testing

get up eat oatmeal go to court with oatmeal lady second day questions sit on the stand look at mom shrug shoulders can't shrug your shoulders have to nod yes no or say it yes no yes no the head board the suit man from dad's side asks questions I sit stare retard adjourn court back at three

the suit man buys Burger King onion rings hamburger Pepsi tells me to talk on the stand it's okay nod yes no yes no suit man drinks his pop says *You have to talk* I nod

suit man me oatmeal lady drive back to court sit in room until it's time to take the stand mom is in the audience with her friend the child psychologist the suit men ask questions I nod yes no yes no squeeze the black pebble I found on oatmeal's step keeps me from floating away mom cross her legs the creepy crawly school lady is in the audience next to the school man everyone listens to how bad I am

bad girl bad girl bam bam bam the honorable judge adjourns to tomorrow morning nine a m sharp

suit man says: tomorrow is important. I'm going to ask if your dad hurt you remember what to do
I say: nod yes
suit man says: you can tell the truth your dad can't hurt you anymore
I say: nothing

nine a m comes to me in the night sharp as teeth smacked is what I get if my teeth touch dad's snake nine a m sharp as teeth in the night hit upside the head dad says if you tell I'll kill your mother I nod yes no yes no shrug shoulders squeeze pebble look at mom in the audience keep her alive

oatmeal lady pulls me out of bed feeds me oatmeal to be strong with oatmeal makes a muscle on her arm

she says: strong
I say: swallow
she says: what did your dad do you can tell me the truth
I say: stare at oatmeal cold lumpy bumpy tan oatmeal
she says: you have to tell the truth
I say: stare at oatmeal the color of carpet

ride car to court sit on top swing lasso *Be strong* oatmeal says smiles I'm a cowgirl swinging my rope not going to court I'm a cowgirl not going to court! not going to court! I catch people with my rope!

The day

has finally arrived suit man child psychologist spider leg lady say: The day! shiny and bright I ride through the streets on the car chasing people with my rope suit man child psychologist spider leg lady sit in a room with me waiting for the honorable judge and his sharp nine a m

suit man says: this is it
child psychologist says: grab onto my hand
I say: pull it away
spider leg lady says: we're going to do it Little Miss So And So
suit man says: I have a good feeling judge honorable will be on our side
spider leg lady says: then you can come back to our school
child psychologist says: and play with the other children
suit man says: fifteen minutes
child psychologist says: important you tell the truth Little Miss So And So
spider leg lady says: you are safe now

I pull my mask back tighter until the strings bleed skin n my eye lids
flatten out like a China girl's I creepy crawly off the chair under table on the
floor out door

suit man says: where are you going Little Miss So And So
I say: into a hole
suit man child psychologist spider leg lady say: come back here! we have a
lot invested in you!

invested I creepy crawly back wait for a m sharp to arrive in a black robe
down to its knees *It's time! it's time!* suit man excites around the room we
sit down in court honorable judge all rise all sit all pray child pointy finger
psychologist whispers to suit man suit man turns slams fist down runs to the
honorable judge's table points and jumps in the air one two three times
bam bam bam *sit down* judge says suit man sits mad dad is at the table
next to me suit man stands up sits down yells *my client cannot testify
intimidation judge honorable* bam bam *One more outburst and this court
will be contempt* says honorable judge honorable
my knees scrunch together suit man meets with pointy finger lady talks
to honorable judge his sleeves crossed over his chest bam bam bam I sit on
the stand stare at my shoes fancy dancy shoes squeeze the pebble in my
pocket *Little Miss So And So* dad sits at the table hands together *Little Miss
So And So!* I say nothing shrug shoulders suit man says *Show the court on
the doll* gives me a doll I drop it look at dad out of the tops of my eyes he
looks mad mom sits in the audience saying nothing I sit on the stand saying
nothing *Show me on the doll where you were hurt who hurt you* no answer
just stare at shoes watch mad dad through my mask eye holes Who Hurt
You stare Who Hurt You Little Miss So And So I stare and stare digging a
hole a deep a far away Little Miss So And So! I stare Please Tell The Court
Who Hurt You *The head board* is what I say *the head board did it* judge
honor bams session over case dismissed the girl must be crazy
                              *   *   *

The ceiling
has goose bumps rock a bye baby rock a bye baby the ceiling has more
goose bumps on it than the skin of a chicken without feathers stretched on

the counter stretched like a mouth when fingers pull it open stretched on the counter skin peeled off the meat n bones mom doesn't like the fat of the skin the bumpy bumpy skin

crazy girl! crazy girl! the headboard sung crazy girl the judge judged crazy girl the suit man shook his head the child psychologist looked out of her big glasses the oatmeal lady left crazy girl in court the spider leg lady won't go up her back no more creepy crawly crazy girl all alone

crazy girl rides home in a car that's me crazy girl rock a bye baby rock a bye baby *That's what you get* mom says *your dad's mad he went out to cool down Whoo! whoo!* steam whistle shooting through my brain cool down dad's mad I don't get no ice cream mom says *Your dad said to have you in bed before he gets home*

the snake's back I don't get no supper no food no fried chicken meat or mashed potatoes or long skinny green beans for crazy girl straight to bed mom pulls down the shades it's still light out not time for bed mom leaves the door cracked

crack the back the headboard spat I don't get no supper not the skin stretched out on the counter bumpy n pink or the meat in the pan sizzling hot or the bone poking out white n round no supper for crazy girl everyone knows she's crazy

I sleep under the blanket listening for mad dad to come home slam the garage door like he always does like he always yells at mom *Is supper ready Big Fat Stupid Miss So And So is it what I want made the way I want Big Fat Stupid Miss So And So* I shut my eyes tight listen until my ears grow big as the room the biggest ears in the world listening for mad dad to come home slam bam the garage door yell at mom sneak his snake up the stairs to my room where I sleep waiting in my bed like a princess gone dead

my ears hear a creaking stair my ears are good the best ears in the world all alone crazy girl has the best ears in the world! creak creak creak someone is sneaking up the stairs I slit my eyes like a sneaky China Doll Girl slipping out her eyelids the door opens it's mom *Bad girl* she says from the door with her face pointed like a knife to take the bumpy skin off the chicken meat white bone bird in the pan *bad bad girl* mom says her hand gripping on the door knuckles white as the bone in the pan *don't ever let anyone find out again*

stupid crazy girl let someone find out! stupid crazy girl is going to burn in hell mom said so don't do it again stupid crazy girl or mom will kill you in your sleep with her bumpy knife to peel the bumpy bumpy skin like the the bumpy bumpy ceiling

the birds chirp outside it's still light out but crazy girl is in bed for being bad Chirp Chirp Peep Peep they sing and play and jump around while I wait I wait and wait and wait n my ears get heavy from waiting n so they need a rest n so they rest on the floor the biggest ears in all the world sit down on the floor in my room crazy crazy girl locked in her room mad dad is home! mad dad is home! my ears tell me mad dad is home slam bam slam the biggest ears in all the world hear it all Where Is She Is She In Her Bed What's This Why's The Skin Off You're So Fat You Should Skip The Whole Damn Meal bam bam bam my ears hear mad dad go downstairs to his bathroom Click goes the handle Flussssssshhhh goes the water Snap Snap Snap goes his pants Stomp Stomp Stomp go mad dad's feet up the stairs my ears disappear they heard enough mad dad kicks open the door swoooosh crack the door slams into the wall

I sleep sleep sleep n sleep more n mad dad's not here I can't hear a thing my body's dead gone buried sleep sleep sleep n more sleep n more sleep mad dad climbs into bed he gets on top of crazy girl the one without a body dead n gone I Told You Not To Tell Anyone mad dad puts his hands on my neck chicken neck buck buck bah buck I Told You Never To Tell Anyone Our Little Secret the snake swishes over me crazy girl dead body eyes closed sleeping sleeping sleeping Open Your Eyes my eyes don't open they can't I'm sleeping not here can't hear Open Your Eyes fingers choke snake swishes Open Open Open can't breathe can't breathe can't breathe

whish whish whish can't breathe can't breathe Open! Open! Open! can't breathe can't breathe the air sticks in my throat can't breathe can't breathe choke choke choke I open my eyes There That's Better Good Little Miss So And So mad dad lets go of my chicken neck

I can breathe! I can breathe!

mad dad snake swings over my legs settles on my knee a squishy snake on a pile of rocks my body is rocks dead rocks on a bed a head rock a neck rock a knee rock a foot rock a toe rock a arm rock head arm neck leg knee touch your toes bend over one two three creepy crawly spiders slithering snakes tongue licking mouth

Pah! Pah! Spit the head rock at the headboard
crazy girl's mouth got two tongues in it

Keep Your Eyes Open mad dad grabs my chicken neck again Keep Your Eyes Open I Want You To See Everything From Here On Out No More Pretending You're Asleep You Little Bitch Ever Tell Anyone Again I'll Kill You And Your Mother

Crazy girl! crazy girl! keep your eyes open!

mad dad sits up his snake poking out his pants unziiiiip! Kiss Em round things in my eyes nose face mad dad fingers stretch out my mouth streeetch round things in my mouth Kiss Em Kiss Em Kiss Em cant see cant breathe whish whish whish round things in my mouth

mad dad makes noises noises noises mother downstairs creaking around frying chicken meat hot sizzling smell round things in my mouth dog hairs on my lips noises noises noises chicken with no skin sizzling chicken no skin bumpy skin on the counter spread out flat fry it up crispy for dad's supper noises noises noises Good Girl petting my hair Good Girl This Is Our Secret Don't Ever Tell Anyone Again

Never tell again! never tell again! the headboard sung sang sung

snake on my neck mouth eye nose face chicken face chest face stomach face down there face the gooey jelly face going to die me going to die me

Don't talk baby talk! mom no like you talk baby talk!

ceiling. way up high above me all the ceiling bumpy n white I see it through the China girl slits in my bat mask bat mask bat mask come to save the day! bat mask! bat mask! mad dad's snake slithers through the rocks the down there face slither slither show me on the doll poke it in stretch it out with mad dad's fingers vaselined streeeetch the down there face is stretched open like a mouth slither slither for the snake slither. the ceiling!

there it is the ceiling bumpy white ceiling bumpy white ceiling bumpier than chicken skin frying in a pan the white knuckles spit spat grease on the floor the white knuckles clean it up before mad dad mad dad thump thump thump crazy girl's head hits the board

Knock knock
Who's there
The head board
Whose head board
Crazy girl's head board that's who

the ceiling is white n bumpy n I stare at it white bumpy ceiling sky over my head the rock head of the rock body lying on the bed with mad dad's snake slithering through it mad dad eats the chicken skin bumpy n fried flat when he's through with crazy girl n white knuckles creaks upstairs to clean up the grease spit in my face crazy girl's face the face down there

rock a bye baby rock a bye baby the ceiling has more goose bumps on it than the skin of a chicken without feathers stretched on the counter stretched like a mouth skin peeled off the meat n bones rock a bye baby

China Doll Girl

lives on the shelf in the corner one two three down the third white shelf from the top sing song ching chong me talk in China Doll Girl talk baby girl talk *Stop talking like that!* mom says locked in my room mad dad and mom eat downstairs fried chicken meat potato sweets stop talking like that! China Doll Girl baby girl baby China girl talk

me hungry want to eat food fried potato chicken stripped meat gobble gobble crazy girl China Doll Girl didn't eat since oatmeal's house choppy oatmeal in a bowl no sugar n rotten teeth oatmeal lady says sugar makes the teeth in your head fall out one two three plunk in the bowl it's not the sugar that makes the teeth fall out crazy oatmeal lady filling up the bowl

China Doll Girl got sent in the mail zoom from my aunt in another state who I haven't seen in a hundred years a hundred years since I seen my aunt! she sent China Doll Girl to me once upon a time from a land called China far far away my aunt sent it in the mail from a far away land with a book about five Chinese brothers zoom

China Doll Girl has red shiny pants n a green n white checker coat n little fingers holding a little basket n a straw hat on her head like a lampshade pulled out of oatmeal n rinsed off n stuck on her head China Doll Girl has squinty eyes like mother says squinty China girl eyes are so life like mom says those squinty squinty eyes

A hat! stuck on her head!
China Doll Girl has a pointy straw hat
n her head never gets cracked
spacked spat on because of that hat spat

You hungry crazy girl China Doll Girl yells across the room from on top of her shelf China Doll Girl jumps off the shelf onto my bed n whispers in my ear *me China Doll Girl me talk in your head now I sneak downstairs spy on parents for you oh kay?* I nod to the China Doll Girl sitting on my pillow *Okay* I say to the China Doll Girl who whispers in my ear *Parents very bad don't listen to very bad parents! very bad parents!* n she runs down the stairs to spy on very bad parents but not before I take a jelly bean out of my old Easter basket hid under my bed a red jelly bean n I put it in her basket perfect fit! it's a perfect fit! China Doll Girl runs off in her coat n hat carrying a red jelly bean to spy on very bad parents very bad! sitting on the couch watching TV

China Doll Girl sneaks down the stairs the creaky creaky stairs behind the couch quiet as a mouse she sneaks in her sneaky China Doll Girl way squinty squinty eyes China Doll Girl sneaks behind those very bad parents watching TV she looks over their shoulders n sees the TV n puts her basket down n sneaky China Doll Girl reaches out her sneaky little fingers to choke the very bad parents sitting on the couch

after sneaky China Doll Girl chokes those parents n they can't breathe she picks up her basket n runs to the kitchen n gets a ham hock from the refrigerator n puts it in her basket n brings it upstairs for crazy girl poor crazy girl stuck in her room with no food but a ham hock sneaky China Doll Girl stole for her

No food but a ham hock! no food but a ham hock!

China Doll Girl me say to China Doll Girl *did you see any mustard* n China Doll Girl says *No* n I say *Okay* n I eat the ham hock until it's down to the bone n I chew on the bone gnaw gnaw gnaw n China Doll Girl climbs back to the shelf n stands there like a doll except I know better China Doll Girl sneaky sneaky China Doll Girl who stole a ham hock for me (crazy girl)

Crazy girl! crazy girl!
sing song China Doll Girl talk in her head
crazy girl put the bone meat chewed off
white ham hock bone under her bed
crazy crazy girl collecting bones under her bed

The hole

under the bed gets deeper n deeper I (crazy girl) digs a hole for the bones the chewed off white ham hock bone n my dog's bones dead last year n mother's bones she leaves around the house dying in the kitchen of fat skin white knuckle bones on the door yelling at me

I dig n dig n dig some more I going to dig to China become a China girl I dig and dig some more n then I (crazy girl) take a break from digging n I glue the white bones along the sides of the hole like the gold fuzzy crown wallpaper mom glued to the hall I make some pictures out of bone n dirt n glue to make up for the art I didn't do when spider leg lady ran up my back the art teacher would like the bones lined up on the walls like the drawings the other kids do that get put in the glass cases outside the principal's office

mad dad says: you are nothing
I say: I make my own bone art in a hole under my bed

I pull off my arm bone n put it in the hole for safekeeping keep me alive then I dig some more with my one arm n a pointy sharp shovel mad dad bought at Fleet Farm n left in the garage standing crooked in the corner

Yoo hoo crazy girl China Doll Girl yells n then she jumps on the bed n then she jumps into the hole n then she sits on my shoulder China Doll Girl says *Crazy girl dig hole to China with sharp shovel* n she swings her legs n she whispers in my ear *crazy girl dig hole to China with sharp shovel* I keep digging n then China Doll Girl says *I want to go to homeland* so I say *No I don't want to dig to China* n she says *Why not* n I say *I need a hole to bury the bones in the ground where mad dad can't break them* China Doll Girl says *Ha* n then she thinks about it n then she says *okay crazy girl you dig a hole for your bones* n so I dig a hole under my bed in the dark where no one can see

I (crazy girl) digs I digs for a long time until *plink!* my pointy sharp shovel won't dig any more I sit down in the hole n look up n see China Doll Girl's pointy oatmeal hat sticking over the hole n her squinty eyes looking at me she says *Hi you crazy girl China Doll Girl go to sleep now* n she stands up n bumps her head on the board on the bottom of my bed *Ow* she says and crawls away

Plink! one armed crazy girl dug to the bottom and hit a rock
plunk! her friend China Doll Girl hit her head on the bed
plink plunk skink skunk crazy girl makes art under her bed

plink plunk pink punk crazy girl (me) hits a rock n sits down tired n sweaty n brushes the dirt off the rock bottom n finds a handle to a door carved in the rock crazy girl sets the shovel down pointy side first n pulls on the door handle round n slippery like the front door to mad dad's house I (crazy girl) yank on the door yank yank until it creaks open like a door on Halloween I swing it all the way open n set it in the dirt n clean my hands off on my pants I kneel down n see people singing round a table *Hey hey ho ho drink up it's time to go* n then a man stands up n says *Lads we have a visitor*

all the people look at me n it's hotter than when the winter heat blows out the vent n then the man comes up to my door n he has a pointy beard n a tail long as a monkey's *Hello* he says n toasts me with his cup I say *Hello* then he holds his cup up for me to drink I shake my head no n he says *Ssssshhhh* like a snake the devil man's face is right up against mine

devil man smiles n I see his horns pointy and sharp as the shovel from Fleet Farm n I see his teeth pointy and sharp as mad dad's n he grows a snout like my dead dog's n he laughs *Ha ha ha ha* like a cartoon so I slam the creaky Halloween door on his head crunch n I hear him say *Ouch* n *damn her* n so I pile the dirt on top of the door n I close the door slam it with the handle round n slippery the same handle on the front door to my house what's mad dad devil man doing in my dreams

I

(crazy girl) hear water run in a sink I blink at the bumpy chicken skin ceiling n I blink at my arms both there n I blink at China doll on my shelf her squinty eyes staring empty at the wall the water turns off the shadow from mom's feet moving under the door mom's hands in the hall closet sound like a rabbit thumping in a cage the closet door squeals shut I (crazy girl) let my rock body lie in the crusty sheets until I bury everything in my mind the hole beneath my bed. buried

then I (crazy girl) get up

I get out of bed pull my Holly Hobby bedspread over the crusty sheets n pile my stuffed animals over the pillow cover it all up make mom forget to do laundry one two three a floppy red dog a bear in a hat a pink pig with a blue ribbon stuck to its side a creepy crawly spider marches up my back knock knock it says

I stop n listen mom's in the kitchen n I listen some more but I only hear air with bacon sizzling in it mad dad is hiding from me (crazy girl) quiet as a mouse I need to know where he is so I can be somewhere else the bacon grizzles n I walk quiet across the carpet n pull up my shade n there's mad dad walking across the yard moving his lips the way he does talking to himself I spy on him from my window he walks to the tree n looks up it he walks to the sprinkler n picks up the hose n drags it across the yard a big snake the biggest snake in the world swishing in the grass he drops the sprinkler in the rocks under my window mad dad walks to the garbage cans n drags them up the driveway the metal scraping teeth grinding together loud noise wakes up half the neighborhood *Not everyone wants to get up at seven on a Saturday* is what mom says

Little Miss So And So time for breakfast mom yells from downstairs n I run to change my underwear crusty from badness change my clothes so mad dad can't see nothing more about me

> *Run Little Miss So And So*
> *crazy girl China Doll Girl run to the dresser*
> *put on jeans and a shirt and new underwear*
> *Run Little Miss So And So*
> *to the closet*
> *stuff your old underwear into the toe of a shoe*
> *so mom won't find them*
> *forget it bury it stash it hide it*
> *run little girl run outsmart your mad dad*

mad dad sits at the table eating bacon hot and drippy from the pan I (crazy girl) sit across from him my head down eat toast n a poached egg n grapes in sour cream a special treat people in Paris eat mom says she got the recipe in a magazine at work a section on special treats mom eats her grapes mad dad says nothing neither do I where is Paris

I like the food n I forget last night being scared n dying n I swing my legs under the table n I like the Paris sour cream grapes n I look up at the clock on the wall n I lift my toast up in the air above my head n then I crunch down on it crunch! I take a big bite n I chew n I swallow n I take another big bite n whack a board hits my face the table tips orange juice sprays on me crazy girl Little Miss So And So China Doll Girl all rolled up in one a eggroll floured n fried n served with orange sauce like mom made once out of one of her magazines whack we all fall down

Learn some table manners mad dad says takes his board hand away through the door n I lay on the floor in a puddle of orange juice n mom says *You don't have to be so harsh* n she throws a fork at the door where he left n we hold our breath but mad dad doesn't come back *Go get cleaned up* mom says and lifts me to my feet n a mower starts up in the garage vroom vroom mad dad is mowing the garage my face stings bees

Mad dad

spits at the grass bends over scratches his knee drives his mower into a tree I (crazy girl) watch him from my crazy bedroom window

* * *

Jack and Jill

went up the hill to fetch a pail of water mom reads to me snaps her fingers to the words something is wrong with my mom something is wrong with my mom! help! something is wrong with my mom! but no one comes and mom says *Jack fell down hit his crown and Jill came tumbling after do you hear the rhthym* she says *you can tap it out on your leg* and she does *Jack and Jill went up the hill to fetch a pail of water Jack fell down hit his crown and Jill came tumbling after* mom laughs laughs laughs hits her leg with her hand laughs laughs laughs her shiny ring someone help my mom doesn't even know I'm here she stares at the white white pages red blue and green pictures of Jack and Jill falling down down down *Mom why does he have a crown* I say *was he a king Jack and Jill* she whispers to herself *Mom was he a king* I say *Shhh* she puts her hand over my mouth *no more questions Jill came tumbling after* and she stares at the drawing of the girl and boy falling down a brown hill with sprouts of grass *Jack and Jill* she says taps on her leg stares across the room at the blank wall her shiny ring

Stay

where I can see you mom says she's reading her book her back against the picnic table the swing sets full of kids screaming I go away from them find a dirt trail wide as my tennis shoes follow it one shoe in front of the other one two three four crunch crunch crunch over the sticks n stones break my bones there's a river! a river! I stop listen with my ears my big big ears until I can't hear the kids or the cars or the grown ups talking until all I hear is the water over the rocks until all I hear is *Someday everything will be all right someday everything will be all right*

The move

to East Rose Avenue one block off Payne happens in one week mom packs packs packs like a rat n I help her fold the dishes wrapped in newspaper into the boxes there are grease stains bananas n oranges n rings of crisco on the bottoms n sides of the cardboard boxes me n mom hauled home from Supervalu *Our plates are going to smell like bananas* mom says n tapes a box shut with duck tape stuck tape why call it duck tape *Our towels are going to smell like oranges* mom says n sniffs a towel n smashes it into a box we play records Simon n Garfunkel n the Mommas and Poppas n Christy Minstrels sing about a box black that gets let open n all the bad things in the world get out

> *All the bad things in all the world!*
> *all the bad things in all the world let out!*

but I don't care about the bad things today mom's in a good mood mad dad's gone n we're moving out of the neighborhood with the nosy people nosing around our family business like mad dad says nosy people nosing around to see how bad I am we're moving to a new place where no one will know I lived at oatmeal's n no one will know the judge judged me crazy girl n maybe mad dad won't come in my room no more

mom bought me strawberry powder for my milk at Supervalu she is happy thinking maybe she won't have to wash my sheets at the new house the way she has to wash them the mornings after mad dad maybe mad dad won't come in my room at night no more in the new house is what she is thinking I just know it

mad dad doesn't come home for lunch cheese sandwiches n mustard n cherry kool aid n he doesn't come home for a snack tapioca pudding made right out of the box by me n mom listening to music n whistling n stirring bumpy bumpy milk

I leave my bat mask upstairs n China Doll Girl is quiet on the shelf one two three from the top she stands there with a red jelly bean in her basket everything is quiet except for the record player spinning music in the air n mom is smiling n paying attention to me who the judge judged crazy girl her daughter she is proud of me she says so proud of me for making the tapioca all by myself (almost) waiting to move to our new house on East Rose Avenue one block off Payne

Bring bring!

the telephone rings n mom answers n says *Hello Martha yes you heard right we're moving um hum yes in one week it's short notice your son Mr. So And So got a job on the east side of town got a good deal on a house over there I don't mind Little Miss So And So is helping now no one will know about it you know what I mean the past few months the problems with the school*

Hello gramma I say

Hello granddaughter she says

Would you like to come see me sometime soon gramma says

Yes I say

Put your mom on I'll pick you up half way

Yes I say

me n mom pack more boxes than we ever thought possible n the dust makes us sneeze achoo! achoo! achoo! but we don't care it's almost dark and no mad dad we are so happy we keep playing records n packing two rats sneezing n coughing n laughing mom lets me sleep in her bed with her no bad things happen mad dad doesn't come home

We drive

toward North Dakota me n mom who drives her daughter so that her daughter can spend time with her grandmother because dad won't even drive his own daughter to see his own mother *a son who won't even drive to see his own mother!* we drive through St. Paul n Minneapolis then up a road for a long time with trees that look like gray sticks *a son who won't even drive his own daughter to see his own mother!* we drive toward North Dakota where the Indians live to see my gramma Indian I have a gramma Indian! who my dad won't take me to see he is a bad bad dad

Gramma

we packed like rats I say n bite my bologna sandwich as big as I can as big as I can! I hold it up in the air so I can see the sun shining in through my bite the biggest bite in all the world! *You did* she says and sets a red glass in front of me *who Me n mom* I say n take another bite chew up that bologna butter bread *Mmm hmmm* she says and wipes her hands on a blue towel strung through the refrigerator door *Why are you moving* I pick up the glass *I'm excited to move* I say n squint into the glass n my heart tumbles down a hill like Jill *hill and Jill rhyme* I say gramma nods wipes up crumbs holds them in her hands looks at me *It's milk* I say gramma nods I set it down *Still not drinking milk* gramma says I shake my head no milk is bad white stuff in my throat *Mmm hmmm* gramma says drops the crumbs in the sink picks up my glass sets it on the gray counter top the color of her cat *Grapefruit juice or apple* she says opening her refrigerator *Grapefruit* I say n take another bite n swing my legs gramma sets juice in front of me bends down so her face is in mine she has a big round nose and black hair dark as the black bird that pops out of that boy's pie and skin the color of light brown paint she's Indian like dad mom said so dad said *drop it no one needs to know about that* gramma reaches her hands across the table gray as the counter and cat *A crown is your head* I say and touch mine *Mmm hmmm* she says *Mom reads to me* I say *Yes I imagine she does did you know your mom wanted to write books* No I say *Something better came along* she says and smiles sits down I shrug don't smile back it's something about me so it must be bad bad bad crazy girl *Does your mom say why you're moving* gramma smiles a smile big as the sky n North Dakota n rubs my wrists the soft part where all the blood is *mmm hmmm* her mouth is smiling but her eyebrows knot up like tied shoelaces n I take another bite n then another and don't answer her question

Gramma takes me

to McDonalds we eat french fries n double cheeseburgers n pop n we share apple pie n gramma sits next to me n rubs my wrist she squeezes me with her other arm kisses the top of my head a old lady and some kids sit down next to us the girl says *Is that lady from China* and the lady next to us looks mad but I don't know why *I'm not Chinese* gramma says to the lady and takes her thumb and presses on my cheek *see those flat cheeks* and she presses on my lips *those fat little lips* she whispers in my ear *that's what an Indian looks like you're Indian too no matter what anyone says you hear me my girl* she sits up and takes a bite of the apple pie she ripped into pieces *She don't look like no grandma* the boy says *Robbie* his lady says *Well she isn't all gray like you* he says *Quiet* his lady says and hits his hand *Why don't you look like a gramma* I say gramma won't smack me for asking questions she looks down at the pie pieces blows on one *Indians do that* she whispers to me *we age good* she nods then says loud *your parents were young* Oh I say but don't ask no more questions because it might be something bad about me gramma kisses the top of my head *I'm the luckiest grandma ever* she says n I sink into her side until I can feel her ribs *You're my girl* she says loud then whispers *my little Indian girl* n I stop chewing n sink my face into her side n she hugs me n whispers *What's wrong my girl* I cry the apple pie in my mouth onto her shirt she hugs me rocks me in the booth doesn't care about the pie running down her shirt or the other grammas or kids or people eating lunch at McDonalds who don't look Chinese I'm her girl

* * *

Pennies

are from heaven gramma says so but the devil he has nickels in his pockets *A special present for my special girl on the first day in our new house* mad dad says n hangs a plastic pink purse round my neck n touches my lips with his finger *our special secret* he smiles a long smile a snake smile n drops a shiny nickel in the purse n zips it up tight *advance payment* he says n his lips stretch out across the new living room bare as a floor without a rug snakes slide out the corner of his mouth crawl across the boxes n disappear down the hallway

mad dad walks away whistling I stand in the living room in the new house east side California sun feeling like throw up standing here not moving I can't think at all stare at the sunlight on the floor bare wood no rug floor *Isn't that nice* mom says sees me staring with the pink purse round my neck she smiles so long her smile turns upside down n she stands there on the bare floor in between the boxes smiling upside down because nice things don't happen unless bad things are coming

the day goes on and on a long rope me mom dad unpacking dad banging in the garage mom spilling flour in the kitchen me putting my stuffed animals out in a line in my room a duck a bear a dog a bunny with real fur under my one window waiting for dad to carry my bed upstairs I need to find China Doll Girl but she's not in the same box maybe she ran away didn't want to wait to see if California sun is going to shine on the east side new house Rose Avenue one block off Payne I take the pink purse off leave it in the corner put my head against the window the glass is cold I look up as far as I can push my cheek n eye into the glass the sun is like finger painting in the sky all smudgy n gray maybe China Doll Girl ran away because there isn't going to be any California sun the way me n mom were thinking whistling packing like rats ignoring the black box all the bad things in the world

I push my face into the glass until my eyes get all mixed up n one looks at the glass n the other looks at the tree branches gray sticks in the air then looks through the branches at the house across the street a green finger paint smudge two pickups in the driveway clomp clomp clomp dad comes up the stairs n I smash my nose in the cold glass n roll my face over to the other side keeping one eye on the house *Little Miss So And So* dad says n the other eye sees him throw my mattress on the floor *Put That Back On* n he points at the pink purse *now* n I ignore him n he goes away n the mattress bounces clomp clomp clomp dad goes down the stairs n I forget all about him n smash my forehead against the window n see two of everything then I lick the glass to see what the cold tastes like it tastes like nothing so I taste another part n that part is like water so I taste another part n that part is like dirt n I taste another part n that part is like the chalk on your fingers when the teacher lets you draw on the board there aren't any grown ups around to yell at me so I open my mouth n stick my tongue as fat as it can be on the window like I'm yelling out it at the trees n finger painting smudges n the road that China Doll Girl ran down

clomp clomp clomp mad dad's coming back so I pull my tongue in someone comes out of the green finger paint house it's a girl n I put my nose against the window to watch her she's bigger than me n has a pigtail clomp clomp clomp *I Told You To Put That Back On* n dad throws something it goes clank I ignore him watch the pigtail girl bounce across the yard n stop *Did You Hear Me* mad dad yells but I keep watching the girl *What The Hell Have You Been Licking The Window You Little Sicko* the thing he dropped clanks again n he hits me on the back of my head n I keep watching the pigtail girl n he picks me up says *I Told You To Wear Your Purse* n he puts his foot on the windowsill n hangs me across his leg but I keep watching pigtail *You're Gonna Learn To Obey Me* unbuckle slide slide he pulls his belt off n yanks my pants down n whips me with his belt I make a noise he says *What's wrong little baby can't you take it* I don't cry I try hard not to cry no crying I lift my head n watch the pigtail girl across the street then I squeeze my eyes shut stop the crying *Little Baby* pigtail goes to a bush n pulls on it whish whish dad whips me butt hurts bad whish whish *You're Gonna Obey* pigtail girl twirls around waving a stick like it's a sword stabbing the air

mad dad's snake rises up it sticks me in the stomach he huffs n puffs pushes my head down so I can't see pigtail girl huff puff huff puff whish whish the head board did it butt hurts bad mad dad's thing pokes me in the stomach dad whips one more time grabs my neck n legs n pushes on me his thing in my stomach so hard can't breathe huff puff huff puff I look out window stare at tree branches make them blurry with my eyes my two eyes blur the branches n the smudgy green house n the gray smudgy sky into one nothing

stare stare stare don't feel don't feel don't feel no crying huff puff huff puff I am two eyes on the window looking out at East Rose Avenue one block off Payne

Mad dad jerks

his thing in my stomach jerks jerks then he sighs sticky on my stomach let's go of me slide down legs to his feet he stands up pushes me off his feet on to my stuffed animals lined up under the window he whistles clanks whistles sets my bed up I make my eyes go blurry stare make myself not be there be gone like China Doll Girl ran away down the road

Me run down road!
me hate it here!

my hands on the floor cold as the window legs on top of stuffed animals no crying no feeling he puts the mattress into the frame mom's downstairs car drives by hands on cold floor mad dad pushes the bed into the corner away from the window picks up purse grabs arm drags me to bed puts the purse next to me *There Little Miss So And So* kisses me on my head *You're Very Pretty You Should Get Something For Being So Pretty* n dad mad dad the devil in disguise I see his face through my eyes smiling lips snake lips kiss me on my mouth kiss kiss kiss I want to throw up stop kissing dad unzips the purse holds a shiny nickel says *Oops I already paid you for this* n puts the nickel in his pocket n hangs the purse pink round my neck long n skinny

Big bad wolf

blew the house down mom says *do you hear the b's* she says n looks at me *big bad blew it's good to read to children* she says *I read that somewhere some magazine* she looks at the ceiling *McCalls* I nod listening I think about the wolf big hairy just like trolls scaring the pigs wanting to kill them and my mouth goes dry and I rub my wrists and she stares at the clock tick tock on the new wall in the new house waiting for dad to get home from basketball at the YMCA waiting for big hairy dad to get home tick tock tick tock we all fall down

P girl (Patty)

goes to my new school on the east side lives across the street from me P girl pigtail girl I saw on the gray finger paint day that's not why they call her P girl

Hey P girl yells to me n waves through the semi trucks that whiz by our street whoosh whoosh mom didn't know the east side California sun new house was on a road truckers take out of town whoosh whoosh all day n all night *can you come play*

Sure I shrug my shoulders n stand on the curb till a truck with a blue head n a gray body drives by toot toot! the driver pulls his rope toot toot! the kids at school call her P girl because she wet her pants one day in first grade she peed right on her seat n no one washes her clothes *P girl stinks like poop* is what the kids say

I cross the street n stand on her yard hands in my pockets with only one pick up parked on it today *I'm Patty* she says *Sure* I say again n shrug my shoulders *What's your name* she says her hair's in a long pig tail n the finger paint smudge day flashes in my head like things do on TV n I don't see P girl for a second for a second all I see is my bedroom floor n hear mad dad's breathing n smell him n see P girl in her yard while dad's snake got hard n I want to scream but no sound comes only P girl in her finger paint smudge yard n mad dad's thing inside his pants sweaty n hard n rubbing n before I

know it I'm not standing in her yard my hands in my pockets I'm throwing
up in P girl's bushes

I throw up one two three times n I stop n I see red berries the kind mom
says is poison don't eat them! you'll die! n I see throw up dripping off the
leaves n seeing the throw up makes me throw up again *It's okay* she says n
pats me on my back *I don't care if you throw up in my bushes* n I keep
throwing up n a boy says *Is she okay* n P girl says *Yeah*

Throw up once throw up twice throw up three times a lady
watch out crazy girl
the drivers drive hard on the east side close to the freeway
the drivers drive hard!

I wipe
my mouth on my shirt sleeve n stand up n stare at the ground gray green
finger paint smudge through a window until it turns into grass n I know I'm
not in my bedroom with dad's thing in my stomach *What's your name* P girl
says n I stop spinning shrug my shoulders *Okay you don't have to tell me
your name* she says *why do you have that purse around your neck* I shrug
my shoulders and don't say nothing because what can I say *What grade are
you in* n I think for a second because of the spinning mad dad's thing in my
stomach finger paint smudge day n then I almost throw up n then I say *Mrs.
Smith*

They call me P girl she says n I nod even though I already know it *I'm in
second grade and you should call me Patty not P girl and I'm the only girl
in my family I've got six brothers all of them are older except for Jimmy go
away stupid!* n the boy's voice says *No* n then P girl I mean Patty jumps at
him n I see him in the door turn run into the house *Want to go play* she says
n puts her arm round my shoulders even though I got throw up on me we
walk around her house to the back n I wipe the throw up off with some
leaves n she picks up a bucket n a long smooth stick with no bark that's the
color of a penny *Let's go catch stuff* she says *there's moles in tunnels down
there pick up that bucket!* she points to another bucket lying upside down
by a hose we can trap them together

Okay I say n wipe my mouth on my sleeve n pick up the bucket n follow
her down the hill

Crazy girl has a friend!
her first friend in all the world!
they are going to trap moles with buckets
plastic and white
crazy girl has a friend!

bam bam bam! Patty whacks the stick over the top of her bucket set up
over the mole hole *Stay there!* she says n so I do I stay with my bucket at the
other end of the mole hole *Hold it down!* n so I do I push on the bucket in

case a mole tries to run out Patty picks up a rock n puts it over her bucket n takes her stick n runs yelling *Come out! Come out!* whacking at the mole trail up and down it back and forth from one bucket to the other n I wait n watch for the moles who live in there somewhere

we try to catch moles everywhere in her back yard that's the edge of a forest that's really just a few trees but I call it a forest anyway n she tells me there's a river down there inside the forest n we have to go looking for snakes n mice n fish n muskrats n her dad has a fish net we can use in the garage we can go down to the river n catch all sorts of animals she says but she doesn't say what we're going to do with the snakes n mice n fish I wonder but don't ask *You don't talk so much do you* she says I shrug say *They call me Little Miss So And So Are you a shy girl* she says n I shrug my shoulders *No* I say *I just never had anyone to talk to beside my gramma* I shrug my shoulders *that's all* Patty sets the buckets up on another mole trail n whacks at the hole

but no moles come out n Jimmy says *Time for supper* out the back window n Patty throws her stick down n kicks her bucket n a mole runs out past her into the forest *Uh* she says n hits her leg n throws her face at the sky *it got away again!*

How's my girl
gramma says
Good I say twirl the phone cord like a lasso
Gramma I say
What
Am I your only grandgirl
Yes
Am I your only grandson I say to be stupid cause I know I am not a boy
Yes she says you are my only grandchild
Oh I say you are my only gramma and grampa
I know she says
Why I say even though I know the other grammas and grampas are dead
They're in heaven gramma says so I love you that extra much
Me too I say step on the lasso I love you that extra much too
Gramma I say and stand in a closet so no one can hear me am I your Indian girl
Yes you are my Indian girl
Oh I say
Are you okay she says
Yeah I say
You can say if you're not she says
I know I say feel sadder than sad than the saddest bluest sky
You are the cream in my coffee she says
You are the cream in my coffee too I say even though I don't drink coffee

The night

comes creepy crawly after chasing moles going home eating supper washing the dishes helping mom make popcorn melting butter watching the Rockford Files Jimbo got shot at n his dad was mad at him the night comes creepy crawly a black spider up my back the night won't leave me alone on East Rose Avenue either

night drops down on a string I go to my room ready for bed mom says *I'll be up in a minute to check on you I don't want you up too late we have church in the morning* I unpack like a rat sharp pointy teeth the lights are on at Patty's n I wish I lived there one more box to unpack *Hello crazy girl! I have been waiting for you!* n I see China Doll Girl's pointy oatmeal hat under my Little Red Riding Hood coloring book n I pull her out

Hello China Doll Girl I say to her n I stand on my chair n put her on the shelf mad dad drilled on the wall *It's soo good to be out of stupid box* she says n I unpack some more n then I kneel on my knees n color Little Red Riding Hood color her cloak red n her hair orange n I color red red red until I rip the paper n then I finish it by making her eyes red too n then I crumple it and throw it against the wall n then I put my chin on the windowsill flaked off paint n watch Patty's house across from mine *What wrong crazy girl* China Doll Girl says n I shrug my shoulders n she says *That's a nice picture* n before I can answer she snores asleep on the shelf I watch Patty's lights China Doll Girl sleeps the night drops on me alone

Whish whish whish the night swings through the trees

Creak creak creak

someone's coming up the stairs mom pushes the door *Time to go to bed* she says n clicks off the lights n wraps the covers round me *tuck you in tight* kisses me *be sure to put away your crayons from now on* n she pats me on my head n walks out *you found your doll* shakes head says *such squinty squinty eyes* closes door clicks handle sighs on the other side the light shines in under the door China Doll Girl snores I watch the light for mad dad's shadows his hairy feet

Mad dad's feet! Mad dad's feet!
his hairy hairy feet!
hairy footed troll on a bridge!
crazy girl watches for mad dad's feet!

I watch n watch n watch n hold my breath count one two three one two three hold breath watch listen biggest ears in all the world grow out the sides of my head I wish wish wish I lived somewhere else at Patty's in her bed under her bed away from mad dad's hairy hairy feet n shadows in the night Patty n me dig holes catch moles chase snakes in the woods I wish me Patty China Doll Girl lived in a land far far away

Whish whish whish tires flapping in the rain

clomp clomp clomp squeak bathroom door opens I watch the crack under the door there's his toe mad dad's toe n another toe squeak a door squeaks I see his foot mad dad's foot then his other foot *Patty China Doll Girl help help help* biggest ears in all the world go away they heard enough squinty eyes that watch the crack under the door close mad dad's breath comes in the room the devil himself from the hole under my bed no ears no eyes just skin that feels mad dad's breath breathing breathe breathe breathe huff puff puff big bad wolf devil man hairy footed tooth fairy with nickels for my teeth Give Me Your Teeth my pointy pointy teeth want to bite on his thing when he puts it in my mouth *biggest lolly pop in all the world* my pointy pointy teeth clomp stomp clomp *Patty Patty China Doll Girl save me monster in my room* mad dad snake devil man comes for me in the night hairy footed tooth fairy with wings leaves nickels cold nickels hard nickels one two three he snaps them down under my pillow when he's done no body no body no body nickels for the no body

Gramma whispers out of me *help please* devil man gets on top of me devil man mad dad squeezes my neck whispers hot breath in the biggest ear in all the world that has gone into hiding *No one is going to help you hear no one not your mother she is nothing not your grandmother hear your grandmother is nothing she is nothing and she will never help you your grandmother will never help you* he licks his lips *your grandmother is nothing*

No No No No in my head Not True Not True *Gramma gramma* whispers out my throat

choke choke throat body gone turned to stone body turned to rocks on the river water washes over them body disappeared gone huff puff blown down by the big bad wolf Little Red Riding Hood coloring book red cloak help help China Doll Girl help the ceiling the ceiling bumpy n white chicken buck buck bah buck neck choke the body's dead gone to the wind turned to dust ashes Jesus hanging on the cross dead priest says make the sign of the cross touch your face rock chest rock shoulder rock lips rock body gone stone ash burn it up on fire pray for me China Doll Girl Patty pray for me crazy girl body burned to ashes on her bed will have to get up in the morning to pray in a pew

Good morning

mother says I say nothing *Rise n shine we've got church today* n I go to the bathroom n mother rips the sheets n throws them down the chute to the basement n mother grabs my head n my toothbrush n brushes my teeth n I cry n my gums bleed n my tears run down my cheeks n fill up the bathroom n I close my lips around the toothbrush to hold my breath what if the water rises I don't want to swallow it n mother keeps brushing n my lips sealed n she says nothing nothing nothing to no body

Mary Beth

a boy shouts across the church parking lot n I stop turn look at the boy who shouted Mary Beth wait for him to say something else to me but he's looking at an old lady who bends over kisses him I look at the graves next to the parking lot a tall white stone with purple flowers lying next to it a short gray stone the top corner chunked off *What're you doing* mom says yanks my arm pops my shoulder we walk up the tall steps into the church with the dying Jesus n crying mother Mary n wood seats I can't see over

Mother Mary

Jesus Christ stand up sit down priest says bang bang bang his fist in his hand we're all going to hell unless we do what the priest wants mom bows her head does what he says serve thy husband serve him well!

N

mad dad devil man brings nickels to me in the night on East Rose Avenue one block off Payne leaves them under my pillow one two three buy a candy buy a jewelry buy a spinny wheel toy with the nickels in the pink purse tied round my neck by a broken string don't take it off! the devil man gives me nickels on the east side new side no California sun side house mom says *It's nice your father is finally taking an interest in you* when she sees my spinny wheel toy red white blue in the sun shining through the windows I blow on it red white blue America spinning Love American Style

California dreaming

mom sings leans up against the window *on such a winter's day* finger paint smudge gray spinning red white n blue

Fly fly

to the ceiling leave body below bye bye rock bye bye body rock a bye body fly to the ceiling mad dad below mad dad scary dad body below bang bang bang on the head board bored head ceiling I am the ceiling I see the body below buck buck bah buck mad dad chicken neck bang I am the ceiling I am the sky I am the trees n the breeze n the moon cracked in the night ceiling sky trees breeze moon finger paint smudge gray I am it all bye bye baby body mad dad banging bye bye baby body I am it all is me I watch wait store it in my brain watch wait ceiling sky moon breeze I am all watching waiting

Whish whish whish the head board did it!

Age Ten (1978)

The purse

flaps on my chest I am growing boobs they stick out pointy hard nipples that hurt I hate them mad dad crazy man mumbling bought me a new pink purse for my birthday this one has sequins on it covering over it like the scales of a fish a pink fish! I hate it I ripped it on purpose made it look like it got caught on a fence so I didn't have to wear it but mad dad crazy man had mom sew it and strung it around my neck again

he gives me nickels to fill it up with it gets too heavy to wear so I dump them but he makes me wear it I take it off at school put it back on when I get off the bus I have piles of nickels piles n piles of nickels in a Keds shoe box in my closet the back corner's filled with shiny hard nickels hidden away in the dark dad puts one then another over my boobs I buy me and Patty ice cream and malted milk balls and fake candy cigarettes with the painted pink ends so we can pretend we are older smoking on the street where the truck drivers whiz by

Mrs. Olson

makes us keep a diary for one week which I don't want to do because first what will I write and second what if mom or dad read it but I have to for the assignment Mrs. Olson says to write about the past the present the future the only thing I like to think about is the future but I have to write about the past and present for the assignment Mrs. Olson says she will not read the diary she will look at the pages and give us a grade for how many pages we have written in so I sit down and write:

Crazy girl is gone she died a long time ago I can't remember it very good being five was gray and lonely and sad and I (crazy girl who is not really dead just buried) barely never talked there was a black judge bowls of oatmeal without sugar at some lady's house I never look at pictures of myself Little Miss So And So a five year old crazy girl all alone except for her gramma and her white China doll stuffed animals lined up under the window I have too many things to do now I am busy! I don't want to remember neither does mom dad he doesn't think about anything just walks around talking to himself maybe someday he will leave

now I go to Phalen Lake Elementary school fifth grade teacher Mrs Olson I live on East Rose Avenue one block off Payne in Saint Paul on a road that's a straight truck line heading to North Dakota a gray nothing marsh land with black sticks of trees and three gas stations where the truck drivers get gas on their way to somewhere else but I don't know where because I've only been to the edge of North Dakota where Indians live on reservations where my gramma lives she is a Indian so am I she says so but dad says Shut up! Just shut the hell up! *when mom calls dad and me Indians but he doesn't hit her like usual he just gets up leaves* Shut up! Just shut up! *stomps out the door drives away stays gone all night*

once when I was nine we went to gramma's for a whole weekend over Christmas me mom dad I got a feather headress keychain at a store that sells Indian stuff like Indian statues carved out of wood tall as the ceiling and necklaces made out of big bear teeth with little blue beads in between each tooth They're fake *mom said she likes Indian stuff more than dad does* the teeth aren't real *she picked it up ran her fingers over the tips of the fake teeth to symbolize something she said but we couldn't buy it because it was too much twenty dollars or more twenty dollars I saw mom's thoughts on her face thinking twenty dollars would buy me a baby sitter in the summer maybe for one whole month instead of having me go to mom's work with her and play in the gym and disrupt her which is what she says I do*

that time at Christmas dad wouldn't come in the Indian store sat in the car waiting to drive to gramma's for Christmas she lives in a house without a TV and smaller than ours which is small smaller than anyone's house in all of Saint Paul! in all of Saint Paul! we have the smallest house in all of Saint Paul! but gramma's house is smaller and she doesn't have a TV and her yard is mostly dirt which dad doesn't like Grow some grass Mom Christ *he says and I can hear embarassment in his words and his ears flop over like a dog when the whole family had a party for us dad sat in the corner by himself all night drinking beer is all he did wouldn't talk to anyone or look at anyone but I didn't care I had fun with gramma in her lap all night* My girl my girl *she said petting my hair*

Two days

go by and I don't do any writing keep the diary under my bed until mom dad go to a meeting for something the babysitter watches TV so I write:

Patty comes with me to play kick ball in the empty gym dusty smelling sneezing gray walls we can't turn the lights on Can't waste the school's money on electricity when school's not in session *is what the janitor said when mom asked him if she could turn on just half the gym's lights so her daughter could see to play*

Patty goes with me some days and some days I never see her like she disappears off the face of the earth we swing from the ropes Me Tarzan you Jane *we play cowboys and Indians with my feather headress* The Indians invaded the school! Watch out! I'm the Indian *I yell* whoo whoo whoo whoo whoo! *I run in circles hold my hockey stick over my head* watch out Patty *I yell* the Indians are in town! *we play kickball the red rubber balls with dusty dimples all over we throw them at each other to practice for bombardment we want to beat the boys*

Patty is in fifth grade now with me because she flunked it last year too many absences and they kept her back That's what Patty gets for not going to school *mom said and ate her toast at the breakfast table while dad read his paper he never pays attention to anything just walks around mumbling like he's crazy Patty thinks he is* He's certifiable *she says her arms crossed around her chest but most of all at mom's school where me and Patty go over Christmas Easter summer break we practice floor hockey I am the goalie I bring my gloves and use the school's goggles and stick with the orange blades and get down on my knees with the stick handle flat on the floor the way girl goalies play floor hockey not standing up like the boys on ice girls always have to do dumb stuff Patty shoots on me from everywhere and I catch the orange pucks out of the air quick as a cat like my coach says I snag them in midair slide them back to Patty who shoots again and again we can play all day just the two of us shooting catching saving sliding the orange pucks across the dusty floors the dust makes me cough*

Patty is the star forward on the Eastside Raiders and I am the star goalie we have black t shirts with Raiders written in white on the front our numbers on the back and someday we are going to be professional hockey players we wear our Raiders t shirts and North Star hockey jerseys to school the boys especially Tim and Jeff say Yeah you're going to be pros professional retarded ostriches *and they laugh which makes me and Patty want to beat them bad hit them hard with the red dimpled balls in bombardment leave dusty circles on their backs for treating us like girls*

Patty can play floor hockey because mom signed her up and drives her to all our games she scores goals because she is tall and not afraid she does not get called P girl anymore because her clothes don't smell like pee anymore she figured out how to use the washer in the basement and washes her own clothes now some of them she steals from the Goodwill on White Bear Avenue she says it's easy to do because you just rip off the tags and put them on in the dressing room and no one can tell if they're yours or Goodwill's cause they're already used Patty's clothes are used but they're clean now even if her clothes smelled like pee no one would dare call her P Girl the boys are afraid of her even though they won't say so she beat three of them up when she was in the fourth grade and now no boys will mess with her she's taller than all of the boys in all of the grades the girls on the floor hockey teams are afraid of her too they get out of her way because she has five older brothers who knock her around and now another baby brother to go along with her other little brother Jimmy and a mom and dad who don't pay her any attention if Patty runs away I am not going to let her get away I am going with her headed out on the truck driver's line straight to North Dakota to the Indians to my gramma's to whatever is past I don't know what the future will be but it's all I can think about

Turn in

your diaries Mrs. Olson says leans against the front of her desk *I hope that you'll keep these when you get old it will be interesting for you and your children to read* she smiles the way she does I smile back hand mine in

Two days

later Mrs. Olson gives us our diaries I open mine in big red letters it says *F Do not talk poorly about your parents* it says *I have half a mind to show these to your parents* half a mind! she has half a mind to show them to mad dad n mom n my eye balls roll around thinking about the trouble the trouble I'd be in!

at lunch I tell Patty to save my place in line I go to the bathroom down by the janitor's closet that's only for one person that locks I rip out the pages tear them long and skinny soak them in the sink until my words are fat and faded then flush them down the toilet Fluuush they are gone no one will ever know no one can ever know I can never write again!

* * *

Susan

a woman watching the game yells from her chair the short fat girl on the other team has the puck she shoots from anywhere *Susan* the woman yells again I don't want to look because the short fat girl will score *Susan* I drop my stick and walk toward the woman yelling my name Patty yells *What'reyoudoin get back in the net* I want to get back in the net but it is like I am walking under water all of a sudden I am standing in the middle of the court the short fat girl looks at me pushes the puck around Sally I left the net open! I run toward her dive on top of her stick grab the puck the short fat girl falls over me tweet tweet! the ref yells *Ref* the other coach yells *eject her* I hold the puck orange and dusty between my hands look at the woman who yelled Susan her legs crossed I look at Patty who stares at me I walk around the short fat girl crying on the floor hand the ref the puck he stands there his whistle dangling on his chest I walk out the side door go to the girls' bathroom sit on a toilet hide from mom dad Patty short fat girl parents teams I don't know what just happened

Today

is a beautiful day here on East Rose Avenue mom says *ready to go to work* and she pulls the curtain on the sun it explodes into the living room suddenly I am five year old crazy girl standing in the living room boxes around mom singing *California dreaming* waiting for California sunshine to pour into the house *Hurry up Little Miss So And So* and I see mom standing in the living room with furniture no boxes but now it's Easter break *Today is a beautiful day* mom says again *hello anyone home* she says I blink like a retard why did mom call me Little Miss So And So today instead of Miss So And So I'm ten not a baby anymore I see her white knuckles on the door my stomach sinks like a rock in the river

> *Skip skip skipping rocks in the river*
> *Patty and the fifth grader chasing snakes*
> *with fishing nets and sticks and buckets lined with grass*
> *skipping rocks in the river on such a summer day*

Can Patty come I say mom sighs pushes the curtains around digs at something with her fingernail *If she's ready in five minutes I really mean it five minutes period we can't wait for her today Okay* I say feeling the way I did when I was little a crazy five year old I remember those feelings bad bad feelings like I was going to die I forget them leave them leave the living room call Patty's house swing the white phone cord like it's a jump rope hit the refrigerator hit the wall hit the refrigerator hit the wall no one answers

> *Crazy girl's buried*
> *the fifth grader says so*
> *the fifth grader buried her in the hole*
> *under the rubble dirt sticks*

> *it takes many to survive*
> *the father mad dad crazy man talking to himself*
> *the fifth grader doesn't want to know crazy girl is alive she can't know*
> *the fifth grader must survive at school in the world or we all die*

I knock on Patty's door knock knock no one answers there's only one pick up truck on the lawn knock knock the semis whoosh by splash puddles on the sidewalks knock knock until Jimmy answers *Is Patty home* I say *No* he says *can I come instead Where is she* I say whoosh whoosh whoosh *I dunno can I come instead Where'd she go* Jimmy shrugs his shoulders *Can I go No* I say wait for the trucks to quit whooshing worried she left without me mom pulls the garbage can to the curb *Hurry up Miss So And So my boss is in today* I hurry

The mole

crawls under Patty's lawn at night the mole crawls under Patty's lawn at night! and since we can't catch it with buckets or sticks or even the steel trap Patty's dad bought that slams down through the grass spears the mole right through its head or neck or maybe its eye but since we can't catch it during the day we decide to watch for it at night Patty says *I swear I'd set up a camera all day and all night if I had one* meaning she'd tape the mole crawling under the grass making trails and mounds of grass and dirt clumped up but since she doesn't have a camera I'm sleeping over tonight the night before Easter we're staying up all night to watch for the mole with flashlights

All night! staying up late!

Patty and I sit on the porch I don't ask her where she was yesterday she was supposed to go with me to mom's work I can't be a goalie without her shooting on me so instead I read a book this year I read more books than anyone in my entire school for the book fair and my teacher told my mom I should be in honors which would cost money mom told dad at dinner and he said nothing like he didn't hear and mom said nothing after that and I know I won't get in honors but I still heard it and now I know people think I'm smart not stupid like dad says the book I read at mom's work was about a boy detective who has red hair and red freckles and carves a key out of soap when he gets locked in a room that's the way he escapes and I know I have to remember it in case I'm ever locked in a closet I can make a key out of soap and escape and be a hero instead of sitting in the room until I suffocate to death

I don't want to suffocate to death mad dad wants me dead he might choke me or shoot me with his rifles lined up in the cabinet in the living room he rubs them down with a raggy old t shirt and oil from the kitchen vegetable oil the kind mom cooks with me and mom think it must be wrong to use vegetable oil on rifles but we don't say anything to him we just watch him get his oil out of the kitchen cabinet and slop it on to his old raggy t shirt that says *University of Alabama* in old faded pink letters why does he have a t shirt from there he went to school at St. Cloud State

What's wrong Patty says I forgot all about her sitting with me on the porch *you're floating away again on a current of air squak squak* she flaps her arms I don't say anything the sun is on the other side of the trees and the trucks drive by splashing water on the yards and I'm with Patty she keeps me safe from dad who's in the garage doing something it smells good out here the way it does in spring when the smell of gasoline is sweet like a cantelope and you know summer is coming and you think you just might be able to live for another year not die in your bed just not wake up one day

Get your flashlight Patty says *let's go over to my house Wanna play hockey too* I say *Yeah* she says so I run to the house through the living room with brand new old style American furniture painted all brown up the stairs two at a time smelling dinner smelling beef stroganoff the smell runs with me up the stairs to my room I grab my goalie gloves off the head of my red stuffed dog Clarence then I run into mom and dad's room reach under their bed on mom's side grab the big yellow flashlight click it on it works *Miss So And So* mom says I stop look out mom's window it's spring birds call their babies brown shadows play in the back yard there's no mole trails in my yard dad would kill it right off he shoots squirrels I soak in the shadows until I become the colors in the back yard the birds the rectangle and triangle shapes on the grass my eyes soak it in I don't have any thoughts any feelings any fears I just am I just am! *Miss So And So time to eat* Patty is waiting for me

I run down the stairs *Can't eat mom I'm going to Patty's for dinner and a sleep over* I hold my breath to see if she'll let me *Do you have your pajamas* mom says my foot hits the bottom stair *Yes* I yell running away from her the beef stroganoff mad dad in the garage on my way to Patty's

Patty makes

frozen mushroom pizza for me and Jimmy I pour Shur Fine Lemon Lime *Shur Fine Lemon Lime sure is fine* we say pour it up to the second line in the blue plastic cups with three ice cubes each so it's all even her mom's in bed the blue TV light shines out the bottom of her door *Ow* Jimmy says when he takes a bite of the pizza it burns his mouth he spits out the cheese *Dummy* Patty says and slaps him on the head I eat the pizza slow blow on it listen to the TV buzz out the door pick off the mushrooms eat them one by one Jimmy's eyes are all red he tries not to cry he misses his dad hasn't been home in a while *You big baby* Patty says and slaps him again but this time lighter then she stands behind him hugs him he's in first grade his mom stays in her room with his baby brother Danny Jimmy's eyes get red like Christmas light bulbs *Shhh* Patty says stands up *there's nothing to cry about* she loves him but doesn't like being his mom

Can I play with you Jimmy says sitting at the table with his feet crossed *No* Patty says I throw out our cheese stained paper plates and Jimmy jumps down and grabs the plates picks off the tiny strings of cheese still stuck to them I down the last of my Shur Fine Lemon Lime the ice hits my teeth and lips *C'mon* Jimmy says his eyes getting watery and red like a fish gill *please* he says *Go play with Danny* Patty pushes him *But he's a baby So are you go away I'm telling mom* Jimmy says and throws the paper plates on the floor he yells *I'm gonna tell dad when he gets home* and runs into his mom's bedroom

me and Patty walk up her back stairs covered in brown carpet with outlines of gold squares hooked together like a chain it's black out now Patty's jeans are ripped at the bottom because they used to be her older brother's and she cut them off the Levis tag is gone if you collect 150 of them you get a free pair and I practically stare at her butt because it's right in my face she is really skinny *The sun is still up in California even though it's down here* I say and Patty doesn't say anything her butt and ripped up jeans keep moving she doesn't say anything when I say stupid things which I do a lot meaning I don't know why I say a lot of the things I do and when I say things like how pretty the trees are against the sky or other stupid things that slip out of my mouth kids make fun of me Patty never says anything when I say stupid things it's like she knows why I say them

We

get to the top of the stairs and Patty says *Want to look for the mole* and pulls her jeans up over her hips but they slip down right away *Sure* I say but

I'd rather play floor hockey Patty opens the hall closet and digs out a huge red flashlight and looks me in the eyes and there's no knives in hers there's brown shapes and sunsets and gasoline smell and all the other things that make me feel safe *C'mon* she says and we go into her room that doesn't have a door that's never had a door as long as I've known her a faded baby blue sheet hangs where the door should be

Patty sits down on her bed flicking the light on and off shining it in her face so she looks like that Camp Fire teacher Mrs. Whitner I had once who took us camping and told stories to us in the dark and lit her face up from under her chin to look scary she did look scary I got scared and quit but I quit more because I didn't want to collect beads and sew them on those stupid vests and wear those stupid white gloves and carry those stupid flags around my fingers touch Patty's real name *Patricia* sewed across it in bright blue stitching Patty sewed it on herself and it's one of the best things you could ever see her name stitched in cursive writing like a professional right across the sheet it's how I know who Patty really is she is smart and brave and pretty and she uses her real name Patricia not Patty or P girl because she is someone other than the bad things people think about her she could make a key out of soap I know it!

Pretend like we're at the airport we're air traffic controllers Patty says and so I do *Okay* she says and opens her window and pushes out her screen it twangs to the ground *Now open your window and push the screen out* and so I do *Okay now start in the back* Patty says *we have to work together like a team like we're playing floor hockey okay Okay* I say and we start in the back crossing our beams of light over the back yard inch by inch looking for the mole we go over Patty's entire back yard from back to front until we're leaning right out the windows our hands on the shingles of her house so we can shine our beams of light straight down over the sidewalk below and the lawn mower and the broken kitchen chair and the pile of bricks with weeds sticking out between the holes and a milk carton squashed by someone's shoe but we don't see the mole digging a tunnel

Maybe it's sleeping I say and shine my flashlight at the jet black branches against the moon thin and curved like your nail when it chips off I feel the moon and the colors and the smell of the earth and the river whooshing over the rocks and the semi trucks whooshing down the road and I know someday everything will be all right

There it goes Patty yells and practically falls out the window and I flash my beam of light back down to the ground *Okay see over there by the swing* Patty yells *it's running to the river* and I swing my flashlight around like I'm a air traffic controller but I don't see anything just the clumps of dirt and dead brown grass waiting for spring *You missed it* Patty says *Yeah* I say *Oo* she cries *I wanted you to see it now it's gone* she throws her flashlight down on the floor *I wanted you to see it* she says practically crying her pony tail covering her face because she wanted me to see the mole she's been trying to catch for a long time and I'm in shock meaning I can't barely believe how much Patty loves me for real

> *For real and forever FFE friends forever and ever*
> *they sign their notes at school FFE forever and ever*
> *P girl loves the fifth grader FFE*

We play

hockey downstairs with a bright blue raquetball it bounces like crazy meaning that Patty can shoot on me over and over because my back is against the wall and it bounces right back to her ping ping ping the raquetball pings around the basement it's more fun than anything including than playing a real game of hockey the ball flies so fast and Patty catches it with her blade and traps it to a dead stop and shoots on me over and over we marked a black goal frame on the wall last spring and I kneel on the cardboard and Patty shoots ping ping ping I knock them and block them and catch them right out of midair *This is why we're so good you know* Patty says in between shots and I nod too out of breath to talk I'm not shivering anymore just sweating and dry mouthed

we play until we can't play anymore and my knees have red and brown bruises then we go upstairs where the blue TV light shines down the hall Patty gets a bag of potato chips and Shur Fine grape pop one for me and one for her *Thirsty* she says and holds her pony up with one hand while she gives me a pop with the other hand and I think she's pretty standing there in the kitchen the blue lighting up the edges of her hair

Patty leans over the sink looks out the window at the back yard where the mole ran off the TV blue and the moon shine off her hair from high above but other than that it's dark and quiet and I think this is how church must feel for some people I want to trap this feeling in my heart and hold it where no one can take it from me her brown hair in a pony her hip pushed to the side standing on one foot the sound of our breathing the sweat from the floor hockey I trap it the way Patty traps the puck hold it inside me

Does Patty's mom

love her I wonder as me and Patty run up the stairs two at a time flip her sheet like we are kings entering a room *Dang* Patty says *it's cold as ice* she runs to the windows and slams them down one at a time Slam Wam Bam one of the nails falls out and the towel over Patty's bed drops to one side Patty crawls under her bed *What are you doing* I say *Just a sec* she says and I find the nail on her pillow and take off my shoes and climb on her bed and nail the towel up because I don't want someone to look in at us

Patty crawls out from under the bed *What are you doing* I say *This* she shoves a magazine at me *Sports Illustrated March 22-29 1978 Property of St. Paul Public Library Where'd you get that At the library look who's on the cover* Martina Navritalova's hitting a tennis ball her legs are full of muscles and her arm is stretched out her fingers pointing at the ball *Cool* I say *For you* she says and puts her arm around me *best friend* I stare at the cover *When did you go to the library* I say because I don't know what to say *The other day* she says and I pick up the magazine and look through it for Martina's picture because she is my favorite and Patty knows it

Patty leans

on her elbows and crosses one leg over the other and wiggles her foot around *Do you like it* she says *Yes* I say and I feel embarrassed but I don't know why

Martina jumps

Martina scores Martina hits one down the line Martina pushes her hand through her hair Martina squints raises her fists wins Wimbledon Martina's calf muscles bulge she is strong she would protect me she would protect me! Martina would protect me! she is strong her muscles are bigger than dad's why can't she be my mom *Look at that* I say *look at her muscles* and Patty hangs her arm around my shoulder *Yeah* she says *she's so strong I wanna be that strong* and I point my toe pull my jeans up flex my calf like I'm Martina Navritalova like I'm strong like I'm somone who would protect someone Patty watches and doesn't say anything pops Bazooka in her mouth *Want one Yeah* I say staring at Martina's calves and her thighs that are thicker than a man's *I hope she kills Chrissie Everett* and I whine out Chrissie's name because she is a sissy baby *Me too* Patty says her mouth full of Bazooka Patty leans back with her hands behind her head snaps her gum and stares at the ceiling cracking and peeling paint drops down on her sometimes when she sleeps

Patty whistles and I read about how Martina is from Czeckslovakia which I already knew and how she whipped Evelina Googalina's butt Martina is so strong I can't stop looking at her muscles strong as any man's men are afraid of her mad dad is I can tell the way he acts when she's on TV *How come you wear that* Patty says and I feel like someone stuck a knife in me *What* I say even though I know she means the purse

my eyes swim I feel so scared Patty doesn't say anything I stare at the picture of Martina hitting it down the sideline stare stare stare she would protect me she would protect me! I am so scared I hold my breath *What's wrong* she says really soft no one knows how soft Patty is except me my head feels like it's swimming in a fish bowl I can't barely see Martina hitting it down the line in her white sleeveless dress *Dunno* I finally say as low as I can to keep from crying Patty moves her leg snaps a bubble *Don't wear it* she says I feel frozen like a deer right before it gets shot in Patty's freezing attic room

He will hit me

my teeth chitterchatter my arms hug tight around my legs the *Sports Illustrated* drops to the floor Patty wraps me up in her blanket *Where'd you get the magazeeeine* I say even though I already know my teeth chittering and chattering I feel like a stupid dummy *At the library* she says and wraps up around me in a ball to keep warm she hugs me with her arms her breath on the back of my neck *Shhh* she says and I feel her body relax around mine *When* I say *A few days ago The day you disappeared* I suck my breath in I don't know if I should tell her I notice she disappears Patty is quiet and one of her arms tightens up around me then relaxes *Yeah* she says soft *Is that where you go Yeah* she says soft *Is the magazine mine Yeah* she says chewing her gum *Did you steal it* my teeth are quiet now *Yeah* she says snaps her gum *Thanks* I say and swallow my gum so I won't choke on it stare at the light on the ceiling the one with so many dead bugs in it the light shines out on the sides

I wish

she wouldn't wear that *What* Patty says *That* I say and think of Martina bending over her muscles popping out *the dress* I say the words fast to keep from crying Patty says *Uh huh* pops her gum *she thinks she has to though* and she pops her gum again *like you*

> The girls fall asleep Patty Patricia P girl
> Little Miss So And So China Doll Girl the fifth grader sleep on the
> mattress
> the towel hangs crookedly showing a slip of black glass between the
> white towel and window frame
> this is how they sleep in each other's arms
> they don't hear anything
> they don't hear her coming in to the house or walking up the stairs or
> pushing back the sheet or standing there for a moment

Patty Little Miss So And So

out of bed screaming in my ears Patty jumps up and so do I mom waves my pajamas in her hand Patty and me stand up like we've been caught doing something bad *I should have known* mom says and then she says *what is going on* like she can't believe whatever it is that's going on *I dunno* Patty says standing in her jeans with one sock on and one sock off lost on the bed somewhere *Don't you mouth back to me* mom says *filthy trash* mom looks at me and I don't know who she's talking about me or Patty or both of us

I stand there like a stupid barely awake not knowing what to do or what's going on *Me and Patty we were just sleeping keeping warm it's cold in here* I blurt out one two three steps and she's got my arm her white knuckled fingers around my arm digging in to my bone *I didn't do anything* I say *I should have known* she says over and over only I don't know what she's talking about I try to look at Patty but mom steps between us shaking me she's going to ruin everything *This is unnatural something is wrong with you Little Miss So And So* and she slaps me across the face stings bees I must be crazy to have this happen to me

Whish whish whish the headboard did it

The windows Patty yells *Do you think I'm a fool do you think I'm a lunatic do you think I don't know what goes on in my own house and just who are you Patty to be saying anything right now what were you two doing on that bed together sick worse than anything* mom looks at me *anything* I say nothing my face stings my mom hit me I'll never move again mom hit me I never knew she would hit me I always knew she would hit me the way she looks at me sometimes mom hates me *The windows were open* Patty says *Why were the windows open* mom says Patty doesn't say anything and mom's fingers dig in she pulls me toward the door *Because of the mole* I shout *What* mom says and looks at me disgusted like she blames me for everything everything bad in the world *Oh I see* she says and looks at my purse swinging around my neck *just like what you told the judge* her face screws up *you're a liar you're a little crazy liar We're trying to catch the mole* I yell like I'm going to die if she hates me I can't take anymore white knuckles on the door washing the sheets she still washes them finds them in my closet collects them in a bundle brings them downstairs to the washer rinses them out bleaches them dries them irons them folds them puts them back in the closet no California sun shine mom hates me one two three she pulls me to Patty's sheet

That's the stupidest thing I've ever heard there aren't any moles around here she drops my arm not making any sense because there's a mole in Patty's back yard it digs tunnels *not in this weather* she looks at Patty who looks down at the floor

Mom holds

my pajamas out to me I stand there not knowing what to do or why she was mad or why she doesn't seem so mad now she hit me I want Patty to do something but she does nothing Patty must hate me too suddenly mom's face looks disgusted again like she thought of something really gross and she drops my pajamas on the floor and says to Patty *You're not welcome at my house or work ever again* mom pushes through the sheet *not ever again* I think I'm going to die don't understand what happened what we did wrong mom says from the hall *Be home by ten Little Miss So And So* she says in a bony white knuckle voice and I look at Patty who looks mad and I look at the floor nothing makes sense brown shaggy carpet matted over in places

How's my girl
Gramma says
Okay I say
Just okay something wrong
Nothing gramma
How's school
Okay I say
How's your mom

Okay I say
Uh huh gramma says
Gramma guess what
What
Me and Patty almost caught a mole
Oh she says that's just good that's not easy to do
No I say
Gramma I say feel sadder than sad but don't tell her
Yah
You are the cream in my coffee
You are the cream in my coffee too granddaughter

Tell her

anything mad dad steps up from downstairs grabs the phone bang he slams it down *No* I shake my head scared he was listening to me *She ask you how you are* I nod *Did you tell her you're okay* I nod *From now on you tell her you're good hear me* I nod

She tell you anything I stare can't ask questions even though he doesn't make sense *did she* I don't answer he looks at me sideways *about being you know Indian What* I act stupid he grabs the trim high up over his head *Did she say she's we're you're Indian* I don't know what to say because she tells me I'm Indian but not today he smashes his face in his arm closes his eyes I think he's crying *Not today* I say his face in his arm *Good* he says his voice shaky *don't listen to her if she does* he rubs his face in his shirtsleeve *it doesn't matter you hear* his eyes red *doesn't matter none of it*

School to

morrow I can't go I can't go I can't go please someone help me mad dad came in please someone to my room bed can't go can't go someone help me please Patty she disappeared all weekend went away on Easter my trip to gramma's mom canceled told gramma she's having more trouble with me I'm bad please some one Patty disappeared she's ignoring me hates me for what mom did we were cold please some one help me mad dad to night the sheets still wet still wet my body is frozen rocks on a river bed can't move my butt rock I swear we were looking for the mole swear it please mom please love me don't hate me don't leave me Patty can't go I'll die rock bed I'll die dead rock bed rock head rock back rock legs wet sticky can't move them the sheets are wet sticky cold rock bed head rock my head rock heavy like it used to be it came back heavy head crack the back the head board spat dead dying done roasted chicken on a spit twirl twirl spin spin everyone hates me mad dad frozen jelly between my legs can't move can't move my legs between my butt it's cold wet sticky where's Patty she hates me mom hates me Patty hates me everyone hates me I can't see the other kids the head board cracked my head ow ow ow it hurts my head rock heavy my back bent like a old lady's I get a cane go to school hobble with it it's back all the old feelings Patty's gone it's back the judge oatmeal five year old crazy retard

mad dad's feet at the door he's back for more the head board bored head cracked whoosh I climb to the sky make my bed fly bye bye house down below mad dad's feet mom's asleep in the living room chair mad dad's back! his feet are at my door big wooly feet and his long licking tongue I climb to the sky make my bed rise up a million miles high mad dad opens the door I have the tallest bed in all the world! mad dad walks inside the tallest bed in all the world taller than anything anywhere no one can reach me up here I lean over the side of my bed I see mad dad far below he hops on his feet he jumps in circles! he shouts I AM GOING TO GOBBLE YOU UP AS A MIDEVENING SNACK and yells YOU LITTLE BITCH I AM GOING TO MAKE YOU WISH YOU WERE NEVER BORN and screams YOU WILL HAVE TO COME DOWN SOONER OR LATER he shakes his fist but he can't reach me no siree mad dad cannot get me on my bed the tallest bed in all the world no school to morrow I cannot go I CAN WAIT he says and so he does and so he does

YOU LITTLE BABY

mad dad yells up the stairs GET YOUR ASS UP YOURE NOT SICK YOURE GOING TO SCHOOL I'm dead bones on my bed don't make me go to school don't make me be me let me be Patty or Martina or Fran Tarkington or Bobby Orr smashing people in the boards let me have big muscles to run with hit with fight with keep me strong don't let me be me my arms are too skinny please don't make me go to school I'm naked everyone will laugh let me be anything but me let me be a tree in the mountains where no people go let me be a bird fly away high as high as my bed climbs let me be Mark or Annette or Rachel or one of the Brady boys or Scooby Doo or Fonzie or my teacher's daughter living in a home where bad things don't happen or the girl down the block who won't talk to me or the prissy girls at church that I hate or Mary Tyler Moore swinging her hat in the air or Fran Tarkington throwing touchdowns or Ahmad Rashad catching them or Chuck Foreman with big shoulders the biggest shoulders in all the world!

Up

and at em mom clicks on my light blue lamp in the shape of a girl's ice skate I've been awake for an hour she slides back my curtain it's still dark outside I think I'll die seeing the dark morning hearing the trucks drive by being so tired Patty is gone mom smiles

I am a noodle the wet stickiness dried caked between my legs and butt *Wake up* mom shakes my shoulder *up and at em* her eyes slit I see the devil run through them if I don't move she'll pull me out say I wet the bed rip the sheets off take them downstairs I make myself move but my body is a spaghetti noodle it's somebody else's body I live in sometimes I can't barely move even to get my covers off *It's going to be a beautiful day* mom says and she doesn't pull back my quilt to see if I wet my bed last night *breakfast will be ready fifteen minutes* she walks out the door *we're having oatmeal* and then she stops in the hall and looks at me *are you sick* No I shake the body wobbly so wobbly I am scared I might fall down the stairs mom leaves I slide out of bed sit down next to Clarence sit there for a long time staring at nothing at the ceiling at the navy blue carpeting at the lines on the wall

Little Miss So And So

my shoulders jump but the rest of me doesn't move mad dad's work boots in the doorway YOU LITTLE BABY GET YOUR ASS UP YOURE NOT SICK YOURE GOING TO SCHOOL he grabs my shoulder wraps his fingers under my arm pit and pops my arm *Ah* I say a little mouse *Damn it* he says *let's go* I don't feel much except for a burning in my shoulder my arm doesn't move at all mad dad gets on top of me straddles me grabs my collarbone squeezes hard and jams my arm in to my shoulder I slide to the floor my arm burning screaming then nothing no pain no feeling he stands over me laughs *Get up you're going down for breakfast* leans closer to my face *don't you tell anyone* devil in his face warning me and so I don't and so I don't

I don't tell

mom why would I tell her she doesn't care what he does to me I sit at the table staring seeing two then three tables three bowls three spoons three cups the garage door opens slams shut dad left for work mom will be mad she always wants to eat as a family a can slices open *Want some cottage cheese and peaches* mom says I think she must be crazy who eats cottage cheese for breakfast *No* I shake my head her ring hits the counter she is angry the can opener starts again *Can you at least talk to me* she says does she remember what she did she talks about work a lady did something she didn't like she talks like nothing happened at Patty's like my sheets are clean like I didn't stuff my crusty underwear in the back of my closet like I didn't put two more nickels in the purse like I don't have the purse around my neck so kids can make fun of me *dork! geek!* oatmeal steams my face mom sprinkles white sugar over it

Patty isn't

on the bus I zip up my jacket so none of the kids can see my purse even though everyone knows it's there it's been there ever since I moved to the California sun east side of Saint Paul I sit in the front behind the driver Jack who has a big chin and smokes while he drives the other kids yell at each other and Patty doesn't come out of her house and Jack drives away *Move over* Kelly a fourth grader says to someone in the seat behind me and all I can feel is relief that she's not talking to me that I don't have to talk to anyone I'm too tired to talk my arm hurts a truck whooshes by Patty doesn't run out of her house at the last second waving her hand and yelling at Jack to wait I watch her house it's gray and cold out I push my face into the glass until my cheek bones hurt

Mrs. Olson

says *Quiet* I sit with my desk top up so Mrs. Olson can't see me holding my arm *But* Jake says and Mrs. Olson says *Out* and Jake has to go to the principal who'll write him a yellow slip and send a copy home Jake's shoes squeak my arm hurts like someone shot me and then it doesn't hurt as much and then it hurts again bad *Fifth grade girl* Mrs. Olson says *fifth grade girl* out in the hall someone yells *Mark!* I yell *What* and kids in the class laugh and I am confused because for a second I thought my name was Mark Mrs. Olson says *Yelling is not allowed in the classroom I had to say your name twice before you responded to me now please put your desk top down* and I don't say anything why did I think Mark was my name Mrs. Olson is standing next to my desk her stomach rolled out over her black pants and her hands on her hips she's wearing a pink sweater with a white spot on it like she spilled her milk *Did you hear me* she says and I nod my head yes trying to keep from having to talk cause I'll cry *then put your desk top down* I reach up with my good arm and lean the desk top on my head and pull the rod out and grab the desk top off my head and put it down with my good arm Mrs. Olson says *I'm not impressed* and I stare at the pencil groove at the top of my desk to keep from having to talk Mrs. Olson folds her hands together like she's in church *Where's your sidekick* I shrug my good shoulder *Um hum* she says and walks to the front of the class *okay class* she says *we're going to go over* and I pull the purse off and crack my desk top and shove it in until it fits along the side of the desk in the curve between the papers and the smooth cold metal of the desk

I forgot

my permission slip and so I have to stay in the principal's office until the end of the day meaning until the bell rings the secretary made that clear *Did I make that clear* she said and I nodded but I didn't say anything because she might find out about my arm and take me into court again the entire fifth grade went to the Saint Paul Capitol to see how the government works firsthand and then they get a brown bag lunch with chocolate milk and then they go to Schmidt's Brewery the entire fifth grade class gets to skip class and drive around in a bus all day eating apples and chocolate milk and cookies and I have to sit with the secretary who has a blue scarf wrapped around her neck because I forgot to get the permission slip signed

I sit and think

about this and wonder about Patty and stare at nothing until the principal Mr. Fayen walks in says *Who's she* and the secretary says *A fifth grader from Mrs. Olson's she didn't bring her permission slip for their field trip Oh* he says and I look at him without looking at him he has black curly hair and a crooked pointer finger and a beard and two big turquoise rings because he collects rocks and polishes them into jewelry he tells us this the same thing every year in the auditorium at the beginning of the school year *Don't you have anything to do* he says and I shake my head and he looks at the secretary her scarf tied in a knot around her neck and says *Send her to the library there's no sense in her sitting here all day Okay* the secretary says and writes me a pass to walk in the hallways without a teacher and so I do

I give the pass to Mrs. Larkin the librarian and she smiles last year she had to order in high school books even though I was in fourth grade my teacher gave me special permission to read higher because elementary school books are too easy *You're back* she says I nod *I haven't seen you in a while* she says and I try to shrug my shoulders but it's really hard to do because my arm still hurts *Can I help you find something* she twirls a ring on her finger like she used to do last year *help yourself to the candy* she says about the bowl on her desk and I take a butterscotch piece and use one hand to open the candy *Is your other hand okay* Mrs. Larkin says *Nah* I say meaning to answer her question about whether she can help me but I realize when it comes out of my mouth that it sounds like I'm saying I'm not okay I put the candy in my mouth the sweet buttery scotch runs all over my mouth *What's wrong* Mrs. Larkin says and I say nothing go to the magazine section and get kids magazines on sports and sit down in one of the orange modern bean bag chairs the sports magazines are stupid made for little kids and I don't find any pictures of Martina Navritalova in them I close my eyes roll over on my good arm and let my chin dig into the beans little pellets against my face

Girl Who Is

A Good Reader! Girl Who Is A Good Reader! I open my eyes don't know where I am or who I am Mrs. Larkin is leaning over me her brown bead necklace hanging in my face two kindergarten kids staring at me there's drool on the bean bag chair I grab my hurting arm without thinking *Are you all right* Mrs. Larkin says and I don't say or do anything I don't nod yes or no or pretend like I'm fine I just stare at her still half asleep wishing for a second that I could tell her she could hold me take me away save me from mom and dad save me!

I nod Yes *You were screaming in your sleep* Mrs. Larkin says and puts her hand on my forehead *you're hot* I don't say anything she has long fingers and a puggy nose with freckles *is something wrong with your arm* she says and I feel her fingers on my shoulder *No* I say concentrating hard on the orange carpet *I'm fine* don't cry don't cry orange carpet *Oh no* she says *you're sick I'm going to send you down to the nurse* and I freeze up can't think creepy crawly spider fingers *Stay there I'll write you a pass* and so I stay in the bean bag chair wipe drool off with my sleeve and hope the kindergarteners aren't still staring at me like I'm a dork I reach down the purse is gone I left it in my desk oh no

At the hall

where I'm supposed to turn to go to the nurse's I go straight past the jackets hung up outside each room and the shelves above the jackets mittens and scarves and book bags and lunch boxes Scooby Doo and the Mystery Machine and Kung Fu and Charlie's Angels I don't have a lunch box like those mom sends mine in brown paper bags Patty will come back soon the light at the end of the hall is bright Patty will be back soon I turn the handle to my classroom round and smooth and cold it clicks to one side and then to the other side I can't get in

Down

the stairs march one two three I'm in a lotta trouble up down march around Patty's gone dad'll be home soon the school called to tell mom she forgot to sign the permission slip I'm getting detention for leaving school mom is mad that I left school that I didn't tell her about the field trip says I was faking being sick oops! now I'm in for it I ruined mom's night again she bought me and dad matching white baseball hats I ruined everything mom says I ruined her night and her nice presents she wants me and dad to dress like twins

this is just great is what I think practicing to be in the army I'm going to join the army march up down around until mom yells at me from the kitchen where she's cooking sloppy joes *Stop that! You're driving me crazy!* so I stop sit down on the top step hold my arm lean against the wallpaper with gold fuzzy decorations in the shape of a crown like mom and dad are trying to be queens and kings from England it's stupid Patty is gone the purse is locked in my desk at school if dad finds out he'll whip me the way he did the last time when I buried it in the vacant lot I was seven I had to go dig it up if he ever caught me without it again he said he'd whip me till I bled dead stead my brain isn't working I can't make sense of my thoughts tots spots Patty is gone dad's gonna whip me till I bleed steed deed my thoughts grind into the ground I get little again a five year old retard tard fard

wham slam bam mad dad's home I'm a retard drooling on the fuzzy decorated wall he's going to kill me my ears get big as cauliflower big enough to hear what I don't want to hear I shrink in to the wall drool drool drool all over mom's new white baseball hat she made me try on before the school called before I ruined her day before I ruined her nice surprise

Whistle whistle whistle

I'm not in fifth grade anymore I'm five dad's whistling in his basement bathroom washing up getting ready for dinner rolls n sloppy joe meat n carrot sticks shaved clean of the dirty skin chopped up in little pieces *Wash up* mom says cheery hoping mad dad will stay in a good mood not hit her I don't move a million minutes pass *We're eating soon* mom says cheery hoping mad dad will stay in a good mood not beat her he's going to beat me if he finds out I wash up the soap slips through my hands like a fat mole

I have to get downstairs eat do the dishes and get back upstairs without mad dad whistling man finding out the purse is gone I want to hide disappear be someone else fly away Patty is gone she is gone I walk down the stairs don't let mad dad see my arm hurts hope hope hope mom doesn't tell him about the permission slip I walk into the kitchen backwards mom and mad dad are eating at the table *What are you doing* mom says she's going to tell him *Just seeing what time it is* I say like I'm dumb *Come and sit down* mom says she always wants us to be a perfect family that eats together and wears matching hats so no one will know what it's really like in here the spoon covered with sloppy joe meat sits on the stove I will have to clean it up it will stick to the stove before I know it I'm at the table covered with a gold partridge tablecloth partridge in a pear tree!

Sit down

you little weirdo mad dad snaps uh oh I made him mad by walking backwards now he'll beat me till I bleed steed feed *Sit down* he says so I slouch couch fouch down fast so he can't see my stomach fumach dumach covered by the table fable pable he scoops sloppy joe meat in his mouth with a roll looks at me his eyebrows crumpled *We had an incident at school today* mom says why does she tell *What* he says slopping meat I give up stop being scared my body collapses *The secretary says she didn't give us* nah nah nah *her permission slip* nah nah *to sign* nah nah nah I stop listening my ears go away inside my head I don't care he's going to beat me can't stop him so I don't care mom tells on me nah nah nah mad dad crushes bread between his fingers I slouch down don't listen LITTLE MISS SO AND SO he says then says to mom *on top of all this we have a kid that can't hear* mom eats her food doesn't look up doesn't want to get hit why did she tell

Your mother went out and bought you a present and this is how you repay her he says pointing his fork at me eating another sloppy joe the meat spills out on the plate mom sits up super straight in her chair the way she does when she's nervous I don't want the hat but I can't say I hate the hat I have to make him stop thinking about the hat so he doesn't see the purse is gone he told me never take it off he points his fork chews hard

It'll be okay husband mom says mad dad is getting steamed *these things happen sometimes she's just a child No it's not okay* mad dad says stops chewing *why aren't you watching her better* and now mom and me really see it coming here it comes steam whistle shooting through my brain Whoo! Whoo! *What the hell is wrong with you stupid bitch* mad dad says to mom I stop eating *I* she says *I nothing* he says *no excuses* he stands up hits her across her face snaps her neck she makes a noise *Stupid bitch our kid is fucking up in school because of you* she covers her face he hits her again sloppy joe meat on my fork

mad dad picks up the edge of the table till the dishes fall off on top of mom n me jump up the pan of sloppy joe meat falls in mom's lap she screams *Get upstairs* she yells at me *Stupid fucking dumb bitch* mad dad hits her arms *Get upstairs* she swings at me *get* I run upstairs two at a time who cares if my arm hurts I close the door get in bed listen to them scream *I'm sorry! I won't do it again Bitch! Stop! Please! I'm sorry* crashing no more sound my light is out hide under my quilt don't move don't blink my eyes animals in the dark

Sound

is gone no screaming no crashing no begging just black sound hold my breath count in my head onetwothreefourfive no sound garage door goes up truck starts garage door goes down headlights jerk in my window he's gone

Baby

I'm sorry I'm sorry baby that you have to go through this I'm sorry baby wake up mom's crying *sorry sorry sorry* petting my hair *baby I'm sorry he's gone he had a drink he didn't mean it* I see her face in the moonlight white through the curtain *he didn't* I say nothing she told him *Baby* my arm hurts *Baby* her tears drip on my face *forgive me shhh go to sleep it's going to be all right* her cheek is bruised I can see it in the white moonlight *Get some sleep I'm sorry baby you don't deserve this he didn't mean it go to sleep we'll forget about it in the morning okay we'll have pancakes* she wipes her face her tears drip down my neck they're cold

How's my girl
Gramma says
Okay I say
Just okay
Yes
How's your dad
Okay I say
How's your mom
Sorry
Sorry
Yes sorry
Why
She got mad at me
Oh gramma says are you okay
I'm okay
Oh gramma says and sounds sad
Gramma I say am I still the cream in your coffee
Granddaughter she says you will always be the cream in my coffee

Jack

closes the door turns up the heater we have to idle for four minutes even though I'm the only one getting on at this stop Patty hasn't been around for four days mad dad's been gone for two ever since he threw the table on mom the other kids scream and yell I stare out the window at nothing the day is a gray blur cold and rainy Katie sits in the seat in front of me she is in second grade she lives behind me next to the vacant lot she breathes on the glass fogs it up draws hearts with her fingertip Jack revs the bus no Patty I left my purse at school again dad's not home to see it gray nothing outside I stare

the bus jumps forward then kids yell *Hey! Hey! Bus driver wait!* Jack looks in his long side mirror the bus sighs then stops some kids are pointing yelling I kneel on my seat see Patty run down Rose Avenue and then up the bus steps her cheeks are red her hair is wet stuck back in a pony tail a boy yells *Hey it's P girl* then the other kids laugh talk they're not interested in Patty the girl who used to pee in her seat wear stinky clothes Jack nods shuts the door I stare at her long saggy jeans dark blue zipper sweatshirt white bumper broken in Reebok tennis shoes

Hey she says slides into my seat *what's happening* her face is red and white and wet everyone is talking no one is paying attention to her any more she punches my shoulder it doesn't hurt Patty is back! she puts her hands into her sweatshirt pockets *Hey* she says again balls her hands up under her sweatshirt she's nervous stares at the top of the seat in front of us green padded vinyl in case our heads hit it during an accident I lean on it the hard padding feels good on my forehead Patty's back!

Jack takes a corner sharp slides Patty into me smashes me against the window Katie's heart slips makes a jagged line like a V the boys yell *Ewww get off me Sorry kids* Jack waves his hand in the rear view mirror straightens the bus *Shat up* a boy yells from the back Patty's still on top of me past the blonde brick apartment buildings square and flat past the baseball fields past the woods past the pond past the park wet swing sets monkey bars chain link fence gas station insurance company building's sign says *Have five minutes stop in we'll drop your price by 25% guaranteed see us for all your needs* Patty's still on top of me I think this must mean she likes me doesn't hate me her hands balled in her sweatshirt pockets

Puddles

in the school parking lot a line of dark orange buses wet creepy crawling kids like swarming bees Patty's squishing me *Stay in your seats until we reach the front* Jack holds his hand up brakes idles everyone sits on the edges of their seats Patty doesn't move I don't move the bus lurches idles lurches idles Patty takes her left hand out keeps it in a ball puts it on her leg *Stupid idiot* someone yells Patty unfolds her fingers puts her hand on my leg *Dink* someone shouts *Hey* Jack yells lifts his hand Patty grabs my hand holds it tight *All right everyone off* Jack opens the door it cuts in half slides apart before I know what I'm doing I grab Patty kiss her on the cheek her hand pokes me in the stomach all the other kids are in the aisle pushing to get out the cold air rushes in through the door *Lezzies dykes look at that gays freaks fags look at that a girl kissed another girl!*

OHHHHHHH!!!! all the girls yell they don't touch our seat when they walk by they lean away from us my hands drop down I stare at the seat think oh no Patty looks out the window it's raining in straight lines the other kids are yelling laughing grossing out they run onto the playground *P girl and the fifth grade girl kissed they're lezzies dykes fags freaks!*

I put my forehead on the seat oh no I don't know what I just did Patty doesn't say anything did I do something bad does she think so *C'mon girls* Jack says looking at us in the rear view mirror *I don't know what just happened but you need to get off the bus*

Jump

in a puddle Patty says and stomps with two feet flat footed sprays mud water all over the slide all the other kids are inside *Let's go!* and so we do we run Rocky style our fists in the air *Yo Adrian!* around the outside of the school we spy around the corners our bodies pushed up against the brick we spy looking for teachers and janitors and hall monitors we move slow we are sneaky China girls then fast Patty makes a pose Bruce Jenner

I laugh like it's California sun on my face like I know nothing else but happiness like Payne Avenue is not one block away like mad dad is dead mom and me live in an apartment somewhere like me and Patty will be together best friends forever and ever I love her long saggy jeans Bruce Jenner muscles I laugh like mad dad won't smash the night time whip me hit me break me I laugh and laugh and laugh Patty's cheeks dark wet sweatshirt ducking running spying I laugh like there is nothing else in all the world nothing else in all the world! but me and Patty and the puddles wet mud on the cuffs of our jeans we're late for school and we laugh like there is nothing else in all the world but us

Yo Adrian!

my fists in the air rain hits our faces gray day cold day we're late for school day Patty's shoes are muddy n wet her cheeks are rose red her breath comes out of her mouth like lace she grabs me pushes me against the school bricks bite into my head but I don't care she holds me rain in lines from the sky Patty holds me she kisses me her breath on my lips *Let's go* she whispers *Okay* I say her lips and cheeks rose red

we are Bruce Jenner! we are Martina Navratilova! we are Ahmad Rashad Fran Tarkington Muhammad Ali float like a butterfly sting like a bee fists above our head Rocky Balboa style I am Rocky! *Yo Adrian I love you!* we run across the playground around the slide through the swings push them high in the air the other kids are in school we run the cuffs on our jeans are wet they hit our ankles we don't care! we run faster than anyone has ever run before *Yo Adrian! I love you!* faster than anyone has ever run before over the sidewalk across the baseball field red thick sand on our shoes we run over left field into the trees black trees dark trees wet trees trees with wet black skin they stand over us with curled branches we run our feet move our muscles are strong laughing where are we going I don't know I don't care we run we breathe listen to our breath listen to our breath listen to our breath

we run under the trees to the other side me and Patty away from school the laughing kids *dykes fags freaks* we bend over our breath knitting together I can do anything the strongest person in all the world when I'm with Patty my best friend forever and ever we laugh high five like she scored a goal I made a save nothing can break us apart me and Patty stand then we run laugh breathe like there is nothing in all the world but us

Around

the corner across the street we are laughing falling on the smooth wet grass *Oh yeah* Patty yells we can't stop laughing we are on the other side now no one from school can see us call the turquoise principal or the police or mom or dad *dykes fags freaks!* no one can see us me and Patty rolling sliding laughing getting wet no school no parents no teacher we are free!

Her lips

are red she looks in my eyes and there's lightning in my stomach that grows into my chest shoots up my neck out my mouth I smile a real smile not the fake smile I give to everyone so they leave me alone *Let's take the bus* she says *I got two fifty* I say n pull out nickels from my jacket Patty looks at me funny *Let's go downtown* she says turns away from the school her tennis shoes leave soft round red marks on the sidewalk

Downtown

the bus driver says Patty nods drops change in a machine it clinks around like it's going down a conveyor belt I've never been on a city bus before!

I paid for her too Patty says to the bus driver is the color of my gramma he nods me and Patty sit in the back I want to jump on her *Yo Adrian! I love you!* Rocky Balboa style I am the Italian Stallion I am going to skip school forever with Patty we are riding on a city bus mom doesn't let me they're too dangerous

we sit next to each other Patty takes out her super ball bounces it off the seat traps it with her hand the bus drives past houses and trees drying out wet black skin turning gray dried out crackling bark I squint my eyes make the houses and the tree branches blur twist flip flop in the wind brrrr cat purring ball bouncing brrrr me and Patty skipping school

Hey girl! says a man who looks as old as Patty's oldest brother he sits behind us *going around town again* Patty snaps her ball brrr *Hey hey town girl* Patty snaps her ball brrr brrr purr the man gets up sits across the aisle from us *Town girl going around town ya gonna ride the bus all day long* Patty snaps her ball *Ahey* he pokes her in the shoulder *Don't touch me again* she says *I dint* he says *Shut the frick up* Patty says the way her brothers talk she bounces her ball she looks like she could kill someone he sits down Patty bounces her ball brrrr brrrr brrrr

The bus

screeches in the middle of downtown St. Paul I usually see it from the freeway except me and mom came down here once to get some court papers on the house for mad dad but mom's afraid to be here she thinks it's dangerous to be here because of the black people who live on the street and the men who will hurt you when you park she told me to run and scream if a man grabbed me run and scream! I didn't say anything wondered what's wrong with her I just nodded and walked with her to the courthouse *Okay* she said again once we got on the sidewalk *run and scream* okay I nodded my head but thought different thoughts

when me and Patty walk up front the man yells *Hey town girl see you next week* Patty's pony tail jerks a little but she doesn't say anything the buildings are rose colored made out of blocks of stone a million times taller than me me and Patty skipping school *lezzies dykes fags freaks!* I'm never going back to school *Do you know him* I say to Patty when the bus pulls away *Nuh* she says not saying no or yes meaning she knows him meaning she rides the bus when she disappears now I know what she does all day long! now I know what Patty does all day long!

We run

past rose colored buildings a million miles high around the black light posts between the people on the sidewalks we run! we are Chuck Foreman we are Ahmad Rashad we are Walter Payton we are the Heisman trophy winner our hands stuck out to the side no one can hurt us! not mad dad not Patty's brothers not Fayen not a man in a parking ramp not no one! we spin around the man in the overalls jump over the curb we run we score we win me and Patty win the game the division the playoffs the Super Bowl we are World Champions! we run full tilt without looking who cares about cars we run into a square park in the middle of downtown we run through a black iron fence under trees around the benches hop hop scare the birds breathing hard yolky sun drying our hair and jeans we breathe hard one two three breaths *lezzies dykes fags freaks!* we don't care we are Doctor J jumping from the free throw line slam bam wham I jump on a park bench hands in the air breathing hard the yolky sun in my hair *Yo Adrian! I love you! We are the champions!*

The library

is across from the park *Wanna see something* Patty says *Sure* I say *I'm Muhammad Ali* and I jump off the bench but now Patty is serious she is quiet she points *The library* I look at it two stories tall wide as the park that old kind of building that looks like it's from England made out of gray stone with leaves carved everywhere *Let's go in* Patty says *Okay* I say and I think about how dumb I am sometimes

Your mouth

is nasty a black man says to a white woman *Say what* she says *my MOUTH!* I stop in front of her she glares at me I feel like a little little little kid *What* I say like I'm two looking up at a tall grown up *What what* she says pushes me out of the way *Hey* he says *don't push that girl* and they yell Patty grabs me pulls me into the library *Why do you do that* she says *what's wrong with you I don't know* I say shrug my shoulders but I do know I thought she was calling me because my name is Mouth I say my name is Mouth!

Patty fills

out a day pass for me except she writes Kelly Johnson instead of my name Patty thinks of everything Patty takes my hand she is serious we go up stairs made out of marble to the top floor Patty leans into a door so heavy we can barely open it *Shhh* she says her pony tail hits me in the face the room has tiny windows way up high so high the light is gray n dusty a woman sits at a desk on the other side there are shelves and shelves of books everywhere Patty takes me down an aisle of shelves with every kind of magazine you could ever want! *Bees and Other Insects Cars and Motors Brides To Be Contemporary Architecture Time Newsweek Life Horses Poetry in America Gardening in America Sports in America Sports Illustrated The College Athlete* everything in all the world! the library has everything in all the world! Patty gets on her knees to read something off the shelf I go through every single magazine on sports one after the other no one else is in the room but me and Patty and the lady behind the desk I look at the pictures their legs and arms are like the dusty air so beautiful the way they jump through the air no one can touch them

Want to see something else Patty says from behind me I practically jump out of my skin she swallows loud *Yes* I say I put the magazines back like I'm in church we walk over to the woman *May I assist you* she says she acts like we are adults folds her hands into each other *Yes* Patty says *May we have the Madama Butterfly filmstrip Do you have your card with you* the woman smiles Patty hands her the card *Thank you Sally Johnson* she walks to the wall the dusty light falls on her head she pulls out a skinny box hands it to Patty *You may use room number one* she says sits down behind the desk again

we sit in the room with one small light above our heads *I made it so we're sisters* Patty says and unwinds the filmstrip part way *that way we'll always be together* and now she's really serious her lips are tight she puts the tape in the tape player and winds the filmstrip into the projector *Kill the lights* she says so I do

Madama Butterfly it says across the wall I don't know what we're watching Patty pushes the play button on the tape player *Just wait* the music starts Patty clicks the filmstrip a lady with her arms in the air is on the wall then a woman is singing she sounds like a siren I never heard anything like it *This is opera* Patty says and I sit next to her we watch the opera in the little room with a lady who sings like she could kill somebody I love her I want to be her singing so loud being so big on a stage she can't disappear she could never disappear there's no way she could ever disappear!

* * *

LAAAAA

I am a lady on stage the spotlight's on me I slide across the kitchen floor in my soccer socks mom and mad dad never caught me skipping school Patty forged our notes now school's over now it's summer now me and Patty play soccer instead of floor hockey mom drives us to games and practices we wear matching purple jerseys

LAAAAA mad dad doesn't notice that I don't wear the purse anymore he's working two jobs during the day he's at the city and at nights and on the weekends he roofs when we cleaned out our desks I left the purse in the desk now I throw out the nickels I flush them down the toilet fluush no more purse no more nickels me and Patty don't need money for anything we steal everything Blow Pop suckers Hershey Kisses combs pony tail holders shoes matching red soccer shorts with three white stripes down the side notebooks for us to diagram plays garden gloves just in case we ever catch the mole and have to carry it somewhere before we let it go orange coffee cups from Walgreens a statue of a teddy bear with a ruby on its stomach fake miniature roses made out of glued cloth to give to mom for driving us to soccer it's nice of her! it's nice of her!

La la la la la luh lah lulu laaaa I run into the dining room *Is Patty here yet* mom yells from upstairs she forgot about saying Patty could never come into her house again *La la la la lah* I back into the new wallpaper mom and mad dad put in brown stripes with a beige background I run as fast I can across the carpet until I reach the kitchen floor then I sliiiide on my socks *LAAAA!! LAAAAA!! LAAAAAA!!* I wham! into the table *What's going on* mom yells from upstairs *LAAAA!!* mom comes down stairs watches me for a second makes a face walks into the living room *LA! LA! LA!* I put my arms in the air like I'm a gymnast in the Olympics like I stuck the landing! a perfect ten thank you thank you I bow all around *Come on it's time to go* mom says Patty knocks on the back door *LAAA! LAAA!* I answer it Patty smiles she has her cleats around her neck we only wear our soccer shoes on grass or we'll wear out the cleats we play the Burnsville Blizzards today

The Burnsville Blizzards!

the Burnsville Blizzards! they beat us last time 3-1 they are gold and black bumble bees they're two games ahead of us in the conference if we don't win today we won't be able to win the conference I want to win! last night I slept at Patty's *dykes fags freaks* we kissed all night long in her bedroom behind her blue sheet with the towels blowing in the breeze we kissed and hugged I let her touch me we slept just the sound of our breathing and the wind blowing and the owl down by the river *hoo hoo hoo* we went to bed early because we had to be well rested for the game today the game today!

me and Patty warm up together the other girls on our team go to a different school we don't know them we pass with our instep that's hard to do we pass with the inside of our feet that's easy to do we don't kick with our toes we don't kick with our toes! no one who plays soccer for real kicks with their toes! we read that in *Soccer for Beginners* we trap with our thighs drop the ball down at our feet trap it with the bottom of our feet we head back and forth two three times in a row Patty plays forward she is fast she scores goals lots of them I play defense one of the dads said last game *That little number nine sure is something you can count on her to get the ball every time* and I say you can count on me number nine every time! every time!

Tweet!

the ref blows his whistle Mr. Sampson my coach has a brown beard that runs up the sides of his face like a rug *Be tough* he says to me I nod my mom is on the sidelines with the other moms and dads she sits in her lawn chair in tan shorts she crosses her legs dad says her legs are the purest white you have ever seen she puts on brown sun glasses big as the eyes of an owl Patty gets the kick off dribbles it around one girl then another then another then another! I jump in the air I get so excited she toe kicks it the goalie slides misses it Patty scores! the parents cheer Patty turns and walks to the kick off line one of the girls on our team puts her hand out Patty slaps it I jump on her *Way to go* I yell *I kicked it with my toe* she says I jump on her again *Who cares* I say *you scored!* another girl slaps her shoulder Patty frowns watches the grass while we walk back to the center line Kickers one Blizzards none!

Half time

and it's still one to nothing we eat orange slices out of baggies and drink Sunkist Mello Yello and Hawaiian Punch Mr. Sampson tells us to stay spread out *Don't bunch! Pass as a team and if you get stuck on defense kick it out of bounds!* I nod an orange slice in my mouth like a big orange smile Patty is quiet she wants to win bad we do our cheer all hands in the middle *One Two Three Go Kickers!*

I pull up my shin guards even though the padding makes my shins sweat I'm ready to float like a butterfly sting like a bee we have to win! a Blizzard girl dribbles toward me I take it from her kick it down the field as hard as I can my whole body kicks it the parents cheer Patty snags it shoots hits the post boing! then they almost score on us but our goalie hits it out at the last second bap! only two minutes left! two minutes and we'll win the game! two minutes and Patty scored the only goal! two minutes and we can still win the division! the ref blows his whistle tweet tweet time out a girl on the other team can't breathe *She has asthma* the parents yell me and Patty stand by ourselves *dykes fags freaks!* but we don't care the other girls are not as good as us they're not as serious as us they're not as tough as us

We don't care!
we don't like them anyway!

Let's get the show on the road ref a parent yells *I still need to cut the grass today* and the parents laugh the ref raises his hand the girl is under a tree tweet! tweet! one of the girls on my team throws the ball in Patty kicks it down the sideline runs after it past the girls on the other team gets it in the corner the parents yell *cross it pass it shoot it* Patty kicks the ball in the middle of the field one of the girls on our team kicks it out of bounds we didn't score! they throw it in their girl kicks it there can't be much time left! all of a sudden one of their girls kicks it hard it goes over my head in slow motion like I am floating in my bed up to the ceiling the tallest bed in all the world! the tallest bed in all the world!

I don't hear anything no cheering no yelling I turn my cleats dig in my body moves it's like the dusty air in the library floating the opera lady singing *LAAAA!* Muhammad Ali boxing Martina Navritalova hitting Fran Tarkenton scrambling Chuck Foreman dodging Bruce Jenner throwing Doctor J jumping Ahmad Rashad catching I run! I run in slow motion but I run faster than the other girl kick the ball with my toe so what! the coach told me to boom! I kick it out of bounds past the bushes tweet! tweet! game's over we won me and Patty won! Kickers one Blizzards none!

Gramma
I say
What she says
We won we won the Kickers won one to nothing!
I am so proud
I love you gramma
I love you granddaughter cream in my coffee

Muhammad

Ali is me I am Muhammad Ali I dance on my toes float through the air spin in circles I combo punch upper cut right upper cut left one two three I bow *Thank you thank you tha thrilla in Manilla right here* mad dad walking through the back yard one block off Payne *tha thrilla right here right here tha thrilla!* stomp stomp stomp I see mad dad mad dad sees me

Tha thrilla in Manilla!
step right up folks
tha thrilla in Manilla
right here right here in eastside St. Paul
you don't have to take a plane or a train
it's all right here!

mad dad drags me into the house his fingers are wrapped tight around my arm my skinny skinny arm *How long did you think you could get away with this Huh* I cry I don't want to be in the house with him *How long* he is crazy *How long* crazy man crazy mad dad bashes me into the cupboards switches hands shuts the door locks it click like a bone breaking

You don't have to travel south to see tha thrilla in Manilla
it's right here!
step right up!

I'm trapped in the house with mad dad help someone he drags me through the kitchen *How long I asked you how long* I choke *Where is it huh* he shakes me drags me up the stairs one two three my legs butt slams into them *How long did you think you could go where is it* he pins me against the wall at the top of the stairs choke choke *Do you think I'm stupid* he looks me in the eyes choke choke spit on my face

Tha thrilla in Manilla! I say tha thrilla in Manilla!

wham I swing at mad dad I miss wham I swing again he gets madder n madder mad dad lifts me off the ground by my neck against the wall mad dad's choking me! mad dad's choking me! *Let me at the cracker!* I kick him in the stomach his breath goes *whumph* I kick him again *whumph* and again *whumph Let me at the motherfucker* upper cut right upper cut left I'm swinging kicking swinging kicking *whumph* he drops me I fall on the ground *Tha thrilla in Manilla! right here folks step right up pay at the door! tha thrilla in Manilla right here eastside St. Paul a block off Payne!* I kick like a caged animal my whole body kicking the soccer ball down the sideline *whumph! Muhammad Ali! Muhammad Ali! the greatest in tha history of tha world* I upper cut him right upper cut him left *whumph* he's trying to get a hold of me I kick I hit I twist mad dad says *Where is it* he's got me by the neck on the carpet *Where's the purse* buck buck buh buck he holds me unzips his pants

* * *

Phone

for you mom sets it on the chair against the kitchen wall I've been waiting for Patty to call all morning *Hello* I say *Hi* she says *Got it* I say *Yeah* she says *Come help me get it in there Okay* I say *I'll be right over*

Oh no you won't mom takes the phone out of my hand hangs it up *you are always with her you can spend some time at home every once in a while* I slap the cupboard door *I don't wanna stay around this stupid house* I say *How do you think that makes me feel after everything I do for you* her eyes and nose turning red *don't you love me your own mother everything I do I do for you* I stare at the brown metal flower cupboard handle until I don't hear or see anything all I want is to go to Patty's house she needs me mom cries the way she cries when mad dad hits her she acts like because I want to go to Patty's I'm as bad as mad dad *You don't even care about your own mother It'll be okay* I say but I have to get to Patty's mom's nose is running *Maybe you should take a nap* I say and get her a Kleenex and I feel bad so bad like I stabbed myself in the stomach because I say it so she'll go to sleep so I can go to Patty's so I can leave her

the phone rings bring! bring! mom picks up the phone hangs it up *Tell me you love me* she grabs me pulls me to her *I love you you know that right* I say nothing squished against her I stare at the cupboard handle bring! bring! mom pulls out the plug

Let's take a nap

you're right she says I follow her up the stairs one at a time we curl up in her bed I stare at the painted green dresser there's a spot where you can still see the wood I pet her hair I have to it's my fault all the badness in the house is my fault just like she says just like mad dad says it's all my fault all the bad things in the world all the bad things in the world! I feel it in my stomach how bad I am but I feel the hate now too lots of it creepy crawling over me a giant spider walking up my back she snores n I wait n I wait n then I creepy crawly off the bed don't want her to cry again I creepy crawly out the front door then I run across the street I don't slow down for the cars or mom or nothing Patty's got it!

I run

in Patty's back door hear noises like a clawing cat *Patty* I yell *Hurry up* she says I run down the stairs into the basement Patty is in the corner behind the mower leaning over the mole's cardboard box *It's almost figured out how to get out* she says holding down the box *gloves* she says and points next to her on the floor *hold it here where were you* I have to stare to keep from crying *I called* Patty says I stare thinking about my mom on her bed *C'mon* she opens the cage she stole from someone's yard pulls it right up against the box jams her thigh against the cage *ready Sure* I say Patty opens the top of the box a crack the mole's head pushes out then it jumps right into the cage *Close it* Patty yells we shove the cage door the mole runs into the back of the cage sits there in a ball hissing like a cat it has weird eyes its nose is pointy its hands stick out to the side white and big they claw at the metal *We got it* Patty snaps the lock shut *we got it!*

C'mon

Patty says *Jimmy told my brothers we caught it if they get back they'll kill it* Patty grabs a oily sheet off the workbench wraps it around the cage we pick up the cage together the mole hisses and growls *Got bus money* Patty says *Sure* I say *Good* we drag the mole upstairs it's heavy! out the door around to the street past my house I look at mom's window I tricked her my stomach hurts *hsss hsss* the mole moves around in its cage it can't see it lives its whole life underground by itself I stare at the greasy oil cloth until the sadness goes away *What's wrong* Patty says I shrug my shoulders

Patty lifts the sheet looks at the mole *My mom* I finally say Patty says nothing she knows how it is looks up at the sky like she's looking for something important

Whoa ladies

the bus driver says he's old *what's in there Nothing* Patty says *No pets allowed on the bus system ladies It's not a pet* Patty says *Well then all right what is it* the bus driver leans over in his seat to see the cage *Nothing sir* Patty says *we just want to go down the road Sorry ladies you'll have to find another ride* we pick up the cage move it off the bus step onto the sidewalk *If we let it go here it'll get killed* Patty says I nod thinking about my mom how much I hurt her I never wanted to hurt her Patty leans over the cage says *Hello mister mole you'll be okay* and I know I hurt my mom because I love Patty but I can't stop loving Patty

What should we do Patty says I shrug the mole squeaks a few times Patty jerks her thumb at a truck it keeps driving and so does the next one and the next one but then a big blue semi without its box stops the driver waves us in his mustache curls up at the tips Patty climbs up on the step and almost falls backwards *Hey there honey be careful* the driver laughs touches his hat *needin a hitch somewhere Yeah* Patty says *just down the road Well hop on in* he says we push the mole's cage in the truck until it's sitting sideways on the floor *Whatcha got there some sorta contriband Yeah* Patty says *Whatcha runnin girls you look like you're up to somethin with those gloves on your hands* the driver laughs puts the truck in gear looks in his side mirror *Nothin* Patty says and puts her foot on the cage I stare at a New York Giants sticker on the dash board *You a Giants fan* he says and leans over and taps the sticker *No* I say *Well I sure am don't matter that I'm from Bama I'm a true blue Giants fan painted my whole damn cab blue just so the world would know that man's a Giant's fan* he points at the windshield *I was almost on TV once some TV men wanted to shoot my truck I got a Giants football helmut on this side ya know you just can't see it from over there No* Patty says he slows down for a stop sign says *They canceled at the last second I washed my truck down even cleaned the inside of cab and all then they call say we found something different we're gonna use some man who's dressen up like a skunk for Jets games you know they had that real bad season in '75* I look out the side window I like being up so high *So what do you got in there Nothing* Patty says *a mole A mole* he laughs *I see a mole what are you doing with a mole Saving it* Patty says *we'd like to get off up there* she points to a circle of picnic tables alongside the road *Well all right* the driver says and touches his hat again *then that's where I'll let you off how come you got the mole It dug up my yard* Patty says *the entire yard this time my brothers would of killed it I see* he says *that's nice a you* and pulls over we jump out pull down the cage *Thanks mister* Patty says *Sure thing go Giants this is our year* and he pumps his arm in the air and drives off toward the North Dakota reservations

Drag

it over here Patty says so we drag the cage next to a picnic table we sit the sheet slips off the mole huddles in the corner *It's scared* Patty says the mole squeaks *poor mole* Patty covers it up *think it'll be okay out here I dunno* I say the trees scatter sunlight on me and Patty and the cage *Let's let it go off in the woods* Patty says *Okay* I look straight up into the sky think about my mom *What are you thinking* Patty says *Nothing* I open my eyes then close them again *What are you thinking* I say keep my eyes closed feel the hot breath of the sun on my cheeks *About how we're going to be super stars in high school* Patty says *win state be the leading scorers all that kind of stuff Yeah* I say and keep my eyes shut imagining it all

But sometimes I think I'm going to leave her feet scuff the grass my stomach is a pit *Huh* I say *Just go somewhere else don't you ever want to leave your dad stop getting bossed around and hit and stuff* I don't say anything my head starts to spin like it's too hot I feel like I'm going to black out I can't lose Patty! I keep my eyes closed *No* I squeak *It's just thoughts* Patty says *but sometimes* she doesn't say anything for a while *I don't know if I can stand it anymore* we sit there for a while I keep my eyes shut if I open them the ocean will come out

the sunlight the shadows the breeze spins me around like I'm in a Tilta Whirl spin spin spin like what I do when mad dad comes in my room spin spin spin like what I do when mom scares me spin spin spin stare at the ceiling spin spin spin make my bed grow like a beanstalk papoosh through the roof to the sky spin spin spin clear out the space between me and Patty make everything so far away so nothing can touch me spin spin spin

Help me take it to the woods Patty says *Okay* I open my eyes blink everything is so bright and close *I'm just thinking* Patty looks at me *I won't leave without you* I nod don't talk or I'll cry *I promise* she pulls me up we drag the cage across the grass until we reach the woods there's a pond on the other side *At least he'll have water* Patty says and opens the door the mole sits in the corner *Umm you know* she wipes her chin on her sleeve *since you're Indian and all maybe you should umm say a special prayer or something What* I don't know what she's talking about *You know* Patty says *I saw it on TV once Indians do stuff like that* she bends down plucks long strands of wilty grass holds them out to me on her palm *Here* she says *you're the Indian you know what to do* I don't know what to do I'm still spinning I swipe the grass off her hand look at the mole huddled in its corner Patty steps back holds her hands behind her back bows her head I don't know what to say *Um bless you mole* I drop the grass on its head and back it scratches to the other side of the cage Patty nods like I'm supposed to say more *Find a good home mole* I say *Go on* Patty says to the mole but it sits there the grass still on its back my head spins what if Patty leaves she gets a stick pokes at the mole from behind *Bless you mole* she says it moves a little she pokes it harder it moves a little more until Patty tilts the cage up and the mole half slides half runs out the cage onto the grass and into the tall weeds along the pond *There* Patty says and kicks the cage *stupid cage* and she turns and walks toward the picnic tables I stare at the cage on its side in the tall grass the mole can't see anything how will it live *Come on* she says and so I do

Sit here

I close my eyes listen with my ears the biggest ears in all the world! in all the world! I listen rock on my butt bones Patty kicks a stone Patty kicks a stick Patty sits grass bends birds *coo coo coo Quiet* I rock *quiet* bend my ears to the stream it sings! it sings!

What does it say

Patty says I squint I rock harder *Shh shh* I say squint harder *someday it's going to be all right it's going to be all right that's it* I say *that's what the river sings someday it's going to be all right it's going to be all right* and Patty nods slit eyes at the ground

How's my girl

Gramma says
Okay I say
Just okay
We caught the mole
Well that's good
I suppose
What's wrong
I miss it that mole
You always stay this sweet my girl
Okay I say
Gramma I say
Yes she says
I want to tell you something I say
Yes she says
The water talks to me I say
Gramma doesn't say anything
That's fine my girl she says that's fine
Okay I say is something wrong with me
Gramma clears her throat
No my girl you are special don't forget that she says
I say nothing this is a secret between me gramma Patty
You are the cream in my coffee gramma says
You are the cream in my coffee too gramma

Hot

is the word for the day the channel four weatherman says *Hot oh ya you bet it is* China Doll Girl is back *there's something else that's going to be hot around here in just whan minute* and she wiggles her fingers getting them ready to choke mad dad he sits on the couch without a shirt his fat belly hanging over his jean shorts

Hot is the word for the entire week in Minnesota as we head into another stretch of record breaking heat the weatherman is almost bald mad dad finishes his beer and burps squishes his can sets it sideways on the TV tray China Doll Girl is mad mad dad came in my room last night I made the bed fly *Are you going to finish the toilet before lunch* mom yells from upstairs mad dad tore up the bathroom because the toilet's clogged mad dad grunts *Oh ya ahsoo hiyah I karate punch you right in your big fat stomach mistah* I run up behind mad dad's recliner the one no one else is allowed to sit in and punch him as hard as I can my whole body kicking it down the sideline! *Ah!* he yells makes a face I run away down the stairs into the garage outside the house sneak under the front window look inside the house he's still in front of the TV I watch him like a commando if I had a machine gun I could break the glass and shoot him *He should be shot bang! bang! right in his big fat stomach Little Miss So And So* China Doll Girl says *he is a very bad man a very bad dad*

I watch mad dad for a while he scratches at his thing then stands up shuts off the TV walks upstairs I sit on the tire swing in the backyard the people who had the house before us left it hanging from the tree the rubber burns my hands and legs

Ah so Little Miss So And So
I say we choke your father your very bad father

we eat lunch with the fan blowing on us mom made turkey sandwiches with mayonaise and lettuce and chips and cherry red Kool Aid with extra ice I drink it and smack my lips together *Ahhh!* mad dad growls at me the fan blows in my face it's so hot out even the cool air is warm

I do the dishes mad dad goes upstairs comes back down says *I'm going to Menards* and drives away mom wipes down the table waters the plants says *Wooo it's too hot to do anything* puts Jim Croce on gets out her macrame I'm so hot from doing the dishes I wait on the front steps for Patty she's sleeping over tonight

Patty and me
make salt and butter and parmesan cheese popcorn after dinner we bring a bowl to mom in her bedroom reading in front of the fan we don't bring one to mad dad working in the bathroom Patty says *I hate him Ya me too* China Doll Girl says we go in my room sit down look through the books and magazines we checked from the library *Soccer Skills 101, Sports Illustrated July 7-14, 1978, The Early Life of Puccini, How Garby High Hockey Won the Gold, The Hobbit,* and *Moles: What They Are What They Do How You Can Get Rid of Them*

I stare out the window the sun is turning Patty's house into a bright white light that hurts my eyes *Whaddya think* Patty says *Huh* I say *I just

asked *if you thought we should have let the mole go by the pond* Oh I say
sure Patty picks up the book on moles *Look there it is* she says and points
to a picture of an Eastern Shrew Mole *that's our mole right there* and she
taps the picture leaves a buttery fingerprint in the book

There it is I rest my chin on her shoulder close my eyes hear mad dad in
the bathroom next to us wham bam slam *Do you think it's okay* I say *Yeah*
Patty says *it's all right* I pretend I'm blind like a mole reach for the bowl get
a piece of popcorn put it in my mouth practicing to be blind Patty flips the
page I put my arm around her *Yuck* Patty says *it says their skin grows right
over their eyes Yuck* I say thinking how it would be if my eyelids grew shut
over my eyeballs

Bam!

the door flings open something hits above us sounds like glass breaking
my eyes fling open nickels bounce off the walls fall all around us like rain
mad dad troll fills up the door I let go of Patty she tries to stand up but he
pushes her grabs my shirt rips it *Damn you* he yells slams me into the wall

Crack the back the headboard spat

Hey Patty yells we all fall down he hits her she hits him he pins me
against the wall his breath spits in my face *Hey hey hey let go* Patty yells
What's this he holds me up one arm across my throat puts a dirty black wet
nickel in my face I float *Look what I found in the pipes where'd it come
from* he peels my lips open *huh* I clamp down my teeth like a dog it's dirty
smells like poop *Stop it* Patty yells hits him he throws me on the bed gets on
top of me Patty jumps him he pushes her off puts his arm across my throat I
choke his thumb in my mouth he laughs pushes the nickel in it's slimy wet
poop my tongue blocks it slips almost down my throat can't breathe can't
breathe!

Patty screams *You little fuck we never had problems until you dyke boy*
he says throws her into the wall crack smack flack crack the back the
headboard spat *Uh* Patty says air slams out her I spit the nickel on the bed
mad dad's kneels over me pulls out the snake slaps my face with it I try to
kick it not in front of Patty! not in front of Patty! *You shouldn't have done
that* he growls rubs pushes his thumb into me then the thing breaks me my
head board bored head slams *the head board did it!* Patty's in the room not
in front of Patty! not in front of Patty! I blur my eyes grow skin over them
hurts hurts so bad I'm cracking he laughs *That's right that's right this is the
way it is this is the way it will always be* he grunts like a pig it hurts hurts
hurts my head board cracks

No

Patty cries I hear her far away falling down to the ocean floor mad dad
stops pulls that thing out of me hurts me! I can't move cracked can't see my
head went blurry skin eyes growed over another set of eyeballs slit China
Doll Girl eyes n she runs off to watch from the shelf Patty yells from far

away through water mad dad says *dyke bitch cunt* I slide over the edge of the bed see light and shadows through the skin growed over my eyes mad dad on top Patty stops yelling she grows quiet he grunts no no nonononnononononononononono not p not p me instead not p not p me instead nonononnononononononononono

i cant move nonononono no no not p she doesn't make a sound he grunts i cant move cant barely see through thick skin dad gasps like he does when hes finish gasp theres no sound anywhere no sound anywhere all world died me Patty mad dad mom downstairs wite nuckel deaded wurld dyd

Patty cries little

through the blur dog whimper mole blinded in the cage scareded hurt whimper mad dad says *Dyke boy* the sun gone the sky navy blue blur outside the window the light gone world ded

All

my fault all my fault all of it! forever and ever a l l m y f a u l t dad writ in blood on my brain i live in a dream the dream lasts all night mad dad on top of us me p me p he laugh he groan troll on the bridge troll on the bridge! i live in a dream where it is hot sweat burns my face like wet fire i can't reach p blur far away float i hear her dying we are dying we are dead already dead i live in a dream i live in a dream it's a bad dream a bad world that has died it is all my fault i put the nickels down the toilet mad dad leaps between us in slow motion like a troll on a bridge spills the popcorn kool aid on the floor grunts moans the world is dark the world is hot i hear small noises i see nothing for hours days years in my dream skin grown over China Doll Girl watch she m a d kung pow

i

wake up the sun came back the popcorn kool aid nickels gone the books magazines in a pile i wake up from my dream dead world to a sunny day i wake up open my eyes see the ceiling bumpy and white the sun splashes above me the day here the dream over the world died gone on living tricked everyone i dead i go on living tricked everyone my eyes skin peels can see better i dead i tricked everyone went on living

patty is gone my eyes do not see her the books magazines in a pile the popcorn bowl kool aid white knuckle picked up patty gone she gone she is gone all my fault all my fault all of it! forever and ever all my fault

This morning I woke up P not home I checked Jimmy shook head no

this morning I woke up Patty not home went to work with mom made her happy kicked the soccer ball in the gym alone all day

this morning I woke up Patty not home went to our end of the year soccer party Mr. Samson said I practice real hard I play forward next year this morning I woke up Patty not home Jimmy door crying shook head no I stayed home alone all day listened to Meat Loaf Patty got it for me at the mall

this morning woke up Patty not home rained all day stayed inside dribbled up down stairs drove parents crazy crazy girl drove parents crazy she good at that during supper *at least she's not singing opera*

this morning woke up Patty not home house on Rose Avenue

this morning woke up Patty not home Jimmy not answer door

this morning woke up Patty not home Katie knocked on front door gave invitation to her ninth birthday party I said *thanks* threw it in the garbage

this morning woke up Patty not home I stood at the front door against the screen pushed out n saggy watched Patty's house no one came no one went foot on soccer ball all day

this morning woke up Patty not home stood at front door one block off Payne mom came home on lunch break said I am going to gramma's until school starts

this morning woke up Patty not home older brother answered door Jimmy crying behind him said we don't know where she is dribbled soccer ball across street hard to dribble on pavement put ball in car go to gramma's next season I am going to play forward

Age Fifteen (1983)

Oh Mickey

you're so fine you're so fine you blow my mind hey Mickey! hey Mickey! I run down the stairs bang bang bang I slam each step *Did you shut off your music* mom says from the kitchen bang bang bang I run back up the stairs *Oh Mickey you're sooo fine* too bad I can't sing for shit not for shit! not for shit! I pull the plug on the radio slam my door shut run back down the stairs drag my fingertips over the gold fuzzy crowns *Do you have to be so loud* I don't say anything grab my duffel bag *Johnson High School Governors Pride of the Eastside Girls Basketball* written on one side *Let's go* I run past her to the garage *Hey missy* mom says *if you're late it's your fault not mine I've been ready for half an hour*

we drive to school in the 1971 Chevy truck it is gray and warm and almost spring and tonight I play in my first varsity basketball game she drives slow not like how I'm gonna drive when I get my license I don't do anything slow or half assed anyone who knows me knows speed is my thing *Can't you hurry up* I say this time she ignores me

we get to school she puts her blinker on to turn into the lot blink blink blink tips her chin looks in the rear view mirror waits for the oncoming car to pass looks in her mirror again what is she waiting for! I want to smack her hand off the wheel and press down on the accelerator myself move! but she sits and waits for nothing no cars only gray mist with green and red refracted lights floating splotches in the air *Do you know what refracted means* I say she ignores me turns into the lot god I hope no one from the varsity team is standing around outside

no one is! I jump out of the truck *See you at the game* she says I slam the door want to run into the school but I have to be cool in case anyone is looking but shit! I made it! I'm going to letter in at least two sports as a sophomore

So And So

Kelly yells from the doorway *So And So!* she's in the big white oxford shirt she wore to school plus sky blue basketball shorts and knee high matching socks and unlaced bright white nike high tops she hugs me smoke on her clothes *Way to go you're playing up Thanks* I say like I'm cool but really I want to dance around like a four year old we high five and walk into the school *You still want to go out tonight right So And So* she screeches the way she does when she's excited she's a little bit crazy but that's why I like her *Hell yeah* I say *Hell yeah* she says and makes a fist *I've got the Monte all night*

I ride in the front of the bus with the sophomore team the varsity team went to state last year and I watched all their games on TV *woohoo* I yelled whenever Ann Kind scored she made the all tournament team with a 17 point game average and now here I am about to play with her I block out Kelly and Kate yelling in my ear watch the cars and trees and light posts speed into a blur if only Patty and then I make my thoughts stop stall them right in their tracks *I can't wait to get my license* Kate says to Kelly I half listen to them talk about nothing while I stare at the back of the bus driver's head he's mostly bald except for a ring of dark brown hair he flipped over I stare hope no one notices me staring at his hair sometimes there's too much sadness to hide

Hey

So And So what's wrong Kelly flicks my bangs stares at my face wrinkles her nose punches me says *my mom says your dad is Indian you're not Indian are you So And So* I stare at the dark green dimpled vinyl seat *Ahh* I say *where did that come from* Kelly calls black people niggers *You kinda look funny like an Indian* she knocks my shoulder again *it's true isn't it* I look up Kate and Monica are laughing fear cuts into my stomach are they laughing because my gramma is Indian because I look kinda funny dad would get mad whoo whoo dad would get mad Kelly says *So And So don't play on varsity stay with us!*

The sophomore team

yells *Governors!* I yank my sweats over my high tops Kelly flings the bag of balls across the gym floor they scatter like children on a playground Patty! running across our elementary yard! coach Terry White taps me *Coach is going to keep you entirely out of our game* he says *All right* I say Terry leans down *This is your big chance* he whispers *show em what you got* I nod a ball bounces off my leg jams under the bleachers I pull my sweats up dig the ball out with the toe of my high top the sophomore team plays first then the junior varsity then the varsity

I sit in the stands by myself nervous about what Kelly said scared she'll tell everyone my dad won't even talk about being Indian if she said something to him I puff up my shoulders keep my hands in my pockets look tough something hits me in the back of my head I don't look around pretend like I didn't feel it the varsity girls are behind me *Hey* someone yells now I will have to turn around a whistle blows the sophomore game is about to start I look back feel stupid *How come they call you So And So* Ann Kind says she's got curly blond hair cut up above the tops of her ears I say nothing *Yeah what does So And So mean* Julie Brown says eating a malt from Dairy Queen with a long red spoon they're all sitting next to each other in the stands their feet up on the rows in front of them *are you so so or what*

I sink like they tied a stone around my neck watch my friends play basketball without me at halftime mom and dad show up stand next to me in the stands dad with his fat belly and jacket flared open I hunch in the stands they say they'll be back for the varsity game *Make your old man proud kid* dad taps me on the shoulder I say nothing don't want him to touch me want them to leave I push my duffel bag over try to sit big

Time

to go someone taps me on the shoulder I jump embarrassed zoning out like always I'm hyper or zoned it's Julie Brown *We dress during the second quarter of JV* she says *Okay* I stand up a dizzy spell coming on I have to be tough get hyper I follow Julie Brown up the stands stepping around people and over piles of coats and bags until we reach the hallway *You excited Sure* I say shrug my shoulders pretend like I don't care *I heard Coach brought you up for your quickness Sure* I say embarrassed we walk into the locker room stop by some lockers painted peach Julie stretches her arms out over her head looks at me *Crank the music* someone yells *Not Journey again* someone yells *Too bad* Julie yells *we always listen to Journey before away games* she looks at me like she's trying to figure me out grabs her ankles stretches her long leg behind her *Just do what we say out there and you'll be fine* she pats me on the head like I'm a kid and walks away I throw my bag in a locker and get dressed

We change

I tighten my laces stretch stare at the sides of the lockers peachy colored metal a weird color soft and smooth but so cold *Let's go* they shout run out the door I follow them into the room next door where Coach is waiting on a stool *All right* he says *we've brought up someone from the sophomore squad everybody say hello to So And So she's going to help us out on defense she's a regular Houdini all right that didn't make a lot of sense just say hello to So And So* he taps his belt buckle *Hello So And So* some of the team says *Okay good now let's get down to business* I tune him out even though I should listen everything in the room is forest green Moundsview's colors conference game low ceiling we win this we've still got a shot at state thick mats lined up against the walls white floury dust on the mats *Let's go! one two three go Governors!*

we run out onto the court the band's playing if only Patty I stop my brain my feet shuffle right shuffle left knees bent palms up stare at nothing blur the stands the people the floor into nothing shuffle right shuffle left there's noise the crowd my teammates the coach the band I hear it but I don't hear it stay bent down quick as a cat I am pure motion in the warm up pure speed pure power float like a butterfly sting like a bee my eyes water I'm crying! I miss Patty I sprint to the line bend down touch it spring back I can't stop my eyes from watering if only Patty stop those thoughts! bend down touch the line turn sprint to the next line bend down touch eyes watering we do lay ups two lines pass criss cross I bring it into the basket Doctor J style I jump float twirl lay it in bright orange backwards off the glass turn run I am pure motion pure speed pure victory no one can touch me no one can stop me tweet tweet! *All right* Coach yells *everyone in Great warm up So And So* someone says pats me on the back I don't say anything

we circle up mom smiles from the stands gives me a thumb's up I look away try to listen but I'm caught up in the sounds and smells of the gym tennis shoes squeaking people talking in the stands cheerleaders yelling a trombone fluttering up then down buttered popcorn stale sweat all of it makes me want to puke Coach's voice rolls around in my head like water *So And So! Right!* I look up embarrassed Coach is looking at me I nod *Say it* he says *Right Coach* I say he smiles all hands in the middle a big daisy *One two three go Governors!*

I sit down in the chair at the end *So And So!* Kelly screams from the stands *So And So!* I wonder if she's already drunk hiding a flask of whiskey in her coat pocket Kelly loves me but I can't show my love or mad dad will kill it I look at the clock at the other end of the gym it's already 8:20 time means nothing to me before I know it the first quarter is over we are up 16 to 15 I didn't get in my shoulders slump I hear my mom in my head sit up straight and smile I slump more *So And So!* Coach says crouched down in front of the bench he points at me *you're starting the second quarter* I jump up *point guard we're staying with the zone you're on top* I take off my long sleeved jersey shove it under the folding chair pull down on my uniform top it springs back up I hate how short it is one two three break!

I am pure speed

pure motion on the court my high tops squeak we circle up the ref tosses the ball in the air it spins slow mo above our heads then drops like a spider on a string Ann smacks it Julie Brown grabs the tip off bounce passes it to me I dribble down the side smooth leather on my fingertips cross over reverse spin one two three I bank the orange off the glass screaming everywhere *So And So!* sound is far away I am pure focused floating stinging bee everything I do I do for Patty it's my fault she's gone I toe the line where the other team will throw it in my hands up a Moundsview girl grabs the ball steps to the line I see nothing I see it all I blur space and time into one into nothing I step in and out of time and space I am four inches from the Moundsview girl I am on top of a bed taller than a mountain I am waving my hands following the orange tracking it's my fault it's all my fault! hands wave I have ten hands ten feet ten heads it's my fault I float on the ceiling it's my fault I sting like a bee smack the orange smooth leather cracks against my palm it's my fault knock it in the Moundsview girl's face tweet she holds her nose stares at me I look at nothing toe the line the ref hands her the orange leather tweet I knock it back in her face one two three times the crowd is screaming *So And So!* my teammates hit me on the back the Moundsview girl runs up and down the line I follow her ten hands ten feet ten heads tall as a mountain floating on the ceiling time and space are doorways I step through I knock the ball out of bounds again Moundsview can't get the ball in they call a time out it's my fault all of it's my fault every last thing floating on the ceiling while dad's on top of me on top of Patty it's my fault I'm here a basketball star then I'm there dead on the bed here there here there stepping through the doorways I should have kept the nickels in the purse I should have kept the purse it's a new Moundsview girl now she smacks the ball yells *Break!* I kick her bounce pass into the stands

Gramma
I was the third leading scorer in my basketball game
I am a little kid
Oh Gramma says that's wonderful
Thanks I say I'll have mom send the article from the paper
Oh granddaughter Gramma says I am so proud you are the cream in my coffee
You too Gramma I say love you too!

Coach
    wants me to play up for the rest of the season I spaz bounce a cherry red super ball on the countertop *That's great honey* mom says we are both nervous watching dad out the corners of our eyes he is in one of his moods again mom pulls on my jacket collar straightens it out dad is at the kitchen table a martini with three green olives on a saucer in front of him *You did so well tonight but couldn't you just you know look a little nicer out there* mom bends her knees a little keeps her back straight so she can look into my face I don't smile set my duffel bag down by the oven *You look like a damn princess out there* dad snarls

    I say nothing I know what is coming I want to get showered and get out it's Friday night time to party *Oh Mickey you're so fine* runs through my head like fat red yarn on a needle *I was the third leading scorer* I say hoping to divert his anger *See what I mean* he says slurring his words shaking his fist in the air *see what I had to deal with wife all last summer and the one before that training her at the park in between my jobs do you see the kind of lip she's got she's got more attitude than Princess Ann Margaret out gambling away her life you're going to be nothing nothing at all if you keep up that princess attitude* he takes a drink *your coach won't stand for it do you hear me he'll cut you then you won't even have a spot on the sophomore team* I step away he screams *You're shit you're a goddamn piece of shit Yeah sure* I say *whatever you say* I think he's frickin crazy I'm not a little kid anymore *Listen you little bitch* and he springs on me faster than what I thought he'd be able to *don't you smart ass your old man* he stumbles a little mixes his own feet up reaches for my neck I push him in the chest he falls back *Get the fuck off a me* I growl mom says *Come on now we've all had a big night husband aren't your proud of your daughter she played varsity tonight* her voice pitches high like the peak of a Tudor *Oh sure she played varsity tonight she's a big star* dad waves his hand in the air *look at me* he says *a big star* Your brain's shot I say he does this after every game *Don't you smartass your old man* he gets in my face his breath is pure alcohol *Get the fuck out of my face* I snarl he raises his hand I don't move we stare horns grinding

Thrilla in Manilla!

mom says *Oh come on now you two stop it* her voice is far away we stare

Thrilla in Manilla!

we stare

Thrilla in Manilla!

Oh you two now soft and far away

Thrilla in Manilla!

my arms bust out my jacket as big as Muhammad Ali's I glare walk s l o w l y up the stairs I've learned to never show fear I stop at the top surrounded by gold fuzzy crowns *Fuck you* I look him in the eyes

Thrilla in Manilla!

did he kill her did he kill her a fat red thread through my head I don't shower can't take the chance he'll come in I dress in my room fast even though I don't want to it's like admitting I'm afraid clean underwear jeans tube socks basketball camp t-shirt gray sweatshirt Governors Girl's Basketball I grab the wadded cash on the desk shut the door behind me he's at the bottom of the stairs waiting in the dark all the lights are down low the fear could drop me to my knees but I cut it off walk down one step then the other *Think you're going someplace* his voice cuts through the dark I say nothing his body is a shadow waiting for me on the bottom step I think of Patty disappearing into his darkness *You're not going anywhere* he slams me into the wall holds me by my collar *you wouldn't know the truth if it hit you upside your head* his eyes glint he punches me in my belly *got that* fire twists up my spine I push him run out the door *Get back here princess* he slurs I run onto the street there's one light at Patty's when is she coming home what happened to her how can she just disappear

So And So

Kelly and Monica honk at me standing on the street corner the lights flash red one way yellow the other way *So And So! you're a frickin star* I say nothing *You were on the ten o clock news* I say nothing they pull up next to me smoking in Kelly's mom's Monte Carlo *What are you doing out here* Monica says she doesn't know me as well as Kelly *Nuthin* I say make my words short and to the point keep from crying I climb in the back seat hang my head I don't want them to see my eyes watering *Oh So And So what's wrong* Kelly looks back at me *Nuthin* I say *What* Kelly says again *You know* I say *get outta here* I'm afraid he'll come outside chase us *don't drive by my house* Kelly does a U turn *Can we go to a drive thru* I shake I'm cold I'm hungry my father wants to kill me I don't know what happened to Patty

Monica is quiet embarrassed the way everyone gets when they find out about my dad *Want a chew* Kelly hands Kodiak wintergreen and a styrofoam cup over the seat the bear on the packaging stares at me I pinch it put it between my gum and lower lip lean back stare out the window the street lights form a steady stream of light I buzz Kelly punches in her Van Halen tape sings along I spit in the cup relax stop shaking Kelly pulls out a Heineken the only brand she drinks *Want one So And So* she looks at me in her rear view mirror *In a minute* I say *in a minute*

My body

flows into the seat I am blue suede upholstery we pull up to McDonald's *Shit* Kelly says *it's your coach* I duck down pull out the chew my lower lip is rough like sandpaper little bits of chew stick to my lips *Shit* I say *there's bees in my head where is he Right here* Kelly whispers turns down the music *Hey girls* Coach pounds on the top of the Monte Carlo looks through the window on Kelly's side she doesn't roll the window down *Great game* he gives me the thumbs up I nod hoping I don't have to talk he walks around the back of the car I am paranoid that he's trying to see inside but he disappears into the parking lot *Jesus fucking Christ* Kelly says *Damn* Monica says

So And So you want fish Yeah I say *Two filet fish one hamburger* Monica says *Three fries* Kelly says *And a Coke* I say *Okay* the McDonald's woman says pulls down the front of her brown striped hat *Runnin with the devil* Kelly and Monica sing I look over my shoulder but Coach is gone *Sing with us So And So* Kelly says drunk but I don't sing Kelly rewinds the tape bzzzt punches a button *Runnin with the devil* she yells *I found the simple life ain't so simple* we drive through Saint Paul eating drinking listening to Van Halen chewing spitting staring into the tall black night *Tell me about your game* I say to Monica and Kelly I miss playing with the sophomore team already because I can't be happy anywhere even playing varsity basketball even being the star on TV nothing is ever enough I crack a beer put in a new dip

Lights
   in a black night flash into the car one after another I am floating on my back through the streets *Where are we* I sit up *Nowhere* Kelly snorts she is drunk *Uptown* Monica says go that way outstretched arm the Monte Carlo jerks toward the arm I lie down lights bing bing bing one after the other the wheels of the Monte Carlo virrr on the pavement soft music on the radio *I don't know how I got here* I say silence they must think I'm crazy *We're in Minneapolis now* Monica says that's not what I mean I think but I don't say anything *That's it* Monica says tires squeal the Monte Carlo jerks again one side jumps over a curb stops *Stay here So And So* Kelly says gets out of the car *someone might recognize you now that you're a teevee star* a door slams I twitch flash to mad dad the garage door *So And So's a teevee star!* another door slams *So And So's a teevee star!* the black air is cool runs over my body prickles my hair I feel like a child

I slit my eyes someone says *I don't think so* the words string through my head like Christmas lights car doors thud a red white light circles through the inside of the Monte Carlo I feel like a child at oatmeal's a lady with hair the color of oatmeal a lady who made me eat oatmeal! the red white lights stop then bounce inside the car I am drunk buzzed off chew they put little pieces of ground up glass in the tobacco to cut your lip the lights a lady named oatmeal riding in her car swinging a lasso catching people *Hey So And So* Kelly hisses above my head I tip my chin up she is upside down *unlock the door* she hisses her dad is a snake like mine *sssth* I say they are both snakes I know one when I see one *So And So* she says quietly I reach pul pull pulll the round plug until it pops up like a cork a door opens keys clang bottles clink the lights buzz round my head my legs are soft Ben Gay tingling they do this every time I drink I feel good I don't care about anything the oatmeal lady took me somewhere in her car chasing people with my rope! I'm tired I'm hot we shouldn't be doing this all these thoughts pull through my head like threads on needles the car starts I am blue upholstery soft suede on my cheek eyes slit Kelly drives the car I am a child a baby in a basinet *So And So are you okay* floats through the air brushes my hair *Yeah* I say *I love brushed suede* Kelly laughs rolls to a stop pitch black cold air brushed suede Ben Gay legs

A door opens
Got it words say in Kelly's voice *Yes* darts through the blackness back lot no street lights I shut my eyes my eyes shut me *Is she okay So And So's okay* give me a cup of ice *Oh ya* China Doll Girl's voice cuts out of my mouth no one says anything clatter clatter ice cup liquid glug glug glug radio turned on soft *La la la la* I say a baby in the dark no one says anything glug glug glug *Want a wine cooler So And So* my eyes slit *Oh ya* China Doll Girl's voice says *uv coarse I want a wine cooler give me whan right now* Monica and Kelly laugh I sit up straight full of energy alert *What kind of wine*

cooler you got I wag my hand in their faces *Jesus So And So hold on* Kelly says *I want cooler right now* China Doll Girl says looks around the parking lot a white Lake Street Liquors sign trees a dumpster flattened card board boxes *give me drink right now* China Doll Girl says Kelly and Monica laugh Kelly hands me a wine cooler *Ah so very good* I say they laugh again *Your accent is really good* Monica says how do you do that Kelly turns off the headlights the car idles in the back of the liquor store *Ah very good wine cooler taste like grape* they laugh again Monica's foot is on the dashboard without a shoe just a sock I finish off the wine cooler my head spins like a top *faster! faster! spin it faster crazy girl!* Kelly burps sings with the radio *The parents are bad very bad parents!* China Doll Girl's voice shouts Monica's foot slips down *Shit So And So* Kelly says *Damn* Monica looks at me I lie down what do I care what they think blue suede on my face I burp grape my body relaxes the Monte Carlo is the only place where I relax blue suede brushes the small of my back I sleep like a baby

The key

is around here somewhere I just know it kick the Welcome! mat letters faded to gray it slides off the steps on its rubber belly into the bushes half of it stays on the steps I think I kicked it too hard stare at it draped over the steps like a fish sucking air over the side of an aluminum boat or a snake swinging *stop those thoughts!* does everyone talk to themselves *of course everyone talks to themselves*! okay I look away then flip it off into the bushes with my toe *so long mat!* it flops into the bushes and dried up leaves leftover from last fall the Monte Carlo banana split peels a few roads down in my head I see Kelly turning the corner by the stop light too fast *she is going to roll that car one of these days!* Kelly ate fries cole slaw large Diet Coke banana split extra whipped cream ten cherries once we got sick of driving around all this pops into my head like a picture like one second I am in Kelly's car the next I am outside my house the next I am watching Kelly eat

The key! where is it

fall into the railing black shiny dark cold steel on my belly my jacket and shirt pull up the railing hits me bare in the belly *cold!* another squeal far away now she's out of our neighborhood hope mad dad mom didn't hear her peel off *where is the damn key!* it's always right here under the mat the moon makes a perfect circle on the parent's bedroom window I stare up at it *refracted light!* the fastest girl in the conference can't get into her house drunk high on chew that chew is good stuff spit it out once more there might be one last piece hiding in my mouth the moon above me a perfect round mouth *oh! my name is Mouth I say my name is Mouth!* what the fuck my mind is like a Greek chorus *a Greek chorus!* it never shuts up *we never shut up!*

I get down on my knees feel for the key the bushes poke me in the face *where is the key!* I am cold the cold travels from the concrete through my knees to my teeth chitter chattering so loud they'll wake up mad dad mom asleep the moon on their window *where is the key!* I follow the sidewalk to the front the lights are on at Patty's house they are always on Jimmy leaves them on for Patty says she'll come back someday she'll come back someday! I jiggle the front door the handle is loose practically falling off but it's locked shit! and damn! I have no where to sleep maybe in the yard maybe under the leaves a truck shoots by naked no box I imagine Patty jumping out of the truck saying *Hey* instead the lights at Patty's burn into me she is gone because I loved her because she loved me I follow the sidewalk to the back stepping around the cracks dead brown weeds poking out between the concrete I will sleep by the steps in the bushes under the leaves will keep me warm my knees are wet cold muddy from looking through the bushes the garage shines white and dewy behind the house under the moonlight black roof lawn mowers upside down waiting for mad dad to fix them vroom vroom! he'll never fix them they've been there for years tires spinning in the wind grass growing up their sides I walk up the back steps listening to myself talk in my head myself talking to myself

Self One: *No! We won't sleep outside!*
Self Two: *It'll be fine in the bushes!*
Self Three: *Under the leaves like a wild animal!*
Self Four: *I'd rather sleep out here than listen to mad dad snore*
Self Five: *Or when he comes in the room*
Self Six: *Be quiet! don't say those things!*

See the key!
      there it is the key a black spot in the middle of the step I grab it a soft light is on in the parents' bedroom it must be mom's night light near her side of the bed the one mad dad makes her unplug he makes her unplug it every night! I stand there looking up the key's cold teeth bite my palm refracted moon beams in their window why do I make her feel stupid I push in the key the rough burnt orange curtains on the door's window move like long hair like Patty's hair I lock it put the key on the counter stare at the key on the counter stare like a retard mom helped me I step on the outside edges of the stairs where they won't creak the gold fuzzy crowns are soft and feathery like moss like a worn in leather basketball
      in bed I watch the moon through the cracks in my shade Patty looks at the same moon somewhere maybe California maybe North Dakota maybe Texas a Dallas Cowboy fan go Danny White Tony Dorset Too Tall Jones! she watches the same moon maybe even right now she cannot be dead that I know me and Jimmy know she cannot be dead she cannot be dead! my head is in my pillow the pillow is around my head I let it rest stop all the thoughts that make my head so heavy a crooked back like an old lady I

hobble to school with a cane mom helped me kept me from sleeping like a wild animal under the leaves the mole could still be alive moonlight on its eye lids

River water

speaks to me on my knees in my dream next to the stream in Patty's backyard *someday it will be all right it will be all right someday it will be all right it will be all right*

* * *

Cockaigne

an imaginary land of great luxury and ease I write it down under ubiquitous which is one two three four five lines under pontificate we haven't had vocab in more than a week because Mr. Norman was at the hospital his appendix ruptured during homeroom people say who cares he's a fag anyway I don't say anything no one needs to notice I'm a fag dyke freak too Mike Taylor on a Notre Dame football scholarship said they should have let him die he said that during Mr. Norman's class in front of the substitute teacher the teacher smiled a little like she thought that was funny Mr. Norman says *Missy define cockaigne A land of great luxury and ease* she left out imaginary he'll tell her so *An imaginary land of great luxury and ease Missy* Mr. Norman says *class it is highly likely that this word will be on your SATs* Mike raises his hand *When are we going to use a word like cockaigne* and he pronounces it as COCK ayne kids laugh *Mr. Taylor* Mr Norman says and sits on an empty desk *you plan on going to college correct Yeah* Mike says *I presume you will do something other than play football correct Oh yeah* Mike says and licks his lips and smiles *Mr. Taylor really must you be so vulgar* Mr. Norman places his hands on his knee *we all know you're a big man with the ladies* Mr. Norman knits his fingers together *I meant study learn for the sake of learning advance yourself mentally morally and psychologically by being aware of the great literature and philosophies of the world while simultaneously developing the language to articulate your own life to pursue the most essential philosophical questions of all time who am I and what is the purpose of my existence* Mr. Norman put Mike in his place and I am glad I draw loops on the left side of the paper connecting all the vocab words

Hmmm Mr. Norman purses his lips raises his eyebrows so that everyone knows he's a fag Mike says nothing stretches his leg out looks at his size 16 tennis shoe I draw tiny pointed pine trees and a valley my own cockaigne a valley with green trees where my father does not live and cannot get into my cockaigne is a place where my father is dead and girls make their own rules and Patty is back *Ms So And So* Mr. Norman says *Yes* I say and look up from the tips of the pine trees dark blue against the white page *Define ubiquitous Present everywhere Correct* Mr. Norman nods his head once *very good Ms So And So* I am in a college prep course with seniors and two juniors because I scored in the 99 percentile nationwide in English they bounced me out of tenth grade English boing! *Sam define montage Um it's sort of like a mixture of things Incorrect* Mr. Norman says and points to someone else she answers correctly *Open your books to Night by William Blake* I draw some rocks under the pointy blue pine trees Mr. Norman recites I write *who am I* in the sky

Bring! bring!
the hallway is crammed with students and teachers who stand with their arms folded in the doorways of their classrooms Mr. Norman never stands in the hall he says he has better things to do than baby sit teenagers *So And So!* Moe says I say *How's it going Good* she smiles one of her wicked smiles opens her locker and shoves her zip lock baggy filled with a toothbrush toothpaste and mint waxed floss on the shelf *got plans for Friday No* I say she brushes and flosses her teeth at school something must be wrong for someone to be that fastidious about her teeth I scan her short wide face and shoulder length brown curly hair but only see happiness or is it obliviousness whatever is wrong is buried deep her father says to her and anyone who will listen *sex is like potato chips once you start you can't stop What* she says because I'm staring *Nothing* I say and look at the vents in her locker slatted like fish gills everyone thinks I am weird *Want to know who is having a party* she pulls out her yellow American History textbook I shrug *Brandon Ziegler* I shrug again he's a hockey jock *The Brian Ziegler* she says and giggles shuts her locker *Ready* I say *You'll go won't you your game is on Thursday I don't know* I say *Kelly and I usually go out Fridays Well both of you can go c'mon it's going to be a great party plus you can go to Brandon's house* she sighs and looks at the ceiling *he's so cute* I don't know what to say because I don't think he's cute and Kelly hates Moe *I suppose* I say and we walk to American History Mr. Hale's class is honors but dumber than shit because you can sleep through every class as long as you memorize his worksheets the night before the tests

It's So And So Ann Kind and Becky from basketball say *Hey* I say my voice drops a pitch Moe grabs my arm and says *He is so so cute* Ann and Becky laugh walk away *He is so cute* I hear Becky say in a high voice and all I want is for them to know I don't think he's cute I am not like Moe she clings to my arm walking backwards down the hall saying *I could love him I really could* and I don't do anything just walk with her grabbing my arm

Gramma
hasn't called in a long long time

So And So!
So And So! the ref hands me the ball I crouch throw the ball in front of me with wicked back spin so it bounces back to me *One* I spin the ball back *So And So So And So!* the crowd yells Kelly screams *Yeah!* in my head I see her nostrils flare the way they always do when she screams *Two* I spin the ball back crouch even lower the crowd yells *Three* spin it back crouch low

left hand on the side of the ball right hand finger tips lined up along a black rubber seam I hear nothing imagine the shot perfect back spin orange orb descending in the west falling through the air like Blake writes swish through the basket all net I let it go perfect follow through the orange arches spins slow motion I can see each black seam as the ball twirls from a wicked follow through drops in the net the crowd goes wild I capped a three point play I have over twenty points now *So And So! So And So!* the other team calls a time out my teammates push me I smile jog to the sidelines Coach ignores me doesn't want me to get a big head wants me to stay focused on the game the team stat girl leans over whispers in my ear *You've got 22* Coach shoots her a look *Listen girls two minutes left we're up by three keep feedin them to So And So full court press man on man all hands in the middle* he waits puts his hand over all of ours looks at me says *So And So next time down the court run the box and one you take it to the hoop if it's wide open if not pull it back* I nod he pushes his hand down on top of ours all white arms except one black girl like a big daisy with a stem *One Two Three Go Governors* we yell break apart five of us head to the court everyone else returns to their cold metal chairs

So And So! Kelly yells from the stands throws her head back tips her hand like she's taking a swig of whiskey straight from the bottle *Oh god* I turn around hope no one saw her Mrs. Hoffman the superintendent of schools and Larry Wilson the principal and Mr. Schell the assistant football coach who is also in charge of Johnson's drug abuse program are all here to watch the big game between Johnson and Edina the winner advances in regionals the winner of regionals goes to state oh god now everyone knows I party the bands starts up *Hoo Rah Rah* they yell I am on the ball arms windmilling the Edina girl throws it in I charge the girl she threw it to tall dark hair in a pony she's a foot taller than me tall girls never worry about short girls she holds the ball over head where I can't reach it Ann jumps on her too we are both on her I put my hands in her face so she can't see Ann slaps at the ball the girl leans back I slide behind her rip the ball out of her hands big girls aren't very smart I dribble down the right side go in for the lay up see Ann out the corner of my eye flip the ball behind my back to her the crowd yells as I land behind the basket the ball drops through the net we are up by three now Ann ignores me covers her girl down court I'm on the end line windmilling *Kind Kind Kind Kind* the crowd chants *So And So* Kelly screams she probably wishes I'd kept it myself but I want Ann to like me I chase down the ball it gets away they score we are up by one *time out!*

So And So box and one Coach yells I nod look at Ann she doesn't look mad or glad or sad neither do I we are serious ball players with serious game faces don't let anyone see how I feel! if I score on this play I'll have 24 my name will be announced on the loudspeaker tomorrow morning at school as the leading scorer the next Ann Kind the next star! *Let's get to state* Ann growls *Go Governors!*

Edina presses us Becky holds the ball with one hand wipes her forehead then passes into Ann I clap my hands for the ball Ann takes it down the right side spin dribbles past two of their players gets to our half stops in the corner covers the ball with her arms leans over *Here! Here!* I run to her she steps through two Edina players slips me the ball I fake a penetration down the middle pull it back switch hands three Edina girls run to me smack my arm *Phreet! foul! number thirteen shooting one on one* Ann broke the play Coach yells *Kind! get over here* she jogs to him head hanging the ref says *On the line* I step to the line *So And So! So And So!* I block out the noise I want my name on the P.A. system tomorrow morning leading scorer I want Ann to like me I want to win the game go to state win it all be a star be on TV I toe the line I have to make this I have to get on TV get on TV! so people see me I don't want to disappear like Patty disappeared in my bedroom one night poof! poof! mad dad waved his magic wand I crouch spin the ball my fingertips on a seam see it swish in my head let it go watch it circle float an orange orb like Shelly bounces straight up spins hits the backboard spins rims rolls through *So And So! So And So!* the crowd screams we are up by two! I act like nothing happened cool as a cucumber no fear game face bat mask pulled tight *That So And So she belongs in the mafia!* I hear in my head *Nothing gets in nothing gets out* psychology lady with the pointy glasses pops in my head my game face bat mask keeps me safe keeps everyone away the other team can't read me will I pass to the left or the right dribble down the middle pull up for a bank shot throw a Hail Mary downcourt no one knows what I'll do not even me not even me!

the ref bounces the ball to me I crouch crunch spin spin spin set my fingers on the seam push flip my wrist follow through my elbow was out *Off!* I yell jump in for the rebound it shanks off the rim the orange orb is now a basketball jumpy out of control freakin leather wound round a rubber pig's bladder Ann skies from the other side rips it out of the air underhands it to me Ann can touch the rim slam a Nerf *Phreet!* the ref says *Game to Johnson* he points to our bench I slam bounce the ball at midcourt high in the air watch it twirl for a second black seams spinning slow motion before my teammates jump on me tackle me smother me I keep my game face bat mask tight China Doll Girl slit eyes dad will yell at me tonight all night long I missed a free throw I won't be able to escape him it's Thursday a school night in my hometown of Saint Paul Minnesota on East Rose Avenue a block off Payne where truck drivers pass through on their way to the Dakotas there's no escape for me

*   *   *

Spring birds

need food too mom says *it's still cold out* mad dad rolls his eyes flips the channel *You pay for it* he says *I don't bankroll birds* mom carries the bird feeder made out of rough hewn wood to the kitchen cuts through the plastic wrap with a steak knife I watch her from the door my arms crossed look at him in his chair flipping channels he won't settle on one for long mom peels off the plastic crumples it leaves it on the blue counter top where it slowly unfolds returns to its original rectangular shape she pulls on the feeder's cord handle lifts it off the table watches it swing I wonder what she's looking for what she wants what she sees in her mind cardinals blackbirds chickadees sparrows blue jays gripping the tiny dowels poking at the seed behind the glass until they figure out how to puncture the tiny holes covered by plastic along the bottom she goes outside the orange curtains on the door swing behind her she disappears I won't go near mad dad he screamed at me all last night right through the news while mom and I watched the highlights *Sophomore standout at Johnson scores 23 in regional win against Edina* the announcer said over footage of my reverse lay up me bouncing the ball at midcourt my teammates piling on top I was the star! it didn't matter mad dad screamed *Fucking shit! stupid retard! dumb piece of shit princess* drank half a case of Hamm's knocked the table lamp over broke the bulb mom picked it up last night before she went to bed *fucking shit! freak dyke fag* rang in my head all day I won't talk to him go in the same room with him mom picks up after him made him breakfast sausage eggs ham buttered toast with homemade rhubarb jam bought a bird feeder tried to engage him about feeding birds I don't know why

I see her through the window on her tip toes hanging the feeder off a tree branch anyone who knows my father knows he doesn't give a shit about birds he would just as soon shoot them as look at them he settles on a North Stars' game *Broten sends the puck down the side* mom leans over stands up dumps bird seed into the feeder claps her hands together *icing on the Stars* I set the table for supper drop his plate down loud want to break it smash his face with it the pot screams mom comes inside I put the knife she used to cut the bird feeder plastic at his plate he wouldn't like that *Turn down the flame* she says I toss a plate at her place scatter the rest of the utensils on the table *Careful don't scar the table top* she says takes off her boots I drop the flame down to nothing the screaming stops I start up the stairs to wash up *Who cares* I say *who cares about the fucking table top What* she says *what did you say* she yells up the stairs after me

Mad dad piles

his plate with mashed potatoes mad dad clicks his ice in his rum n Coke mad dad stabs a steak with his fork mad dad coughs in his arm pit mad dad makes a noise like he's going to spit I tuck my chin to my chest I grip my fork n knife I rock a little in my chair just like a retard like a baby retard! I rock so I won't explode! I rock so I won't lean across the table jab a steak knife into his chest scream *you repulsive piece of shit* mom sighs says *Work was draining today Maryanne is back* I rock I rock I want him to die I rock I rock to keep from killing him tipping the table across his chest driving it to the ground pushing it pushing it pushing it I pile my mashed potatoes higher than his I stab a bigger steak cover it in ketchup AI sauce cut it into squares he eats his steak down to the bone I eat mine down to the bone we click we clack we eat with no words

Mother says: we are a happy family living in a house with gold fuzzy crowns on the walls repeat after me we are a happy family living in a house with gold fuzzy crowns on the walls repeat after me we are a happy family living in a house with gold fuzzy crowns on the walls and a rough hewn bird feeder in the back yard

Party tonight

shouldn't eat so much it'll be harder to get drunk but I can't help it I have to eat as much as he does repeat after me: we are a happy family I flatten my mashed potatoes *Miss So And So how was school* mom says butters her mashed potatoes *Great* I say bright and cheery and sarcastic she looks at her plate

> *Poor mother she tries so hard and we are so mean to her!*
> *Yeah she tries all right*
> *She tries to pretend last night didn't happen*

Just super I say again I can't stop the sarcasm dripping from my words my heart the bloody steak I can't stop! *Oh look* mom ignores me points to the window with her knife *a bird Oh look!* I say dripping ketchup AI sauce mad dad keeps eating he never listens to us *What is it* she says squints her eyes leans forward *A bird* I say she ignores me *Husband look a bird is already at our feeder* why does she say our feeder it's hers she bought it he doesn't care why does she say ours *Huh* mad dad says looks up at her like he didn't know she or I or the table or the room was there *Look at our feeder there's already a bird at it* I eat my steak covered in ketchup AI sauce chew it cow meat I'll puke it up later *Oh* he says like he's surprised like he lives on another planet like he forgot all about the bird feeder he wouldn't bankroll *Oh* I say imitating him like the dumbshit he is neither of them say anything he looks surprised like he does not know why I would be rude

> *Who knows why he looks surprised!*
> *he's a crazy man!*

mom spoons green beans on her plate pushes the saucepan to me *No* I say I'm going crazy I want to fling the sauce pan across the room I can barely keep myself from hitting breaking punching screaming killing everything *Oh* she says *Oh* I say I can't stop! I keep imitating her keep hurting her I'm so angry I can't stop she clicks her tongue to let me know she heard me let me know I hurt her

> *She doesn't like it!*
> *Stop imitating them!*
> *They're going to kill you lock you out!*

mom puts her napkin on the table *Don't scar it!* I say she ignores me mad dad is on another planet *Husband look it's a sparrow So what* I say dripping ketchup AI sauce murder in my blood *a bird is a bird* I say *A sparrow* he says makes a face *What's the difference* I say *They're garbage birds* mom says *not attractive* I stop chewing *You only feed certain birds That's right* she says meets my eyes *only the nice pretty ones* I stare at her stupidly *the ones that smile* she means me a freak fag dyke I am to blame for everything I see it in her eyes the way she sets her jaw she wishes I'd never been born *We don't bankroll sparrows* mad dad takes another drink *You don't bankroll anything* I say trying to provoke him *except beer* he doesn't say anything goes back to his own planet mom walks to the window *Get off* she yells hits the window with her fist *you piggy sparrow let the chickadees eat* the sparrow flies off turns a circle lands on the feeder mad dad gulps his drink ice hits his teeth *Sparrows are so ugly* mom says *Sparrows are so ugly* I repeat hating them wishing they would die both of them including my sparrow hating mom

She's in

mom says steps toward me with the phone dad stops chewing looks at mom raises his eyebrows *your mother* she says holding the phone to her chest he shakes his head stabs a piece of steak rolls it in A1 sauce she stops I look at her then him my mouth open he's never kept me from talking to gramma before mom doesn't move doesn't follow his orders he slides the meat off the fork into his mouth pushes it around in his mouth *No* he cracks his fork on his plate *Sorry* mom says *she's not available right now* my mouth opens *You don't need to talk to that crazy old* he doesn't finish his sentence taps his fork *fills your head with all sorts of shit* I look at him he knows how much he hurt me a sparkle in his eyes like a jewel

Two shots

one for each basket I scored last night *Go So And So go!* Kelly screams nostrils flare *one two three* I slam she slams we slam a shot of Jack Daniels burp *Whew!* we yell high five *Great game So And So* Kelly screeches her hands clenched like a child's Moe is jealous she doesn't drink stands off to the side we are in Brandon's sister's bedroom she must be really young four or five Raggedy Annes loll over her yellow frilled pillow case *Four more Kelly* I look at her face while I pour another shot she's adopted I wonder if she's only white gramma flickers through my mind I focus on the amber liquid chase the thought of her away Kelly pours another we toast each other we toast the bottles I toast Moe in the corner arms crossed *People will see you* she says *everyone knows who you are now So* I say *fuck em* I think of my father want to punch him *one two three* I slam Kelly slams we slam the door slams *Good riddance* Kelly laughs we are wasted but not wasted enough *More* I say *So And So* Kelly says *how many Twelve* I say she laughs pushes me over leans on my stomach *So And So you can't drink that much Oh yes I can* I want to touch her but I don't *C'mon* I say *get up three more*

Nuh uh Kelly pulls her Kodiak out her back pocket taps it with her knuckles I line up our shot glasses she keeps them at her house in the back of her closet her mom never snoops her glass says *Las Vegas* mine says *Hollywood* I'm a star! I look at Kelly pulling her lip out putting a chew in she is funny I love her like I haven't loved since Patty but I keep love far far away like a fairy tale from another world two more shots burn my throat Kelly spits in a red party cup *Ah!* I say *two more* the room spins I love being drunk last night's screaming *dyke stupid retard* the look on sparrow hating mom's face doesn't feel so bad the room's blurry I spill the whiskey on the yellow bedspread *Oops poor little girl* I wipe it up with my sleeve *oh poor little girl!* Kelly laughs at me I am funny when I drink *One!* I slam a shot *Two!* I slam a shot the ceiling bucks over my head I fall backwards onto my back I like how it all sounds the words in my head I fall back on the Annie Raggies striped red white legs bounce around me ceiling white bumpy bumpy ceiling buck buck buck bah buck poor little girl!

* * *

What's your name

she moves toward me blocks the light *Fuck* I say she has white nylon legs *Sit up now* her voice cuts through my head hurts worse I curl up taste puke in my mouth I am drunk somewhere a white padded wrestling room white mats on the floor white mats on the wall a white lady in the door maybe I died and went to heaven this is what heaven would look like for sure if it existed white ladies in white suits yelling in my ear *For your information you are at the Ramsey County Detoxification Center* Oh shit! I yell they'll kick me off the team I sit up she is for real a white giant in a white padded loony tune bin room

Wake up

to a smooth ceiling *Nurse she threw up again* a woman says I turn my head a big mouth crazy is in a bed next to me a nurse pulls my sheet down *Get out* I say nothing look at the ceiling smooth as a baby's butt caked throw up on my knee

Give me my bra I say
Get up the nurse says
She threw up big mouth says
You already said that I say
Get up right now the nurse says
Fuck off I say
She swore big mouth says
Shut up you kiss ass shit I say hate her
A boy wonder nurse walks in snaps his fingers
I stare at him
Hey he says I'm Tom

grabs me pulls me out of bed caked throw up yellow brown on my knee and thigh don't care crazy dyke fag freak then that's what I'll be *C'mon* Tom says he's the only half way nice one in here *She threw up* big mouth says again while the nurse balls up the dirty sheet *Is she crazy* I say to Tom he lifts his eyebrows drags a white plastic chair next to my bed *Are you trying to kill yourself* Tom sits me in it I say nothing I hadn't thought of that he makes my bed *Now there's an idea* I say I close my eyes I'll wait a few hours then I'll sneak out no one will know a thing I won't get kicked off the team I won't get kicked off the team! *Why don't you tell me your name* a new voice I open my eyes a small white lady brown hair down her back in jeans and blue clogs and a peach polo shirt I shut my eyes again she can't get through China Doll Girl slit eyes bat mask pulled tight bleeding skin *If you can't tell us your name we will have to contact the police* she puts her hand on my shoulder soft gentle makes me want to punch her in the face *I'm sure your parents are very worried* I pull my shoulder away blue clog bitch

I wear
a blue striped frock to a meeting with people in suits

What's your name suit people say
Shrug
What's your name suit people say
Shrug
What's your name suit people say
Look out small window in the door to see who walks down the hall
You are making it worse for yourself by not telling us your name suit people say
Look at a gray crack on the white tile floor
Your parents must be very concerned suit people say
Ha ha I say
Worried sick suit people say
Ha ha I say look at nails keep one arm under boobs to hold them up since cannot have my bra
Has something happened recently to upset you suit people say
A loss suit people say
An argument with a boyfriend or family member suit people say
Trouble at school with grades or friends suit people say
Feeling sad suit people say
Lonely suit people say
Depressed suit people say
Out of control suit people say
It's okay we all have hard times suit people say
You can talk to us suit people say

Tell us what is wrong suit people say
Yawn look at ceiling white as the faces arms nylons frocks
Everything is white I say still a little bit drunk laugh because I am drunk but
they are stupid will think I am crazy like big mouth
Look at each other suit people
What did you drink suit people say
How much did you drink suit people say
Have you drank before suit people say
Were you trying to hurt yourself suit people say
Lift eyebrows I say lean elbows on knees
Were you attempting suicide suit people say
Nah I say
No to which question suit people say
No answer make my eyes blank
No to one of the questions suit people say
Or no to all the questions suit people say
Or no to some of the questions suit people say
You're right she could mean no to some of the questions suit people say
I hadn't thought of that suit people say
Mm hmm suit people say
Close eyes will outlast them I am a patient patient sneak out later me n
China Doll Girl
Tick tock tick tock I sit in a frock I laugh
We're not getting anywhere with her suit people say
We'll have to call the police suit people say
Bite nail keep one arm under boobs to hold them up don't like droopy
boobs against my stomach
What's wrong suit people say
Spit out the piece of nail I chewed off
Please tell us what is wrong suit people say
I can't have my bra that's what is wrong I say

Dream

   all night long nurses in white nylons hook my bra up to the ceiling *No!* I
scream *you don't understand this isn't who I am* they gather round in a
circle laugh one climbs a ladder hooks up another bra *No! I don't want to
die I don't want to hate I don't want to want to kill* but they don't hear me
clip another bra on a hook *Patients might hang themselves from the ceiling*
they say hook up another bra then another *No!* I scream *I have something
important to tell you listen to me!*

That is her

   I'd like to talk to her alone mad dad's in my dreams mad dad's pinching
my arm mad dad's closing the door mad dad's in my room I pretend to
sleep *Don't pull this shit with me Little Miss So And So you're in no
position to play games* he pinches harder harder harder until my bone feels

like it's going to break crack! right in two white walls white bras white metal hooks I keep my eyes shut he squeezes harder I scream in my head gramma gramma help me! push my face into the pillow bite my lip *It won't work I can send you to a loony bin* he whispers in my ear *that's where you belong remember the judge*

If

he says far away like he's in water *You* he says I sink like a stone *Ever* he says I am drowning *Tell* he says *Anyone* he says *I* he says *Will* he says *Kill* he says *You* he says *Like* he says *Your* he says *Little* he says *Friend* he pulls me out of the water by the ankles leaves me on shore looks over his shoulder points at me *Smile* he says *like your mother says* he walks into the hall *leave her alone for a few minutes she needs some time to think about our talk Shouldn't I at least say hi* mother says *Later* his voice fades as the door shuts behind him then his face returns to the window up high watching

Your father

and I are very disappointed in you Little Miss So And So mom tucks in her chin so she'll have better posture wipes the corners of her mouth with her thumb and finger the way she does when she's nervous mad dad screeches around a corner *Oh Husband* mom sits up straighter afraid of him I slouch in the back seat *What* he yells slams the brakes I bounce into the back of the front seat bright blue vinyl replaces my face

One and a half stories

asbestos siding upside down lawn mowers we thought we were moving to California but it was just another part of town me and mom walk up the sidewalk mad dad squeals off tailing a truck out of town *He needs to cool off* mom says now that he's gone she seems sad but I can't care about her anymore it will kill me to care about her the house looks strange like I haven't seen it in a thousand years something has changed and it will never be the same again *Your team lost to Minneapolis North last night* mom looks at me there is a wistfulness in her eyes reminds me of the blue lilacs that bloom in late spring out back but I don't care I can't care! the pain knifes my stomach I've ruined everything all my fault now me and Patty will never be stars in college high fiving down the court *I'll make a grilled cheese* she opens the screen door someone painted it black while I was in detox *Okay* I shrug I don't live here anymore

How are you my girl

gramma says
Fine I say I know mom told her
You are the cream in my coffee gramma says her voice low and wobbly
I want to tell her dad isn't letting me talk
I want to ask if she calls a lot if she hasn't forgotten about me
dad opens the basement door

You are all I have I whisper hang up

What

 did you do Mike whispers hunched over in his chair he's a black painted nails Mohawk freak *I didn't do anything* I say glance at the teacher she doesn't mind if we whisper she's not like the other control freak teachers her job description is to work with fuck ups like me and Mike *Greg will you read your piece about an event from your childhood to the class* Greg sighs dope freak that he is takes his feet off the chair in front of him *My grandfather died in a farming accident* he stops reading coughs Mike leans across my desk whispers *Did you ever tell them your name No* his eyebrows go up *Really* he lets his hand fall at me like a fag but he's not he's got a girlfriend in another state *And when my grandma found him the tractor's back tire'd already run him over Never* I whisper and draw a line through the air *My grandma dialed the sheriff I kinda stood around until the sheriff came* the teacher nods *It took the detox people three days to figure it out* I say *my parents didn't report me as missing for two days* I hold my hand up in a peace sign *two days! and Kelly and Monica never told on me* I smile Mike whistles he is impressed doesn't think girls do things like that *probation for a year and* I say lean toward him *I won't ever play basketball for this school again* Mike crosses his arms *The coach told my dad that it was a waste of my time to try out next year That bites* he whispers *he's a dick Fuck em* I say anger spikes in me like a long tall weed

Age Twenty (1988)

Stadium lights

glimmer like diamonds through the humid air *So And So* Shelly yells behind me I turn receive the ball softly on my instep I am one with the thick air the sweat and humidity condense on my forearms and the backs of my hands *Down the line* Tanya shouts with one smooth fluid movement I shut out my defender send it down the line to Tanya a perfect pass she loses out of bounds I bend over hands on my knees pull at my shorts one with the airbound water my sweat my muscles my lungs I can feel every cell in my body every thing around me *C'mon Tanya concentrate* Barb yells slaps her hands I am at one with the noise of her slapping hands no one knows I am stoned

the squad with the yellow practice jerseys throws the ball to their defense they swing it around to the other side I can stand and watch now the breathlessness of soccer the bodies thighs calves the movements of both teams is like an orchestra all so beautiful it's living breathing moving poetry the yellow squad loses the ball in a shuffle near our goal line Gail moves out of the pile arms pumping thighs ripping through the air she booms the ball across the field her whole body lifts off the turf from the force of her kick the ball twirls through the humid air in slow motion high as a mountain a perfect arching volley directly at me I lose it briefly in the jeweled stadium lights then find it crouch wait the ball hits my chest just under my collar bone I drop it at my feet swivel my hips leave the defender flat footed *Nice trap* Gail yells her voice trailing behind me a comet in the sky my thighs hips have the power of a horse *a fricking horse!* I take one two three steps set my right foot kick the ball that jackass toad standing at my feet clean through the air with my left foot curve it just over the keeper's white gloves into the upper right hand corner the ball drops in the back of the net whoosh I stop in my tracks the perfection of my body and the ball and the damp air my hair wet on my neck and forehead *Helluva shot* Shelly says gives me a high five *Thanks* I say barely move I don't want to break the feeling of perfection in my body *Great turn* Daniel says from the sidelines *Awesome* Gail runs up from the back slaps both my hands down low *you got balls to chest trap that Thanks* I say I don't want to come down

Ready

Tanya slaps my back *For sure* I say *Great practice* she scruffs her short black hair with a towel I pull mine back wrap a rubber band around it thick as a snake *Let's go* I push her shoulder water beads glisten on the back of her neck make little gray spots through her white v neck t-shirt I want to touch her the beads like crystals under my stoned fingers *Pub* Judy says holding her towel around her chest *U of Wisconsin Badgers* written in red cursive along the edge of the towel *Ask So And So* Tanya says *she's the one with the fake ID* I say nothing immersed in the water on Tanya's back *Well* Judy rubs one foot against the other *What* I say *Are you going to the Pub* I glance at Tanya embarrassed as if she knows my thoughts *Yeah* I say *the Pub sounds good to me All right* Tanya scuffs across the floor in her navy blue Adidas flip flops *Let's go So And So Uh yeah sure* I tuck the loose ends of my hair behind my ear Tanya pushes the door with her forearm leans into it looks back at me turns her eyes into a question mark I say nothing watch the crystal beads dry up along her neck line

What's your full name

the bouncer squints *Janelle Michelle Johnson* he flips the license over squints *Minneapolis address* he studies my face *2354 32ⁿᵈ Avenue South First name Janelle Last name Johnson Middle name Michelle* the bouncer studies me then the card between his thumb and forefinger *All right* he hands the driver's license to me lets Tanya in right away

Shelly leans against the back wall sucks the froth off of her beer the Pub is a dark paneling lined dive *Pool* she says I shrug watch Tanya buy a pitcher at the bar hope she'll hurry I'm coming down off the pot Shelly breaks the white ball spits off the others spins in a corner Shelly is eighteen but acts like she's twelve *How's your mom* she stands next to me holding her pool cue like a sentry *I dunno* I pull out a pack of cigarettes from my duffel bag the last thing I want to talk about is my mom *It's your turn* she says I look at the configuration of balls *Rider of the Storm* starts up on the jukebox Tanya carries a pitcher and three glasses I want Tanya alone I shoot for the striped seven miss *That's okay So And So* Shelly bounces to the other side of the table I hear in my head like it's coming over an intercom *I am very happy having a lovely time ma!* and imagine a picture of the Pub with me in it drunk kissing Tanya *I'd follow you anywhere Tanya* I hear take another drink to get rid of the voices and the pictures that pop into my head hoping those words never escape my mouth hoping no one knows who I really am *The bouncer sure gave you a hard time* Tanya says breaks the balls fracture across the table settling into fault lines *Yes!* Shelly yells raises her fist in the air *nice break!* I line up my shot take it smash it

* * *

Click click

clack clack the class repeats what the white professor says African Storyteller supposedly a hard class but I'm acing it *clickety clickety clackety clackety* I never repeat after the professor I have enough problems speaking in my own language he runs around the stage hunched over in his baggy assed jeans and blue suede running shoes a gray haired scrawny white man who's lived in Africa half his adult life he's a nut which usually I like in people but not him he's a marathon runner who hates all student athletes because we get out of class to travel on the weekends he thinks it's easy for us but he doesn't know how different it is for the women's teams no lobster steak dinners for us! we eat Subway Chinese at best on the road I've eaten Subway sandwiches white bread all the veggies mayo mustard vinegar and oil with a dash of pepper across half the country thanks to UW soccer the sunlight falls into the room through the top windows it's a big classroom holds one fifty in a marble building the oldest on campus the pillars and doorways chiseled into Grecian columns and archways I would come to class even if I didn't like learning the stories and culture of southern Africa just to look at the sun glancing off the marble and dashing off the swaying bouncing leaves outside the windows it's hot in here *cluck cluck clank clank*

Very good class very good the professor says and wrings his hands and walks to the podium in the middle of the stage he flips through some papers *Okay* he says *open your books to the story of The Girl Who Dragged Her Entrails Through Life Behind Her On The Ground* he looks over the top of his glasses while we open our books I am excited I read this one five times this is a story I understand it *Okay her father cut open her stomach with an axe ripped out her entrails and flung them down beside her then he left her to die by the river now why did he do this class* he pauses *class* I keep silent even though I know the answer *He believed her to be barren* a man from the middle of the room says the sun flashes across the ceiling then goes away I look at the tops of the trees through the windows flailing and bouncing like they have something to say something important! a girl child in her seat in some classroom any classroom anywhere the trees bounce say listen to what she has to say! *Yes* the professor says *what else She disobeyed him when he told her to pick yams* a man in the back says I turn in my seat look at his thin beard *Yes* the professor says runs around the room again *but what is implied in this story in the information the storyteller gives to the listener but never comes right out and says* I am afraid to talk in class I am afraid everyone will laugh stare think I'm crazy weird gross lock me up throw away the key *The storyteller uses information both as a means by which he gives information to the listener and he uses it as a smoke screen to hide knowledge a knowledge that may be too much for the listener to hear outright or a knowledge that breaks the rules of that particular society She was a girl and her father preferred sons* a woman's voice floats through the room joins the sunlight dancing off ionic columns and marble leaves the professor does not respond he's getting agitated he's spent his whole life studying stories from southern Africa learning the Khosa's clicking language so he can teach it to white kids in Wisconsin he starts rubbing his jaw *Because she was stupid* a man yells out four rows in front of me looks at the man to his left they laugh the professor folds his arms across his chest says nothing someone else laughs Patty flashes through my head her dark pony tail skinny legs *Yo Adrian I love you! what happened to her! what happened to her!* screams through my head more laughter from the back of the room it feels the whole room is laughing in my ears everyone everything the whole world laughing at me while he hurts us laughing who cares mother turns away blames me *where is Patty!* my father laughing his face over mine while the world watches

She was raped I nearly scream *her father raped her* the guys stop laughing everyone turns looks at me I am freaked out I don't know what's happening the professor claps his hands together *Yes yes yes this is what the storyteller says without coming right out and saying it the girl who dragged her entrails through life behind her on the ground is a story about the father daughter incest taboo found in every society which is so taboo that in fact one cannot directly address the taboo itself* I think I am going to vomit I feel Patty everywhere she is the marble leaves ceiling columns tremoring green and gold leaves outside *I remember the beauty! I remember the beauty of her love!* I clutch the writing board over my lap press my palm into the metal bite of the spiral notebook stare at the back of the seat in front of me *listen to us breathe listen to us breathe listen to us breathe!* the blonde wood pressed into a semicircle to fit the curve of a back a standard back an average back a male back I stare until my feelings are severed ripped out dragging behind me picking up dirt loose pieces of grass stray sticks I stare at the curved wood in front of me until my feelings are dead

Thanks

a student from African Storyteller says grasps my hand holds it presses into it I feel the warmth from her body in mine *Thanks* she says again I say nothing grip her hand shake it don't know why I'm shaking her hand not sure why she is thanking me the class files out behind us *They don't know anything* she says continues to shake my hand her eyes water look into mine I feel nothing stare at her *I know what it's like* she walks away skinny legs sticking out of cut off jeans

I stand

in the hall glass case filled with books written by a professor of geology at the U I hear my breath I know I am alive but my body is marble the class files by someone laughs I assume at me but I can't worry about it my body is failing I can't move my legs arms are heavy

Are you all right someone says I swallow have to interact with her I nod *Are you sure* she says my eyes are on her combat boots no socks hairy legs hairy legs! why does a she someone have hairy legs I feel more confused than a five year old lost at the supermarket *What's your name* the woman says I say nothing she says *I really liked what you said in class today it took courage* I say nothing *Can I help you* she touches my elbow *Janelle* I say look up can't focus on her face hope she doesn't notice try to send me to the loony bin *I am discombobulated* what a good word the way it sounds feels a fat red thread pulling through my brain *my name is Janelle a good name don't you think*

she says nothing trying to decide if I'm crazy I'm not making sense in my own head my own body my thoughts are slow like a train wreck being pulled back to the station *whoo! whoo! steam whistle shooting through my head mad dad is angry I told* I try to focus on her face I need to get rid of her need to stand here against the cool wall I like cool I like flat it rests my brain I need to stand here until this stops until my body isn't marble anymore until my thoughts get back to a normal speed I don't want anyone to see how crazy I am here on the inside where I keep it locked up

You know

she returns her blond hair and pointy nose *if you want someone to talk to you can go to the U's Counseling Center* she says *or the Women's Center* she says *we'll help you* I nod vomit coming back up my throat please just go away I think *My name's Jessica* she says *here's a Women's Center card* she holds out a card *All right* pointy Jessica says clank clank clank her boots walk away I am alone in the hall the smooth cool wall against my back my eyes close click clack click clack student A.D. 1988 turned to stone on this spot when she thought what she shouldn't think said what she shouldn't say did what she shouldn't do broke a taboo

Key in door

turns she is not home in our home away from home oh how I miss my home! *Yeah right* I hear in my head I dig up a pipe smoka smoka the fancy black one with gold scrolly lines open windows wide turn on TV smoka smoka a cockroach skitters across the floor me and the cockroaches have an agreement we have trust we have a compact I do not kill them grind their greasy bodies into the kitchen tile they do not steal my food shit in my grains crawl up my arms neck face at night the way they do to my roommate they know I know we know I have to be stoned to forget everything in my head forget it all! bury it in the hole! talk in funny China Doll Girl voice! be the drunkest most stoned to make people not see how crazy I feel how weird I am how I have conversations with my self age 5 to 20 plus every age in between my head hurts from all the fighting inside it *I am a parrot repeating grown up thoughts! Your head doesn't hurt! Yes it does! No it doesn't! It's my head not yours stupid!* this weed burns nicely leaves my lips like moss smoka smoka Oprah blinks swivels in her chair my phone rings *Hello yes it's me yes tonight all right sounds good no of course not a problem surely I'll be there wear shorts no long pants or jackets with pockets* click smoke another bowl so what drug testing tonight picked from random my ass Gary watermelon head coach picked me he hates me I hate him end of story end of fucking story!

Hello gramma

I say
Hello my girl how's school she says
Good I say
How's the team
Good I say but my voice breaks I want to cry like a kid
Are you okay gramma says
I'm okay I say
It's good to hear your voice gramma says
It's good to hear your voice I say
Am I still the cream in your coffee I say
You will always be the cream in my coffee one and only granddaughter
You are the cream in my coffee gramma I say sucking up the sea

The field house

is across from the Regent built out of gray stone A. D. 1872 carved across the top some committee wants to tear this down build a modern facility we train in here in the winter two and a half hours of scrimmage capped off by ten timed sprints up the stairs so steep at the top that we have to jump just to get from one step to another I pull on the mile high set of doors slip into the cool dark air

the rafters five stories up give the air a bite on the tip of my tongue thanks to windows sealed shut sixty years ago must and accumulated stink from thousands of dusty shoe prints stomping on the floorboards *Go Badgers go!* generations of people with lives that no one will ever know about dreams lost here torn pieces of paper floating end over end from the upper deck why would someone want to tear this down

Whish whish whish the headboard did it

I imagine my father stashing my girl body in the rafters *So And So! So And So!* I hear Kelly's high pitched scream her wide flaring nostrils menthol light in one hand imagine Patty and me running down court 14,000 fans yelling our names in an article in the Cardinal the next day *Patty and So And So Break Big Ten Record In Assists and Scoring in Win Over Big Ten Rival Michigan* that way if we die if we disappear we'll be in the archives in the library someone fifty years from now will run across us save us from mad dad's annihilation *save us!* I run my hand along the red smooth countertop pick up a *UWI Men's Basketball Can't Be Beat* plastic cup I want to be somewhere else in another world another time a better place than my mind where my dad still hunts me *So And So! So And So!* the crowd chants my hand fits around the cup smooth and round my life is a zero

So And So

someone says from far away through the dark dusty air I come back to this time and place *Hey Tanya* I leave the people and their dreams and their heartaches behind *What are you doing* she spikes her hair *Nothing* I raise the cup as if I walked that way to pick it up *you here for the drug testing Shit* she says low walks toward me grabs my arm *my dad will kill me if I test positive* her dad is a lawyer she doesn't even need the scholarship my dad is a roofer part time garage mover he won't care if I lose my scholarship college is worthless soccer is a sissy European sport when I got kicked off the basketball team he stopped going to my soccer games even when we won state my senior year I scored the winning goal *So And So!* Coach Chuck said *get your ass out there and score* and so I did and so I did

I could have played basketball here could have been a star me and Patty I take a breath hold it get the feelings under control stop them dead in their tracks I don't care about anything rough tough dyke fag freak I drop the cup on the floor stalk toward the bathroom Rambo style

Kick

me off the team then I say *I don't care You get a probationary period* Gary says arms crossed he's saying what he has to say *You set this up* I lean across the desk with the picture of his two children even uglier than he is *I wish Tim had never left* I say *he was a good coach he didn't care if we partied* Gary unfolds his arms picks up a pencil taps it on his desk *I suppose that's why he's gone* I hate him *Do you suppose that's why the girls who play are the ones who go to church with you* Gary's eyes open a little more *It was the poppy seed muffin I ate at Perkins* I say *I don't do drugs* I lie I am not stupid I won't admit guilt go to jail or rehab or something *Nevertheless* he sits up in his chair *the probationary period extends into next season* he bounces a pencil on his desk *Who was the second leading scorer the last two seasons first in assists* he nods *So one would wonder why you picked me for the drug test* I know there is a hole he can exploit in my accusation but I don't know if he's smart enough to catch it I don't care he's a liar do it the right way Christian freak *You're a liar* I say now I'm all over the place but I can't stop he is a hypocrite who wants to get rid of me and Tanya because we're not Christian ass kissers who follow him to church

I stomp out the door ten feet high an old fashioned window at the top tilted to let the air escape *Now you've got the scholarship you wanted* I say *now you can go recruit some passive Christian girl to play for you* I slap the woodwork with my bare hand he's trying to put me up in the rafters take my dreams from me I won't let him I'll yank them down first

Ugly bird

I quit

the team I speak into the receiver clearly enunciate the words are pearls on a string they are on time in order I own them they are mine those words

there in the air on the tip of my tongue at my fingertips they are mine! I
won't take any shit anymore no more! I am on fire steam engine whoo
whoo! ready to take down anything in my way my anger pushes me through
a lifetime of silence shrugging shoulders

What mother says
I quit the team hand clutches the receiver
What mother says
I see her sit down in the kitchen in the house that was never my home one
block off Payne
I quit the team ugly birds do ugly things
Have you lost your mind
No!
the sun slants over the kitchen sink bits of suds in the basin
Why would you
For good reasons I say I am going to put the receiver through the wall
But what about your scholarship we don't have the money
I don't care about the scholarship
What about school
I'll find a way I don't care I hate my coach I'm not gonna take it anymore I
nearly scream
You should have stayed on the team call him back apologize
No!
                                        Ugly bird

I'll call him then
No!
                                        Ugly bird

Did you really quit
Yes I really quit
                                        Ugly bird

Why
                                        Ugly bird

I quit for goddamn good reasons
Don't you swear at me missy she says the off white curlicue phone cord
between her thumb and finger did they catch you drinking again
                                        Ugly bird

Is that it
                                        Ugly bird

No I say
You're going to end up like your father
No I say
You're just like your father
No I say
You're going to end up like me working for nothing no one appreciating
you

I am not going to end up like you

Ugly bird

How can you can treat me like this after everything I've done for you she chokes call your coach maybe it's not too late
No! I feel like I want to die drown in the ocean for making her cry I bury my feeling

Ugly bird

I'll have your father talk to him
No!

Ugly bird

What is your coach's number
No!

Ugly bird

I hate him
What is the number
I hate you
Gasp

Ugly bird

I she says

Ugly bird

Silence cord drops to floor bounces three times settles spins

Ugly ugly bird

I open my mouth let go of the ocean drowning me in a lifetime of silence I quit I say it's over
Click
I hang up
Click
I turn the key to my apartment walk down the hallway the skittering of cockroaches a thin orange light at the end of the hall the setting sun
Listen to me breathe listen to me breathe listen to me breathe

* * *

Hamburger rare
fried onions pickle no on the mayo I set a large cup of ice under the Coke nozzle oozing brown syrup we haven't cleaned it in a week *Huh* Angie says she is short almost fat wears Elvis Costello glasses even though she hates him cuffs her jeans over her Mary Jane's we are both English majors *It's your turn to clean the nozzles* I hand the woman her Coke heavy on the fizz low on the syrup *E tu Brute* Angie points her spatula at me turns back

to the grill *It's damn hot in here* I say wipe my forehead the next woman pushes her tray in front of me a grad student in one of the hard sciences I can tell by her clothes plain brown shorts short sleeved shirt thick watch a look in her eyes I can just tell!

I stare at her up here in Tripp Commons we're not about customer service I continue to stare until she says *Turkey on wheat with lettuce and mayonnaise please Sure thing* I say *it's a tradition here at Tripp* I slap the sliced turkey and lettuce onto the bread *that each customer tell us what department she or he is in before she or he can get her or his food* I slop the mayo on two slices of wheat bread the woman looks at me she is not amused I cut her sandwich cross ways wipe the blade off on a white cotton towel let the knife drop into the hole between the lettuce container and the cutting board *Well* I lean on the palms of my hands *Well what* Angie says standing next to me she slides a plate with the hamburger rare fried onions pickle no mayo over the top of the sneeze guard *You get a salad bar with that* she says to the woman who walks out without acknowledging her *Professor* we say smirk *What about you* Angie points her metal spatula at the turkey sandwich woman the woman looks over her shoulder at the line *Oh c'mon* I say *look at how hard we work can't you humor us I'll give you some chips* I run my hand through the bin of Old Dutch premium potato chips *Oh all right* she forces a smile I would have given her the chips anyway but I don't tell her that *Hurry up hurry up* Angie says *we don't have all day* I dump a pile of chips next to the turkey sandwich drop a pickle spear over the top of the sandwich *I'm in chemistry* she says looks over her shoulder *working on my doctorate Ah ha* I say I want to ask her who she is looking for but that's too rude even for Tripp Commons *I knew it* I hand her the plate she takes it almost dumps it struts away

You did not know it Angie scrapes the grease off the grill *Turkey woman wants to be a professor more than anything so she can go to cocktail parties kiss ass all day long be better than the rest of us cretins* I am a jerk for saying it even though it's probably true Angie nods pushes me away *Get back to work* she says *I have some serious frying to do here Can I help you* I say to the next man *I sure hope so* he says a visiting professor I bet he's too young to be a full professor here *We have a rule here at Tripp Commons* I say then see Jane slouched in the doorway in her slovenly way she gives a little wave by her hip her thumb in her belt loop *It's time for my break Angie* I say *you'll have to man the grill by yourself Woman it* she says yeah right I think I have more important things to find out right now than whether the snobs eating at Tripp teach ethics or biochemistry or Chaucer

What's up

I push Jane to the salad bar in the dining room a former three story ballroom enormous red velvet curtains draped across each window *What's up* I say again she is in the habit of not responding the first time someone asks her a question *Not much* she pushes at a strand of reddish brown wavy hair hanging in her eyes *Did you get it* I muck the spoon around in the cottage cheese bowl *Yes* she says her brown eyes never dart no matter what not even when we discuss drugs in public spaces I toss a celery stick at her under the sneeze guard *Is your sister okay* I say *No* she says a man walks up leans over me grabs the vinegar *She's back on the psych ward* she says loudly she likes to freak out people *same room as last time* she tosses a baggy of shrooms on her plate grabs raw spinach with the tongs *Don't get those mixed up* I mound a plate with squares of cantaloupe lettuce shredded cheddar cheese french dressing and spoonfuls of sesame seeds that skitter down the lettuce mountain

Tabatha!

a woman's voice scatters across the towering ceiling my head jerks toward a tall blond woman in a white tank top I wave *Yes! yes! here I am* the words spout out I don't know why I said that my name is not Tabatha! the woman strides toward me it's like I stepped aside for a second and the words poured out my mouth without my approval the woman is a few feet away *Hello* I say she walks by doesn't look at me I twirl in my chair she hugs a woman two tables behind me I look at Jane she looks at me I shrink the way I do when frat boys and sorority girls glare at me my brown hair shaved to an inch of my skull Ragstock faded painter jeans silver rings *Just joking* I say but it's not convincing so I say *too many drugs huh* but it's not the drugs I don't know why I answered a name that's not mine

* * *

Angie

you're bootiful Tracy sings falsetto at the 501 Club torn red vinyl bar stools *Drink up* Jane says spills beer on the floor *Sound check one two* the sun sets over the top of State Street hot pink n gassy blue behind a silhouette of darkened buildings a fan rotates over the bar the air is sweet with pot *Want one* I hold my dugout to them *No* Angie says Tracy ignores me we haven't been introduced Jane nods my best friend I can always count on her the front door is propped open with a cement brick a line of college students drop outs druggies wanders out the door down the street *Good thing we got here early* I jab the tiny pipe into the dugout until it's full inhale Jane takes a drag blows the smoke over her shoulder at the bartender *This is Tracy* Angie rolls her eyes puts her hand on his chest *he's my boy Hey* Jane says I nod drop the dugout into my jean pocket light up a Camel *I have died and gone to heaven* I say *pot beer Trip Shakespeare* Jane lights up *That's not what you said when we smoked this afternoon What happened* Angie says *Honey I'll see you later* Tracy says *nice to meet all you girls* he kisses Angie on the cheek walks out the door *I didn't know you had a boyfriend* I say *I don't* Angie says *he's gay what happened this afternoon It was laced with pcp* Jane pours another beer *she kept saying I'm going crazy I'm going crazy oh my god the girl is crazy court dismissed I'm going to be in a psych ward for the rest of my life* Angie looks at me I don't remember saying those things the guitars join the drums Jane drains her beer *You're not crazy* Angie says pats me on the arm *just a little weird*

A guitar whines

the sun disappears turns into a moon *Cheese cake I could go for some cheese cake* I blurt out no one says anything the band is loud drowning us fish rocks seaweed people crowd the empty spaces corners bar stools booths cracked red vinyl reveals matted down yellowed padding inside

Toolmaster of Brainerd c'mon let's dance I pull Jane n Angie off the bar stools Trip Shakespeare is in purple velvet their hair down to their asses shirts open to their belly buttons we find a bubble in the crowd slip into it fill it up we dance a few people away from the front *He took a charter bus too young and sweet to be hustling us* the lead singer flings his hair across the stage I want to be him on stage the stars shining bright the moon hung low across the street I miss soccer being the star Jane's head is down she's tapping her scuffed army boots on the sticky floor Angie's eyes are squeezed shut a small smile on her lips with her big Elvis Costello glasses I'll bet she wants to be on stage too I close my eyes slam from side to side Trip Shakespeare is from my home town!

He played his guitar like a natural disaster I run my palm over my stubbly hair *tooolmaaaaster of Braaaayneeeerd* the riff ends *Yeah* I yell I am fucked up someone grabs my ass the only people behind me are women I smile bow a woman grabbed my ass!

* * *

So

my mother says *we're coming Thursday* my roommate throws an empty shoe box out of her bedroom it lands near my feet she follows it I sit up on the back of the chair place my feet on the cushion *That is so rude* she says points to my feet goes back in her room hair flying through the doorway *We'll be there sometime around eleven in the morning Eleven* I say my roommate reappears throws a green plastic bag into the living room *Your father wants to get back in time for his program at seven* I say nothing space out the thought of being back there in that house with him a black duffel bag lands in the middle of the living room *Crazy* I say under my breath her bedroom door slams *What was that* my mother says *Amy's on another rampage* I say my mother says nothing *Get off the phone* I hear my father *did you hear me* he says my roommate is crying in her bedroom *Now* my father yells *I really should get going* my mother says panic in her voice *All right* I hang up my tongue goes down to my stomach I run to the bathroom wet cotton balls in the sink half packed boxes lying on the floor I vomit in the toilet

Gramma

I say I'm coming home for the summer can I come live with you
No no my girl no

chest sinks I say nothing
she says nothing
I can't speak an anchor is pulling me to the bottom
I'm losing the house gramma says I have to move
No I say sinking
You can't stay with me my girl I don't know where I'll be
No I say a little boy in a Chinese fairy tale

Jesus christ

what did you do to your hair I stand frozen next to my parents' car he leaves it running in the middle of the parking lot jumps out slaps my head *What is this* he looks at his hand like we're in a horror film and he just put his hand in slime *look at this* he says to mom sitting inside the car then he looks at me like he is seeing me for the first time my ripped t shirt three sizes too big silver rings bracelets necklaces men's dress pants cut off at the knees oversized combat boots *Oh my god what have you done* mom says I look at her a deer in headlights I haven't seen them since I quit soccer why didn't I know they would be mad *What sort of get up do you have on* he says *you look like a goddamn* he raises his fist drops it a car pulls in to the parking lot *Husband* she says low a warning he pushes me around the side of the car *Get out* he says to my mother she does not move not understanding *get out* he yells she steps away he throws me in the car punches the lock slams the door points at me through the glass *You move you die* I say nothing head spinning huddle against the door we roar away leave mother in the middle of the parking lot her purse on the floor next to my bare feet inside my big boots

Jesus Christ

he mutters stares at the road hands at ten and two *Jesus Christ* he turns by the field house drives over the shadow cast across the road I don't move not a muscle I don't move *Jesus Christ what is wrong with you* he yells we cross Regent *Jesus Christ* he mutters I don't move not a muscle not a toe not a finger the sun comes into the car the sun leaves the car *woo woo steam whistle shooting through my head* I am going to die we roar past the grocery store past the elementary school baseball diamond the sun comes into the car the sun leaves the car *Jesus Christ* he mutters the sun comes in the car the sun leaves the car tree branches leaves telephone poles I don't move not one muscle he is going to kill me he is crazy *Jesus Christ* he mutters *help* I want to scream at the people we speed past *help me!* but I don't move a muscle not a muscle

I could end you he says *right now* he says *I could make it so no one would ever find you* he says I move not a muscle not a toe not a finger the sun comes in the car the sun leaves the car the world fades I close my eyes the car slows I move not a muscle not a toe not a finger the blinker blinks we turn shade crosses my eyes I can't see! I can't see! I can't open my eyes I

move not a muscle not a toe not a finger we drive sun shade sun shade
across my mole eyes

What do you think about that he says
Closed eyes is what I say
No one would ever know
I move not a muscle

What do you think about that he says
Closed eyes
His hand on my thigh
I move not a muscle
His hand down there
Closed eyes nothing I move not a muscle feel not a thing
I could kill you he whispers right now

Get out
he says I blink I can see the parking lot mother sitting on the curb in
shade poor mother! she burns so easily *Start packing* fingers strangle my
arm *and change into the sort of clothes normal people wear* the voice gets
closer *I'm not driving four hours through Wisconsin with you dressed like
that* he took my body in the front seat folded it swallowed it now he wants
to dress it

I bring down box after box the parents sit and wait cockroaches scratch
between walls I bring down box after box until I am finished turn key click
slip it under the door watch my body my hands my arms my legs from afar
do what he says in slow motion automatic autonomic what is the word
numbness I did not change like he said but he doesn't notice shifts into drive
goodbye cockroaches fare thee well Angie Jane field house of dreams soccer
team my heavy head stalls

Mad dad the magician
n his snake poof! a little girl again face pressed to cool glass a girl with a
pony plays across the street

Houses
Highway 151 the mall Ponderosa Steak House Freeway 94 West to
Minneapolis sadness flat land red barns hot sun cool glass pressed to my
face he has me again mad dad the magician cast his spell where is Patty
buried under the shrubs truck stops diners fresh sweet corn stands Conoco
stations vented air

I told you to change he says inflamed brain cools on glass rolling hills
Wisconsin countryside green signs: The Dells 9 Miles *I'll be goddamned if
I'm going to drive another minute with you dressed like that* he says blue
signs: Campground! Hotel! Bingo! Antiques! Circus! Fun for the Entire
Family! Next Two Exits!

Tires on gravel

past Big Dan's Truck Stop to an A frame brown house Gerziak's Camping Outfitter *all your camping needs and more sold here* brown hairy arm across the top of the front seat hand clutches mother's headrest mother's head does not move his hand slaps loose vinyl on the back of the seat *Get inside* mad dad the magician looks at me in the rear view mirror *pick out some normal clothes appropriate for a female* he pulls out his wallet hands me two twenties *you'll pay this back by working it off around the house* I take the cash get out of the car I know what he means mother looks straight ahead *work it off around the house* circles my brain *work it off around the house* circles my brain *work it off around the house* circles my brain I am his concubine

Can I help

you miss I shake my head no walk round in circles know I am supposed to do something but what the muzak over the loudspeaker confuses me am in an elevator am in detox am in the mall Elton John with violins where am I who am I a puppet a person a freak a soccer star a partier an A student a little girl a loner

I float up near the ceiling to a display of tents bikes boots suspended in the air by wires I crawl in the tent look at the store below *Bad Bad Leroy Brown baddest man in the whole damn town* shouts from somewhere but where not from up here with the bikes boots hanging nearby more shouts *Calm down sir she must be here somewhere* I peer through the tent flap it's mad dad at the cash register mad dad at the cash register! I float down crouch behind the rack of biking shorts extra thick cotton crotches loud voices move toward the back I move along the side wall past a woman leafing through gray sweatshirts see ya! I float like a butterfly sting like a bee crawl on my belly below shorts thick gray sweatshirts I won't be a puppet staring straight ahead

I run out the front door bent over like a old lady with a cane except I'm not an old lady I'm a college student going back to school I sneak down the stairs run four cars left of their car mother in the front seat sitting up straight facing forward she doesn't move doesn't look doesn't see me I leave her there waiting for his wrath grapes of wrath! I run across the gravel parking lot crouch in the bushes watch the brown A frame *where you can get all your camping needs met*

mad dad another man appear around the side of the A frame scan the parking lot I don't move not a muscle not a toe not a finger mad dad walks to the car mother rolls down her window they talk mad dad goes back into the A frame mother stays in the car

I don't want to work it off around the house father's own personal whore I run in the ditch toward 94 under hot sun trees rolling hills Wisconsin country side I have to get off the road soon I cross it run into a grove of pines 94 buzzes ahead I cough up phlegm spit it out pull the twenties out of my pocket crumple them drop them like wadded up kleenexes in my mother's purse I won't be his puppet

Where you going

the trucker says the bill of his Packer's hat is split down the middle curls up on each side *Madison* I say pull myself up on the step of his rig flatten myself against his truck in case mad dad pulls in *I got money* he laughs *I don't need money* he says taps his boot on the floor starts up his truck *I got money* I say again he laughs *You in or out* I hesitate there's only one other rig at the truck stop and the driver is nowhere to be seen if there's one thing I know it's my father and he'll be pulling in here any minute the driver starts up his engine *I got money* I say again know I sound stupid I should say no fuck you I'll find another way but I'm desperate if mad dad catches me he'll beat me to death I swing myself up and in pull the door the cab smells like gas the trucker makes a sound with his teeth looks in his side mirror *Any money get exchanged* he says *will be from me to you I got money* I say again *I can pay you for the gas You just don't get it do you* he says swings the long semi onto the frontage road *I think it's only fair* I say playing dumb looking in the side mirror *Who ya looking for* he says shifts the truck I say nothing *A boyfriend* he says *You a Packer fan* I say see my father's blue car pull into the truck stop *Damn right* the trucker says tips his split hat turns a corner I lose sight of the car with my mother my father mad dad the magician all my belongings *The Packers could be a force in the Central Division next year* I say keep the focus on the Packers compliment his team even though they suck he is just another stupid man *Damn right* the trucker says speeds up the steep curving ramp

Trip Commons

is closed for the summer session the woman in the business office says her nose round as a mushroom *You know that I do know that* I say *you already told me what I need is my last check Okay your last check* the mushroom nose woman in the business office shuffles through a pile of envelopes *did you fill out the form telling us where to send it Um yeah* I lean on the counter *Did you tell us to send it or hold it Well* I say *send it I suppose All right just one moment* she leans back says something to the man behind her *Okay* she goes through the envelopes *it should be here we haven't mailed them yet Good* I say *I really need this money Uhm hum* she says stops shuffling *Is this you* she holds the envelope up to the window *Yeah* I say relieved I need clothes and food and tampons she slides the check under the glass but the man says something in her ear she pulls the check back *I'm sorry* she says *since you signed the release to have us mail it to Saint Paul we have to by law send it there What* I say *but I'm not living there I had a change of plans I'm sorry* she puts the envelope on the pile *C'mon* I say *you've got to be kidding give me a new form to sign* she shakes her head *I don't have any money I'll never see this check again There's nothing I can do Who can I talk to* I say *I'm a legal adult this is my money*

He's it she says jerks her thumb at the man behind her *Fucking goddamn it* I kick the wall *I'm a legal adult Hey* the man says *do you want me to call security Yeah* I say *that's just what I want call security on me you stupid fuck* I kick the wall again a short dark haired man turns the corner heads toward me I freeze think it's my father tracked me down come to kill me but he walks right by

It's so hot

my Oreos are melting Jane's sister Lori says from the bathroom *How can Oreos melt* Jane lights a cigarette in the living room big enough to hold a folding chair a coffee table and the green easy chair with ripped up armrests we dragged off a street corner *Look* Lori says walks out of the bathroom wiping her face with a towel points at a stack of Oreos double stuff just about the only thing she eats on a paper towel on the kitchen counter Jane scowls she can't forgive Lori for ending up in the psych ward during finals week *Where'd this come from* I hold up a baseball type card with *Jesus As Our Savior* written under a picture of a black Jesus Lori tries to pry apart an Oreo but the chocolate crumbles in her hand *Okay* Jane says *I see what you're saying* Lori makes a clucking noise turns to me holds out the cookie it dissolves in her hand chunks of the dark chocolate fall onto the kitchen floor *See* she says kicks at the crumbled chocolate then eats the white frosting *Uh huh* I say *I believe you it's hot* I wave the baseball card of a black Jesus Lori blushes Jane rolls her eyes *What happened* Jane blows smoke at the ceiling *Well* Lori says moves one foot so her feet end up pointing in opposite directions it's hard to watch her like this but it's worse for Jane *this guy came in* Lori picks up another Oreo *and he said Jesus sent him here because he knew an angel lived inside* Lori blushes the color of Tom's eyes when he's on coke I look at the back of the card *Outreach Ministries 313 Mifflin Street Madison Wisconsin Say that reminds me* I interrupt her *oh sorry what happened Did you give him money* Jane says *Well yes but it goes to a good cause see* she points to the card *it's a group that wants to spread the word that Jesus was really a black man* Jane stabs her cigarette into the coffee table *God Lori you can't keep giving away your money But* Lori says *No buts* Jane says *remember mom said don't give anyone your money and lock the doors we could get raped we don't live in the country anymore this is downtown Madison You really need to lock the doors Lori* I say but can't get too mad at her because after all they let me live with them on no notice I just showed up on their doorstep *You're just racist* Lori says eats the melting oreo *C'mon* Jane says looks intently at the smashed tip of the cigarette Lori looks at me raises her eyebrows *I don't doubt Jesus was a black man* I say even though I don't believe in Jesus or God or angels *but you still need to lock the doors* I want the conversation to be over so I can ask Jane about the Mifflin Street party *Nuh* Lori kicks her heel into a cupboard Jane walks to the sink runs her cigarette under the faucet *C'mon Lori* Jane flicks the soggy cigarette into the garbage can Lori stomps down the narrow hall to the bedroom *Wanna go to the Mifflin Street block party Angie invited both of us Yeah* Jane says scowls at nothing in particular her sister was a straight A student pre med biology major until she had a breakdown last winter now she's just a nut

* * *

I buy

a lime green notebook a miniature clip on fan a reading light at Walgreens put the rest of my check from La Casa in the bank for tuition it's been just over one month since I made it back to Madison I don't jump every time the phone rings afraid it's mad dad tracking me down

tonight Jane Lori I stay home don't get high don't get drunk don't slam dance we read Jane Austen Patty Hearst Emily Dickinson write in our notebooks twisted in sheets from Goodwill three of us in the bedroom two windows rusted screens broken shades the moon filters in slats of light across the floor

* * *

Two ounces

per tin foil square Shorty says *no more or we'll lose money* I nod fold a square of cold chicken meat want her to go away so we can smoke *All right then Mrs. Shorty* Dan flings his witchy dyed black hair to the side *Get that under a hat* she scolds *Oh yeah* he says *right off* and goes back to tearing tin foil into squares Shorty counts out the cash Dan looks over at me his back to her he grimaces this means it'll be harder for us to steal from the till today I tear a hunk of the stringy meat in half her son Tom doesn't care what happens here he's running drugs out of La Casa forty or fifty bucks a day isn't anything to him

Don't let anything sit out long Shorty says *eighteen people got food poisoning from the Taco Bell on Washington* she closes the register *three hundred fifty two and forty cents do you want me to write that down Nah* I poke at a pink vein in a dark chunk of meat *Three fifty two forty* Dan whistles *we're loaded baby!* Shorty wipes down the counter sets the rag down *Guess I'll be going then* she walks slowly toward the front door like she wishes she had something else to do *Toodle loo* she waves *See ya* I say *Bye bye* Dan says once she is out of sight we grab the pot wrapped in a tight little ball of tinfoil hidden above the electrical box in the back room we toke up blow smoke out the window until a customer rings the bells Shorty tied to the front door

Hey

a man's voice says *can someone get service around here Sure* Dan says *coming right up* his black Converse high tops smack the floor *What can I get you son* Dan says *Son* the man says *I'm old enough to be your father It's all semantics* Dan coughs I laugh it's so good to be stoned *I'd like a chicken* burrito and a Coke *no ice No ice* Dan says *it's hot out there man why don't you let me give you a little ice No ice* the man repeats I look out the back window covered by wire mesh see a man outside the window freeze think it's my father I stare not moving not blinking like a caught rabbit and then he waves it's not my father it's chief of police Jutson waving at someone next to the window outside the front door jingles my heart pounds

I weigh chicken

Tom walks in *Heya* he says his father died and left him the family business instead of leaving it to his wife Shorty's got to be pissed *Anything new* Tom nods at me pokes at the refried beans *Nope* Dan says *Chicken pulled and sorted Yup* I say Tom's eyes are pink and red no white *Whatcha need* Dan says *Nothin son* Tom opens the freezers pokes at the frozen tortillas turns toward us hands on his hips I don't know why they don't call him Shorty he's barely five feet with a gut the size of barrel *Just doing a little business out back* he smiles a cocky smile runs his hand through his permed hair *All right* Dan says *takin out the garbage That's it* Tom rifles through the register yanks out a handful of bills doesn't count them looks at me *Beef burrito to go no onions lettuce* Dan grins now we can help ourselves to the register *Dan out back Sure boss* Dan squeaks his black canvas high tops across the floor

Mifflin Street

down two blocks take a left at the lights can I come a guy says his blonde dread locks swinging around his waist *Not with us* Angie laughs at him *Oh c'mon* the guy says hits his bare chest *I'm already trippin Whatever* Angie scuffs her thick soled boots on the pavement *I hate it when white boys have dreadlocks* she skips up onto the curb *Uhm hum* Jane says spits out her bright pink gum on the tar pavement *Who's got the hash* Angie says *I do* she pulls out a baggy flips it around *Shit girl* Angie says *put that back in your pocket What* I say *we're almost at the party There's cops all over Nah uh* I say *this is Madison they don't care about drugs* Angie shrugs her shoulders *I'd still be careful* she tugs at one of my belt loops *cute pants* I don't know what to say wonder if she has a crush on me *Uhm hum* Jane smiles at the stoplights *What's she on* Angie says I shrug my shoulders *Oh you two are so cute* Jane puts her arm around my shoulder squeezes me *just so cute She gets friendly like this when she smokes* I say *I see* Angie says we turn left at the lights walk against the flashing red outline of a hand *Oh* Jane grabs my cheeks pats Angie on the head *you two Jesus* Angie says

Bam babam bam

a man beats a bongo we flow with the crowd across Mifflin Street up onto a sidewalk a boy band above us with floppy orange hats no shirts *Groovy* Jane stops dances a second Angie grabs my elbow pulls me I grab Jane we squeeze through the people sweaty bare skin loose hair dirt covered feet my hand slides down Jane's arm I grip her fingers *What beautiful lesbians* someone says *three of them* I tug Jane along with me she is already stoned Angie stops I bump into her back push up against her from behind *What is it* I say *Pot brownies* she buys three of them and a lemonade we sit down watch half naked white people trying to find a new way to live

Angie jams

the hash into the bowl packs it down like brown sugar in a measuring cup *Just like mom used to make* I say Angie laughs lights up brown sugar tar sears our throats lungs *Sweet* Angie says *So so sweet* I say

I drink lemonade crunch the ice small and smooth like a tongue slipped in my mouth I lie down the dry earth against my crooked spider spine creepy crawly skin on dirt twigs scratchy grass I fall fall fall a sleep

Grass fire

grass fire on my face arms the hair on my fingers fried brown sugar burned baby

> *Grass fire grass fire up my arms down my back too much heat*
> *mad dad in the night hot sweaty skin on skin burning*
> *When are you going to wake up and smell the coffee*
> *Mister Norman wants to know*
> *Yah when you going to wake up*
> *We all wait for you to wake up*

I jerk awake what's my gay high school teacher doing in my head I blink bright light heat explosion heard voices like they were coming out of the sky *You're fried girl* Huh Angie is a blurry stubble headed black tank top my body is fire *Where's Jane* my tongue bloated *Here I am lobster girl* Jane sits in the shade a trunk grows out her back smoke twirls out the tips of her fingers Angie's hand reaches *Don't touch me* I say grass fire black sugar tar in my throat *I'm on fire* Angie's hand stops laughs *You are fried* her head tilts back says *Clouds are bountiful orgasmic Marvelous* Jane Dragon Girl says smoke twirls out her fingers lips hair curly branches bright green leaves

Creepy crawly spider fingers searching for bumps on the back butt head

Shit I say sit up arms legs chest bright pink red in spots what's the nurse doing in my head *I am so fucked up* my arms are bright red third degree burns call an ambulance call a doctor call a nurse someone's body burned up in a fire

Dragon Girl

lights up twirls smoke around *That's bad for you* I say in a little girl voice *I swear I swear* Angie Cockroach says on her back feet in the air kicking at the clouds *you are just like a little kid when you are stoned* laughs laughs laughs Angie Cockroach laughing cockroach scratching scratching in the kitchen walls one for it two for me

5 7 5

I lean against Dragon Girl *this is it* we follow Angie Cockroach up the gray stairs pink legs red legs into the big white house *Dan* Angie says he wraps his arms around me pats Jane's shoulder *Hey girls* yellow ridged chips in a bowl my ears hear Dan say *What's up with her I heard you* I say point pink fingers *don't think you can talk about me behind my back I hear everything my ears are the biggest ears in all the world!* Dan Angie Cockroach Jane Dragon Girl laugh laugh laugh *I'm going to piss in my pants* Angie Cockroach says

Woman eat

I hold yellow ridges up to Angie cockroach's gray eyes freckles *You have cute freckles* her wide face gets bigger closer to mine room spinning *Where's Jane* I say ceiling fan spins chips drop to floor *Don't know* Angie says *You have cute lips* I whisper ceiling fan spins air across my forehead *So do you* her thigh moves between mine ceiling fan *Where's Jane* Dragon Girl lips together hands move to back inside shirt on skin sweet sweet skin lobster girl's hands deep in the ocean away from mad dad grass fire grass fire lips together teeth click bodies fit thigh inside me stubble hair *Whoo two lezzies at it in the corner* keep kissing kiss me forever over dry earth dusty sand kiss me forever breasts pressed together so soft so soft sweaty neck in my hand Mr. Norman said wake up and smell the coffee so I did so I did

She's turning green

someone points at me I me we all of us in my head go downstairs looking for Jane Dragon Girl I me we all of us chipped railing sliver in thumb *ouch!* no Jane at bottom just dirt bushes grass voices crawl under tangled bushes dirty hands knees where'd Jane go is she mad at me for kissing Angie Cockroach *Janie Janie don't be mad at me don't hate me* I say through alley *Jane* I say *Jane* music noise dark sky bright street lights like tiny eyes a big moon hangs like Angie's breast cupped in my hand where is Patty! *Jane! Jane!* a garage not attached to its house thumb hurts sliver have to find Jane have to find Jane I am afraid I like the kissing but it makes me afraid *Jane! Jane! Jane! don't hate me* I bend over green eggs n ham Dr. Seuss throw up

Hey here

it is over here next to the garage Hey you you're coming with us Male or female I don't know grab the arms turn it over Hey hey you you're coming with us it's a she

* * *

OT

at three CD group at four social skills at five Sheila flips through my file I hunch my shoulders won't look at her dyed red hair make up bright gold ring with a rock the size of Havana from her rich doctor husband *Doctor Abramson is going to go over your meds with you at nine tomorrow morning your parents would like to see you this weekend* she pauses *if you refuse you realize we will force you to meet with them in a counseling session if we feel it would benefit you* I shift my butt on the paper thin white cotton spun bedspread she takes off her glasses tinted red to match her hair *Your father helped you at the very least you could meet with him* her chair screeches on the linoleum floor

He cut off my insurance I say she puts her glasses on *He intervened you could have gone to jail you should be thankful* she says I look out the window barred on the outside no one tries to get in to a place like this *I hate him* I say she shakes her pencil at me *Now remember what the therapist said about totalizing thoughts That's not a totalizing thought* I say *it's a feeling* stupid bitch I think but don't say it

One more question she looks up quickly but doesn't look me in the eyes *the nursing staff wants to know if you have sexuality problems* I think about them rolling their eyes when they talk about me and the other patients *You know* she waves the pencil *any sexual difficulties or deviancies* I stare at her hating her hating my parents hating the cops *No* I say *none Okay* she spreads out a wrinkle on the bedspread *does that mean you date men What Do you go on dates with men are you heterosexual* she looks at my hair *I want to smoke* I say I get up *Sit down* she says *and answer my question or I'll revoke your smoking and your reading privileges* I glare at her but sit down *Do you date men* she says again pages flipping *I don't date period* I say *now can I smoke my friends will be here* she sighs *Go ahead* she says

the nurse at the counter gives me a cigarette tucks her chin into her neck *I'm from outer space did you know that* I put the cigarette in my mouth backwards walk to the patio the nurse follows lights the cigarette for me I take a long drag stare into her eyes she is scared of me goes back inside doesn't say or do anything to bother me

Are your hands

starting to shake Lori says No I say *They will* she says walks to the edge of the patio her hair frayed at the ends *Thanks for coming* I know it's hard for her to be here she turns around abruptly her hands on her hips trying to look like she's got it together *No problem* she tries to smile I see her pain duck my head I know why she was in a nut house want to tell her I'm sorry *I want you to take the plea bargain and go home with your parents* Jane says *Nuh huh* I say *I'd rather rot here than go with them* Jane shakes her head says *This is way worse than the place Lori was in Yeah* I say *state psych wards are what you get when you don't have insurance* Jane picks the brick wall *I can't believe he did that* I shrug my shoulders *I can* I say everyone is quiet *One thing* Lori looks at Jane stops talking *Yeah* Jane says *we're really really sorry but rent we need it by Monday Of course* I say pat my hospital pants they won't let me wear my clothes Jane holds out my checkbook *Sorry* Lori says *I wish we didn't I understand* I cut her off make out a check my thoughts start to go I can't believe this is happening plays in my head over and over I think about my friends from high school how did this happen to me *Angie called* Jane breaks the silence I catch myself looking to see if the nurse heard as if they could hurt her somehow *I told her you're still in jail* Jane says *you know I wasn't mad at you I'm happy for you I really am it's just that* she cries *Jane* I slide the bottoms of my feet on the concrete patio *don't feel bad my father always said I'd end up in here*

Crazy

is a layman's term it's not a word we use here yeah right I think Doctor Abramson leans back in his tan leather chair *I see you've been doing well in occupational therapy* laughter bursts out of me he squints even more *Why do you laugh* he says *No reason* I say I decide not to rag on gluing together prefab bird houses and pencil holders he writes on a pad of paper *Now you're a smart young lady* he clicks the pen so the point recedes *or so your transcripts say you I drank too much* I interrupt him my voice sounds desperate I didn't want it to sound that way *I drank more than I should have one night everyone drinks too much in college But* he says holds up his hand blinks his eyes rapidly *the veracity of the statement that everyone drinks in college aside not everyone gets caught and* he leans forward changes the position of his butt in the seat *not everyone passes out in the road with a half gram of hash in his pocket Her pocket* I say his eyebrows shoot up *it was an alley someone else put the drugs in my pocket I don't drink very often I'm not crazy you have to let me out of here* my words spin out of control now he'll think I'm crazy for sure

Doctor Abramson twirls his chair toward a tall book shelf against the back wall runs his finger over the spines I am glad he has his back to me I am almost crying what if I am crazy *This* he taps one of the books I look around the room panicked I can't escape *is a good book* he slides it out turns in his chair sees my eyes watering puts the book on his desk slides it toward me between a gold framed picture of his family two teenage daughters and a wife who looks like Meg Ryan *Your wife looks like Meg Ryan* I say something stupid to keep myself from sobbing he looks surprised then says *Yes I have been told that before you may borrow this for a week* he leans back in his chair *Mental Illness What Everyone Should Know and More* I want to laugh but don't I want to cram the book down his throat but don't I want to tell him he is full of shit just like my father power tripping asshole but don't I China Doll Girl mask my face *As far as the drugs and alcohol are concerned I understand you have had problems with drinking in the past What* I stare *Your father told me all about it detox being kicked off the basketball team in the was it ninth grade Tenth* I spin inside mad dad is going to get me *You can't talk to him* my voice edges out stops starts filled with anger and panic *Hmm* he says arms crossed over his chest he leans over as if he is looking at his shoes then sits up straight *I find that to be a curious thing for you to say we have a signed release from you*

John Hancocked on ah he flips through my file *the 8th would you like to see it* he holds it out to me *That's the night I was arrested* his eyebrows arch *I don't remember* I say it's my signature loopier and sloppier than usual *but I was drunk* he shrugs his shoulders *I can't attest to that one way or another I was not present when you signed the release* I look around the room bookshelves manila folders a Picasso print framed in heavy wood two mostly brown iveys a Seattle needle paper weight on the huge maple desk *I am going to need some more time to make my diagnosis complete I am concerned that you have an underlying mental illness which you have been compensating for by abusing drugs and alcohol* I stare at the edging along the side of his desk this is my worst nightmare come true *You may have a combination of mental illnesses or what I call multiple mental illnesses you have issues with authority especially male authority you are manipulative in your thoughts and actions you have gender confusion and your speech and thoughts race at times and those combined could point toward a sort of gender dysphobic Oedipus complex with a touch of manic depressive disorder What* I say *Oh do you like to shop Huh* I say *Shop for clothes other items excessive grocery buying I* I say *It's a simple question really do you enjoy shopping do you find yourself shopping frequently I suppose I no I don't do much shopping* I can't believe I'm answering him *I don't have any money so no* my thoughts feelings have stopped the room has stopped the air has stopped the clock has stopped he has stopped we sit in silence while he reads my file *Okay do you hear voices* he looks up at me waves his finger around his head *No* no way am I going to tell him about the voices I hear like they drop out of the sky *no* I shake my head *One more question would you prefer to be a man Huh* I say *are you joking* I see he isn't joking *I don't want to be a man* he looks at me for a while *Are you* I stumble for words *are you fucking crazy* I say my body is numb *Uh hmm* he says *I hardly think I am the one with a problem here* he scribbles something in my file closes it *Your parents will be here for a meeting on Saturday they are very concerned about you it should be a relief to you to have such a loving caring family Uh* I say stare at him the blood in my body has stopped shocked into submission *Your meds are going to stay the same through the weekend I'll reevaluate next week* I stare at the brown iveys then the Meg Ryan wife *You may leave now* he says and drops my file into an open desk drawer

In my sleep
nickels rain the moon watches

in my sleep
nickels rain the moon watches a reminder of what was

in my sleep
nickels rain the moon watches a reminder of what is

in my sleep

nickels rain the moon watches a reminder of what will be

Marcy

the black haired old lady with a hump growing out her spine yells *Goddamn pea soup gain can't eat this shit* everyone ignores her she does this every night *I agree with Marcy* I say *the pea soup sucks here This isn't a resort* the nurse passing out meds says *No shit* I say she moves on to Richard a former high school track coach math teacher from Baraboo in here for attempted suicide I haven't seen him in a week *Next time I'll succeed* he told me when I first came in *watch out for those pills you get hooked on them and you'll always be under them* I see what he's saying but right now I don't care don't mind the high every night *Richard* I say *how's it going* he looks at me his face as long as Frankenstein goes back to eating his pea soup drips it all over his tray lap the front of his shirt *Richard* I whisper *what's wrong with you* he keeps eating *Leave him alone little girl* Mable says from one table over she is Indian *What's wrong with him Mable Little girl I like your hair* she pats her head *like mine Thanks* I say Richard keeps eating Mable is in her fifties *I've had a hard life little girl I know* I say she's told me before about the abuse at the school the breakdowns the white husband who beat her *I'm sorry* I say and I am sorry for her sorry for Lori sorry for Richard *He got buzzed yesterday* she says wiggles her finger around her ear *Huh* I say *Buzzed you know electrocuted No* I look at Richard he doesn't seem to hear us Mable turns her back unwraps a dinner roll *Richard* I say he eats his pea soup sits up perfectly straight

I bus

my tray feel a shot of terror they could do that to me I move into the TV room so I can keep an eye on the going ons of the psych ward it's amazing how fast one fits into the psych ward one week ago I didn't even know this place existed I flip through the channels settle on a rerun of Michael Jordan and the Bulls playing for the title Richard walks in stands behind me *Richard* I say *have a seat Jordan can fly but let's face it he isn't Doctor J* Richard says nothing walks away in his light blue robe his hospital slippers scratching across the floor I lose myself in the spin dribbles soft five foot jumpers pick and rolls to set Jordan free one on one with the big slow center *So And So! So And So!* Kelly's voice in my head I remember what was what could have been *So And So! So And So!* I'd better figure a way out of here or I'm going to end up a long face Frankenstein hunched over old lady hobbling to school with a cane Jordan slams it over his man *So And So! So And So! Jordan can spin but he can't fly like Doctor J no one can fly like Doctor J!* I say to no one there's a close up of Jordan his high pinched cheeks I flash to Jutson in the La Casa parking lot Jordan lunges at the camera holding up his finger screaming *Number one!* and it hits me chief Jutson buys dope from Tom!

* * *

Oh god

mad dad mom tomorrow morning oh god they deemed a meeting therapeutic with my parents I hitched a truck headed east made a fool out of him at the camping store oh god he's going to get me Run Westy Run Jesus Lizard playing at O'Cayz Corral tonight I should be there me n Jane n Angie not here Margaret in the corner eating Cheez Its all day how am I gonna get outta here oh god oh god wall to wall pace pace pace Tom's outta town until Sunday oh god

oh god kick at the punching bag dance around it on my toes fists up

> *Where is he*
> *I'm the greatest*
> *Muhammad Ali*
> *float like a butterfly sting like a bee*
> *let me at him*

Rise and shine

sunshine a tap on the door I'm not in my body I can't move the night before the nurse who tucks her chin in gave me trazodone and extra Klonapen put me out now I can't move *If you don't stop pacing* she said then threatened to send me to the padded room where they monitor patients with a camera sound system these state hospitals do invest their money in some things *Rise and shine sunshine* shit the morning my parents arrive I get the only cheerful nurse on staff she taps on my door again *Okay now hello in there are you awake yet* her high pitched voice heavy Wisconsin accent makes her sound like a happy dolt the worst kind

Honey

Nurse Sunshine whispers touches my shoulder pulls me back *I've seen girls like you before you need to get up and out of here as soon as you can* her breath tickles my ear *play the game* I move my leg *All right now time for you to get up* Nurse Sunshine says for everyone to hear *come on now it's a bright and sunny morning*

Mad dad sits

on a couch I schizt out cartoon character bulging eyes brains explode car horns honk feel faint his dark hairy forearm resting on a table his jaw muscle working exactly like I remember still a hairy troll mom sits in a corner hands in her lap *Good morning glad you could finally make it* Doctor Abramson says in front of the nurses case workers social workers a whole team! mad dad jerks forward then settles into the couch mom gets watery eyed *who cares not me cry all you want!* I blur my vision a crazy retard fard

Why don't you

say hello to your parents Doctor Abramson says I stare at the beige linoleum floor *Uh hum* Doctor Abramson says I say nothing *Oh honey* mom cries I say nothing one of the tiles has a crack *All right* Doctor Abramson says we should start by introducing ourselves *I'm Doctor Abramson head of psychiatry and I am pleased to be working with your daughter* someone coughs *And I'm Mrs. Thompson staff social worker My name is Clarice Burns I am also happy to be here I will take care of her case management And we are nurses Dowling and Schoenberg* Hello Gregory Adams I am interning with Doctor Abramson I attend the University of Wisconsin Medical School someone clears a throat Nurse Sunshine's head pops in the door *Okay then sorry I'm late* she says acts as if she is sneaking into the room sits down next to me *We were just completing introductions* Doctor Abramson says *Okay then I'm Connie Baker one of the nurses on staff here I've just been assigned as your primary nurse* Doctor Abramson nods *Let us begin* he says

Great I say *just fucking great* mad dad says *Do you see how she is this is what her mother and I have been dealing with all her life her own grandmother doesn't even want her anymore* he points at me *she explicitly told me to tell you not to contact her again* my eyes look at mad dad don't want them to I don't want them to! but they are so surprised they do anyway and mad dad sees he hurt me he sees uncertainty who could blame gramma I'm as low as it goes Doctor Abramson raises his hand *I appreciate your input father but I expect everyone to wait his turn from now on* he turns toward me *your response was very interesting highly intriguing can you tell us what you are feeling* I want to not exist is how I feel but I say nothing *Oh honey* mom says *I don't understand we gave her everything piano lessons sports Mother* Doctor Abramson says *please wait until I direct a question at you* she cries harder *Please tell us what you are feeling* he says to me Gregory sits off to his side looks at me intently I want to kick his face in that's how I feel but I say nothing *Please* mom blurts out *admit it please just tell these people that you seduced your father*

Connie Baker

Nurse Sunshine says *Oh my* Gregory looks at his shoe I watch everyone out of the corner of my eye I have many corners I have many eyes I have many names I am many people some living some dead some dying when one dies another is born this is how I stay alive mom cries my body goes on breathing Doctor Abramson watches me I watch him mad dad looks at his hands acts sad *It's true she tried* he says Nurse Sunshine watches mad dad I watch her Gregory sits with his mouth open looks at mom then at me then at mad dad I watch him the case worker with big gold bracelets stares at mom crying one of the nurses is bored looks out the window at the outdoor area where non violent patients are allowed to walk with guests if they have a pass from their supervising doctor I watch her the other nurse holds a pen I watch her I have many corners of many eyes to watch my back mad dad's mouth opens Doctor Abramson runs his fingers over his chin mom cries into her kleenex I watch all of them at the same time space sound stop I'm shooting a free throw

Whish whish whish the headboard did it

mad dad's tongue gathers energy uncoils snaps into the room SHE sss hiss California sun fell around the packed boxes DID now everyone is turning their eyes to him even the bored nurse watching the outdoor area where one crazy walks with a chaperone IT mad dad's throat swells stretches his neck arches TO I look at him at all of them they will believe him not me ME Doctor Abramson drops his hand to his knee bored nurse shifts in her chair Gregory looks at the side of Doctor Abramson Nurse Sunshine looks at mad dad she watches him the way Doctor Abramson studies me

Liar

I yell stand up *you're a fucking liar and you know it I'm not your puppet I'm leaving You may not leave* Abramson says I run out the door down the hall toward my room I am going to get my book and go home to my apartment where I live with my friends Jane and Lori they are sisters I won't take this anymore! I won't take this anymore! *Wait* Nurse Sunshine says I turn into a room crawl under a big wood table don't want to be heard found seen known don't want to exist Nurse Sunshine follows *Listen to me* she says *come back with me* her voice is low again not sunshiny sweet *I didn't do that* I whisper *I know you didn't* she kneels *I'll help you get out of here in one piece* words form in front of my eyes old words cut into the bottom of the table the letters sharp like a razor *Help me*

Knock knock

Who's there Nurse Sunshine lilts her voice *Doctor Abramson unlock the door* Nurse Sunshine says full lilt *Okay then right away doctor* she whispers to me *get yourself together play his game for the time being don't go against him* I nod Nurse Sunshine is going to protect me I believe it I don't care that he's outside I don't care that mad dad mom are downstairs I don't care about any of it because Nurse Sunshine is helping me I crawl out from under the table wipe my eyes it doesn't matter that Doctor Abramson is on the other side of the door I have Nurse Sunshine

Yes yes

yes I don't smile don't cry don't talk except for yes yes yes Doctor Abramson says *She will stay at the facility until I deem she is stable enough to function in the community* yes yes yes *this involves identifying and then treating her underlying mental illnesses* yes yes yes *when I deem her fit to leave the premises I will release her to her parents* yes yes yes mom cries mad dad chews his jaw says *I'd like a few moments with her by myself* Nurse Sunshine stands up *Okay then according to Doctor Abramson's orders she is still committed to the hospital so I need to take her for her afternoon class which began* she glances at her watch *about ten minutes ago all righty then* she pushes me to the door I don't look at mad dad mom Doctor Abramson Gregory the others none of them know what to do *Walk fast* she whispers *get to class before they decide differently*

* * *

Dan

I say *Hey* he says *what's new* a cash register clangs *You got to get Tom to talk with Jutson* Nurse Sunshine puts pills in little white fluted dixie cups at the nurse's station *What happened* Dan says *I'm still in here they committed me* I wrap the phone cord around my hand *listen get Tom to talk with Jutson tell him I'm a college student that got caught partying at Mifflin all that jazz Eww* Dan drawls *I'll talk to Tom but you know how he is one minute he's a great guy the next minute he's a dick Dan they're going to fuck me up bad in here I swear this one guy got a lobotomy or something* my voice cracks Nurse Sunshine picks up the tray of dixie cups starts her rounds *Yow* he says *I'll talk to him tonight gotta run* click bzzztt my brain hangs on the thread of two junkie dealing fast food workers and a crack smoking chief of police

Three days

pass punching bags boxing gloves six bird houses eight ball pool Cheez Its Che Guevara when I can concentrate long enough to read more than two pages at a time ESPN golf basketball reruns car races a new woman Alice in her thirties *Tired* she says her grandfather raped her since she was a baby then her brother joined him when she was seven or eight her mother didn't know her father never did anything to her he just stayed out of the way of her mother's father a big wig in construction *Lots of juice* Alice says *they do this to me I spend my life in and out of the loony bin* scars up and down her forearms thin criss crossed white lines she cuts herself *I spend my life wanting to die* she shows me the inside of her arms *on better days I say I'm making a trellis* I try not to make a face *you know for morning glories* she stares at the ceiling tile for a moment nods says *purple ones*

On the fourth day

me and Marcy play cards by the nurse's station *Go fish* I say *Damn it* she throws her cards crosses her arms *All right* I put my hand up *let's quit for now* she is getting on my nerves I'm starting to feel like I've been in the crazy ward forever like my life before the crazy ward was a dream I had once upon a time in a land far far away where there was a girl and bad things happened to her so she drank an ocean of sadness and drowned

Alice

ain't getting out Marcy crunches ice spits the chips into her cup *she's permanent* Alice white gauze wrapped round her left wrist shrugs *What would I wanna get out for* closes her eyes

* * *

Richard

I say *I've been discharged* he nods a bunch of times scoops up peas hands shaking most of the peas roll off the spoon land in mashed potatoes and gravy or bounce off the plate roll across the table *Quiet little girl* Mable says sitting at the table next to us *Hi Mable* I say *Get your clothes on your body little Indian girl* I sneak a look at Mable her head is cocked a wicked grin curls across her lips like smoke I nod to tell her she's right *All right Mable* I wave to Nurse Sunshine standing in the doorway she taps her wrist *See ya Mable Richard* they ignore me focus on their food Alice is at a table next to them I am giddy terribly glad but suddenly sad to leave these people my friends we have been through shit no one else can understand *What am I gonna do without all of you* I say *Aw you'll figure something out* Alice says scratches at her wrist *Yeah* I nod feeling sad for them guilty for abandoning them to the shit head doctors and nurses the shithead system that's the best friend to men like mad dad or Alice's grandpa who in return are the best friends to the system I walk to Nurse Sunshine she called a cab charged it to the hospital's expense account without anyone knowing *Girl* Mable says *don't forget us*

The cab

is outside Nurse Sunshine hands me two brown paper bags with all my stuff *your meds* she says we walk down the hall *now you need to sign your discharge papers with the social worker she'll ask for a forwarding address* she lowers her voice *if you don't want your parents to know where you are make something up All right* I say we stop at a door she knocks *Come in* someone says we enter *She needs to sign her discharge papers* Nurse Sunshine says to the social worker the social worker nods adjusts her granny glasses hands me a stack of papers *Kind of like leaving the army* I say she smiles at me lips dried and pressed tight like petals in the back of a book *Uhm hum* she looks at Nurse Sunshine says *Now just how did you pull off this one* Nurse Sunshine points to me says *Ask her* the social worker looks at me *Read this* she says pushing paper at me *responsible for your own well being will report any future relapses to a responsible professional agree to release the Wisconsin State Psychiatric Hospital of any responsibility once you leave the premises* I flip through them quickly *Stop here* Nurse Sunshine says *this is the clause that says you have to get mental health care within 60 days of signing this agreement they will check on you so don't forget* I nod but think not if they can't find me the social worker takes off her granny reading glasses folds them says *What I want to know is how did you get out of here when your doctor refused to release you* I smile sign the last page say *I got connections*

Nurse Sunshine and I

walk down the hall *How did you do this exactly* Nurse Sunshine says I lower my voice *I know someone who knows Jutson* Nurse Sunshine's eyebrows shoot up *The chief of police* she says *Yeah* I say *he made the call to spring me Oh* she says sounds surprised I am proud I just got over on the doctor mad dad mom beat them at their own game *So And So! So And So! scores the game winner again! Well all righty now here you go* Nurse Sunshine turns on her lilting voice unlocks a door *you need to sign out with security* Damn I say *this place is for big time nutsos* Nurse Sunshine frowns lowers her voice *Don't do that to yourself* she says *this is serious business* I'm not sure what she means but I don't ask sign the sheet *You need to go* she walks me to the cab *finish school and stay out of here* I feel stupid awkward a freak dyke fag but I am grateful to her for being kind I have a fleeting wish she could be my mom take me home to her house let me be five again *Thanks* is all I say she nods *Union Cab* the cabbie says *Yeah* I say Nurse Sunshine doesn't smile steps back from the cab crosses her arms *Stay off the drugs* she looks really serious maybe I shouldn't keep calling her Nurse Sunshine I think as the cab pulls out

We fly

down Washington Avenue trees spin by people bikes cars trucks shopping centers I'm in shock it's so big there aren't any walls rules white dixie cups morning noon evening cable TV birdhouse kits *What were ya in there for* the cabbie says a hippie his skin white and flaky as chalk it's strange to talk to someone outside the psych ward although he looks like he could be in a psych ward with his long hair fat gut grubby clothes *Um* I say *I smoked too much at the block party They got you for that* he says *shame on them* we speed past a UPS truck *they don't pay me to sit around ya know Yeah* I say *I'm sure they don't* I watch the UPS truck disappear in the side mirror *they pay pretty well though at least we're unionized Uh huh* I say hang my arm out the window *It's a hot one* he says I watch some small children play kick ball outside the YMCA *Hmph* he says *so you a college student I was* I say think about the children the stores the people we pass everyone from my past a world I'm not part of anymore *Was* he says *me too school isn't all it's chalked up to be I've got a Ph.D. in Philosophy Kant Locke Hume pshew look what it got me* he turns a corner *there it is* the capitol dome looms over Washington Avenue *our esteemed seat of government* he leans back in his seat *she always tips well* he says *Huh* I say *Connie Mrs. Baker right isn't that her name* I shrug my shoulders *She's always getting folks outta there paying their cab fare* he turns right toward the Rathskellar *always tips us well* he says *like a modern day Harriet Tubman Yeah* I say but I don't really see the analogy

Jane and Lori

are not home I've been calling them for five hours from the free phone at the Rathskellar sitting in a booth drinking water pretending to read Che I don't know anyone at the Rat right now which is good I want to hide I feel like people can see I've been in the loony bin I'm crazy like the ones that sit in here day and night in their coats and hats staring at the tables dirty clothes paper bags filled with old newspapers I can see it in their eyes like a bucking horse the fear took them over

Nickels

along the edge of the bar left in payment for the pretzel rods in a big glass jar two for a nickel if I could get those nickels I could buy a Mountain Dew stay up all night make sure no one touches me if I could get enough nickels I could buy half a veggie pita sandwich those alfalafa sprouts on the top so good I can taste them

Can I have a water I say the bar up to my chest my hands in front of me on the top *Sure thing* the woman says her light blue hair pulled back with a royal blue hankie *Very pretty* I say meaning her hair then I am embarrassed I shouldn't say things like that to a straight woman she turns her back one two three four five six seven water pouring eightnineten eleventwelvethirteenfourteenfifteen I drop the nickels in my pocket they clatter into my empty pocket a mile deep blue hankie woman turns toward me water in hand I smile *Thanks* I say *For sure* she brushes the side of her face with the back of her hand I want to scream do you know what happened to me help me I have nowhere to go but I say nothing walk away slow keep the clinking clattering shiny bright nickels buried deep in my pocket from making too much noise

The Rathskellar

will be closing in ten minutes a woman says over the P.A. system I hang up the phone Lori and Jane are still not home a janitor pushes a long gray broom I run up the stairs to the fourth floor women's bathroom couches mirrors with tables and chairs in front of them from when the women used this as a powder room handwritten notes on the bulletin board *Roommate needed!* I smash my bags down push them under the couch furthest from the door lean on the marble window sill the campus is pretty white flowered trees a gurgling eight foot high water fountain the PA system spits out *The Rathskellar is now closed please leave the building* people flood down the steps below alone in twos in groups unlock their bikes wait for the bus wander through the courtyard a navy blue night sways in through the screens

I crawl under the couch red frayed fabric above me I wait for the janitors the door opens the light flicks on then off nickels roll out my pocket I find them in the dark throw them side arm across the room listen to them clatter I climb onto the couch listen to the crickets take up the night

Morning sun

arrives on the wheels of a garbage truck I haven't slept a wink brrrrrah the garbage truck scoops up the Rat's dumpster sunlight creeps across the gray carpet dust in my eyes and mouth I sit on the couch wait for 7 am when the Rathskellar opens so I can sleep

7 O 1 am
sleep

Afternoon

bright sun through windows full blast so hot dry mouth sandy eyes hungry dirt sweat body stinks to high heaven straight up to the ceiling chicken neck buck buck bah buck ceiling bumps sun through the tall windows burns me up

Evening

need food need food need food no more pretzels water cups need food dig in garbage for food rich spoiled college students throw out everything a hoagie dated yesterday eat it up gobble gobble stupid me crazy nut from the nuthouse at least there I had food no wonder gramma doesn't want me anymore sit in Rathskellar call Jane Lori no one home sit in Rathskellar crazy nutso me not enough sleep too hot some one says *hello hey how's it going* I don't talk don't wave don't look keep head down don't want no one to see my bucking horse eyes sleep in Rat drool on hands drool drool drool crazy girl judge judged me crazy girl here I am! I am! here I am judge! two smashed down bags no where to go nurse said be careful don't go off medications without supervision sometimes crazy people do that when they leave here crazy crazy people go off their medications without proper supervision Doctor Abramson has super vision prick head I'd kick in his face asshole won't take this medication going cold turkey peel off the stickers with my name on them Doctor Abramson's name Mendota State Psychiatric Ward id #334529 prescription for thorazine take two at bedtime with food may cause drowsiness other side effects what are the other side effects what are the other fucking side effects

Too hungry

call gramma call gramma mad dad hairy troll's lying she wouldn't cut you off call gramma call gramma! she'll help 412 no 311 no 441 no can't dial the phone right stupid ass me retard of the century 414 no Jesus Christ my fingers don't follow my mind concentrate crazy girl 4 1 1 I did it I did it briiing briiing I am on top of the world the smartest damn fuckup anyone's ever known *What number do you want Uh* I say biggest dumm ass on the planet *I need my gramma's number Yeah real cute* the woman says in her east coast accent I imagine her long nails and big hair piled on top of her face *Hello hello* the voice says I say nothing *Does your grandma have a name* the woman says *or should I just type in grandma Um* I say and scale the cliffs in my mind dig around in the holes until I come up with the scrap of paper *Martha* I shout *Wadena* the woman scoffs *in America or some other country America* I say *land of the free Yeh huh they let anyone in don't they* the woman says *She's Indian* I say *she let you in How old are you* the woman says *five Eighteen* I shout but I'm not I must be older than that but I can't remember I can't remember how old I am I don't understand age *northern Minnesota* comes to my mind *northern Minnesota yeah up by Dilworth yeah Dilworth Minnesota Martha Wadena in Dilworth Um hum* the woman says *just a moment* what if mad dad lied what if gramma still wants me I could go live with her have food and a bed *Hmm* the woman says I can hear her nails clacking against the desk top *no Martha Wadena are you sure you got the name right no Martha or M Wadena anywhere in that entire zip code either maybe it's unlisted or maybe she doesn't have a phone* I want to say something smartass to her for making a crack because gramma's Indian saying she doesn't have a phone my ass I wanna smack her fatass head say go back to fucking England where you belong and give gramma back her land and house but my gramma is gone disappeared just like Patty I am too stunned to say anything anything at all

I lean

against the mustard wall mad dad was right I remember his cutting eyes he's right gramma hates me thinks I'm trash she's hiding from me hoping she will never see me again I'm no more cream in her coffee

* * *

Pssst pssst

I say to the man at the round table in corner by the fireplace *psst remember me* he nods *Yeah yeah I remember you have a seat howya doin Good* I say *real good but I need some money food money you know my ID is at Jane and Lori's Right* he says looks over my head is someone behind me *I got these* I shake the thorazine in his face and these shake the other bottle Klonapin *Whoa man get that under the table All right* I say shake them under the table *sixty bucks for all 100 Nah* he looks away *Don't bullshit me* I say *I know it's a good deal* his eyes scit around *Nah* he says I keep shaking the bottles *Fifty* I say *Mmm* he says *maybe I'll meet you at the dock in ten At ten in ten* I say *I'm a little out of it right now Yeah sure* he stands up stretches looks around for cops security he leans down into my face bad breath he has bad breath *in ten* he says *In ten* I say fifty bucks is lots of pita sandwiches where are Jane and Lori my friends disappeared unhappy making me unhappy decidedly unhappy

Dock

in ten here I am dock in ten shit I'm crazy sweating freezing the sun setting over the lake is so pretty ducks floating at my feet people feeding them popcorn don't feed it to the ducks give it to me! I sit down over the water swing my feet watch the ducks bob like wooden toys sailboats painted as duck bodies swaying against their anchors across the lake are miniature buildings one of them is Mendota State Psychiatric Ward here I am escaped convict crazy selling her pills shake the bottle at them *Na na na na stupid Doctor Abramson son of a bitch*

Hey the dealer says I wrap my hand around the pills he sits kicks a booted foot hits me in the butt I move away closer to the edge *Got it* I rattle the bottle *Fifty* he says taps his shirt pocket *Yep* I hold out the bottles *No not here anyone could see us* he gets up on his haunches clasps his hands in front of him looks at me like he expects something *Well* I say *where I'm over by the frats* he points to the shoreline where the frat boys sorority girls live in old mansions *Uh* I say I might be crazy but I'm not stupid *no I I'm waiting for someone All right* he says wipes his jaw with a hand looks like he is he laughing I want to get away from him but I need the money need to eat he snaps his fingers *How about we go down the path* he points to the shoreline to the right of the Rathskellar away from the frat houses *I know a good spot Um* I say think about leaving but don't know where to go who to call what to eat *okay* he stands a duck quacks

Why can't we just do it here I say *Maybe we should just forget it* he says I grab his sleeve *All right* I say I'm too hungry desperate alone afraid I push down my fear follow him off the dock salty popcorn floating in the water making miniature oil rings in the lake *Who needs Valdez when we've got Rathskellar popcorn in the lakes* I think I think it but realize I said it out loud drug dealer says nothing I look over my shoulder at the loony bin dot on the horizon I'm gonna get over on them sell their dope for food the trees are black the water pink and four shades of blue the sailboats swing from side to side lazy boats with tall poles people chit chatting on the terrace nuclear physicists sociologists world's leading expert on crop management all so smart so smart eating popcorn drinking pop beer I hate them they're stupid they don't know shit the dealer and I walk down the path into the darkened trees out of sight out of mind I shake the bottle in my hand hope this is worth it

The path

sticks close to the shoreline water laps against dirt sticks empty cans washed up on shore my mind returns as it does when it must I walk behind him the path is rutted and coarse I hope he will forget about me give me my fifty bucks go back to his table in the Rathskellar a jogger sprints toward the Rathskellar my body is burning up like the pink line in the sky refracted off the lake refracted! mother didn't know what refracted meant and I was mean shamed her drug dealer whistles the water through the trees is royal blue the sun's almost set *How about here* I stop walking don't want to go deeper into the woods no one will see us he ignores me *Hey* I say now I know I am not only crazy but stupid because I follow him

He is a shadow

the moon has taken over the sky we walk out to the point an isthmus two miles from the Rathskellar I used to run it with my soccer friends *Hey* I say really afraid now *whish whish whish the headboard did it* crickets twittering a dull moon the shadows on its surface make it look lumpy his dark gray body ducks under a tree branch disappears I follow him afraid of him but more afraid of being left alone I duck under the tree branch my feet slide down rocks dirt to a sandy beach *There you are* he says grabs my arm *isn't this nice* he walks out to the edge of the water pulls me with him I say nothing can't believe I was stupid enough to follow him the moon lays down a path across the lake he releases my arm skips a rock *Smoke* he pulls out a pipe packs it lights it *Nah* I say try to be cool but I'm piss in my pants scared he exhales *Are you sure* he waves the pipe at me the tips of his blonde hair shine under the moonlight *Yeah* I say *it's cool I haven't eaten you know Right* he says takes another hit blows the smoke into the sky *Hey* I say *here's the stuff Right* he takes another hit taps the pipe against the bottom of his boot wipes it out with his thumb short and thick *Why don't we sit down and enjoy the scenery* he pulls me down to the sand with him I shake *Cold* he says I nod teeth chattering *whish whish whish the headboard did it* he takes off his shirt puts it across my back and shoulders *Thanks* I say I don't want him to know how afraid I am want to leave but don't know where to go can't figure my way out of the woods alone

He puts

his hand on my thigh *What about the drugs* I say *I'll give them to you for forty Nah* he leans into me the water licks the shoreline *I can get those for free* his hand is on my stomach his face in mine mouth over mine *No* I say push his chest he laughs *Too late now* he says *you came all the way out here* he grabs my neck his mouth sucking at mine some sort of snake from the sea I say nothing try to breathe with his mouth tongue on me in me wet horrible sucking he leans into me until my back shoulders grind into the sand then stops sucking my face his hand crawls under my shirt creepy crawling up to my boobs under my bra he pants moonlight in his shaggy blonde hair *This is gonna be good* he says *Stop* I say *I just want money for food take the pills give me ten I'll give you ten* he says on top of me pulling off my shirt undoing my bra he grabs my boobs pulls them out *Wow* he says *wow* his face shaded by the moon behind him *oh man wow you're huge* he slaps my boobs from side to side they wiggle they are not mine not me I am not here *Wow oh wow* he says on top of me pulling out his thing he is going to kill me float my body out to sea on the path laid out by the moon *mmm* he says my boobs wiggle he licks the nipples *oh wow* he says *Stop* I hear my voice say from far away *no I don't want to I'm with someone else Wow oh wow* he says *crazy good* he pulls my hair back *Say you're actually kinda pretty if you didn't dress like such a guy* he says runs the tip of his thumb over my nose and forehead *sort of foreign looking* he runs his thumb over my eyebrow *like South America* he leans back squints *or some asian country* I try to push him want to kill him say I come from this country you're the foreigner but he laughs I say nothing he pins my shoulders against the sand *Undo your pants* I try to kick him my legs pinned under his body I feel his body tense against mine he is stronger than me *Do you want to get hurt* he says *No* I say *then undo your pants* he pushes on my throat *undo your pants* and so I do and so I do *Now lie still* he says *you don't have to do anything just lie there I don't want to have sex with you* I say *Yeah* he whispers his face close to mine blonde tips of hair suction mouth round stubby nose *but I do and that's what counts*

The water

licks the shoreline he pushes into me I make no sound he pants grunts my body goes numb like a magic trick my mind makes a path I follow it to a place where no one else can go

Thanks

he says *it was great* pushes paper into my vagina pulls it out a ten dollar bill smears across my boobs drops it on my chest walks off sand money stuck to my body saplings and sticks crack under his boots sex is money my body is money money is dirt

The moonlight

soft shimmering on the leaves above me trails down my arms over my wrists the fine golden hairs on the back of my hands the moonlight stops at my nails pallid like round shells I am obliterated yet I think I am dead yet I breathe I am terrified yet I have nothing to fear my mind is on the loose cracked a meaty nut escapes its shell for some reason I think of Shakespeare and the Fairie Queen and Sir Lancelot luminous because this did not just happen to me this did not just happen to me my mind is sorrow my body dirt except for the places the moon touches turns to gold King Midas and straw made into wealth my mind is at sea burying what it knows

Shakespeare

runs through my head to be or not to be the night is dark rich black his semen dries on my chest down there to be or not to be Shakespeare wasn't writing about me to be taken or not to be taken that is the question the sand is cold I don't move bugs bite my skin I don't move if someone kills me I won't care Shakespeare should have made Hamlet a girl to be taken or not to be taken is a more interesting dilemma than the simple philosophy of men to be or not to be if only it was that simple I lie in his shit I am shit money is shit sex is money in my mouth round hard nickels covered in shit pasted to my chest to be or not to be what about me my body goes on less of me inside it more of me in the trees ceilings moonlit paths across the lake looking for a better place

My mind

walks to the moon on all fours *Goodbye mind* I say wave to it n close my eyes sand stuck to my body all I have it is of the earth *someday it's going to be all right it's going to be all right* someone says to me crazy girl broken girl crazy broken girl I hear the lake talking crazy broken girl *the headboard did it! the headboard did it! someday someday it's going to be all right it's going to be all right*

The body

is shit sand bits of grass blood guts hair meat water organic charcoal the body is of the earth it lies half buried in the cold cold sand for a long time then gets up walks across the earth down the path it used to run in freedom but now the body straggles to the Rathskellar early morning bright light blue waves wooden ducks forehead on forearms on table on terrace eyes shut the body has its own life

Hey

someone says I hear it but don't hear it *is everything okay* I hear it but don't hear it *Is she all right* I hear it but don't hear it water lapping lakeshore birds singing dead tree dangling *I dunno* I hear it but don't hear it *Can we help you with something* I hear it but don't hear it metal chair legs scrape the concrete pressure on my shoulder wiggle wiggle my whole body *Huh* I look up takes time to focus the patches of color *Hey* someone says *can we take you somewhere* I blink two faces staring at me *Are you all right* I shrug my shoulders behind the faces there are wooden ducks floating sailboats behind the sailboats the psych ward *What's wrong* the face says again the boy gave me a lobotomy not the doctor I got away from him the boy got me instead I want to say the boy got me instead! but I stare at their faces words coming out of their mouths in coarse salty chunks

Um

she says *can we take you somewhere* my mind flashes to a hairy legged girl giving me a card in the hall outside click clack class my mind swerves finds this memory for me my mind the one crawling on all fours to the sea the one burying what it knows but memories are fingerprints they never go away just hide the girl from click clack class fingerprint comes to my mind the sights sounds smells the me person I was then one million years ago it seems one million years ago! *Women's Center* I say

Raped

the word runs in my head vacant building *We think you were raped* I drop head on forearms I am crazy *If you were it's not your fault he is responsible for his behavior* I am crazy forehead sinks into the flesh of the arm *It doesn't matter if you went with him somewhere You seem to be hurt badly* I am crazy forehead hits arm bone *It's okay* her hand on my back wiggle wiggle can't get the wiggle out of my head life isn't supposed to be this way vacant building mind gone all fours across the lake *No* I say *I'm crazy I deserved it I'm stupid I'm nothing You're not crazy you're hurt* a voice says a nice voice a soft voice a smooth voice makes me remember I'm hungry very hungry *Food* I say it's all I can say too tired hurt crazy sad to say another word *We'll get you something* another voice says forehead on bone

* * *

How are you

Crystal fiddles with a ruffle on the cuff of her blouse I shrug *Have you made a decision about the group* I scan the gray carpeting scratch the back of my head *I'll do it* I say *Oh good* she says claps her hands *we have ten minutes before it starts it's very brave of you to start a group this quickly* Uh huh I say it's only been two weeks since they found me at the Rathskellar put me in a hotel room until Jane and Lori got back from their parents' Crystal turns to her desk piled high with papers books a lunch box pictures of her children and husband at a rock concert *Here are your test results* she hands me papers leans over reads them upside down as I hold them *See here* she points I like her she is nice safe *this shows that you have significant depression What are you feeling* she says *Embarrassed* I say *Why* I shrug my shoulders *I feel crazy* I say *You're not* she says *your concentration will return* we sit in silence until I say *I'm afraid to go to a group with women who have been raped* she nods *It's an important step* she says *you're very brave* she looks at her watch *it's almost time let's go*

We walk

through the university's health care building down hallways past doors I flash to the psych ward feel dizzy afraid want to touch Crystal so I don't float back to that place trapped scared drugged out she stops turns around I'm half here half in the psych ward *What's wrong* she puts her arm around me I shake my head I haven't told any of them yet about the psych ward only Jane Lori Dan know and I don't talk to Dan anymore never even said thanks *The group* she points to a door it's a sunny room with big blue pillows and four women sitting in chairs *We have a new member everyone* Crystal squeezes my shoulder I don't say or do anything stand there with my China Doll Girl mask frozen ready to cry or run *Hey Hi Welcome Have a seat* I sit down in a chair as fast as I can cross my legs try to look disinterested but I wonder who these women are what they're doing have they all really been raped

All right Crystal says *time to get started* she is tall dark hair dark eyes part Italian *ready Sheila* Crystal pokes Sheila the other group leader with her elbow *Ready as I'll ever be* Sheila says looks at everyone smiles they're both older than my mother I've never seen such peppy older women before *Let's start check in* Crystal says picks up an orange coffee cup *I'm Crystal a graduate student in psychology and co-facilitator of this group I've had a wonderful week and I'm ready for classes to start next week right* she laughs *Marta Okay* Marta rolls her eyes *this week has been kind of hard you know last week I told my mother about what my father did and* she stops runs her hand over her eyes *she said she doesn't see how that could have happened* everyone is quiet I feel sick what did her father do why won't her mother believe her I see mother's white bone knuckles on the door *How are you holding up* Sheila says *It's hard* Marta cries I freeze Crystal says *It's power when you name when you say it rape* I float around white knuckle bones snarled white sheets brown nickels I sway not in the room I'm long gone

*   *   *

Jane slouches

in the dining room her feet pointing out sipping the froth off the top of her beer *Here's to our kick off the school year right party* we tap cups drain them I crank Run Westy Run we jump up on the couch slam shoulders to their speed guitars screaming vocals Jane drops her head swings her arms like an elephant I laugh *I love our new apartment* I yell *I love our new apartment* she yells *a dining room and a living room and three bedrooms Yeah!* I say we all get our own rooms *Yeah!* she says this is the best I've felt since the rape Crystal helped me get financial aid we moved now mad dad mother can't find me *Imagine that* I yell *a dining room and a living room and three bedrooms* I jump off the couch onto the bare wood floor my feet go thud my heart stops what about Patty

the doorbell rings *Can you get it* Jane yells from the kitchen I buzz Andy Ruth Steve Jason up we sit in the living room smoke drink beer I want to get so fucked up that I won't know what's happening Jane dances on the couch puts in a tape it's loud it's crazy I'm stoned getting drunk where is Patty if only she could be here now Jane's friends from IHOP buzz up *Hey Hey* I smile but I don't care drink smoke eat corn chips sit inside my own head a vacant building away from everyone this isn't fun anymore these boys are dumb in their ripped up army pants they don't know jack shit

Shit

Jane yells from the kitchen I dump my beer on the sofa run! to the kitchen someone called me someone mad someone yelling get there fast don't get hit *What* I slide into the kitchen a kid on stocking feet singing opera *Shit* Jane yells again *What* I scream right behind her afraid she's mad will hurt me a kid on stocking feet singing opera fear wonderment fun all happening at once *Shit* Jane says again smacks her forehead with her palm *someone broke the taps fucking shit I'm right here* I yell *I'm right here!*

Remember

last night Jane yawns on the couch *Think so* I lift my foot onto the couch arm *The entire night* she lights a cigarette *What do you mean* I have this flash of fear that Angie showed up and I said something dumb *Remember shit What* I say sit up *Shit I yelled shit when I saw the broken taps and you came running like a dog like I was calling you and your name was shit* Oh I say *sort of* I remember standing in the kitchen stocking feet Jane pointing at the kegs Jane lights a cigarette *You answered like it was your name or something Oh* I say *guess I was really drunk huh* Jane sticks the match in a potted plant *No* she says *by that time you'd had a beer maybe two* Jane sits up cross legged a burning cigarette between her fingers *you acted like shit is your name*

* * *

No More Rape!

meetings are in room 402 umm Tuesdays that's today 4:30 Thanks I say to the woman behind the info desk take a bite out of my black cherry ice cream cone half a frozen cherry falls on my boot I fling it off it lands on the back of some man's pant leg he doesn't notice *Oops* someone says I look over at a woman with short brown hair sticking up all over she smiles struts up the stairs

I run up the first part of the stairs as fast as I can the dealer who raped me might be able to see me from the Rathskellar Crystal says it's important for me to go to the Rathskellar to not let the dealer take it away from me but I still run by where he sat I push open 402 the woman with short hair is sitting at a table I don't know any of these people or what they do Crystal said I should check out a campus group that organizes against rape *Hey* I say slip my backpack off one shoulder the woman smiles *Hi* she says sets down a piece of paper *are you here for the No More Rape! meeting Yeah* I say frog in my throat I sound like an adolescent boy *My name's Chara* she stands holds out her hand *Thanks* I say *I mean hi* I shake her hand *Sit down* she says *the rest of the women will be here in a few minutes* she slides a flyer at me *do you have a name No* I say surprised to hear myself say no what an idiot! of course I have a name but she doesn't say anything just nods her head

Say No to Playboy *in the Rathskellar and at the libraries! Say No to sex discrimination on campus Join the No More Rape! for a sit in at Chancellor Patricia's office Tuesday September 11 noon* I put the flyer down three women in jeans and t-shirts walk in yelling at each other *Chara can you believe her* one of them says points her finger at another one *she is so full of shit* the other woman pushes the woman talking they laugh sit down around the table *I never said that That's exactly what you said and don't even try to get out of it* I listen to them feel like I like them they remind me of the girls I used to play sports with in high school loud and obnoxious Chara says *I don't get in the middle of their quarrels they're fraternal triplets Uh huh* I say *We have a new member* Chara says *Yeah* the other women say one of them pounds on the table

more women walk in the door short hair shoulder length curly hair shiny round faces sit down talk to each other complain about professors the BGH level in the ice cream sold on campus the progressive student organization's sexism the chancellor who is a sell out ROTC on campus *Playboy's* campus tour the proposal for a new fraternity I don't know what they're talking about I feel stupid and afraid wish I hadn't come don't know what any of this has to do with me getting raped on the beach by that drug dealer *All right* Chara says *time for the meeting to come to order* everyone quiets down except for two of the triplets *Natalie and Jessica please* Chara says *Sorry Right sorry* they say one of them pushes the other one she laughs then they both laugh Chara rolls her eyes *Dana isn't here but we have to start without her Oh why* one of the triplets says laughs *Geez* someone else says *enough already* the door opens everyone turns a tall dark complected white woman with long black hair walks in *Heya sorry I'm late* she says *All right* Chara says *down to business first fundraising then the play then anti-sexual assault awareness week activities then our sit in at the chancellor's office Yeah* Dana says *the sit in I can't wait for that*

2 4 6 8

who do we want to berate Dana laughs shakes a poster in the air *impeach Pah trish ah!* cameras snap Dana stands on the steps of Bascom Hall *Yeah* she makes a fist her long hair around her shoulders she is beautiful the entire crowd yells *Playboy off campus now!* drums bang cops stand on either side of the crowd mostly women some men yelling fists in the air chanting *No more rape rags!* one of the triplets told me how *Playboy* encourages rape and incest and wife beating I yell too shake my fist *Playboy off campus now! Pah trish ah's a sell out!* I hear my own voice toads fling out my mouth hop down the steps around the people jump across Bascom Hill toward the lake the drums all the TV stations are here Dana yells over the top of everyone *Time to take her office* the drums bang Dana marches up the stairs we follow her two cops stand in front of the door their arms crossed over their chests Dana doesn't pause walks between them opens the double door we follow shouting beating drums Dana is how I imagine Patty would be we march up the stairs people in the hall get out of our way *Pah trish ah off campus now* we chant Dana smacks open Patricia's door people cheer clap beat drums *Occupy* Chara yells we fill Patricia's office *Hush* someone says then someone says *Shhh* then everyone says *Shhh* no more drums just 40 people saying *Shhh* we sit down slap the floor with our palms *Shhh* pad pad pad *Shhh* pad pad pad someone says *We have demands we want to see Patricia* then everyone says *We have demands we want to see Patricia* pad pad pad *We have demands we want to see Patricia* pad pad pad

Dana stands up in the middle pulls a piece of paper out of her back pocket reads *We the women and men against sexism racism and homophobia on the University of Wisconsin campus demand that Playboy be taken off the Rathskellars' shelves and out of the libraries we also demand that the university take steps so that Playboy staff cannot recruit on campus furthermore we demand to meet with Chancellor Patricia* someone yells *She's a sell out dyke* Dana looks up then continues *We demand to meet with Chancellor Patricia about the skyrocketing rate of campus assaults and rapes* I think about what happened on the beach rock back on my heels stand up *Yeah* I shout raise my fist *Stop rape now Pah trish ah Pah trish ah Pah trish ah* pad pad pad Dana looks at me smiles Chara stands up steps over to Dana grabs her waist then her head her white fingers in Dana's dark hair they kiss in the Chancellor's office in the middle of forty people other women jump up kiss each other drums beating palms padding people chanting *Patricia come out of the closet* I think I know who I am

Age Twenty five (1993)

The clock

glares green three am darkness I roll ribs hit springs hope for sleep tick tock don't want to lie awake all night gray ceiling shadows tick tock Frida bats a cotton ball

tick tock shadows move slowly to four am here on Madison's east side trees rustle monstrous shapes clumped leaves arch sway drop a truck rumbles on Willy early morning delivery of fruits vegetables the Wisconsin State Journal a shadow darts a lone bird calls

tick tock I rise to watch the sun come up over the horizon crouch next to the window facing south overlooking the school yard lean my temple cheek against the woodwork school begins in a few weeks fall will descend the shadows on the walls will lose their flesh become skeletal fingers and crooked spindly arms the school the street the yards there is nothing no dog no squirrel no bird no child no adult nothing except a flickering of soft pink gray light across the rooftops I want sleep now that the day is arriving there will be no night time flashbacks no waking in terror no body drenched in sweat no mind in perpetual panic no questions no night time obsessions about what and how he did what he did

tick tock it is almost five time to dress brush my teeth simple things are hard moving my body is like moving a mountain a bird croons in the front yard for the sun from the other side of the world I fish for underwear in a tomato box under the window grab my jeans off the chair a bra a t-shirt on the floor Frida wraps around my ankles I cradle her walk to the bathroom drop her heavy body on the floor I pull the sink light chain it's not grounded could electrocute one of us the dense black of the bathroom scatters I resent the light its intensity the final break with a sleepless night my face looks orange under the light this can't possibly be my life

I walk

two blocks to the diner Tara will join me at six thirty but until then I am on my own I hear something behind me but nothing is there at the diner I flip a switch half the lights flicker in the restaurant I slam the door dead bolt it catch the terror in my throat breathe talk to myself *You're okay now no one is here no one is here* I flip a switch in the kitchen and bright lights bounce off stainless steel I turn on the deep fryer check the fridges to see how much lettuce tomatoes pickles black olives potatoes meat eggs I will need to bring up from downstairs five thirty am no sleep still not a college graduate cooking hamburgers sweet potato soup leek soup eggs benedict grilled chicken scrambled eggs with cheese and scallions homestyle fried potatoes sour dough toast and whatever the special is for the week

The stairs
to the cellar are steep a hundred years old the walls are five feet thick uneven limestone mold in the cracks no windows thick moldy darkness stings my tongue two naked light bulbs with dirty brown strings stacks of boxes an old industrial mixer from the fifties four waist high freezers cracked pale green cement flooring with a rusty drain in the center

the terror hits me on the steps grips my stomach my throat makes my head dizzy I have to lean back to keep from falling down the steps I have to fight the fear that mad dad is here still chasing me after all these years Gollum in the corner eating raw meat from the freezers drinking rusty drain water seeping in through the cracks in the limestone but once I reach the basement floor take three giant steps through the dark one two three pull the light switch click on one naked bulb the fear stops

Three chicken
Santa Fe fake charcoal grill lines up salsa on the side homestyle fries sourdough one with a side of avocado slide them on the counter ring the bell sweating over the grill it's one thirty another hour I can go home sleep sweet sweet sleep they're cooling down I get in trouble if the food's cold ring the bell again then again my head floats around the kitchen ring again ring ring ring like that song sing sung sang on Double Nickels on the Dime what is the name of the group why can I remember the name of the album see it in my head light green with a man sitting in a car his arm hanging out the window I remember that but not the name of the band I ring the bell again Darren grabs my arm *She's coming* he says dumps frozen fries into the deep fryer sizzles the sizzles are bees feel like knives in my ears I get like this when I don't sleep *One burger rare horse on the side* Tara says picks up the Santa Fes *sorry* she tucks her notepad in her pocket picks up the chickens I nod Darren jiggles the fry basket wipes his forehead with the back of his arm his pants sag off his ass like the rest of us at the restaurant we are freaks fags dykes except Darren technically he is bisexual his brown hair hangs in his face I throw a burger on the grill it sizzles my ears! my head floats around the room I am off balance not in the body I watch it move without me the hands makes a side salad line up pickle chips on the wooden cutting board jutting out in front of the grill I watch the hands move without me they spread a piece of lettuce bright organic green on the roll

three slices of purple onion over the top Tara is at the window again *Butter* she says looks afraid she isn't good at waitressing they're threatening to fire her I don't know how we'll make the rent next month if they fire her I slap some butter in a side cup *Thanks* she says I flip the burger sizzles can't wait to get home sleep *Watch out* Darren says swings the fry basket across the kitchen the grease drips across the floor this food makes me sick the smells make me sick the sounds make me sick my therapist says I have to get another job one that won't disgust me food makes me sick in general I never cook at home I don't even know how I landed this job oh yes I do *Two up* Jody yells taps the bell slips two order sheets on the line she catches my eye winks I look away don't like her she's the one who hired me without any cooking experience she gets off that Tara and I are incest survivors I see it in her eyes

    Let me help Darren finishes the burger for me I read the orders scrambled eggs homestyle wheat toast no butter and potato leek soup with sourdough extra butter I reach around Darren grab a bowl he makes room for me which isn't hard to do since he's the size of a pencil line he is such a nice person compared to Jody I almost wish I was bisexual Darren slides the burger on the bun lettuce onion makes a nice picture he watches what he does intently he is depressed like me except he is differently depressed everything he does is methodical perfect he cares about cooking at the diner

    the pain is on his face gaunt cheekbones deep black smudges under his eyes like a charcoal drawing *Another butter* Tara yells desperate I dump the soup in the bowl splash it on my apron chunks of potato with the skin on greenish liquid from the pureed leeks *Shit* I say Darren laughs he likes me *Hurry* Tara pleads she is hard to work with she's so anxious I slide her a butter she grabs it runs Darren sets the burger and salad on the counter Tara Darren me our dads fucked us into oblivion we do our best to get through each day on four fifty an hour heads floating sweating immense concentration to do every little thing it is a numb life a life on the margins of the margins we are the dykes fags freaks throwaways fucked out of our bodies stumbling around Willy Street home of the hippie freaks and then us the queerest of the queer

Hope

    I hang by my teeth from it like one of those circus freaks swinging from a rope her teeth clamped down over a mouthpiece spinning holding on by her teeth to keep from splattering to the ground

    after my shift I buy a notebook at Ace across from the diner a brilliant blood red with a twisted wire spine *crooked back like an old lady I walk to school* pops in my head *Thanks* I say to the cashier a woman in her fifties with a burnt out tinted red perm she nods my therapist told me to journal make sense of the thoughts and images that pop into my head she says I'm not crazy they mean something they're important like a puzzle or a trail leading to something whole to some sort of understanding he broke my head apart now I have to put it together on the sidewalk the afternoon heat hits me like a brick I wait for an opening between the cars

Wake again

sweating the terror of a small animal heart beating no movement don't dare open eyes a monster in the room! I breathe listen slowly slit eyes moon shines in through blinds a green three twenty seven am Doctor Suess surrealism quick breaths turn into choking can't breathe fingers round throat thumbs press windpipe open mouth round hole thumbprints of a father

Daddy daddy no! daddy daddy no!

can breathe again catch air catch it fast gulp it down feel a very small presence in my body *daddy no! daddy no!* pinned to the ground big hands big body big mouth over me *daddy daddy no! daddy daddy no!* he did it to me small small small a three year old small a two year old small *daddy daddy no!* the words fade round mouth sucking opening closing small round fish mouth on a bed baby in a crib he did it to me when I was a baby round mouth sucking growing gills to breathe around the big round thing mouth sucking the big thing with no name

Mind snaps

can't take it can't take it can't take it mind snaps to the other side of the moon I flip on the lamp light helps takes away the dark makes the baby with gills on its neck go away inside hide

my mind is a record spinning I am a parrot the same thing over over over trying to cope with what he did think of as many words and pictures that mean the same thing repeat them over over over try to understand what he did what he did what he did

Blood red paper

book wire spine scribble scribble scribble like a two year old a two year old scribbling! a two year old! I scribble feels good the lines appear on the paper the two year old feels better! she feels better! it's good to draw the two year old is mad she is mad doesn't have words no words! she scribbles mad dad mad dad she hates mad dad scribble scribble scribble page after page after page the two year old the two year old! is trying to tell us something! she scribbles mad scribbling the way a fish girl with gills would scribble a mad fish girl with gills scribbling say it over n over n over our mind is like a skipping record swinging by its teeth help me! help me! help me! something bad happened to the two year old something bad happened to the baby a baby! when was I a baby! my mind can't hold it a bucket with holes the ocean pours through the China man who drowned his brothers my mind couldn't hold it then

I print in block letters *a tower came into the land when I was very young when I was the size shape and weight of an infant without words without thoughts only physical awareness but with memory and emotions and a sense yes a sense of self an infant has a sense of self if not where she ends she knows she is a beginning she is THE beginning when this is violated by towers bursting through the land from deep below out of the openings of the very body itself she instinctively knows she is under attack her mind creates a land a mythical place along the proportions of all the great myths Greeks Hindus Jews Gnostics Christians a land of biblical proportions where she goes where a tower now exists--put there by the invasion of the father-- where before there was only flat prairie with beautiful caves glistening shiny purple rocks more than anything the people of that land want the tower to be removed they want to defeat it burn it tear it down like a nuclear explosion it disrupted their lives and now the charred burnt evil has come into the body the body remembers the emotions recalls what the mind cannot hold the mind is a sieve the mind is an imperfect entity alone however in cooperation with the body and the emotions they together operate with a perfect genius*

* * *

Tara

you remind me of someone I do she stabs a clump of scrambled eggs *Uh huh* I say *but I don't know exactly who* I pepper my eggs she sneezes Joan Armatrading sings in our house *She's going to be at the women's festival Really* I say thinking about who Tara reminds me of *I had some weird flashbacks last night* I sprinkle cinnamon on my toast *I'm sorry honey* she says sings softly to herself *You know you should really join a choir* I say *you have such a good voice* she wrinkles her nose doesn't think she's good at anything *Who do I remind you of* she flips her skinny rat tail braid behind her I shrug my shoulders *Can't remember* she sighs I chew my toast say *Who's going to be at the festival* Tara stops chewing for a second looks at me *Joan Armatrading Oh yeah* I say tap my fork against the edge of my plate nod my head trying to remember who Tara reminds me of

I drag

the rusted push mower up the basement stairs Tara runs water for the dishes that is our deal I mow shovel in the winter and she washes the dishes I brrr back and forth across the yard mow in straight even lines back and forth back and forth the repetition the sameness of the paths soothes my mind Tara clinks dishes in the kitchen yells *Let's go downtown* the sun is bright and hot an airplane glides a thousand soundless miles overhead I drag the mower backwards the cut grass flips out from the blades like a pack of cards *maybe life gets better* I think it echoes *maybe life gets better maybe life gets better maybe life gets better*

Man

that is way fucking cool a man behind me on the bus says Willy Street crawls by the coop the East Indian grocery store the fund for non profits the Elks Club a basement level bar rumor has it they don't allow blacks a vacant gas station hip high weeds growing through the cracks in the concrete *She put out you never seen nothing like it* a different man says his voice softer sounds older the first man whistles the rest of us are quiet mostly women children a couple of older men who look crazy or homeless or both Tara stares out the window I turn sideways in my seat the two men are looking at each other either unaware or apathetic that the entire bus can hear their conversation *She took me all the way in man you should have seen her* I turn around *Shut up* I say the one with the soft voice has long brown hair down to his shoulders he stops talking looks up at me the other one with a pony tail flips me off *Just shut up* I say the one with the soft voice leans back crosses his arms *Later* he says seems a little embarrassed some people on the bus are looking at me others stare at the floor or out the window the ponytail man glares at me I turn around don't want to get into a huge confrontation on the bus in front of children Tara rolls her eyes she's afraid of men of confrontation I move my foot out into the aisle in case I need to stand up have a wide base to defend myself *Mind your own business cunt* the one with the pony tail says I ignore him cross my arms flex my biceps feel how strong I am imagine beating the shit out of him there is one thing that makes me not spacey and that's fighting *I always thought I should have been a boxer* I say to Tara

   Fucking bitches who don't mind their business pay for it sooner or later I don't look back Tara says nothing someone taps my back the ponytail man leans into my face his lips part I think he's going to spit but instead he says *Did you hear me mind your own business* he reaches toward my face I stand up my foot next to his *Leave it man* the other man says grabs his arm *they're just a couple of dykes anyway* he pulls the ponytail man down the aisle *Freaking dykes* the ponytail man says *you all need a good poke* the entire bus is looking at us there isn't anything to say that will cut him to the bone *Shut up* I say *Carpetlickers* the pony tail man says I flip him off I wish I'd kicked him punched him in the stomach one two uppercut left uppercut right *Muhammad Ali!* but underneath Muhammad Ali is a child's fear and I don't want to have my day taken over by fear but more than that I don't want those men to see it I study the ridges in the rubber strip that runs the length of the bus keep my elbows on my knees feel like a big bad dyke

Pissed

   Tara leans against a pole lights a cigarette *About those men Yeah* she says like I'm stupid for asking *Yeah* I say but wish she would have said something on the bus we walk around the State Capitol toward State Street the sun burning our shoulders we pass red and white tulips swaying in clumps around the capitol one section is a red W in a sea of white tulips *Good use of tax money* I say *Tch* Tara says we pass a gold statue of a white boy memoralized for some war *Tch* Tara says a cluster of four women power walk around the square in their business skirts and running shoes *Tch* Tara says we turn right on State Street away from the capitol toward the university located at the other end of State Street one mile from the capitol I barely remember being a college student like it was three life times ago like it was someone else three white men on the street surround Tara *Whoa girl* one of them says grabs Tara's arm they laugh *Hey look I caught me a big one* the other white man grabs her ass Tara yells *Go to hell* I push the ass grabber he turns to me *Fucker* Tara screams lifts her elbow clocks one of them in the chest I step next to her cock my fists *float like a butterfly sting like a bee I am the champion!* I take a swing miss him turn around a white man is holding Tara's leg in the air I take two steps kick him he drops her leg *You bitch* he says *Fuckers* Tara says steps to the side makes her stance big cocks her fist swings it back then smashes into the stomach of the man who had her leg *Ummph* the man buckles we hurt one of them no one knows what to do everyone on the street has stopped no one's used to seeing women fight back

a siren blasts behind us *Come on* Tara says I don't move don't want to run away from the men let them think we're afraid but they get up go down an alley toward Gorham *Come on* Tara says a woman stares at us her mouth open *Now* Tara grabs my arm the siren is louder closer right behind us we walk fast like those power walking yuppies through people with fanny sacks and Birkenstocks and backpacks and suits *This way* she says we turn left past the camping equipment store past the feminist bookstore past the locksmith the siren screams but the police car has stopped the sound isn't being thrown the way it does when the car is moving we turn a corner into a vacant lot crawl behind two blue dumpsters *You nailed him* I whisper *Yeah* she says *Yeah* I cock my fists under my chin *They're lucky the cops came because I'm Muhammad Ali* Tara laughs then covers her mouth shoes clip clop nearby we sit quiet as stone between the blue dumpster and the brick wall

The clip clop

leaves *You were so pissed* I push her shoulder *They're pricks* she says *Yeah* I say happy Tara is mad *it's so much better to be pissed than scared isn't it* I punch her arm *I've never seen you that mad* she laughs *Pissed* she says *I was pissed* she grabs my wrist raises it in the air *we're pissed women Yeah* I grab her hand lace my fingers through hers *we are pissed women*

A Room

of One's Own in white cursive on the purple sign sways above the bookstore a three by three foot piece of cardboard is taped over the front window jagged masking tape spreads across it like a spider web Tara and I walk into the entryway small books piled on top of each other stacked in corners used paperbacks smashed into cardboard boxes *Discounted* in red ink on a flap *Hey* a woman behind the counter says she has short spiked hair big dangling earrings *can I help you* she leans over the counter points at Tara *Tara right Yeah* Tara says crunches up her nose the way she does when she has a crush on someone *Sarah* Tara says twirls a display of earrings and rings and five starred pagan pendants *Yup* the woman says *We need a book on pissed women* I say Tara laughs pushes at her hair *Okay* Sarah drums her fingers on the counter *that's kind of a broad category try the section on activism to begin with* Sarah points to the back *What happened to the window* Tara tilts her head *Oh geez* Sarah says *someone threw a couple of rocks through it last night* Sarah folds her arms under her breasts *with a note that said death to dykes abortionists and feminists Great* Tara says rolls her eyes *Damn if only we had that much power* I say *Right* Sarah says *not to mention they spelled feminists wrong*

Look at this one I pull out Angry Women sit in a rocking chair next to Tara flash the cover picture of a woman with snakes coming out of her head she throws back her head and laughs I love it when she's like this angry and loose and fun I flip through the pages it's a feminist art book I touch the pictures of the women's art *So beautiful* paintings and drawings of women and flowers and landscapes burning red and green and black *Look at this* she points to a book in her lap *Feminism from 1960 to 1967* she turns the page to a photograph of an old flyer that says Radical Feminists Unite! Castrate Rapists! we laugh hard high from fighting *Pissed women* she says laughing so hard she cries

I am all alone

in the entryway looking at the books stacked piled wedged into one another a crystal shoots squares of light onto the walls and ceiling I run my fingers over the spines on the shelves fiction non fiction theory poetry art politics law all of it is so lovely this is my church Tara and Sarah are talking and I feel safe like I belong *Womyn's Words* no *In Another Voice* no *Sisterhood: Essays on American Feminism* no *Feminism and the Law* no *Grace: a novel in two parts* maybe I pull it out a buck seventy five pumpkin colored yellowed paper compact thick 379 pages by Cohen a feminist I never read in school someone wrote on the inside cover *Julie I hope this changes your world like it did mine in love and sisterhood forever xxoo Catherine June '79* I sit back on my heels read *I was nine when the difficulties began with my father* I snap the book shut it's mine

All set Sarah swings behind the counter all smiles I'm in my own place far away *Yeah* I say Sarah rings me up *That'll be 1.95 with tax* I give her two dollars *five cents is your change* she drops a nickel so shiny and bright into my hand I freeze the nickel rolls off my hand onto the counter I stare at it I want to tell someone something the nickel circles itself on the counter looking for a place to settle I don't move *What's going on* Tara says somewhere over my shoulder I stare at the nickel spinning in a spot next to the pile of bright pink A Room of One's Own bookmarks I shake my head I don't want them to think I'm crazy don't want them to know a nickel dropped out of the sky into my hand made me want to die *Keep the change* I grab my book walk under the shimmering crystal into the street

Shit

I grab my neck buck buck bah buck lean against the camping gear store *What's wrong* Tara says out of breath rough brick bites my shoulder I wave at her can't say anything I don't know what's happening I see her face then I see nothing my head brain eyes aren't working like I'm blind dumb deaf without a nervous system I grab at her wrist miss finger air instead the taste of shit in my mouth horrible deep stench in my throat nose mouth I gag then cough lean over to throw up but nothing comes out *Oh my god* Tara says her hand on my back I cough until my stomach hurts throat bleeds red stead trying to get the taste of shit out of my mouth I stand up car lights smear by in streaks *You okay* Tara says her hand moving up and down my back makes me feel small desperate for love attention comfort warmth *I don't know* I say exhausted I don't want her hand to stop I want her to comfort me mom! mom! white bone knuckle on the door mom don't leave! don't hate me! smears of car lights clip clops of people going to their houses normal lives money cars jobs love family the things people have

Tears

explode *Please help me* I am breaking apart the Chinese brother when he realizes he can't hold the ocean in his mouth anymore a tremble in his throat his nose twitches lips peel leaving only his teeth to contain an ocean

The therapist

talks but my ears are off can't understand her words can't take anything in I am going to explode her office is fuzzy peach light orange walls gray nubby carpet with specks of black I sit on a green sofa she sits on a matching chair next to her is a maple table with an aloe vera plant coffee cup and shiny black rocks must be obsidian she is a nice woman but today I can't look at her I mumble *Yes uh huh* pretend like I listen but I can't she doesn't know what I'm talking about *I had a good day* I say *Tara and I had fun* I don't want to tell her about fighting the men I don't trust her that much she lives in another world the other world the one with money and girlfriends and houses and cute Shih Tzus she brings to Pride *I felt even great* I lie terror catches in my throat like a latch keeps the words from coming out on time in order I feel like I'm choking my sentences weave in and out up and down around and around they get small and short like a child's they jump all over like Mexican beans for sale at Walgreen's they gush out like an ocean held in the cheeks of a Chinese man's mouth the bottom line is I can't speak speech is beyond me and that is because I can't make sense out of my life get my past to stop replaying in my head handle my oceans of emotions *I smelled shit I tasted shit I felt like someone was dropping shit into my mouth my life is a yo yo I go up and down so much I have whiplash* I say my therapist stares at me her wavy brown hair pushed to one side she says nothing *I think I'm going crazy* she says nothing *do you think so* I say she says nothing takes a drink from her black coffee cup *WORT 89.9 the alternative to mainstream radio* written in white cursive

Um she says looks over my head *I think you're having some sort of body memory What* I say I want to scream but don't *are you saying someone put shit in my mouth* she crosses her legs sits back in her light green chair *I really don't know* she says *but it's possible*

I am angry at everyone everything I yank out the folded sheets in my pocket throw them on the floor at her feet *Here* I say she looks at me I look at her she looks down then moves in her big comfortable chair picks up the papers sprung open like a spider when it puffs up moves its legs out a little ready to crawl off she sits back looks at my face for a second then opens the papers looks at each page carefully *What* I say she presses them together *What do they mean to you* she says hands them back to me *They mean nothing* I say terror rising up to my throat *they mean I'm going crazy Well* she looks over my head again *do you remember drawing them Yes* I say *of course how could I not* I sit back on the couch *well kind of it was a blur I guess I mean I remember but it was weird Mmm hmm* she uncrosses her legs picks something off her slacks drops it to the side of her chair what's going on I want to scream but I say nothing *Do you ever lose time* she says squints at me or *find clothes in your closet that don't belong to you* she dangles her arm over the side of the chair her fingers curve graciously like the arch of a bird's beak *What do you mean do I ever lose time or have clothes that aren't mine* I look out the window *Well* she says *do you ever skip over time* she pauses *like you're skipping over parts of your life* what I think I stare at the pebbled tops of the buildings a gray pigeon with splashes of purple on its wings sits on the edge of the brick building next to us *What floor are we on* the pigeon's breast pushes out each time it takes a step *The tenth* she says *This must be one of the tallest buildings in Madison* I say *From what I've heard* she says *no buildings can be built taller than the state capitol What a stupid rule* I say *I guess that's why this place will never be anything but a second rate cow town I suppose* she says brushes her hand against the side of her chair she thinks I'm too aggressive that I lash out at things when I'm afraid the pigeon struts around the top of the building *Do you want to answer my question* she says I imagine pushing open the window leaping Superman style onto the top of the other building then onto the building behind it two stories higher a woman is sitting in a chair a light on above her head the blue computer screen glare on her face and chest and hair *What did you say* I say *I asked if you wanted to answer my question because you abruptly changed the subject What was the question* the pigeon flies away its purple wings beat against the soft blue pastel of the sky *About losing time Oh* I say the blue glare disappears the woman stands walks out of my vision *I guess I don't*

The revolving door

on the ground floor of the therapist's building moves as if a breeze caught it twists it slowly the heel and pant leg of the person who just went through the door disappear I don't like going through this door I have enough spinning in my head enough of a problem staying in my body after therapy I putter across the black marble floor then push through the door fast leave it spinning uselessly on its own *Tara* I say she is sitting on a bench facing the capitol her back to me she turns her head waves a long legged jogger in red short shorts runs between us his package flaps against his thigh *Gross* Tara says he turns left down State Street *I'm hungry* I say *let's eat* I need to cover up how spaced out I am I stare at the sun just above the horizon a perfect hazy circle at the end of the street glistening off the leaves lining the street and splintering off glass storefronts

Did you tell her about what happened Huh I say *oh the men No* she laughs *silly after that Oh* I crack my knuckles look at a patch of sunlight on the cement *not really well yeah I guess I did* Tara takes a drag the cigarette pops when she takes it out of her mouth *She thought maybe it was a body memory* I walk around a homeless woman in a brown wig bent over her shopping cart filled with crinkled brown bags and a white sneaker *Whenever you think your life is shit* I say *Uh huh* Tara says drops her cigarette on the sidewalk *Wish I had something to give her* I say watch the woman over my shoulder *Uh huh* Tara says I almost run into two young women walking toward the capitol *Gawd* one of them says *watch where you're going Like totally* I am a cigarette lighter one turn of the ridged wheel and I'm pissed we walk past Sweets on State and Sue Goldwomon's Travel Agency *Madison has to be the only place with a lesbian travel agency* Tara says nothing

You're talkative I say agitated I pretend like I'm shooting a basketball *So And So! So And So!* chants in my head *Mmm hmm* she says *What's wrong* I look at the posters of Cancun in the travel agency's window *make all your winter travel plans now! I'm worried about you Why* I pretend to dribble through my legs *You're acting weird* I shoot again *So And So! So And So! I can't help it* I say *I'm bored* I shoot again *life is boring* I say *this town is boring the universe is boring* I know I'm acting like an idiot but I can't stop I know I'm freaked out but I can't stop *What else did your therapist say* she stops looks in the window of the civic center we saw KD Lang there a few months ago I lean against the glass press my nose into it the way I used to when I was a kid *It's weird to not remember your life isn't it Uh huh* Tara says *it's a new exhibit sculptures from Wally Stewart Never heard of him* I say *Me neither* she says I look past the red mural that always hangs in the window to the sculptures gray human bodies on pedestals *Tch* Tara says then I see they're women's bodies arms heads look like they've been lopped off *Fucking god* I say *I'm so pissed all the shit we go through* I am so angry I can barely talk *woo woo! steam whistle shooting through my head! every fucking day is an assault Tch* Tara says I punch the glass *Fuck them* I say anger welling up spitting out an ocean let loose *fucking god* my head feels clear not all spinny and confused the anger is a shot of vodka clearing my senses *C'mon Tara* I say *let's do something What* she says *Break the windows smash the sculptures spray paint the sidewalks* Tara laughs *Okay* she says sarcastically we walk toward the sun a streak of gold and peach lingering over the tree tops and buildings *Pissed women unite* I make a fist in the air *let's make posters and put them on the kiosks seriously* the jogger passes us running back toward the capitol his head down package flapping like a dead bird against his thighs *Oh!* Tara says *Pissed women unite* I laugh hard and loud but my laughter rolls like a thunderstorm over a sadness deep as the ocean

Lake Monona
flickers between the buildings the bus turns the corner *someday it's going to be all right it's going to be all right* is what my ears hear the biggest ears in all the world!

1411 Jenifer Street
where we've lived for nearly a year yolk yellow two story house taller than the trees and the sway backed telephone wires scruffy waist high weeds along the back fence we can't afford a weed wacker hell we can't even afford the heat in the winter sit huddled under our blankets for a day or two go to a girlfriend's house winter is our hurricane season mittens three pairs of socks sweatpants over jeans until we can buy the oil eighty bucks a shot from *Sam and Son's Eastside Heating Since 1947* two men slide a thick rubbery salmon colored foot and a half wide python hose across the grassy brown stubble and patches of frozen snow through an open basement window *Crank it!* they yell pump the oil into the metal tank a small caboose bolted down in the basement the hose a pulsing flesh colored snake makes me sick just thinking about it

Hello Tara says jamming her key into the lock she is pissed at me for being spacey *What* I say *Knock knock anyone home* I flinch like she slapped me I hate it when she makes fun of me for daydreaming *I knew this was the right house for us* I say *when I saw the river at the end of the block Huh* Tara says *that's not a river it's a stream at best* I stomp my feet *It's right out of a fairy tale can't you just imagine a troll hiding underneath Tch* Tara says *you are so weird*

I cross my arms stare at the garbage bag she left on the porch last night she kicks a cantaloupe rind it skitters off the porch lands with a thud somewhere in the dark *Damn possums* she says I almost tell her she's the one who left the garbage bag on the porch made it possible for the possums to rip it open feast on our throw aways but I decide not to *The crickets are loud tonight* I say *they sound like they're getting ready for winter* Tara slaps at the handle *Whatever* Tara kicks the entire bag of garbage the bag flops over a blue Progresso soup can pokes out a hole *It doesn't matter to me if the neighborhood squirrels or possums or rats get fat on our food Ahh!* Tara says I am being really irritating and dumb I know she hates rodents Tara and I fight like this sometimes I think because we are both only children

Give me your key mine is sticking again she holds her hand out behind her back I put it into her palm she opens the door a mustiness greets us then washes over us the smell becomes undetectable as our senses adjust to the sharp dead foliage used bookstore smell that rises from the basement *Home sweet home* I say sit on Tara's dark green pappasan chair in the living room Tara drops my key on the phone table hits the answering machine button beep click click click beep *Three hang ups* Tara says *people could at least leave their names* I drop deeper into the wicker chair look out the window at the house ten feet away yet we have no idea who lives there *You'd think so* I say

Out

the front windows the vacant school yard steel jungle gym bars reflect the moonlight the white uneven lines on the soccer field glow in the dark was the wrong kind of paint used by a janitor at the middle school digging through a closet for paint he can't find there was an intra school game that afternoon fifth graders against the sixth graders the lines disappeared over the summer so he runs to Ace picks up glow in the dark ceiling paint by accident marks the field jig jagging lines over the grass dirt red clay baseball diamond now there is a ghostly outline of a misshapen soccer field did the janitor get caught for leaving school grounds during work is that the sort of thing he could get in trouble for I worry about him being in trouble as if I am four years old my thoughts embarrass me I do not think like a normal person Tara walks upstairs her footsteps are heavy she stops rests her hand on her thigh as she gathers herself to go up the rest of the stairs *Goodnight Tara* I say *Goodnight* she says heavily she has her own ocean of sorrow *Pissed women unite* I say softly she laughs Frida sits in the window nothing moves in the vacant school lot no possums rats squirrels no tee ball teams in t shirts down to their knees no soccer balls I forgot I used to play soccer it seems unbelievable another lifetime another person not me like I have been stretched so far I don't recognize myself I had parents lived in a house drank Kool Aid played kickball in the streets I forgot about those things the normal things what I remember now over and over a tape perpetually rewound and played are the beatings rapes terror they wipe out the rest

The normal stuff

must be inside me too a chalky outline of a person I once was a fragment trying to keep up with the rest of me like a snap shot of someone running when the camera doesn't quite catch the person in one spot blurred lines of a hand foot shoulder thigh I squint at the playground blur my eyes make the white lines rise off the earth split multiply float the toilet flushes upstairs a loud sucking kissing noise all that waste eventually flows into the rivers ocean

it won't be long now until it's cold and we forget all about how hot we were today it'll be so cold we won't be able to even imagine the heat we will doubt it ever existed ever could exist again Tara's bedroom door shuts I imagine eleven year olds playing tackle football in the snow wearing Green Bay Packer colors gold skull caps green jackets so large they look like the Incredible Hulk ice on the monkey bars mounds of snow piled higher than the chain link fence salmon colored snakes thick enough to run gallons of oil through in minutes swallow Frida or a small dog whole this moment changes into a pulsing cold oil drilling winter night my bare arms goose up we forget some things so easily

Wake up

cold sweat on a hot morning *where is Patty* banging in my head screaming behind every one of my thoughts cold sweat on a hot morning dreaming blind possums moles a green one hour glow before I have to get up shadow of Frida's sharp ears on the other side of the blinds *where is Patty* a thunderstormhurricanetornado in my head migraine shots of monkey bar electricity Frida's shadow disappears the blinds swing against the window and wall I close my eyes wait pray beg hope for the maelstrom to end *where is Patty* I shiver

* * *

Cling cling

for sure I am going to put that bell down someone's throat the noise splits my head *Up* I say slide a plate of huevos rancheros across the counter *Shit* I say under my breath I am trying to stay calm *Cling cling Fuck* I say monkey bar electricity shooting in my head *Need a break* Darren says *I'll get the order* he grabs the light green sheet off the line I chop an onion lost in the knife's black handle steel blade chop chop chop white juice puddles on the scarred cutting board *Cling cling* I want to scream fuck you instead I slam the knife down scrape the pieces into the bowl my head hurts my eyes tear I grab another onion one that fits into my palm like a softball I chop off the roots throw the chunk in the garbage *Nice shot* Darren says moves next to me cracks two eggs in the frying pan I want to throw the frying pan across the room what is wrong with me chop chop chop

Darren pushes the eggs with a spatula the clear snotty part runs up and over the white and yellow I want to vomit chop chop chop Darren clears his throat I can't stop myself I'm going to bust something I throw a piece of the onion against the back window *Sorry* I say I am but it doesn't stop me from wanting to choke someone chop chop chop Darren pushes the eggs they bubble up around the sides *Gross* I can't stop myself *Yep* he picks up the pan swings it to the other side of the kitchen chop chop chop his elbow bumps the knife slips a thin piece of pain cuts across my skin a perfect circle of bright red blood pools on my thumb knuckle runs off onto the wood mixes with the onion juice Darren leans across my back there's no room for two of us he pushes my stomach into the board my hands into the chopped onion blood red choking eyes *Excuse me* he says slides a plate of eggs onto the counter *Yeah* I say it's not his fault but I don't want to be touched *Cling*

cling shots of white light spin through my head I run down the stairs toward the darkness below

The stairs

steep slick worn wood like cathedral steps in Italy grooved footprints pressed into stone in Italy there are steps worn down from millions of people walking on them their feet in the same place as someone five hundred years before these stairs are two inches thick seventy year old nails heads snapped off we have no thousand year old stone buildings just rotted wood rusted nails new construction plastic bricks particle boards flammable materials nothing's real nothing lasts I wish I was walking down the stairs of a cathedral in Italy where a million people or more had walked before me then I would know what to do the rage left when I cut myself the pain made it stop made me want to hide something is wrong with me what will I do how will I live thin wood stairs fifty people have walked up and down a thousand times in the past seventy years that's not enough I need to belong somewhere I need to know something I need to not be so terribly alone

It's impossible

for me to deal with cling clanging bells people touching me demands for snotty cum looking eggs I press on my thumb the cut is small feels like a pinch what is happening am I crazy am I sane am I neither is there such a thing as sanity why are the people who ignore the violence happening around them everyday sane why am I crazy because I'm hiding in the basement of my work because my head hurts because I have flashbacks 24 7 because I was born to a serial rapist daddy created from the union of genociders and those they genocided welcome to America the pressure is as much as I can take I shake my hand try to make the pinching pain go away my nerves are flipped out worn tire treads

Door creaks

light spills under the stairs thump thump *Anyone down here* it's Jody Darren must have sent her after me *Hey you down here* she says I say nothing squeeze my thumb I'm acting like it was cut off *where is Patty where is Patty where is Patty* Jody thumps down the steps I hope she doesn't find me under the stairs she'll fire me for sure call the cops shrinks surly men in white *Hey* she says *Hey* I say *Didn't you hear my calling you Not really* I pull my knees to my chest *Darren needs your help Uh uh* I say *It's busy* she bends at her waist so she can look into my face *your break's over Oh right* I wave my thumb at her *I cut myself* she thinks I'm weird no doubt about that but maybe she won't think I'm crazy *Are you okay* she stares at me I hate it when people ask how I am stare at me like they're concerned it's a power trip masquerading as compassion *Sure* I say but the words *not really* pop into my head take their place alongside *where's Patty where's Patty where's Patty*

Chicken meat

fills my nostrils buh buck chicken meat the bumpy bumpy skin *Thanks for covering* I say trying not to breathe through my nose Darren reaches into a stainless steel cupboard *No problem* he says pulls out a stack of to go french fry boxes thin red lines criss cross around the outside *Clang* Tara pushes her ticket into the line *Last one* she smiles turns out into the seating area her step has a bounce to it she is going to a movie after work with a friend of hers I gulp Pepsi to get the taste smell of the chicken meat out of my nose and mouth I have an hour left at work I have to finish this shift drinking the burning pop helps me disconnect Darren flips the chicken breast on the grill *white knuckle bone on the door! Geh* I say gulp more Pepsi Darren separates the to go french fry containers stacks them so we can grab them easily I wish I was still sitting in the basement shadows Jody pops into the kitchen puts her hands on her hips cocks her head she is short stocky straight black hair cut above her ears she smiles at Darren *Everything okay* she says *Sure* Darren says neither of us like her *Okay* Jody says *I'll be upstairs doing bills in case you need me All right* Darren mumbles I try to imagine dating him he is nice and he likes me but I can't imagine being with a man Darren slides a chicken breast onto bread I grab the plate drag it along the counter *Pickle* Darren says drops a spear onto the plate they say smell is linked to memory more than any other sense and they must be right because this might as well be a plate of shit

I slide the plate onto the counter don't ding the bell the way I am supposed to *Mary* barks out of me calling the one breeder employee *Ring the bell next time* Mary says she is in her late thirties long red hair two kids doesn't like queers *What* I say she acts like a mother *You heard me* she says *Shut up* I say she presses her lips together puts the ticket in her pocket picks up the plate and walks away *Asshole* I say *if I wanted to talk to my mother I'd call her*

the bell clings Mary sticks another order on the line Darren wipes his hands on his apron reaches for it *I've got this one* he says reaches around me pulls it down I push into the counter I don't want him to touch me I don't want to smell the chicken the counter cuts into my stomach Mary laughs I fling a piece of broken bread at her face *Fuck* she yells the dining room is silent Darren's hands drop to his side the bread sticks to her shoulder and neck *You bitch* she grabs at the bread throws a fistful at me it sails over my head lands in the fryer a million bees fly into the air everyone in the dining room watches Mary clumps up the stairs to Jody's office the dining room buzzes Darren doesn't like confrontations Tara runs into the kitchen *I can't believe you just did that* she says looks at the fryer then at me bread crumbs on my chest shoulders *Oh my god* she says *you're in trouble* I shrug

Clingclingcling

What I say white monkey bar ice lights shoot through my field of vision *where is Patty where is Patty where is Patty My order* Mary points to the ticket on the line her mascara smeared under one eye no one made her order *You stupid dyke* she yanks the ticket out of the clip throws it into the kitchen *are you too crazy to complete one simple order* whoo whoo! steam whistle! the ticket floats above the counter *may I take your order* typed against light green lined paper *cup leek sour bread* in Mary's writing the ticket floats a leaf a wounded bird confetti paper at a ticker tape parade in New York City a dropped wrapper off a hot dog snow falling from the sky on dirty gray streets

> *White knuckle bone on the door*
> *snotty blood sheets crumpled in the closet*
> *whish whish whish the headboard did it!*

then it dive bombs to the floor and the bitch is like my mother *Fuck you* I yell so mad I don't know what to do I knock the bell off the counter clangclangclangclangclang I want to choke her beyond all reason feelings from forever take over I hate her

Hey Jody is in the doorway Darren grabs my arms pulls them behind my back I twist one free *Stop* Jody yells *Fuckin bitch* I yell Darren wraps his arm across my chest *What's going on* Jody says to him then steps back looks into the dining room *Everything's fine* Jody laughs *sorry for the commotion Fucking bitch* I say Jody steps into the kitchen *Cool it* Jody says *what happened She called me a stupid dyke* I say Jody's eyebrows jump up she thinks I am a stupid crazy dyke she's siding with Mary straight woman she should stand up for me we are dykes *Fuck* I say she's not going to take my side the ticket is upside down on top of the bread bag *Leave* she says

My world

drops out from under me shifting sand pummeled by a tidal wave of shame I'm drowning in it can't cope with it so I hate Jody Darren Mary the people in the dining room I won't ever go back there I have to get home get into bed hide everyone knows everyone sees who I am badness a stumbling drunk sick from the hatred red rage coral pink shame burning up my soul straight women matter more Mary touched off more than I can handle more than I can handle! I can barely walk sidewalk cracks don't step on the mother's back! don't step on the mother's back!

No key

on the key ring where is it I am drunk I drank nothing but I am drunk stumbling on the porch stairs gray crooked rotted teeth can't keep track of my keys retard pound the door *Tara! Tara! Let me in* silence snow falling on salmon snake silence it's day it's night dyke! dyke! everyone thinks I am a crazy dirty dyke I am a crazy dirty dyke! *Patty Patty what will I do without you* slap my palm on the door *Tara! Tara!* silent snow flakes it's hot I'm thirsty *Patty Patty what will I do without you*

Punch

the air damn I forgot Tara's at the movies grab my head it hurts I have to get to my room curl up under my blanket hide from everyone I hate the world need to get away I hold my head shut my eyes sit down on the porch a car drives by the swoosh of the tires round noise rubber on pavement smooth black pavement laid last spring orange cones tape tar roller tan men in Levis work boots one woman in an orange vest holding a slow sign I have to think of something else slow my brain is cracking open a walnut pistachio peanut not really a nut it's part of the legume family that's the end of that game come back into my body a little but the pain is too much almond sesame seed cashew can't forget the cashew or those bleached white bare naked no shell or skin nuts in Christmas mixes what are they called shit what are they called shit that's what they taste like no one ever eats them they seem to multiply fill up the bowl while the rest of the nuts disappear

another car drives by on the edge of the road where the sand collects tires popping gravel down the street into lawns loud rifle cracking pop pop pop like nickels against a wall *where is Patty where is Patty where is Patty* stumble off the porch eyes slit light hurts Patty peer pear she disappeared

dis ah peer dd hold head fed ked bled twirl bump into railing on the back stairs Patty pear dis ah peer dd ded dead fed bled have to tell someone dead dead dead have to call therapist bled bled bled tell Tara the police missing persons missing children national hotline 1 800 call us 4 help P pear my peer dis ah peer ded

Falling tidal

wave earth disappears the Chinese brothers will drown! the Chinese brothers will drown! water coral bits gray dead fish missing eyes bike tire shells snapping lobsters claws seaweed clumps pen cap flat chip rocks one hammerhead shark bloated pale blue jellyfish clumps I fall to my knees hold my head keep out light keep out light shattered glass in my brain badness badness help help help

Patty Patty Patty I love you so much heart breaks tidal wave lands smashes roars washes over me covers me I am dying dying dying I give up Patty oh Patty I love you miss you can't live without you all these years tidal wave pounds roars I am beneath its pounding battering weight

As I die this is what I hear:

Once upon a time
in a land far far away a girl lived under water with the fishes rusted garbage can tops tadpoles and lilies of the sea she had very big eyes so that she could see through the gray green murk but unlike the other creatures of

the sea she had very big ears this was because she was not truly a creature of the sea but rather lived beneath the water because a large hairy troll tried to strangle her so her hiding in the sea was the only way she could escape his daily tirades

she used her oversized ears to listen for his thunderous approach which she could hear from miles away boom boom boom went his large feet with extra long toes slither slither went his tongue and the thing between his thighs

the only way for her to get out of the underwater world was to swallow it only every time she swallowed the sea more water fell from the sky she had to swallow the sea again and again until she became as big as the sea until she became the sea living beneath her own surface clinging to the craggy rocks and seaweed stalks on the bottom

this was the way she lived for many many years until one day she could hold the water no more nestled between the folds of her cheeks and cracks between her teeth and splashing part way down her throat suddenly one day it all came out releasing that much dammed up water creating a tidal wave in her land which had not previously known tsunamis

the first day the tidal wave hit the land it turned to night then another day and night came and went like the hands on a clock tick tock tick tock the girl lost track of the days and nights the tidal wave and its ensuing flood covered everything making it impossible for the girl to tell the passing of seasons the passing of time became like the hands on a clock unimportant days turned to nights and back again but without a world in which to place the hours and minutes and seconds time was irrelevant this is how the girl felt alone irrelevant and unknown she became utterly disconnected from the world around her and its human and not so human happenings

another day another night she lay dying among the seaweed stalks and sharp craggy rock formations at the bottom of the sea she thought about why she released the tidal wave she decided she did so for two simple reasons she released the tidal wave because she could no longer hold it back she released the tidal wave because she could no longer be the sea

she gives up swims through her dream past the yolk yellow house down Jenifer takes a left away from the bridge sits at the edge of the river listens listens hard

dying is not always bad even if it is painful

* * *

The river

the river the river get to the river I hear in my head my feet walk my head sings the river the river the river get to the river a stone from my hand skips one two three times across the river's gray plate someday everything will be all right someday everything will be all right the river the river the river feeds me

Many days

many nights an eternity a lifetime a dream the day I am in is dark it is no longer day it is night tick tock tick tock where am I who am I what is going on tick tock tick tock the pain in my head is gone my thigh is bruised scraped red from lying on the concrete edge of the sidewalk where else was I somewhere else the river! grass clippings pasted to my calves and ankles one street light's golden orange glow

haven't I been here before locked out in a back yard am I Sisyphus don't I know how this will end it will never end the door unlocks by itself the key left on the other side of orange curtains I stand up lose my balance the house is bigger than the other one I pull on the screen door wiggle the door knob so gold and shiny under the moon it's locked I wait my head foggy damp murky no one comes to the door no lights flicker inside I sit down on the steps hold my head stare at the shadows in the bushes behind the house this has happened to me before I am sure of it but I'm not sure of much else a squirrel skitters into the yard stops still as a statue twitches its tail disappears into the tall weeds by the fence *Patty!* I groan cover my head

Tick tock tick tock

pain anger rage humiliation shame grief sadness sorrow despair all the feelings in all the world all the feelings in all the world! hit me square in the chest water from a hose lying in wait on the side of the house by the brick red neighbors' house the ones we don't know I need a brick to break a window I look around the house then around theirs you'd think they'd have one if anyone would cause of their brick red house but they don't no brick no stones just sticks blown up on land chopped grass I chopped grass once! I chopped grass once with the mower in the basement but that was before the tsunami hit

Whish whish whish the headboard did it!

my head floats above my body moves on its own accord I watch my arms pick up a stick poke at a hole in the screen the stick disappears into the house clunks onto the floor I can't see in I'm so short China Doll Girl short I'm drunk but I haven't drunk a thing I make my brain think back before the storm to the day before I haven't drank anything since the Pepsi at the diner that Mary! she sure is a bitch oh how I hate that word bitch it's so misogynist that bitch! I watch my arms look at them like they're from outer space strong thin arms do things on their own have their own thoughts now they're tearing at the screen along with the fingers trying to rip open the hole that might hurt but I don't know I can't feel anything I am watching someone else

Who is it

the light above the back door turns on moths flap into the bulb *Hey* I say sitting on the back stairs why does the emergence of light signal to them to throw themselves into the flames the inside door opens *What are you doing* it's a woman a large woman I've seen her before! I know her! Tara! in a long Garfield t-shirt bare knees and legs *Hi* I say *Where have you been* she says I shrug my shoulders leave someone else to deal with the interactions of daily life

Looking for this

Tara says *What* I say a little embarrassed trying to keep up with what just happened which is hard since I don't know what happened *Your key* she says irritated *Oh yeah* I stand up *where'd you find it* she opens the screen door *On the table where I left it for you remember No* I walk into the kitchen take the key from her *Did Jody fire you* I shrug my shoulders blink four five six times try to adjust to the bright kitchen light a single bulb twelve feet high *I don't care* I say *I hate that job Where have you been* she says her hands on her hips the Garfield on her night shirt has a hole through his ear I try to think of something to say *My god* she says *you're covered in grass* she points at my legs *and you're cut* she's right the tips of my fingers are red *Have you been drinking* she says *No* I brush off the grass *where's Frida* I walk into the dining room push the black button light switch original to the house light sprouts from the chandelier four upside down glass cups droop off a bronze center piece Frida crouches on the back of the couch *Hi Frida* she leaps off the couch and scampers up the stairs there's a stick on the floor gray and dried out I pick it up look at the hole I try to remember which is like trying to see through murky water and then I hear it hit the floor again and then I see my fingers push it through the hole remembering is like watching a rerun bzzzt replay!

Tara bangs pots

in the kitchen I push the stick back out the hole *Tara* I say my body too big for me like I'm in one of those mascot animal costumes Bucky Badger himself! I shuffle into the kitchen she plops Spaghetti O's into a pan I realize I'm hungry thirsty *Where were you* she says sets the can on the stove pushes the partially attached scallop edged top inside the can I shrug my shoulders that's a good question I think but don't say anything she tosses the flowered can into the garbage licks her fingers flicks her braid behind her back butters a piece of white bread *Well* she says *I guess I fell asleep* I say *Outside* she says *Uh huh* I say *On the sidewalk* she says *Uh huh mostly* I flick a piece of grass off my knee leaves a dimple on my knee

The river

bends to the right drops into Lake Monona fishes turtles tadpoles scatter I sit away from the bridge weird I know but I hear mom's voice *Who's that roared the troll* and I am afraid from the time I was little n my age sinks like stone in water to four the number four next to my mom n her shiny shiny ring

* * *

Bring ring

phone sings wakes me up dead head on the bed gray sun winks in the room Patty's pony swings by the bushes I watch her from the room while mad dad builds the bed *Patty Patty Patty* I say in my head can't tell where I am California sunshine moving day the first time I see saw Patty I sit up knock the window pane one two three a baby strolls in a basket the sun appears out of the gray a mass of flour and egg whipped left to dry the sky's by Monet life is a painting a dream a movie playing in my head I hide in a room Plato's cave shadows on the wall paste is the texture of life

Hello you've reached

6082460182 please leave a message after the beep no name on the recorder don't want mad dad to find me *beep Pick up the phone* Tara's voice silence a gray matted sun with wisps of yellow mad dad's leather belt down down down stinging cutting pain *Please pick up* silence whish whish whish breathing through the mask holes *Darren went home sick Jody told me to tell you if you get up here right away everything'll be forgiven* whish whish whish *those were her words not mine please*

what will be forgiven the bed mad dad built the snake in his pocket mother's ring finger on the door white bone knuckle sheet scrubbing brown ringed blood stains cum crust the pasty gray sky Monet knew it best the way colors run drip fade into one another smeared eyeliner runs blue down the face of a river mother cries again mad dad's fists made her blue I hate myself for it *Jody's going to fire you if you don't come in* Tara pleads *beep* silence echoes through the big yolk colored house matches the stains in the sky I crawl into bed on four legs the other four plucked by mad dad I lie in bed mom told him about the permission slip she told him! who should I forgive him her me fuck you Jody forgiveness is a fist

Please

get up Tara says I feel bad for her wish I could *I can't* I say *Please come down stairs to eat* she says I shake my head no the sky presses dark against the windows

What else

can I get you Tara puts a plate with food outside my door I crouch beneath a window push the bottom of the blind away from the window *Another gray day* I ignore her question let the blind slap against the window *Are you okay* she says *sitting in there like that* I lean my cheek against the wall stare outside at the playground *You know* Tara says *maybe you could talk to Jody about your job* I say nothing the playground is empty *Could you at least get dressed* she says her voice sad *I don't think so* I say don't mean to scare her but I can't leave my room I can't talk to Jody I hate her I push the blind away from the window outside nothing moves

I don't care

about Jody the diner or anything else I soak in all that crusty gray paste moaning droning suicidal Mazzy Star makes blue waves in my room my thoughts my inner sight my room are twirling slashes of yellow gray blue the kind Van Gogh cut his ear off with anything outside my room is too much

Knock knock

Who's there I say softer than the music in the box music in the box! knock knock door is locked knock knock *Please let me in* Tara's voice *No* I say softer than the music watch my word slip under the door I can't move tied to the bottom of the ocean seaweed round my neck like a twisted umbilical cord *Let me in you're scaring me* I don't want to scare Tara but I can't care about anyone no one at all Patty is gone I never want to be close to anyone again *C'mon* the door knob rattles sun sets over the houses I never want to move again knock knock black bristled pine tops through the windows look like Minnesota I am confused for a second one second time on a tick tock clock where am I here or there ten or twenty five two nickels or five child or adult thinking patterns mix match mingle

knock knock *Who's there* I say *the headboard the headboard did it creepy crawly spider leg woman walking up my back the headboard the headboard!* my body stiffens jerks back arches thighs flex a snake crawls inside stiffens hardens pounds me into the headboard the wall pushed up against the bed board head cracked bang bang bang

My god what's going on Tara batters the door with her hands shoulder thud thud something passed me by but what was it I missed it A Wrinkle in Time now I know what it means time wrinkles like the folds in the brain memories slip in and out but they're always there somewhere Tara says *I'm going to call the police if you don't let me in* thud thud here or there back or forth up or down crawl to the door slip the latch the door knob hits my forehead pushes me over *What's going on* I fall onto the bed fall fall fall over and over fall forever caught in time the folds in my brain store the past fall in slow motion gray outlines in a photograph me falling falling falling

My god Tara cries puts her hand over her mouth *Don't tell* I whisper still falling but I don't know what she shouldn't tell falling whispering not knowing but knowing always knowing he raped us he raped Patty nickels spinning through the air like the basketballs I spun slow motion through the nets me that is me there on the bed ten slammed into the headboard this is me twenty five slammed into the wall by the ghost of my father gray outlines in a photograph taken off speed an in between place that captures motion lasts it forever

Red light

blue light *Hi Tara!* she walks alongside me her face is in mine the space between her teeth says *Hi* my head hurts stars explode red light blue light the stars shine tonight Frida's pointy ears in the window *The hall light's on!*

we're wasting money! mad dad will be mad! I whisper *Oh honey* Tara says hand on mouth crying eyes *Best friend* I stare at the stars scribbled in by black felt tip markers *negative space* I say *felt markers Oooo* Tara says a man in a white shirt with hair like Goldilocks puts his hand on my shoulder pushes me down *Relax* he says I ignore him don't like him *Get your hand off me!* I say *See the bump* Tara says points to my face *the door hit her on the head I don't think that made her this way* Goldilocks says his lip curls *Tara* I say *the light pointy Frida's ears Ooo* she says looks at Goldilocks then at me red light blue light I'm going in a car ambulance!

Goldilocks

lifts me into the red light blue light mouth of the car ambulance slides me in smooth and clean and metallic a cookie sheet of fish sticks going into the oven the story of Jonah I am the fish swallowed by a whale that likes its fish fried Goldi helps Tara climb in straps down my chest and thighs *Ready for lunch* I say to Tara smile at her *Ooo* she says she doesn't know I feel like fish sticks on a cookie sheet she thinks I've gone crazy inside an ambulance Goldi looks at me like I'm full of shit and I am! nickel plated shit Darren said adults have ten pounds of shit caked to the walls of their intestines by the time they're forty

Fields

play through my head in black and white slow motion it is beautiful Patty next to me low flat brick apartments baseball diamonds rough red sand laughter red cheeks on a wet day woods ponds parks my childhood revisited a film in my head I sway inside a whale in the sea a bus on a road side to side it turns corners jumps speed bumps like a horse giddyup! kicks its hind legs in the air I see it all in my head running like a movie screen I must be dying I thought I already died I've died a thousand million times chain link fences gas stations insurance companies *have five minutes stop in we'll drop your price by 25% guaranteed* the smooth roll of the whale the ambulance the bus leans to the left leans to the right Patty's hand on my thigh a rib in my arm I find peace in the mouth of a whale Patty finally at my side I should have died with her

Patty

I scream beat my fists against the hospital bed cold and stiff *Who's Patty* Tara says in the room with me 1950s style pink walls white ceiling gray tile floor *Shut off the light* I say *please it hurts my head* exploding lightning over a boggy marsh in North Dakota *oh please* I moan roll my head on the pillow shut my eyes *Patty* I miss her I miss her I miss her *the light the light* I say clang the metal bar along the side of the bed *turn it off please What is going on* a woman's voice says I don't open my eyes the light is too much even with them shut *Make it stop* I say *my head* I wrap my arm across my forehead cover my eyes keep out the light!

the light switch clicks the nurse leaves I have more than six senses to tell me the nurse is gone I see without my eyes I feel without my skin the bodies in the house with me mother father walk in walk out stand in the hallway stand in the hallway! I have the biggest ears in all the world the biggest ears in all the world! I hear footsteps drop a mile away a mile away! I hear footsteps leave a room walk down a hall padded over by carpet soft as mice pad pad pad mom's knuckles on the door pan frying chicken in the kitchen father's snake coiled in his pants breathing through the zipper sliding up the stairs between the gold velvet English wallpaper crowns I hear it coming all of it coming going staying creeping crawling padding listening in the hall mom listening in the hall! mom hears it all the panting moaning breathing whish whish sound out the mask hole keeping me safe mom keeping me safe with her bat mask sugar candy in the night mother listening in the hall with her white knuckles mice feet padding so no one hears her listening to mad dad snake man killing me in bed twisting seaweed sheets round my ankle chest arm sending me to the bottom of the freezing ocean water

> *Mom mice feet padding mom mice feet padding*
> *mom knew mice feet padding*
> *mom listened mice feet padding*
> *mom went to bed mice feet padding*
> *mom slept while he was in me*

the pain is bad! bad! bad! I have the words of a two year old knives cut through my brain knives cut through my brain! mom didn't love me snakes white knuckles on the door padding mice feet ow ow I cry like a baby like the first time he raped me pinned me to the ocean floor tied seaweed kelp round my body left me to bloat turn gray lose my eyes to hungry fish picking out my insides my insides! I cry owwww knives in my brain *Patty Patty* I moan Tara's hand holds mine *Who's Patty* she says she says I see Patty her long legs pony tail skinny Norwegian nose saggy jeans *Patty* I say again in a little girl's voice I see her standing by the bushes in front of her house I hear him clanking my bed she saved me from him she saved me from them! he hurt her because she loved me Patty shoots she scores I slap the stick on the basement floor flip out the orange puck I am not supposed to have or to feel love Patty loved me *Patty* I cry hard a baby's first rape terrible sadness floods my body washes away numbness fear apathy depression Patty loved me I loved her *Patty* I say the ceiling blurred above me *loved me* I blink hold Tara's hand cry hard for the baby I was for Patty wherever she is

I cry

hard tears cover the pillow I cry hard tears soak the mattress soggy salty water from the sea I cry hard for the baby I was for the baby I am a child's voice lives in my head celluloid looping a girl in the lawn alone hoping voiceover voicever! talk in a child's voice with a child's words with a child's thoughts I never grew up a permanent child developmently disabled the man who made me unmade me his obsession with my destruction tortures me a girl on permanent display *Patty!* I cry hard lights down low pink walls saltwater tears fill the room Tara floats away in her chair one hand on her knee *Hold on* she says I say nothing I keep my mouth closed but the sea escapes anyway the sea will kill us all *Hold on* she says reaches out across the gray tile an eddy swirls her away out the door down the hall *Tara* she is gone *Patty!* I cry hard my sorrow is the sea the fluid of my being salty tear licks since the first time his fingers twisted inside me a baby in a cradle rock a bye baby rock a bye baby I cry hard saltwater tears rise up pallbearers at a funeral carry my bed out the door down the hall where I join the others floating swimming moving in slow motion plastic daisies in vases bob on the surface like tiny buoys from the dining room all of us drowning together *Patty!* I cry hard she loved me Tara swirls out a window I cry hard killing the world with my sorrow I cry hard the hospital floats away its foundation set loose by saltwater tears I cry hard I kill my friends I kill the world

She

might have been seizuring a man says *possibly a severe migraine* his voice by my feet the biggest ears in all the world listen *or it may not be of physical origin* there's pressure on my chest the strap *Could it be meningitis* another man's voice meek subservient by my head *Doubtful* shoes tap tap tap *see how peaceful she is right now* his voice is by my left hand wiggles my leg I feel the kneecap move in its joint *almost like she died* the biggest ears in all the world don't need to be big they are small stay quiet eyes closed black lids listen to voices *run an eeg on her in the morning in the meantime get her out of here* rubber snaps peels *she's out of the woods* rubber snaps peels *nurse* footsteps come squishy suction cup sounds *throw these out for me* footsteps go tap tap tap military metallic

lights buzz above me I'm on a rollercoaster ride an IV bag on a stand clanking behind I feel nauseous tap tap tap plastic toes walk toward us *She's still out* suction cup shoes says slows down *Out cold huh* tap tap tap suction cup shoes pushes me further down the hall her breath has a stale gum minty smell she swings the stretcher in a circle *Here we are* she says flicks on the light rolls me against a wall it smells like rubbing alcohol I'm not sick I had flashbacks there's a ratcheting sound the small pops of machine gunfire I slit my eyes the nurse pulls the shades shut white blinds swing wildly through the room I shut them again I have to get out of here before they take more tests I don't have insurance the machine gun fire stops nurse suction cups across the room wraps something around my wrist the metal hook that holds the IV bag clatters near my head red lights jump in the cave of my eyes *There you go* she pats my arm pulls the blanket up to my chin *sleep tight* she flips off the light shuts the door I rest in the dark alone washed up on the shore listen to my breath listen to my breath watch the blue moonlight dance between the blinds swaying softly above the vents the blue moonlight walks across the wall and I hear *don't worry about being crazy don't care about mad dad or mom or the kids calling you freak dyke fag or the detox center or the oatmeal lady judge or Doctor Abramson or the rape in the sand don't care because your grandma loved you first Patty loved you second and nothing else matters Patty loved you you forgot about her yet you always remembered her Patty's disappearance was forgotten but not forgotten a thorn in your belly cutting you inside protecting your mind by stopping you from climbing the stem brushing the petal of the rose the lace of your breath in the air wet seal skin tree trunks red cheeks freedom real freedom if only for a short time a few years a few hours a few minutes at a time you knew what freedom was what love is tell yourself a prayer it goes like this: I am still alive*

I am still alive! here in a hospital room rubbing alcohol Clorox bleach off the sheets bangs blowing in the air conditioner I open my eyes look at the ceiling gray goosebumps in the sky I pull at the string around my head lift the mask off my face I have full vision now the antiseptic gray and white splotched goose egg speckled ceiling has a new texture now I know why I survived this is why I survived to see with eyes like this to belong in the world the one mad dad took from me when I was a baby a place that belongs to me I to it maybe might yes it does the blue moon dancing on the wall has a prayer for me: wish wish wish

Dizzy

I say *let's see you walk* she says a different nurse from the one last night her shoes are somewhere between the plastic tap tap tap of the second in command and the suction cup squeaking of the other nurse *I'm fine* I say *Not according to these notes* she taps a clipboard *I'm Catherine by the way Really I'm fine* I nod *Get up* she flips the covers back sits at the bottom of the bed *Come on* she pats the bed holds the clip board against her stomach *out* she says I swing my legs to the side knobby knees like pale green apples poking out under the hospital gown

Stand she says *I* I say *Come on* she says *I need to leave* I say the nurse puts down the clipboard *You can't leave if you can't walk* she squints at me adjusts her red glasses tucks a piece of her brown bob behind her ear *You have a point* I say *All right* she jumps off the bed *I want to test your balance* she stands in front of me grabs my hands *we need to figure out what happened last night* she bends her hair slips out from behind her ear *do you remember last night Sure* I say I don't want to admit I don't remember all of it she raises an eyebrow *Parts* I add I don't want to lie *Were you under the influence of drugs or alcohol* she says *No* I sit back *If you were tell me now before we go through all the testing I wasn't* I say the room spins a little *I can't do any testing I don't have insurance Nothing through your work* she says *I don't have a job* I shrug *Try standing* she braces her feet *stand up* I stand for a second sway like a tree in the wind sit down on the bed *All right* she says *it's a start stay there*

Catherine

walks in with a woman behind her *Hi* Catherine says *Hi* I say they stand next to my bed *This is Nicole* I nod Nicole has straight thin blonde hair past her shoulders a black blazer a pinched nose *She's a social worker* Catherine says rolls up one of her sleeves *she might be able to help you get insurance* Catherine looks at Nicole *Okay* Catherine says *Yes* Nicole says nods quick and fast she reminds me of a bird pecking at grain *I'll be back* Catherine waves walks out the door *Okay then* Nicole says produces a thin leather briefcase from the side of her leg *if you can give me some background information I can process a welfare application for you* her voice is high and chirpy my eyes widen *Welfare* I say *Possibly* she says *is that okay with you* Um outside the door I catch a glimpse of a bouquet with a pink Dumbo size ribbon wrapped around the vase *Health insurance is part of the package* her hand clicks a white and green pen *Would it cover the hospital* Nicole stops clicking the pen waves it at me *With a little bit of help from mister pen here* she clicks it one more time looks out the door then whispers *I can back date the application Oh* I say *that would be good* the words stick in my throat like peanut butter she perks up pulls out a clipboard from her briefcase attaches a piece of paper to it *Okay then let's get rolling*

Do you have a job
No
How long since you last worked
Five maybe six days
Have you looked for work since then
No
On what terms did you leave your previous job
I was fired
Why
I don't know
Come up with a reason
Insubordination
How much did you make
Five dollars an hour
Oh
What did you do
Cooked
How much do you have in savings
Nothing
Oh
Any assets cars property etcetera
No
Nothing
None
Address

1411 Jenifer Street Madison 53704
Sign here
I sign So And So in perfect cursive

  Nicole slides the clipboard in her briefcase holds the white and green pen
in her mouth shuffles papers in her lap *Okay then* she cocks her head lifts
one plucked eyebrow *I just might have a case for you it will take them a few
weeks to process your application but if they approve it* she points her pen
at me *and I think they will you'll receive two hundred dollars per month
with approximately one hundred dollars in food stamps plus Wisconsin
Care and oh yes you'll be eligible for job training should you decide to
pursue a new career Great* I say because I don't know what else to say
Excellent she shuffles her papers two more times stands up puts them in her
briefcase *the doctor will be with you soon* she pauses *have a great day* she
smiles at my feet under the blanket walks out

Eeg

  wires on my temples I ride fish stick style through a tube ratcheting in
the dark drilling holes in my head rubber hatchets in my knees tiny torture
wheels with teeth up the outside of my arm ouch ouch ouch down the inside
I feel nothing *Hmm* Doctor Jenkins slides his stool on wheels to the corner
desk scribbles slides back to me stares at my knees for a second wipes his
forehead with one hand then pops my ankle bone with the rubber hatchet
Umhum he pops the other one *umhum* I don't like men touching me my
body numbs I stare at a calendar next to the cupboard with a picture of a
brown lab puppy romping in a field of yellow flowers *Protect your family
from seasonal allergies talk to your doctor about Allergin today* I glaze my
eyes make the puppy's ears float in a sea of yellow jellyfish the doctor pops
my ankles again one right after the other like he's playing a xylophone
Could this be connected to allergies I say just to say something I'm nervous
so I say something dumb *What* he says rubs his chin then slides to the
corner scribbles *huh* he leans his elbow on the desk looks at me blankly like
he didn't realize someone was in the room with him *It says talk to your
doctor* I point to the calendar shrug *I'm just being stupid Oh right allergies*
he says runs his hand over his chin again shakes his head *no I don't think so*
  he hunches over the desk his back to me circles of dark sweat loop like
hoop earrings beneath his arm pits I pull my gown tight in the back suck in
my stomach *Can I* I say *Just one minute* he holds one finger up at me I cross
my ankles watch them move it's sort of amazing to live like this not feeling
my body watching it move on its own accord like someone else owns it like
it is someone else
  Okay he stands up shoots the stool across the room with one foot *we're
finished here* the stool crashes into the door one of his hands goes to his
chin he looks at the paper in his other hand *you can go back to your room*
he walks toward the door reaches to open it then looks back at me *if you*

need help call a nurse *When will you know* I say he turns the knob with the tips of his fingers swings it open his black loafers make no noise

Knock knock

Catherine says from the doorway *the doctor is here to see you* she steps into the room stands flat against the closet door Doctor Jenkins walks in *Thank you Catherine* he says head down I sit up dump the sun out of my lap *Okay* he places a manilla file on the silver wheeled tray that swings across the bed *I'll leave you two alone* Catherine pulls the door shut behind her Doctor Jenkins pulls up a chair sits down leafs through the file *This is a curious case* he keeps his eyes on the papers scratches his head *your symptoms match a number of pathologies but do not fully match any one pathology* he stops clears his throat *I realize this is a rather delicate question* he says and I think of the sun drifting across my belly and face Frida climbing in my lap the puff puff of her breath as she lay sleeping on my chest *I hope you don't mind me asking* I look at him I don't know what he's talking about either he didn't finish his thought or I missed something *Um* I say to buy time he looks out the window tries to smile but his lips don't move enough freeze half way between a smile and a straight line I clear my throat follow his gaze into the parking lot where two stories below a yellow sports car backs out of a stall Doctor Jenkins crosses his arms watches the car drive off to the right cranes his head as the car drives out of our view clears his throat again turns toward me *I don't mean to imply anything negative* he says *you have very real physical symptoms but sometimes psychological difficulties can contribute to or exacerbate pre existing physical problems* I catch my breath look out into the parking lot cars lined up like match boxes I flash to Jimmy and Patty and me building freeways and ramps with black construction paper and boxes drag racing blue red yellow cars with white numbers 69! 58! 11! on their sides across the gray linoleum kitchen floor Doctor Jenkins clears his throat my eyes sting from the longing I want to be ten again on my knees on their dirty kitchen floor speed racing cars like nothing else in all the world matters nothing else in all the world! I try to keep from crying but I can't *Sorry* I say drop my head squeeze my eyes shut I won't tell him

Rent

is due in two days Tara sounds like a punctured rubber toy *scuse me my I know* I say *your asthma What did they say* she heaves *They say I'm going to get on welfare they're waiting for more test results* I watch Wheel of Fortune on mute drop the phone's mouthpiece to my chin cough *In two days* Tara wheezes *You sound awful* I watch the primary color wheel spin until it becomes a blurring red blue yellow circle *You're the one in the hospital* she says *How was work* I say Pat Sajak announces the contestants a man and two women clapping and smiling Pat waves his perfectly white teeth cheeks and forehead are like rubber *Sucks* Tara says stops catches her breath *what about rent Well* I say concentrating on the first contestant she spins the wheel it goes around twice finally lands on $200 *I have something in the bank I don't know how much is in there maybe enough for the rent maybe not* the woman guesses the letter S in a four word phrase two squares light up she smiles claps *Jody gave me your last check today do you want me to open it Sure* I say the woman spins again *One thirteen* she says *and twenty nine cents There you go* I say *no problems I'll have enough left over for a pack of gum* I'm sick of bouncing checks which is probably what my rent check will do the woman spins again Vanna claps stupidly in her high heels and diamond studded gown the wheel lands on $350 the woman guesses T three T's light up Pat nods the woman places the palms of her hands on the edge of the podium leans forward stares intently at the puzzle spins again my philosophy is there's no need to balance your checkbook if you don't have any money but I don't tell Tara my check might bounce she might stop breathing *Hello* Tara says *anyone home Not me* I say *Okay* she says *I have to mail the rent tomorrow when are you coming home Tomorrow* I say the woman gets free vowels guesses I two I's light up *TV is a lot more interesting when the sound is off* I say *Huh* Tara says *Go ahead and write out my check they never look at the signatures anyway One more thing* she says *I put a sign up for a roommate at A Room and the co op* the woman waves to the camera grips the side of the podium jumps up and down Pat says something to her she calms down raises one finger in the air leans over spins *What room is she going to stay in* I watch the wheel spin into a pinwheel feel dizzy *no one will pay for the small room* Tara coughs *You said you would stay in there remember* the wheel stops on $1,000 the woman doesn't smile she stares at the puzzle wrinkles her forehead then says something Vanna smiles flips over an F *Vanna White has a shitty life don't you think What* Tara says *Vanna White* I say *what a horrible name* I watch the woman frown chew on her lip *I don't know* Tara says *she's got a lot of money And an easy job* I say *but I still wouldn't want to be her I suppose* Tara says *I really haven't thought about it She's like a doll* I say *Uh huh* Tara says *do you remember saying you'd move into the small room Well* I say *If you couldn't make rent* she wheezes *Um* I say the camera flashes to the other woman contestant *I didn't really mean it when I said it You said you would* Tara's mad I am stupid for being in the hospital for not having a job for maybe being on welfare *I suppose I have to* I say Pat is on TV he's talking fast nodding up and down laughing *All right* Tara says *All right* I say *is that all Yeah* she says *I'll have to pay less since the room is small Uh huh* Tara says *See you tomorrow then* I say *Yeah* she wheezes

Pat laughs

Vanna laughs the big nosed middle contestant laughs a commercial for Ivory soap dashes manically for thirty seconds then one for the Honda Accord then one for Crest I leave the mute on wonder if something is really wrong with me or if it was just the flashbacks what will my therapist say Pat's face flashes across the screen Wheel of Fortune more like the rack I think as the camera pans the three contestants all clapping and smiling the woman solving the puzzle stops clapping nods Pat is saying something to her off camera she says something the puzzle board lights up Vanna hurries to turn the squares over and I flash to my mother hurrying to pick up a napkin or spoon before my dad clocked her *Finish* is the first word *What* is the second word *You* is the third word *Start* is the fourth *finish what you start* this show is so stupid what sort of saying is that

the match box cars in the parking lot the sun reflecting off the lines of windshields the woman jumping clasping her hands in front of her $2,450 flashes across the screen shit I think if I had that much money I could pay rent for a whole year a car pulls out of a parking spot its windshield catches the sun full on reflects a blinding flash off the top of the metal casing around the window into my room damn it occurs to me I have to finish my degree I can't do nothing with my life forever the matchbox car turns the glare disappears as suddenly as it came the car drives off a boxy maroon family car I flick off the TV with one push of a red button that little girl I used to be knobby bruised knees on the kitchen floor zinging cars down the freeway into the wall wouldn't want me to be nothing

Doctor Jenkins

puts his foot on the bed then jerks it off wipes the place where his shoe was *Excuse me* he sits down *we got your test results from this morning and* he flips through the chart *Wheel of Fortune hotel rooms provided by Hyatt Regency* scrolls down the TV screen *Well* Doctor Jenkins says places a yellow pencil beneath his nose above his lip then taps it on the file in his hands *it's puzzling your eeg results show a possible series of small seizures however it's inconclusive* I half listen to him half watch the TV *on site snacks provided by Frito Lay* I wonder if anyone actually uses any of the products advertised on Wheel of Fortune do they really bring in revenue a Clairol hair coloring ad bursts on the screen Doctor Jenkins's crooked part jags to the left his tie is loose *One moment* he flips through the file his tie flies into the air he taps the pencil on his thigh I'm numb to him and his report I don't have seizures that's stupid I just had some flashbacks a woman tosses her honey auburn hair on the TV it freezes midair splayed out across her face like a bronzed baby shoe the ad ends Brady Bunch faces Carol Mike Cindy Bobby Peter Greg Jan Marcia Alice appear in squares each head smiling turning to the left or right Doctor Jenkins closes the file sets it on the bed *This is a real puzzler* he says *I'm going to send your chart away to a specialist at the university in the meantime I suggest you take medication for seizures and follow up with your regular doctor* the faces disappear it cuts to an ad for McDonald's *you're the coffee in my cream* flies through my head he pauses

Huh I say caught between the thought and his words *Your regular doctor should set you up with a specialist or you can continue to see me but because I only work out of the hospital it's significantly more expensive Uh*

huh I watch a tow head blonde boy smile shove a hamburger into the screen *my girl you are Indian no matter what anyone says* I hear my gramma's voice like a tape recording *Sure* I say to Doctor Jenkins I don't want to hear what he has to say but I don't want him to know I don't care what he says I don't want to get locked up *Are you getting this* Doctor Jenkins says the boy takes a huge bite out of his hamburger grins into the camera with his mouth full *Sure* I smile I don't tell him I don't have a doctor

* * *

Pay

   you next week for therapy this week I say into the phone Tara folds chocolate chips into a bowl of raw eggs n flour n a pinch of salt *sort of like Popeye's friend what was his name the fat one with the bowler Uh huh* Julia says *The one who always wants to pay Tuesday for a hamburger today* Tara picks up the bowl with one arm mashes the dough with a long wooden spoon I reach over her head slap shut a cupboard door it bounces open again *I really will pay you* I say and I mean it of course I'm not a thief Tara spoons out chunks of raw cookie dough drops them on a cookie sheet *That won't work* Julia pauses I've been seeing her for over three years she's the only person in my life right now that I've known for more than two years Tara licks the spoon then flips back her wavy bangs crinkles her nose she doesn't know I'm watching her my stomach turns from the raw eggy dough from Julia saying I can't see her unless I have the money up front *I swear* I say *it'd only be two weeks no more You need to pay each time you see me But what am I going to do* I panic forget about Tara lean my head against the bottom of the cupboard close my eyes this can't be happening *Please* I say can't believe I'm begging *I'm on Wisconsin Care they'll start paying you in a few weeks I'm sorry* Julia says but she doesn't sound sorry *I don't take Wisconsin Care You don't take it* I press my forehead into the sharp bottom edge of the cupboard *what do you mean you don't take it it's insurance* Tara slides the cookie sheet into the oven *It's too much paperwork* she pauses as if she's gauging whether she should continue *I frankly don't want to bother with it* I am going to cry *But* I say hold my breath don't cry! *I won't be able to see you anymore I know* she says *I'm sorry* but she doesn't sound sorry not at all Tara slams the bowl of cookie dough on the counter the sound shoots through my brain *Julia* I am crying *I have to be able to see you I'm sorry* she says *there isn't anything I can do* Tara slams the bowl again I flinch what does she mean there isn't anything she can do Tara jabs at the dough with the spoon *I need to go now* Julia says I don't know what to say or do how can she leave me when I'm on welfare just out of the hospital having such bad flashbacks that I can't remember entire nights *I could do the paperwork* I shoot out I know it's a stupid thing to say as soon as it comes out of my mouth but I am desperate *No* she says *I need to go* setting firm boundaries I think I stare at the cherry wood cupboard she is setting good boundaries *Goodbye* I say but I'm in shock I stare at the curving dark stained lines in the cupboard *Goodbye* she says *I'm here if you get the money to see me again* I say nothing there is a small metallic click then the phone buzzes in my ear the wood grain splays out across the kitchen like snakes coming out of my father's mouth

Oh my god

I sit down *What's wrong* Tara says sobs burst out my mouth I flash to gasping for air while my head is held under a bathtub faucet *No* I cry I wanted to tell Julia about Patty maybe she could have helped me find her I have to find Patty! I have to find Patty! Tara shuts the oven door *Oh honey* she makes circles on my back *Patty* I slide off the chair under the table curl up shut my eyes Tara moves the chair sits on the floor with me *You're safe now* she says I am ten *Patty* I open my eyes the uneven brown stain on the underside of the table looks like a wart I stare blink I am ten *Tara* I say my head against a table leg *Julia won't see me anymore Oh* Tara says looks surprised *is that who you were talking to* I nod my head I am five or ten or twenty five or all of the above at the same time I want a mother who doesn't leave me who protects who me loves me I cry choke on cold water blasted down my throat fifteen years ago press my face into the cold dirty kitchen floor

* * *

Welfare

office down the hall to the right a woman in her fifties with a black bouffant points to the right then looks me up and down over the top of her cat glasses *Trash* is written across her face in black marker *Uh huh* I say *thanks* my hands in my pockets I walk down the yellowed hallway past framed black and white pictures of Patricia Carraway state employee of the month Clarice Hyde social worker of the month Jack Daniels founder of the Institute for the Study of Poverty Jack Daniels I smile stop at a water fountain a cool stream of water explodes in my mouth I hold the water in my cheeks stand up swallow I don't want to go to this meeting I wish Tara had come with me but she's out looking for another job two women one white one black in business suits walk past me their shoes pop against the floor I take a deep breath turn right into the Wisconsin Welfare Office cubicles against the wall on the right a wide open floor with three chest high tables stacked with papers a foot high plastic garbage at the base of each table no windows posters on the far wall that say *minimum wage is $3.75 know your rights* and to the left people sitting in chairs against the wall others in a line behind a sign that says *Wait here* some stand with their arms crossed others lean on one leg or the other black white brown mostly women in jeans t-shirts tennis shoes one man in a cowboy hat welcome to welfare I think and take my place in the back of the line

an hour later my name is called I walk toward the third cubicle from the right where a woman is waving at me I wave back realize I shouldn't have done that drop my hand feel stupid in front of all the people I'm new to this I have to learn the rules of those on welfare

So And So a woman calls me over to her cubicle *Hi* I say to the woman she has glassy blue eyes like marbles *Have a seat* she cuffs the sleeves of her black blazer narrows her eyes looks at me like I came to her home knocked on her door tried to sell her a piece of swampland in Florida *What can I help you with* she looks over my shoulder pictures of children teenagers old people a yellow lab and a calendar pinned eye level decorate her cubicle the walls remind me of my childhood when my mom took me to her work at the school *I have a letter* I shift my hips so I can pull it out of my back pocket she clears her throat I lean on the cubicle wall it tips into the other employee's cubicle the calendar swinging on its nail reveals an off white patch unstained from smoke dirt sun *Shit* I say then regret having sworn around these people who act like we're trash she jumps up grabs the wall divider *Sorry* she says to someone on the other side *Okay* the other person says I can't tell if it's a man or a woman *Sorry* I say place the letter folded inside the ripped open envelope on the table she sits down the cuff on her black blazer unrolled she cuffs it again slides her chair forward opens the letter *Let's see* she says *I presume you're the claimant Yes* I say she flicks her eyelashes back to the paper sets it down licks the pad of her pointer finger swivels in her chair opens the filing cabinet behind her slips out a piece of paper turns to me *I have a few questions to ask you* she says

Single
Yes she checks a box
Ever been married
No she checks a box
Children
No she checks a box
Infectious diseases
No she checks a box
Do you reside at 1411 Jenifer Street in the city of Madison in the state of Wisconsin
Yes she checks a box
Any others live with you specifically a boyfriend
Not a chance
She looks at me Just stick to yes and no answers I don't have time for this
Is there a boyfriend living with you
No she checks a box
How many live with you
One she checks a box
Name
Tara she scribbles
Age
23 she scribbles

Occupation
Waitress she scribbles
Does she contribute to your household expenses
Yes she checks a box
How much
Half
Exactly half
Yes ma'am she scribbles
Do you receive any help from outside sources including parents other relatives bonds real estate
I laugh she sets her lips stares at her pen
No she checks a box

she pulls a calculator from under her desk taps in numbers *You will receive 212 dollars and thirteen cents on the first of every month* she looks at the line behind me *and one hundred dollars in food stamps* she pulls out a manila envelope from under the desk puts my letter in it *a packet will be sent to your home in three to five business days read it carefully and be sure to look for work every week or your benefits will be cut off immediately* she looks at a post it taped to the desk *case closed* she says *Smith Reginald next* I stand up she stares at nothing I don't think she remembers that I was just in her chair I walk out the door feel dizzy from the way she treated me I am now officially on welfare I never imagined this for myself I walk past Jack Daniel's face what is it his institute studies

Cricket

will be here any minute Tara gushes water in the kitchen I cross my legs on the papasan chair *What are you doing* I say over the waterfall *Nothing* the water stops *just getting rid of that spaghetti pan It's okay* I twirl a thick white thread hanging off the bottom of my jeans *it's just one pan* Tara walks into the dining room stands behind me I see her reflection in the living room windows hands on hips *We need a roommate* she says her voice high *You're right* I say she reminds me of my mom when she's nervous *just don't get stressed That must be her* she stands up on her tiptoes I sit up a little in the chair see a big woman built like a truck curly whitish blonde hair to her shoulders

Knock knock
I half expect Tara to say who's there or anyone home or the headboard did it is this what therapists mean when they say abuse causes intrusive thoughts Tara pulls on the bottom of her lavender t-shirt she is self conscious when she meets new people I fall into the deep chair Tara yanks the front door *Cricket* she says in her little kid nervous voice *Hey that's me* the woman booms into the foyer *you Tara Yes* Tara says steps aside they shake hands *Nice place* Cricket looks up the stairs down the hall to the kitchen then into the living room *Well this is it* Tara stands on her tip toes

swirls around toward me *Hey* Cricket waves at me *Hey* I half wave pull my feet inside the chair fold them under me I'm not thrilled about moving into the small room Tara tours Cricket through the house

Nice wood Cricket says from the dining room *oak Yeah I suppose* I say Tara smiles I'll bet she'll have a crush on Cricket *I'm a carpenter* Cricket walks toward me *what about you* I want to say I'm a loser but instead I say *I'm temporarily unemployed Uh huh* she holds out her hand looks into my eyes makes me feel like slipping out of my body and running out the back door I see she won't stop staring until I shake her hand so I do *Nice to meet you* she says *Uh huh* I say she sits down on the couch in front of the windows Tara leans against the woodwork that separates the dining room from the living room *So tell me about yourselves* Cricket says I already don't like her don't like people getting into my business *Well* Tara laughs *there's not much to tell Oh come on* Cricket says *where are you from Janesville* Tara says *what about you Upstate New York* Cricket looks at me expectantly I say nothing hate talking about my past Tara says *How long have you been here* Cricket crosses her cowboy boots at the ankles *A month* she's going to take the room I can tell *You're both dykes right* Cricket looks at us Tara says *Yes* Cricket says *I'm a carpenter in McFarland up at six home at eight it's a forty five minute drive each way I'm not home much Oh* Tara says *I've always thought it would be neat to be a carpenter* I look at Tara I never knew that *It's a great job* Cricket says *I'm out to everyone came out the first day no one cares* she wiggles her boots *how much is rent Two twenty plus one third of the utilities* Tara leans from one foot to the other *I can handle that* Cricket smiles reaches into her back jean pocket pulls out a worn leather men's wallet *What do you want for a deposit Ah* Tara stops leaning looks at me I shrug *Oh* Cricket says *do you need to talk about it* Tara looks at her then me *Fine* I say I'm mad I don't want to move into the small room *it's fine with me Yeah* Tara says claps her hands *when can you move in*

A turtle's

shell the size of a manhole lumbers down the river Tara is right it's a stream trickles green goop into the lake I don't move the turtle sees me head held high claws clamor from rock to rock then it plunges in glides to the next rock pile unafraid a bicycler rolls over the stone bridge clomp clomp tromp tromp the turtle is not afraid of trolls something inside me shifts by the little river

Moving day

Cricket yells up the stairs I drag my mattress out of my old room drop it into the small room it just fits I open the window dead flies curled in the corners I kneel down press my lips nose mouth against the window Cricket slams the truck door I make a circle with my breath on the glass watch her strut around her truck a beat up old white thing with sea blue side panels rust patches the size of birds' nests scattered across the body just like the kind of truck my father used to drive that can't be good the bed is packed full of boxes upside down chairs their legs sticking straight into the sunny day Cricket swings up onto the back gate one foot on the gate the other in the bed she tugs at the leg of a lime green chair

These yours

Cricket says holds out crumpled papers *No* I say *Are you sure* she says opens them *I found them in the closet* I am annoyed *No* I say and then I see they are the scribblings I took to my therapist I am embarrassed *oh yes* I say *I always wanted to be an artist* and I laugh to make myself seem not so crazy because who would believe such scribblings would be done by someone with artistic talents *Really cool* Crickets says and then I feel terrible for lying *Uh yeah* I grab them from her fold them *What else have you done* Cricket says *Nothing* I say *All right* she says turns my doorknob back and forth waiting for me to say something but what can I say I haven't done art since elementary school *I see* she says *well back to unpacking Uh huh* I say and stuff the scribblings under my mattress

See smell taste

a mattress in my face sweaty cotton fabric bed sheets slipped off face first instantly transported to another place time space me on my face knees ass in the air his arm lynched round my waist fingertips pressed into the back of my head pain pain unfuckingbearable pain the ass becomes a hole black and big as the night sky circling spinning breaking into itself infinite pain shooting stars riding the night into my brain electricity shot through my veins sharp knife white cold pain naked thrown against cold unbending sheetrock varnished oak headboard huff puff big bad wolf neck head back smacks against the headboard body goes limp mind leaves wanders away into the night a homeless drunk on the streets leaving a shell a fake thing a doll's body pliable rubbery cold blank eyes drunk mind a hole of sheer raw cutting pain

I shiver

in the heat wrap up in the pink flowered sheet in my old room Cricket whistles a song I don't recognize moving even one room over brings up shit I curl into a ball wrap my arms around my shoulders try to save me from him

a bang in Cricket's room *Sorry* Cricket yells I go back to disliking her it won't be so difficult *Hey* she says *you in there* I say nothing want her to go away the door squeaks *Oh* she says *what's wrong Nothing* I say *You in pain Yes* I say clenched teeth nothing in the world but this pain in my head *Headache* she shuffles her boots on the dusty floor *Yeah* the word barely comes out of my mouth *Sit up* she says *I'll rub it away* I hate the word rub it reminds me of my father I don't move *Seriously* she says *I used to do massage back in New York I bet it's muscle tension from moving* shots of white cold pain lash into my brain like the tip of a whip *Sit up* she grabs my shoulders I sit up eyes closed I'm embarrassed I don't want her to touch me but I do want her to touch me her hands are large strong rough they dig into my neck shoulders run through my hair *Relax* she says it scares me that her touch feels so good that I don't know her that she's this close to me I drop my head she pushes into the base of my neck follows the muscles to my skull

The whir

of a fan a glimmer of moonlight thoughts of my neighbors acting under influence of million year old light I lie awake in bed trapped in a room but I am not being hurt the sheet billows a car drives by Tara sneezes inconsequential acts connect us like the mass of tangled roots of grass spread out from yard to yard tiny white stitched threads I drift off on a slow wave of thought I feel held saved part of something bigger than myself something that undermines the terror of my past it is simple I am alive

I meet Patty

and Frida under tall trees near a white domed building it is Saint Paul it is not Saint Paul another land time space where we talk but I don't know what we say I watch from far away I talk with Patty in my body she in hers an adult now how did she grow up where did she get her body where has she been all these years the person in the body knows but I do not Frida runs next to us her fat belly swinging from side to side she chirps the way some cats do the kind of cats that spend too much time with humans I worry about her loose in the grass bird wings flutter from tree to tree the capitol shines tall and bright over us all where are we I wonder it's as if I am looking through the eyes of a bird at myself below we get in a car drive between parked cars smash into the back of a Blue Monte Carlo Patty I say jump out I am afraid she will leave or be taken from me Frida chirps between my feet now Patty stands in grass trees in her hair birds on her lips Patty I say again she is smiling looking at me with love her beautiful red cheeks Patty I say again pat her back you don't seem to know you died she laughs rapid fire staccato bends over laughing harder faster she stands up looks into my eyes You died I say again but here it doesn't seem to matter

TV

I say at the dining room table eating Quaker Instant Apple Flavored Oatmeal *Yeah* Cricket says from the living room she sets a television on a black stand across from the couch and then stretches in matching red shorts tank top and biking shoes *Just bringing you into the twenty first century No thanks* I say *I'm happy right where I'm at* I dip my spoon into the oatmeal mush dig around for a rehydrated apple chunk *I hate TV* which isn't entirely true I find an apple chunk cut it in half I have to stop saying negative things when I'm nervous *Oh* Cricket says plugs the TV in flips it on the Price Is Right fills up the house clapping cheering Bob Barker's disembodied voice calling out *C'mon on down you're* Cricket turns off the

TV *Most of the time it's junk* she says I feel guilty I don't mean to be that harsh I push the oatmeal bowl toward the center of the table *Yuck* I say *I hate oatmeal Then why do you eat it* Cricket stands next to the TV hands on hips I say nothing I don't like people I know in my space much less someone I don't know I cross my arms stare at the oatmeal wonder what I'm going to do with the day now that I don't work or have therapy

Cricket's shoes click as she walks into the kitchen I feel like an obstinate five year old left at the table for not eating her peas the porch door slams letters slide through the slot into the house then the porch door slams again Cricket clicks to the porch then to me hands me my welfare check from the state *Nothing for me* she says smiles I stuff the envelope into my back pocket *Are you on welfare* she points at my waist *Uh* I say I feel my face turn red *loser* floats through my head *My ex was on it for awhile* Oh I say *No big deal* she clicks over to the stove her calf muscles rise up each time she takes a step *Something's wrong with me* I blurt out in a little kid voice then stop embarrassed *How so* Cricket turns cocks an eyebrow *I don't know* I can't believe I'm telling her this I pull out the envelope tap it against my leg *they think I might have seizures brought on by migraines Like last night* Cricket says I nod look at the envelope *State of Wisconsin* written in the upper left hand corner

Paper and pastels

Cricket sets a brown paper bag on the kitchen table *two bucks at a garage sale on my bike route* I hold up the pad and chalk *Really* I say I'm not used to people doing nice things for me Cricket clicks across the kitchen floor *I can't wait to see what you draw* she says *I want to know more about you* fright and fear and longing stir inside all different colors

* * *

Clunk

dropped in a hole chewed off white ham hock bone n my dog's bones dead last year n mother's bones dying in the kitchen of fat skin white knuckle bones on the door yelling at me

I dig n dig n dig n dig like I'm digging to China looking for buried life I dig n dig n dig through lacelike Zinnia Petunia Morning Glory roots I dig n dig n dig through ingrown weeds Kentucky Blue Grass White Pine twisted Cypress Cedar Jackpine roots I dig n dig n dig through dirt sand layers of rock ice pebbles looking for bone art I dig n dig n dig like my life depends on it

I dig n dig n dig until I find my own bone art in a hole under my bed I find my bone art in a hole under my bed! where I buried it to stay alive! to stay alive!

but it is not enough n so I dig n dig n dig some more til I am sweaty n tired n can't see the sky at all n so I dig n dig n dig on my way to China plink plunk pink punk I hit a rock n find a handle to a door n I yank until it creaks open n I see my past still alive buried deep n I watch for a minute

devil dog man n I will use what he did n what I know to make art to tell! to
tell! to live! to live!

* * *

Shit

I say three men just fell through the roof of a shed trying to catch a goat
that had climbed up on the roof on a rerun of America's Funniest Home
Movies Tara laughs until she cries I snort Coke out my nose *Oh my god*
Tara points at me the credits roll I grab a napkin *I love to see men get their
asses kicked* she says *Wisconsin Live* flashes across the screen followed by
four puppet faced reporters perfect white skin teeth hair smiles *Wisconsin's
only news source Time for popcorn* Tara jumps up runs into the kitchen *this
is fun we should have got a TV a long time ago I don't know* I pull the wet
part of my shirt off my chest and belly *maybe sometimes things happen for
a reason* moments like these take my mind off poverty rape *or maybe we
make reason out of the world* I say to myself the advertisements end *what
do you think about coincidences* I say over the corn smacking *Huh* Tara
pokes her head out of the kitchen *are you getting philosophical about
whether we should have a TV Top news story* appears on the screen in red
Pedophilia group to lobby at state capitol Oh my god I say *look* I point at
the TV the newscaster says *Good evening the speaker for a group calling
itself* Tara runs into the living room the corn pops the newscaster says *Live
from the state capitol* behind her on the steps of the capitol a white man in a
black suit stands behind a podium with brightly colored microphone heads
popping from the podium like tulips *Men who practice sexual relations with
those younger than themselves are discriminated against What* we scream
*ignorance and injustice directed toward cross generational relationships
must end on behalf of the group Lotus I have filed a suit against the state of
Wisconsin regarding their legal age of sexual consent laws Oh my god* Tara
yells the corn stops popping we stare at the TV the director of the Dane
County Rape Crisis Center appears on the screen says *We hope to work
with all involved to clarify the laws* the newscaster nods *What* I say *that's
what the rape crisis has to say You know where their money comes from*
Tara says *Channel ten live from the state capitol back to you Phil Fuckers* I
say *what the hell is up with this bullshit language practicing sexual relations
cross generational clarify I can't stand it they rape us kill us leave us for
dead we live in this fucking shit every day is a struggle and now they have
the nerve to rub our faces in it* I say *fucking bullshit middle class language*
the popcorn is burning the smoke drifts out into the dining room *Try using
words like rape incest mindfuck screwed for life* a cloud of gray smoke
hovers in the kitchen

My hand

runs along the smooth wooden hall railing Tara opened all the doors to
air out the house I remember long dark curly haired Dana on the steps the
sun the crowd chanting *2468* a smooth steel railing under my hand *Tara* I

run down the stairs into the kitchen *Tara What* she says her outline on the back step the red tip of her cigarette the only point of light in the dark night *Pissed Women* I push through the screen door *let's do Pissed Women* she doesn't say anything *Let's do it for real* I say *Okay* she says *No bullshit language* I say *Okay* Tara drags her cigarette through the dark night

Hey woman

Cricket says *Hey* I say from the kitchen table don't look up from drawing the logo for Pissed Women the upper body of a woman her fist in the air holding a woman's symbol like a club Cricket shuts the front door behind her tosses her keys on the floor *Where's Tara* she says out of the corner of my eye I watch her slip off her boots one hand on the railing for balance *At the store buying snacks* I concentrate on the nose of the woman erase one of the nostrils *the popcorn burned* I wave my pencil in the air the house still smells of smoke *I wondered* Cricket says walks into the kitchen digs in the refrigerator I get the nose right Cricket sits down next to me *Can I see* I shrug my shoulders a shy four year old slide it toward her *Wow* she peels off a string of cheese *that's good I'm going to turn this into a stencil* I say *Nice* she says and grins

In

the quiet of the basement in a chair at a wobbly kitchen table left by a previous tenant with a white sheet of drawing paper spread out over the brown varnish I shift my weight knock my knee against one of the heavy wooden legs jostle the pastels lined up in their box clean pure colors squared off at the ends it is absolutely still everywhere inside and out the bikes lawn mower lined up against the cement wall by the stairs the oil tank in the far corner I blur the colors aquamarine blue mint green dark dusk blue blood red honey orange daisy yellow peach brown stark white hole in the sky black run my fingertips over each pastel a different finger touches each one I don't want to mix up the colors put a blue streak over the white mix the honey orange with the blood red I want them to be pure unsullied themselves

dusty light filters through a mess of cobwebs I don't know what to draw the door bell rings a faint chime lingers in the basement Cricket said she couldn't wait to see what I draw I look at the oil tank its legs screwed to a wooden platform remember the cold no heat in the house! mom flashes into my head I mark two quick dusk blue parallel lines running vertical down the paper close them at the bottom dash two small circles n two jelly bean nostrils the outline of a face a cold blue face my face

I get lost in the colors honey orange swirls across the page from top to bottom a black stripe down the middle of my face the eyebrows are cantaloupe rinds tiny aquamarine crescent cuts dash along the side of the face fall off at the chin as if someone took a knife cut away at flesh the mouth is a small round charcoal hole a daisy yellow line outlines a cheek bone a white spiral drops off an earlobe time space sound the basement disappear *So And So! So And So!* orange leather spinning on a rim I become the colors they become me

Cricket clomps

stops drops down the stairs she's coming into the basement! I draw a line up the side of the face Cricket's boots speed up *Hey* she says *I saw your keys I thought you were home Hey* I say fill in part of the chin *what're you doing* she scuffs across the concrete floor *Nothing* I say I'm not sure I want her to see my drawing *Wow* she says I feel nothing *Wow* she says again *that's beautiful*

From my mattress

the moon is a ripe peach on the other side of the street big as a house it is the belly of a pregnant woman I could reach out and feel the heartbeat I lace my fingers under the back of my head feel the bumps ridges craters of my skull beautiful is not me I am ugly a dirty dyke fag freak I cross my ankles one of my feet pokes up picks the sheet up like a tent like when Patty and I camped out in her basement Cricket lies in the room next to me so close *beautiful* I uncross my ankles the sheet drapes over my breasts belly thighs *beautiful* I consider it

I wake

mad dad in my dreams! 2 48 am clouds cover the moon mad dad in my dreams! I twist onto my stomach my ass vagina one burning itching black hole razor bits of flesh missing mad dad in my dreams! pounding on the bathroom door bam bam bam where's mom save me blood in the toilet red strings swirl make finger paint patterns like the kids at school mad dad in my dreams!

bam bam bam my knees hang over the end of the toilet toes pressed in the pink carpet silver doorknob wiggles he's going to break in kill me mad dad in my dreams! I twist on the bed want to scream bits of blood and flesh drop out my mouth the pearls of my childhood mad dad in my dreams!

bam bam bam a body twitching on a bed bam bam bam it was night he raped me I ran into the bathroom locked myself in 6 or 7 I see the child me through a fog knobby knees bloody hand print on the porcelain sink next to my face I lift up out of the twitching small animal body on the bed that was the night I let go of any thought of god

beautiful I did something beautiful I who was once a bleeding girl on a toilet her legs numb from the knees down mad dad bamming the door a disappeared mom a disappeared moon a disappeared god I lift up above the girl *I'm here* I say she reaches toward me dark freckles across her nose and cheeks *I'm here baby* hold her kick down the bathroom door kick down mad dad walk over him down the stairs to the front door the one China Doll Girl ran out so long ago or yesterday just yesterday!

I carry her the girl me to the small room head against my shoulder wrap her in a blanket hold her *Shh baby shh* she makes no sound doesn't move shuts her eyes *shh baby shh* rock her in my arms *no more bleeding*

Running water

in the bathroom sink 5 51 am pink streaked sky Tara's washing for work the freckle face girl is gone I am glad to not be going to the diner glad that Cricket is one room over but there's something else the water stops Tara walks downstairs *Bye* I say but she doesn't hear me I feel something I haven't felt in a long time

the front door slams the ceiling is a soft gray wash above me I listen to my breath watch the clouds unfurl turning a gray early morning into a glorious pink magnolia sky *listen to my breath listen to my breath listen to my breath* I stand up step on my pillow open the small cabinet above my head run my fingers across the spines of my books stacked in the cupboard until I find the short fat paperback I bought at A Room I slide it out this is my religion I feel something I haven't felt in a long time but what is it I flip past the inscription past the acknowledgments past the index to chapter one "bed" *I was nine when the difficulties began with my father*

I leave my world go to Melanie Cohen's world that was so much like mine but so different too she grew up poor in Boston an Italian Jew her father beat her raped her starting when she was nine she fought back her mom told her to keep quiet said she'd hurt the family if she told the girl ran away at fifteen lived on the streets sex for food slept with boys girls then when she was in her twenties she gave up men she gave up men!

I shut the book on page 102 it's a full morning Frida's curled against my hip time went along without me it is quiet I have nothing to do nowhere to be no one to answer to and I realize I am not afraid I don't care about being in the small room I don't care about being broke I don't care about anything but reading drawing writing the way I used to like to draw scribbling in the margins up late at night under the covers hiding them beneath the mattress under the corner of the carpeting in a shoe box in the closet under the pale pink tissue suddenly I know

Meander

down Jenifer to Willy looking for something but what reach the little river dew on the grass and stone bridge bits of water diamonds I close my eyes my sadness is peaceful the river sings its songs

* * *

The woman

behind the desk clears her throat *Well* she says *do you have any experience working with computers Ah* I roll my eyes settle on the Sears sign behind her head *no* I hunch my shoulders *Okay have you done customer service in the past Umm* I rub my eyes stare at the floor watch her out of the corner of my eye *nope sure haven't* she turns my resume over I think I've sealed the deal who looks on the other side of a resume except someone who's rattled I stare at the rounded edge of her desk 1950s tan n metal *What makes you think you're qualified for a position in our customer service department* I say nothing make her think retard she clears her throat *You'd be taking calls from all over the country from people who want to order parts for any number of items we sell such as lawn mowers hedge trimmers stoves refrigerators humidifiers you would be responsible* Oh I say look at her black business suit she wants to move up *that sounds hard Mm hmm* she puts my resume down stands up *thank you for your time we'll be in touch with you once we make our final decision* she holds out her hand I hate to be this rude but I can't take a chance she'll hire me I walk out the door to the waiting room there's eight people in the room Sears is paying five fifty an hour for this job which is decent pay for the Madison underclass *Ma'am* I say to the receptionist *will you sign this* I pull the folded piece of paper out from my back pocket I have to have someone from every interview sign it to stay on welfare the woman scribbles her name doesn't look at me slides it across the counter top *Thanks a lot* I say loudly it's a bright day cars fly down the road I have sunk but I don't care I want to stay at home read do my art write in my journal work is a waste

I hop the curb on Cricket's bike pedal hard against the traffic go through a yellow light at Johnson a car honks I skip up onto the curb a man in a blue van yells *Stupid biker if you want rights obey the law* I flip him off dumb man yells at me because he doesn't like women taking risks the sun bakes my back turns my shoulders a crispy chicken wing brown I skip over railroad tracks take a left down Washington think about that cab ride from the psych ward so many years ago I speed over lazy tree shadows and stray hoses until I reach Jackson spit on the porn store at the corner flip them off through the one way glass hop the curb I blew the interview now I can read write draw! I weave through the people in the walkway *Hey wait up* I hear it like it's being said through a tunnel I want to get to Kohl's buy a pint of Ben and Jerry's Chunky Monkey Ice Cream go home finish Cohen's book *Wait up* the words aren't real attached to my body my world the bright sunshine glinting off the parked cars

Don't I

know you words scatter around my ears shatter in a burst of cold air from the ice cream freezer *chunky monkey chunky monkey* runs through my head a thick red thread *Hello I said don't I know you* says a woman's voice I grab a pint turn nearly hit a woman in the face with my head *Hey* I say *Hi* she steps back *it's nice to see you again* Sure I try to smile but it comes out crooked on my face I don't know who she is I've never seen her before *How's Tara* the woman says *Ah* I say *I dunno* look at the gray linoleum floor *she's good I guess How's the restaurant business* the woman says *Ah* I look over her head at the white rafters hanging down like monkey bars from the ceiling *well all right* I scratch my neck look down at the woman's leather sandals *Are you okay Um sure* I look her in the face brown eyes thick eyebrows then look away fast I don't know who she is how she knows all about me *I was yelling at you in the intersection Oh* I say *I guess I didn't hear you Okay* the woman shifts her feet one of her big toenails is black and blue *Do you know who I am* she says I want to get away from her *Sure* I say give half a laugh *of course I do I'm just you know tired right now Uh huh* she says dangles a loaf of bread by the twist tie slaps it against her leg *well say hello to Tara from me Oh yeah of course* I say she turns toward the bakery I stare at the lone ceiling fan in the center of the store

A white spinning

fan against a white ceiling sky bumpy bumpy chicken skin the sky spins inside toilet water down the drain spins one way in the north and another in the south why would they only have one ceiling fan how could that do any good bumpy bumpy chicken skin who was that woman why does she know me buck buck bah buck I spin with the fan my body's gone I look down at it my hands are someone else's hands they are clumps of clay they slip slide the chunky monkey ice cream under my t-shirt n shorts I am ten twelve twenty three help me! help me!

Excuse me

miss I step into the sunlight *bright light!* then back into the shade under the overhang outside Kohl's I have to get away from that ceiling fan white buck buck bah buck ceiling fan spinning in my head *Excuse me miss* I can't see can't tell where I am I have to get away!

Stop! I run chunky monkey slides out my shorts onto the sidewalk shit! creamy chunky monkey splats on the cement there are footsteps behind me *Stop!* I turn a corner smack into a belly drop to the ground head snaps on the curb the belly leans down grabs my wrist *You okay* says the belly a balding man in jeans and a watermelon polo I twist but he holds me tight *Dang* a man in a green Kohl's apron turns the corner chunky monkey in his hand *Let go* I say to the belly watermelon man *Kohl's security* the green apron man says *we've got you on tape Shit shit shit* I say try to stand up *Stay down* watermelon shirt says puts his hand on my shoulder *Don't fucking touch me* I say *Be careful Wally she might be hurt* the man in the green apron says *She needs to calm down* Wally says

The police are on their way leave her alone green apron belly says police! I think jump up push the belly man run *Hey stop* they yell I run between two garbage dumpsters over gravel under swooping trees behind a rickety house down an alley past garages leaning to the left leaning to the right I run like I'm goddamned Rocky *Yo Adrian! I love you* my fists in the air the cops Kohl's security guards are never going to catch me the chunky monkey thief who runs all the way home leaves Cricket's bike locked to a rack

Shit

I left Cricket's bike locked to a rack at Kohl's shit how do I explain that

Downstairs

my hand moves fast like a crab scuttling across sand when the ocean sucks in its belly my hand draws a face gaunt black and green heavy lids a beaded necklace like the one I wear a sad and lonely part of me jet black curls to match the pupils sit back it's an outline of me *not me!* me! *not me!* not the me I see in a mirror but it's more me than any other picture I've ever seen I color the shirt blue n black with green and black bricks behind her head *my head! whose head!* the chunky monkey thief head hungry so hungry but not for ice cream

I tear

off a blank page my hands scuttle over the once white paper more and more black round oblong rectangular marks across the white page until it is full I let it drop onto the table who cares! the world does not have what I hunger for there is no justice for me a raped dyke fag freak!

Birthing

is never easy knock knock *Who's there It's me Cricket* birthing hurts I am trying to make something from destruction! pushing pulling kneading grasping knock knock *Can I come in your room* birthing is back and forth circular up and down in and out I give birth to my mother I see her face hurt bruised under the moonlight hear her crying on the basement stairs see sadness the way she holds her neck *mother mother mother* the green and black brick drawing downstairs is half me half her she was transposed onto me her sadness became mine why why why mother did you do that to me the lying covering up sheet washing white bone knuckles on the door why did you let him hurt me why did you hurt me why didn't we leave live under a bridge ride a Greyhound out of town jump a rocket to the moon why

Hey

Cricket says her voice low and smooth *Hi* I say my voice curled in a ball *You okay* Cricket bends down touches my bare arm her finger tips against my skin feel like pink tulip petals how can a carpenter have finger tips silky as tulips *What's wrong* she says and I feel her softness her kindness I could trust her I press my face into my pillow

Pink silk

tulip petals Cricket leans against the wall I cry Cricket laces her fingers twirls her thumbs I cry *What are you doing* I say sit up perturbed that she has not left me *Just being here* Cricket says what right does she have to be here with me I should be by myself she should be somewhere else *What* I say she is making me cry by being here pink silk tulip petals what does she want *You're upset* she says *you shouldn't be alone* what does she know I've always been alone I cry I never had anyone sit with me not since Patty Cricket's boots scrape the wood her butt thuds on the floor I bury my head in my pillow I can never look at her again now that she's seen me like this

Breathe she says her pink silk tulip hand on my shoulder *don't forget to breathe*

Patty the nickels crack again and again I ride farther and farther into the past *Who's Patty* Cricket says I open my eyes Cricket's hand in mine I open my mouth to speak taste blood I bit my lip she wipes it away *No one* I say *I lost your bike*

How are you feeling

Cricket says pours milk in her cereal *Fine* I say *you* I drop two pieces of honey wheat in the toaster *Great* she says *I have the day off That's nice* I say terror in my belly how can I look at her I will have to acknowledge last night she'll think I'm crazy she'll ask about her bike what will I say how can I tell her something I don't understand myself *You were asleep last night when I left* she says why would she say that is she trying to embarass me make me feel stupid crazy is she mad does she hate me think I'm a freak a wacko the toast pops up *I'm glad you got some sleep* her spoon clicks in her bowl I say nothing squirt honey out of a plastic bear shaped bottle Cricket stands up looks over my shoulder at my toast *Hey that's like a Pollock I'm going to get your bike back today* I say a rapid fire burst of words *Okay* she sets her bowl and spoon into the sink why does she keep talking to me can't she see I'm a freak a weirdo a social inept I can't make friends who aren't like me who haven't been raped a million times had holes shot through their bodies the walking dead we can't fit ourselves into the world

Who's Patty

Cricket says the bike clatters in the truck bed *Patty* I say how would she know about Patty then I remember last night I look into the side mirror watching for the cops or a watermelon security guard to chase us out of the parking lot *You mentioned her last night* Cricket's hands climb over each other as she cranks the wheel *Don't have power steering huh* I glance in the rear view mirror see nothing but parked cars and a delivery van with Steerwell's written across its side in red *Nope* Cricket steps on the gas no watermelon man in sight I relax won't be going to jail unless they play the store's tape on TV freeze frame my face with a WANTED underneath ha ha I think dangle my arm out the side of the truck the metal is hot it's high noon *Yup* I say *it's going to be a hot whan Interesting accent* Cricket says *is Patty an ex*

What I pull my hand inside the truck Cricket turns right again at the intersection with gnome statues in the yard *You're not with someone are you* she says *Huh* I watch the gnome with the red and white striped Santa hat *Me with someone oh no* the gnome's nose is big as a grapefruit *Have you ever noticed that there aren't many female gnomes* Cricket waves a hands in the air *Uh no not really* she is irritated *No no no* I say *I've never been in a relationship* I don't say what I'm really thinking how could I ever be in a relationship I'm so fucked up no one could ever be with me *Oh* Cricket leans back in her seat *never No never you would think they would have some female gnomes my God sexism runs so deep* I say as a joke but it comes out serious Cricket raises her eyebrow *You're right* she says *It was a joke* I say now my social ineptitude is taking over in another few minutes Cricket will be gone

Silence

the entire half mile drive to the house I pretend like I'm not there my hand outside the truck I still my brain all that exists is heat the white sunlight the lime green foliage along the parkway Cricket turns onto Jenifer Street half a block from the house I stare off to the right so I don't have to look at her what if she hates me the fear is too much my mood flips to anger who does she think she is coming into my room last night then getting me to like her then leaving me she will leave! I don't care what she thinks if she thinks I'm weird a social dipshit fuck her she pulls to the curb in front of the house one tire rubs against the curb fuck her I jump out before the truck stops slam the door run up the sidewalk let the screen door slam behind me scrabble with the key fling the door open fuck her!

I run upstairs to Tara's room grab her smokes I wish I could talk with her tell her what an asshole Cricket is gets in my space like she cares and now she sees me the real me the stupid me the bad me the one mother hates!

Hi

Cricket leans into my bedroom *I didn't know you smoke I don't* I say take another drag *Oh* she says *there's another sunflower next to the house* she points toward Tara's window I exhale shrug my shoulders I don't ever want to fucking talk to her again I won't let her hurt me treat me like I'm a crazy liar stupid bitch she walks to Tara's window looks out the window like she's posing in some farmer's almanac I take a drag don't want anything to do with her I knew I shouldn't have let anyone near me I knew I shouldn't have let anyone near me! no one needs to tell me I know it on my own I am going to run away to New York City sit on the street corner smoke cigarettes until I puke my guts up Cricket hates me thinks I'm a dumb crazy stupid bitch why didn't I keep my mouth shut never should have told her I am going to sit on the streets with the other kids forget about Cricket and Tara and everyone I know disappear into the night where there are a million people like me dirty hands dirty faces dirty mouths stupid dirty kids like me

I am going to leave

running through my head a fat red thread I am going to leave I am going to leave! a fat red thread! I sit on the back steps turn myself to stone don't move don't think don't say anything to anyone never speak again a fat red thread! Cricket walks toward me her head down arms crossed she watches her feet walk over the grass stops four feet from me looks up *Hey* she says I don't look at her

I am going to leave! I am going to leave!

Are you okay she says puts one hand on her chin looks down at her feet again

I am going to leave! I am going to leave!

I watch her out the corner of all my eyes I won't let anyone hurt me! *Are you upset with me* she says No I snap *not at all why would I be upset with you* I turn to stone so I don't jump on her pulverize her for making me feel this shame this worthlessness this need I need her but I won't feel it I won't feel it! it's awful the worst thing in all the world she slides her eyes at me knows I'm full of shit says *Oookay* swings her leg around walks to the rhubarb patch I punch out the stub of Tara's cigarette light another to control the frenzy inside

I am going to leave! I am going to leave!

I fill my lungs with poison Cricket kneels her back to me yanks out rhubarb stalks snaps off the leaves sets them in two piles I smoke calm down calm down *I am going to leave!* see myself on a noir gray and black street corner I want to ruin my life ruin myself make it impossible for anyone to get near me I have to be alone *see what happens when you let someone close* I am so inappropriate so stupid so socially inept *inappropriate! stupid! inept!* that's me the kids in school were right *freak dyke fag!*

Rhubarb

Cricket says she's on the steps with me I don't know how she got there last time I saw her she was on her hands and knees in the rhubarb patch *Uh yeah* I shift my body which switches off the noir twelve year old on a gray and black street corner I squint at Cricket the pale blue sky behind her she smiles holds up the rhubarb stalks minus their leafy ends she is just Cricket who saw inside me the granite girl and the screaming twelve year old on her corner are gone my body is mine again *Want some lunch* Cricket says *Sure* I say I smile but I'm scared I turned into someone else

* * *

Night out

with the girls I grin at Cricket in the hall *Where to* Cricket says *I don't know* Tara says her voice is high sketchy she's nervous I'm irritated I don't want her to bail at the last minute *How about a church* Cricket says I lift an eyebrow at Tara Cricket is my kind of woman *Yeah* I say *I read an article about all how the church knows about those priest rapists but covers it up* Cricket grins

Quiet

Cricket hushes the engine I grab the bag *Let's go* I whisper think of my father I want to spray paint make people see what men do to children we don't have access to media or run the rape crisis centers spray painting is our media we shut the car doors gently don't want to wake anyone I am nervous excited like I used to get before a big game we sneak by two story stucco houses slip under eighty year old trees the sky is black the moon a fat pearl

no people no cats no dogs just a blue TV across the street I think of my parents the house wonder if my father is sitting in front of that same technicolor blue my mother snoring in bed one block ahead the church's steeple punctures the sky I tug on a latex glove Tara leans against a tree she will be a look out Cricket and I walk to the church a tall thin brick building with a lit up sign in the front Our Lady of the Annointed Service Saturday 5:00pm Sunday 10:00am Cricket watches for people I shake the spray paint hot pink for effect the ball in the can is loud too loud it will wake up the entire neighborhood they will catch us throw us in jail call my father who will feed Frida then I clamp down the fear Cricket nods I write with my off hand do it fast in and out bob and weave letters five feet tall Kill Thy Father Who Abuses Thee I take a step back bend down write Pissed Women underneath fear pinches my belly am I being too mean do they hurt us enough to justify killing I think of the boys from the church I think of Patty Tara Darren me one out of three one out of six I dot the i's peel off the glove run

Shit

I say in the car *we did it we did it I feel good da na na na na na just like I knew I would* I shout James Brown lyrics Cricket looks at me in the rear view mirror *Where to now* she says *McDonalds* I say wishing Tara would talk *ice cream*

* * *

Stephanie's

coming for dinner Tara shouts from the kitchen I slide into the kitchen on my socks *Tara* I whisper grab her arm *I've been meaning to tell you about this you're not going to believe what happened to me the weirdest thing first I stole ice cream from Kohl's What* Tara pops open a Coke *did you get caught Almost* I say *but I didn't even want it the ice cream it was like somebody else went ahead and did something and I watched Mmm* Tara says the Coke fizzes *Then I got mad at Cricket so mad* I lean closer *I had to make my body heavy like stone because I was afraid I'd do something then* I tap her hand to make sure she's listening *I imagined I was granite and like I was a girl in New York City and I kept thinking I want to run away over and over Well* Tara says *that's weird Thanks* I say *Talk to Stephanie* Tara runs water in a pot *she's been in psych wards the past year she's gone through something similar Oh great* I say feel scared and curious and excited all at the same time *do you want me to do something Cube the zuchini* Tara says slides the pot across the stove

I'm full

Stephanie pushes her spaghetti to the side *How are you going to dress* I point my fork at her *Dress for what* she says *Lesbian line dancing* I say *what we've been talking about for the past ten minutes Huh* she looks at Tara *Ice cream anyone* Cricket says stands up *mint chocolate chip* Stephanie pulls her plate back takes another bite *What are you going to wear To what* Stephanie says I watch her chew her food is this what I'm like

You

Stephanie looks up from her bowl squints *how old are you you look like you're a child when you chew your ice cream like you're really just* Tara interrupts her says *She looks young for her age You really do* Cricket says *Why do you look so young* Stephanie says an edge to her words like she's accusing me of something *huh why* she pushes her chair back stands up squints at me again makes me nervous I don't know what to say I hate it that I look young *I'm part Indian* I say *that's why I look so young* Cricket's eyebrows shoot up her surprise crawls up my back *You are* Cricket says studies my face for signs of being Indian I nod *My gramma's Indian it runs in the family looking young I mean* my stomach twinges I miss my gramma so much I feel like I'll die *I've never heard that Indian people look young* Stephanie says *Oh they do* I nod my head *sure in part it's the hair stays dark even when we get old* I don't really think that's true I'm not even sure why I said it I slouch stare at my plate can't believe I just said that don't know where I got those ideas from *Does she look Indian to you* Stephanie turns to Tara *Yeah* Tara says *look at those cheekbones And that round face* Cricket adds and I sit there like I'm ten embarrassed and loving it that they are saying I'm Indian

It's been fun

Cricket says *but I have to make some calls* she dumps her bowl in the sink winks at me and thuds upstairs *She likes you* Tara pokes me in the arm *you have a girlfriend I do not* I say *be quiet* I'm embarassed but more than anything afraid of how much I like Cricket how easy it is to be around her how she sat with me the other night how she put up with my bullshit Stephanie pushes her bowl away *Ahh* she says *that was good How come you're in and out of the psych wards* I blurt out then realize what I said Tara looks at Stephanie I stare at the crack in the middle of the table horrified *I have multiple personalities* Stephanie rattles the ice cubes in her empty glass *it's sort of an exagerrated inner child concept you know we all have these inner children that we need to take care of except mine actually take over and live my life and of course not all of them are children* I look her in the face then look at the long scratch on the freezer multiple personalities now what do I say Tara thinks I'm like her *What do you mean* I say Tara looks at me motherly *I dissociate lose time I have other people living in my head well they're all just me split off What* I look from Tara to Stephanie *how why what do you do what do you mean* I tap my spoon against the table Stephanie swallows says *I was abused used as a kid in prostitution my dad sometimes things happen that I didn't remember or I end up in places that I don't remember going to* I am flabbergasted Stephanie smiles *I know* she says *when I first started to deal with it I was freaked out but truly it's not that scary once you face it* she scratches her leg *you learn to deal with it people think you're weird but life goes on* Tara and she look at each other smile and I realize they have a crush on each other *Oh* I say and scratch my neck even though it doesn't itch

Get therapy

Tara says on our walk to buy her cigarettes *No* I whine *You need it No* I whine kick at a stick on the sidewalk the red setting sun blurry through the line of lilac bushes across the street *Oh my god* Tara says *you drive me crazy sometimes No* I whine again *no no no Remember last week when you put the spinach pie in the oven and then went walking for two hours No* I whine but I do remember it I'd left completely forgotten about the pie shriveled and black *You need therapy No* I whine *I hate therapy it makes me feel like a freak You always feel like a freak Good point* I say and open the convenience store door silver bells tinkle overhead

* * *

We paint

hot pink Pissed Women again n again n again n again at the university for covering up assaults on campus at dyke heights where two men in a jeep said get fucked or die dykes at the porn store on Washington its customers ask neighborhood girls going to Burger King for blow jobs Pissed Women everywhere the three of us make it look like the town is filled with pissed women pissed women everywhere!

* * *

So And So

That's me I wave the lima bean green carpet and chairs remind me of welfare office decor I can't possibly do therapy here no cool therapist would work in this shithole *In here* a fortyish woman with short black hair opens a door I plop down on a maroon couch with stuffed animals lined up along the back *Okay* the woman says sits across from me *I'm Sally I'll be doing your intake then Janet your counselor will be in once I finish*

Okay I say

So your name is So And So
Yes I say
You are 25
Yes I say but in my head I say I'm not 25 I'm 5!
You have a history of sexual abuse
Yes I say
From a family member
Yes I say

Your father
Yes I say
Anyone else
No I say
Do you have substance abuse issues
No I say
Sexuality problems
No I say
You are heterosexual
No I say
Lesbian
Yes I say
Okay she says why did you come to the Dane County Sexual Violence
Center
Because I'm on welfare
Okay she says any other reasons
No I say
What I mean is what sort of treatment are you seeking
Treatment for sexual abuse I say
Anything else
Time is like a stone across a lake
Okay
I skip time I say
Ah huh uh huh she says writes on the paper
I cross my legs

Hello

a thirtyish woman opens the door holds her green scarf against her
stomach shakes my hand *Hi* I say *I'm Doctor Janet Hello* I say like her
instantly like strawberry flavored one minute oatmeal she is different from
the rest *Thanks Sally* she says

Doctor Janet sits in a wooden rocking chair across from me *Interesting*
she says as she reads what Sally wrote my throat closes *Tell me about
skipping time* she leans back in the chair *Well* I say *what do you want to
know What is it like Um* I say *Do you forget things find items in your closet
that you don't remember buying do you find yourself in places where you
don't remember how you got there* I scratch my ear feel myself turning into
a fourteen year old this will not impress the therapist! this will not impress
the therapist! *Um I don't know* I say sullenly *Okay* she glances at me then
at the paper

The hour

is up Doctor Janet closes her notebook her green scarf is cockeyed one
end hangs down to the floor I blink try to recover *I don't know what's
going on* I say *How so* she looks at her watch sets the notebook on the floor
I don't know I say terror runs up my legs like a prickly spider *What's going*

on she leans back touches her fingertips together the terror runs through my groin into my stomach *I* I say then I realize that this is how it's always been not remembering things scrambling to try to figure out what just happened trying to maneuver through interactions with people *I* I say terror runs into my chest up my neck I choke on it Doctor Janet leans forward *It's okay* she says *I have a free half hour*

My body

falls into the couch my legs curl up into my stomach I feel safe here she understands *Just let it come* Doctor Janet says I let it go like the fifth Chinese brother only it's safe to let it go no one will die fish water rattles briar rocks sand empty custard cups broken glass discarded ski glove crab banana peel ho ho wrapper licked clean by a stray dog *Keep releasing* she says plastic bag broken chain pen cap sticks shells tiny pale and pink a boatload of sand from the hull of a sunken ocean liner rusted nail clipper discolored tassle off a graduate's cap sand sand sand rocks bottle cap beer can shot through by bb's *Keep going* she says sand sand sand water a sunken ship off the shores of Lake Superior sand sand rock sand at the top of a pine tree a day with no wind

breath
unfolding red zinnia
breath

Are you okay Doctor Janet says *Yes* I rub my eyes sit up in the middle of a maroon couch cough up salt water *sorry No need to apologize* Doctor Janet puts her hand on my knee withdraws it her touch didn't frighten me make me want to run puke *Do you want to talk Um I don't know* I look at the black and white photograph of the willow tree behind her head *We have some time* she fingers her scarf shifts in the chair

I am embarassed I don't know how to let someone in I am not a normal human being! I am not a normal human being! *What were we talking about* I say *I feel like I just got out of a tilta whirl ride I can imagine* she says *you said you didn't know what was going on Oh* I say not remembering saying that I am terribly confused like my brain is turning inside out this is your brain on drugs just say no to drugs! *I'm sorry* I say *I don't know what's happening Can you explain how you're feeling* she flips one end of her scarf into her lap *Nice scarf* I say *Thank you* she says *now how are you feeling I don't know like my brain is turning inside out* I press my hand to my forehead *can a person's brain turn inside out I don't think so* she says *but I think it can feel that way when you're encountering something profound*

Uh I say *I don't really remember what happened since I got in this room it's like watching things through a fog or water Is that a new sensation for you* I stare at the beige carpet with brown flecks *No* I say *I guess not How long have you experienced life that way* I look at the blue rabbit over my shoulder *You can hold that if you want* she says I am horrified that she knows I want to hold a stuffed animal like I'm a baby but I grab it crush it to my chest and curl up on the couch *Forever* I say *it's been like that forever Uh* Doctor Janet says *I see*

Names

I shout at our next meeting a miniature smile flips on Doctor Janet's lips then disappears I watch it the kind of smile that nice adults hide quickly when a child does something cute because they don't want to patronize why would she smile at me like that I'm not a child *What about names* Doctor Janet says seriously but I saw the smile *Why do people have names* the words tumble out over each other like die in a yahtzee cup sliding across a kitchen table *why do people only have one name why do people call me So And So names are confusing I have many names* my words are like drunk adults playing leap frog *sometimes I hear Susan and turn around like it's me sometimes I hear Mark and turn around like it's me sometimes I hear Crazy and turn around like it's me sometimes I hear Tabatha and turn around like it's me sometimes I hear Mouth and turn around like it's me sometimes I hear Mary Beth and turn around like it's me sometimes I hear Shit and turn around like it's me so how how how how can names make sense because my name the one I sign on bank deposit slips and the one on my welfare checks is So And So but sometimes I hear So And So and I don't know who it is and I sit and stare stupidly until I realize it's me* I take a deep breath like I'm inhaling pot for the biggest high ever *so you see how confusing the simplest things are for me* I cross my legs *Yes* Doctor Janet says her eyes wide the way nice adults look when they're surprised and don't know what to do *I do*

It's good

to see you again Doctor Janet says a purple scarf wrapped around her head *Thank you* I say I want to say it's good to be here but I can't *What would you like to talk about today* she smiles at me and I want more of her attention *I just want to talk* I say *About anything in particular* she coughs *My childhood* I say *Okay go ahead I'm here to listen* I am in a dark cold cave filling with warm water

I was born in Saint Paul Minnesota in 1968 to Raymond and Susan I grew up on Rose Avenue one block off Payne Avenue I cry Doctor Janet hands me a kleenex box I shake my head no *and then and then and then and then and then* I tell her everything up to the judge judging me crazy *Time's almost up* she says *I'm sorry those things happened to you you didn't deserve them I can see we need to talk more about your grandma* No I say *Why not* therapist says *She is dead to me I killed her* therapist's eyes shoot up No I say *it's an analogy I killed my feelings for my gramma cut them off like that* I say and swing my flat hand through the air like an axe *I chopped them down* and I cry down the beige hallway through the lima bean green waiting room to the elevator to the street to Cricket's bike down

Willy Street down Ingersoll down Jenifer to my porch up the stairs to my bed where Frida is curled on my pillow deep in sleep

And then

and then and then and then and then I tell her up until I was 15 but I skip the night of the nickels *Thank you for sharing with me* she says *I am sorry you went through that you didn't deserve to have those things happen to you but I have one question did Patty move away I can't tell you* I say and I cry all the way home

And then

and then and then and then and then I tell her up until now *Thank you for sharing* she says *those things should not have happened and I'm sorry they did Thank you* I say and cry all the way home

And now

and now and now and now I tell her about Cricket and how scared I am that she will be hurt somehow my fault *and now and now and now It seems your feelings for Cricket are somehow related to Patty can you tell me what happened to Patty and no and no and no and no* I say and I cry all the way to the river it picks up my sorrow carries it away says *it'll be okay it'll be okay*

* * *

Road trip

Cricket slams the porch door waves a piece of paper above her head Tara and I are sitting in the living room drinking the lemonade she stole from the diner Cricket stands in front of me her back to Tara says *Who wants to go on a road trip with me* I look at Tara her eyes narrow Cricket unfolds the map it falls down to her knees *My site closed down for four days* Cricket says steps to the side to include Tara *Wisconsin Minnesota Illinois* she points to each state on the map *who wants to go with me show a northeasterner the Upper Midwest* Cricket grins at me *It's obvious enough who you want to go with you* Tara stomps into the kitchen Cricket looks at me I shrug my shoulders *Want to go* she says *Sure* I say don't show any emotion on my face like I could care less inside I'm thrilled

Cricket sits next to me on the couch folds the map in half *Where do you want to go* she says *we could camp in Wisconsin or go to Chicago or* she pauses *we could go to Minneapolis* I say nothing part of me wants to go back misses my high school friends the neighborhood the city but the rest of me is afraid if I go there things will be too real *Where do you want to go* I say my throat tight *Well* she says *I'd be happy to go anywhere* she folds the map in half again *I've seen Chicago and I like to camp but I've never seen Minnesota an old friend of mine lives there* I nod no emotion *Would that be hard on you* she says *I don't know* I say *I have to think about it* I carry my glass of lemonade into the kitchen Tara is leaning against the sink arms crossed I drain the glass she looks away I go downstairs draw the outline of a face that slithers off the page

Cricket adjusts

a black baseball hat with a hot pink Q for *Queer* embroidered above the bill *Ready* Cricket puts her hand on my thigh her touch is electric *Yeah* I say *let's go it'll be fun* I'm afraid *All right* Cricket rockets us to Washington windows wide open my spiky hair doesn't move in the wind Cricket is smiling about something or maybe she's just happy and can show it my face doesn't match me

Dells 9 miles

a large green sign says I'm floating inside the truck so afraid I can't stay in my body I hope Cricket doesn't talk to me I don't want her to know I am tossing about in the cab bumping against the passenger door then the roof windshield *Wisconsin Dells Next Right* there it is there it is! the turn off where I ran away

Mad dad! mad dad! and mother too!

my face pressed against the windshield the exit flies by Cricket taps the steering wheel in beat with the song on the radio the exit is gone I'm one who got away

Rock formations

on the right Cricket says I look up from my book *Aren't they nice* she points to the jutting chunks of rock their sides covered by limestone ledges *This is neat* she says *I thought the Midwest was flat just prairies and farms Uh no* I say reading my book *there's rolling hills I know* she says *I've been looking at them for the past two hours Uh huh* I say immersed in Cohen's pain

Look at that more rocks Cricket points to the right her finger is in my face *way off in the distance* she says excited *Wisconsin is beautiful Uh huh* I say Cohen is writing about being gang raped on the streets that's more important than some rocks *Wow* Cricket says *and look at those valleys covered with lush trees What are you some sort of environmentalist* I say *And look at that river* she says as we pass over a half mile wide river bed *just gorgeous* I keep reading sometimes her awe of the world bothers me no one can really be that happy

I focus on the book gang raped on the noir streets of New York but my mind drifts to Cricket and her happiness and my irritation I close the book roll down the window dangle my hand outside watch the hills interupted by farmland strict rows of corn and soybean I am making my way back to my homeland to the place I had to flee like a refugee *Look at that* Cricket points to a dip in the terrain a sea of purple wildflowers I stare at the shimmering purple and greens I am going home to take back my life it is important for me to be conscious reflective not bitter *Would you look at that* Cricket is ecstatic like some sort of saint who's seen the divine *I see it* I say *I see it*

Four hours

farm fields trees barns Jethro Tull farm fields gas stations silos Carly Simon farmfields hay horses fences Bob Dylan *wow just wow*

Hudson

Wisconsin whooeee I used to party here in high school right down there I point at a road between an insurance company and a Super America gas station *we used to drive down there and party in the woods Whooee here we come Minnesota* Cricket puts her fist outside the window shakes it *she used to party here* and I want to dislike her for not being cool for being so expressive but I can't

I crack a grin as big as hers and she laughs at my grin and speeds through Hudson down a steep hill toward the river that separates Wisconsin from Minnesota I lean out the window *Whooee* I shout into the wind *here we come Minnesota* I am here now Cricket grabs my hand raises it brushes my knuckles against the velour ceiling *Here we come Minnesota* she shouts

We zip

between Minnesota farm fields then large office parks until Saint Paul skyscrapers poke up over the horizon *My home town* I say *Look a real city with tall buildings* Cricket says *this is so much better than Madison* she cranks the radio *Ann Reed* she says smacks her hand on the outside of the truck door *can you believe it an out dyke on the radio* her face a sunflower

What kind of Indians

live in Minnesota Cricket says slows down for a stoplight *Huh* I say startled out of watching a dog pee on a One Way sign she pokes me in the leg *Indians you're Indian what kind of Indian are you Oh* I say no one has said I'm an Indian since my gramma I look at the dog balancing on three legs I wonder where my gramma is wonder what she's doing *Chippewa* I say *Ojibwe Oh* Cricket says *like the Song of Hiawatha Huh* I say *The poem* she says *by Longfellow Oh I've never heard of it It's not very good* Cricket says *he was just using someone else's culture for his own reasons* I look at her profile she feels it sneaks a look at me *What about your grandma* she says *you never talk about her* I say nothing have to be careful of the sadness keep it dammed inside *Where does she live* Cricket says *she's alive right Yeah I think so* I say *she lives just off a reservation* I feel the sadness edge up *in northern Minnesota I'm Jewish you know* she bursts through a yellow light *my dad was Jewish but my mom was Catholic she raised us Catholic and wouldn't let him teach us anything about being Jewish how's that for a good time* we drive past tobacco stores and pawn shops and a dance studio *I just started learning about Judaism two or maybe three yeah three years ago* she slows looks in the rear view mirror pushes down her left turn blinker *and it's the difference between knowing who I am and not knowing who I am*

Riverside Avenue

left off the exit to Lake left to Cedar right to 33rd Cricket says *Riverside Avenue* I watch Saint Paul in the side mirror *shit it's only been a few years but I don't remember where Riverside is* I am embarassed wonder if people notice how much I forget things I poke Cricket *can you believe it* she doesn't answer studies a piece of paper in her lap *Amanda said it was off 94 I think I can't read my writing can you* she hands the paper to me *It must be 94* I say but I can't tell from her writing I can't believe I don't remember where Riverside Avenue is I have to remember to tell Doctor Janet that I only remember the way to the old house *There it is* Cricket says *Riverside Avenue There it is* I say I must have blocked it from my mind some sort of defense mechanism

we exit at Riverside Cricket slows down there are people walking all over hanging off street corners riding bikes zig zagging down the street *Hello* Cricket says to a man on a ten speed in front of us he hops the curb bikes off across a vacant lot *How do you know Amanda* some of the houses are boarded up one is burned down two of its walls still standing like chipped teeth jutting out of the earth *We met at Bryn Mawr* Cricket stops at a light *she was the head of the campus glbt organization we came out together* a man walks in front of the truck *Dykes* he says bangs on the hood *Hey* Cricket says *get your hands off my truck* he staggers to the other side of the street seems to forget about the dykes in the truck *You'll like her* Cricket winks *and she'll like you*

Amanda

Cricket grabs the tall gym built woman on the other side of the entryway *you look great So do you* Amanda says her arms wrapped around Cricket's shoulders I stand on the bottom step of the four story brick apartment building wonder if they played rugby together or if they were girlfriends or if they want to be girlfriends

Ah Amanda yells *welcome to Minneapolis it is so excellent to see you Cricket* she steps around *and you must be the roommate I've heard so much about* I don't know what to do didn't know Cricket talked about me so much *Sure* I say hold out my hand feel stupid *Oh you are as adorable as Cricket said* Amanda ignores my hand wraps her arms around me her long black hair falls across my back I don't know what to do can't believe Cricket called me adorable Amanda squeezes me Cricket grins Amanda says *Let's go* then squeezes me again pins my arms to my sides I don't know what to do I've never been around people this friendly

Inside Amanda says *before the mosquitoes figure out we're here Nice place* Cricket nods looks around the dirt yard shaded by enormous pine trees *Thanks* Amanda opens the entryway door *other than the drive by*

shootings prostitution and drug dealing it is nice she laughs loud her mouth wide open I follow her and Cricket up the stairs astonished by their laughter how they let the world know

Amanda's ceiling and walls are covered with deep purple drapings and wild paintings of things I see in my sleep I have never seen the shit in my head somewhere else the colors zig zag lines energy I didn't know anyone else saw these things too *Have a seat* Amanda says Cricket and I sit on a velour green couch that sags in the middle *Be careful* Amanda plops on a black cushion on the floor *you'll end up in each other's lap on that thing* she laughs sits cross legged her barefeet dirty on the bottoms like she stepped in ink

I love your paintings I say feel myself sliding toward Cricket hold onto the arm of the couch to stay in my spot *Thank you* she says *they're not mine* she shakes her head and hands *hello Amanda of course they're mine but I didn't make them I'm an art historian actually going to be an art historian I should say* Oh I stare at the paintings *She's working on her Ph.D. in Art History* Cricket says *she'll be the first out dyke art historian in the history of the world* and they both laugh as if this is an old joke between the two of them I smile less worried about whether they want to be girlfriends than when they first hugged

Actually Amanda stands up *can I get you something to drink* No I say even though I'm thirsty I'm intimidated expect she'll only have something to drink that I can't pronounce *What do you have* Cricket says *Um* Amanda walks out of the small living room into the kitchen opens the refrigerator runs her hand through her hair flings it over her shoulder *lemon lime soda ginger ale carrot juice cheap red wine or water filtered of course Wine the cheaper the better* Cricket says to Amanda *sure you don't want anything* she says to me *Nah* I shake my head look down at the scuffed wood floors *maybe some lemon lime soda* I look at Cricket sideways smile *Can you add a lemon lime to the order Certainly* Amanda says bangs around in the refrigerator Cricket slaps her thigh *I knew you were thirsty* she says I sit up rest my forearms on my knees dangle my wrists and hands stare at the paintings *Nice art huh* Cricket says *Nice* I loosely clap my hands together look around the walls at my barenaked dreams

Amanda and Cricket

get drunk around the coffee table on cheap red wine from Hassan's Corner Liquor two blocks down we eat a tofu pea pod dish from a Chinese restaurant on Lake we dodged used needles condoms large men on small bikes selling dope on our way home *She's an incredible artist* Cricket points at me *Really* Amanda says *what sort of art do you do Um* I say don't have the artistic verbiage to describe my art *mostly I draw what's in my head* I feel stupid leave the chop sticks in the white carton get off the couch sit down on the floor lean against the end of the couch *I draw a lot of abstract faces Oh* Amanda says *a portraitist* and giggles Cricket jabs her finger at a painting to the right of the couch *That is fantastic* she says *you should see her art it's just like that one especially*

Amanda stands up next to the painting *This one* she lifts one foot for a second nearly falls *is it* she looks at me both feet on the ground *Well* I say *I suppose The heavy black outlines and amorphous forms and colors are nearly identical* Cricket shouts stands up spills rice on the floor *look at that right there it looks like the one you did last week Wow* Amanda says *It's identical* Cricket scratches her cheek *He's a famous painter they just came out with a book of his work* Amanda turns toward a bookcase on the far wall points at it *I would show it to you but* her voice slows down *I think someone borrowed it* she tucks one hand under an armpit *yes it's still out I guess we see the same things in our heads* I say *Saw* Amanda says *he died in an insane asylum they wore him down* she presses her thumb into her chin *bastards* she adds

I spit my lemon lime soda back in the glass *Look look* Cricket drinks sets her glass on the arm of the couch I grab it *I've got pictures of her paintings I had some extra film* she says to me rifles through her duffel bag *here* she holds a packet in the air *right here Let me see* Amanda flings her hair to the side juts her hip out as if she's trying to fill her baggy men's boxers *Amanda's going to open a women's art gallery right here* Cricket hands her the pictures *right Right right here* Amanda says *I'm coming into some money next spring from my family a bunch of aristocrats* she laughs *and then there's me* I shrink into my chest feel inadequate poor stupid on welfare

Ooo Amanda says *wow* flips through the pictures kneels down in front of me I hand Cricket her glass *You are talented* she says *gifted special* she looks at each one again *How many years have you been doing art* Cricket grins behind her they are both looking at me *Years* I say it like I'm asking a question *a few months* I am overwhelmed by their attention and praise I tap my foot on the floor so that I don't float off *Are you kidding* Amanda slides through the pictures again *have you had training* she looks at me I shake my head *No* I say *You're freakin amazing actually a genius your stuff should be in galleries* Amanda looks at me *I could set you up with a show in Minneapolis do you have enough work* I shrug my shoulders *I'm not kidding* she says *I told you so* Cricket says *I told you so*

Sleep

on the couch Cricket pats the cushion beside her Amanda is in the bathroom the only light on in the apartment *I'll sleep on the floor* Cricket says I shrug my shoulders *I've always liked to stay up late sit in the dark* I say staring out the black window listening to the occasional bug hit the screen shout from the street car horn the continuous stream of cicadas *Minnesota sounds different from Wisconsin* I say Cricket doesn't move off the couch *The air smells different* I say *I miss it here* I say *Mmmm* Cricket says

You can both sleep on the couch if you want Amanda says over running water *it's a pull out Nah* I say my chin on my arms back hunched against the wall *I'll sleep on the floor Really* Cricket says *we can both sleep up here I won't bite promise Nah* I say I am lost in my head the noisy void outside the window the sadness *I want to sleep alone* I say *on the floor*

Nothing

I say *nothing's wrong Are you sure* Cricket says her feet up on a chair drinking coffee out of a mug with Dali Sold Out Surrealism written across it *How can you drink coffee in this heat* I say wish I had not come back here I'm afraid feel stupid uncultured around Amanda *It's not that hot* Cricket says *it's only 8 in the morning* she half smiles fear jabs me is she mad at me does she really like me I don't belong anywhere except in an insane asylum with that artist just like mad dad said I'm a freak fag dyke dumbass bitch I could never really be a good artist they're playing with me

Is so I say just like a little kid *it is so hot already* I'm mad at Cricket for being mad at me fucking with me *Okay* Cricket says she is embarassed doesn't know why I'm being a jerk I want to say Cricket help me! I'm frightened! but all I feel is anger hatred distrust I can't be close to anyone it's a rule mad dad made a long time ago and I don't know how to break it

Mad dad

still owns me! mad dad still owns me! oh no! crumbling bricks burnt out buildings no walls left standing inside oh no! oh no! need to function people around oh no! oh no! oh no! *Need to use the bathroom* Cricket's voice chirps *Nah* shake head no communicate can't let people think we're insane know we're here where's Doctor Janet we want her to know we're here ohnoohnoohnoohno help us slipping into the darkness help us!

mad dad ohnoohnoohnoohno he's here somewhere close he'll get us rule us kill us ohnoohnoohnoohnoohno *Hey* Cricket's voice from somewhere don't know where *are you okay* say say say something *I'm not feeling that good* say something *I'm tired* make her think it's something else not us not us upset! *Maybe you're coming down with something* Cricket is good she is good not a bad person she is good she doesn't know about us about mad dad owning us he owned us!

the way you own a car drive it
the way you buy a candy bar eat it
the way you buy a hairbrush use it to make yourself look good

he owned us! owned us our body owned it like it was his like it was something you buy at the store find in the garbage piece of trash something to hurt he owned us! used our body like it was toilet paper to wipe himself on toilet paper! our body! hurt us crushed us bulldozer dozing burnt out house set fire to the ground ashes ashes we all fall down boom! we all fall down he made us then he bulldozed us!

mad dad devil man we all burn in his hell

You look

like you're going to pass out Cricket says *get on the couch Yeah whish whish whish the headboard did it* I say head lolling back *yeah the couch'd be good* Cricket holds my arms shoulders steadies me to the couch *Is she okay I don't know I've never seen her like this before* Cricket sets me down *I think she's sick It was the tofu* I try to be nice make a joke to make up for being a jerk smile at Cricket her face over mine sad worried like the sad faces I draw sliding off the page *Cricket* I say she sets me on the couch my face against the velour maroon back *Cricket Yes* she sits next to me *I was just kidding about the tofu I know* she says holds my hand not connected to my body a floppy hand in the air all by itself a hand all by itself! *Just kidding about the tofu it was good* I say room spinning Cricket's eyes looking at me nice eyes like Patty! not like mad dad's green eyes glowing in the dark owl wolf bobcat dad owl wolf bobcat dad

consume me like I am something to be bought at *Hassan's* I say out loud *You want something from Hassan's* Cricket says I am making a scene can't help it the spinning worse than a Tilt a Whirl *Gatorade* I say *I'll get some* Cricket says sounds like she's the fifth brother crying crying Roy Orbison jet black hair crying forever for killing the boy the rain is the water coming out his mouth one and the same I make Cricket sad *Cricket* I say *Yes* she says rubs my arm *I was kidding about the tofu* I squeeze her hand *it's the heat it's hot in here*

Gone

talked them into leaving me here burnt out raw flesh too many explosions occur I have to be alone cannot let anyone close I sit in the apartment stare at the pictures shocking to see my insides outside shocking someone else feels what I feel maybe I am not alone but that thought that possibility opens the dam too many emotions mixed together like gas and oil in the ocean water don't put a match to it! don't put a match to it!

I find a radio on the kitchen counter flip it on *KFAI community radio no corporate sponsorship listener friendly* is everything friendly in these people's lives *John Coltrane hour up next* my elbow on the gray and green flecked countertop with silver edging just like my gramma's counter tops I want to put my arms around the counter hold it in place of my gramma's body but that would be crazy

Dumbass bitch

snaps me out of my mind *Leave me alone* a woman shouts I look out the kitchen window but only see pine tree branches *Fuckin bitch get in the fuckin car now* I run to the living room window see a short white man tall white woman on the sidewalk a white car next to them in the street he has her by the arm she twists away runs toward the apartment building stairs her front bloody her front bloody! my body gets large my mind big and slow a drifting balloon time slows the green of the pine trees blurs with the white of the house across the street red from the traffic light in two steps he is on her she makes it to the door pounds screams thuds screams I move not a muscle my mind lightly bumping against the bumpy bumpy ceiling wanting to escape find the trees and the wide open sky *No* the woman yells *help help* thud thud thud he drags her down the stairs bam! bam! bam! her face bounces off the concrete into the milky car my body slides to the floor my creepy crawly spine against the smooth cool wall I listen to the car rip into the street

Paper skins

flecks of pot saliva pop a match inhale I am higher than a balloon sucking a ceiling a bumpy bumpy ceiling I am someone who does nothing I am someone who does nothing I saw blood I am someone who does nothing I am like my mother like all those terrible adults those terrible terrible adults

A someone

I am who does nothing I saw blood a lady's bashed in face I am someone who does nothing

I am someone

who does something bashes in the wall I am someone who does something bloodies up her hand

I am someone

who is her mother

You did

what Amanda's mouth drops open *I got high* I cover the scrapes on my knuckles *Jesus* Cricket steps closer to me *Why what happened does it hurt Nah* I say *can't feel it mostly* Amanda kicks off her shoes *Is that your blood on the steps Oh* I say *no* my head reaches for the bumpy bumpy ceiling *What happened* Cricket rubs her forehead *Nothing* I say cross legged on the floor staring at the thread sagging off the bottom of the couch flex my hand the pain feels good *some guy some man* I bury my face in my arms *I did nothing nothing nothing* I say *he raped her What* Cricket says *No* I say *Patty a man some guy this woman all bloody On the steps* Amanda says *Yes* I say *blood he chased her I did nothing she screamed he dragged her off* I'm choking *in his car white* I see Patty in the corner of my bedroom mad dad hurting her I did nothing Cricket pulls me into her *White guy short in a white Lincoln* Amanda says I nod my head buried in arms *A white car* I say *Did you call the police* I shake my head no Amanda makes a noise like it's my fault like it's all my fault all of it Patty the bloody woman she walks into the kitchen runs water in the sink *She didn't mean it like that* Cricket says *He's a pimp* Amanda says from the kitchen *You should have called the police if you'd gone down there he would have messed you up* she hands Cricket a washcloth Cricket wipes my cheek wraps my hand in the warm cloth I walk to the living room window only see scattered flashes of metal through the pine needles as cars drive by *It doesn't matter* I say *I should have gone down there stopped him* No Amanda says *he would have messed you up* I don't care I think but say nothing

* * *

Let's go out

Amanda pulls her hair back in a pony tail *get your dancing shoes on girl* she says to me slaps my butt walks into the kitchen then the bedroom *can't sit and cry all day let's hit the town women* she yells from the bedroom I stand in the middle of the living room like a scarecrow hung up on a cross my arms and shoulders awkward what is sexual and what isn't

Cricket sets the book she was flipping through on the coffee table *She doesn't mean anything by it* she leans back *it's just her way of being friendly* Okay I say not sure how I feel about her slapping my butt telling me not to cry *Amanda isn't like other people I've known She's not like anybody anyone's known* Cricket lays one arm across her belly the other behind her head her legs spread apart *You look nice* I say then stop the air is still Cricket looks at me the hum of the traffic is low like music a particular song made at just this moment then never again *What* Cricket says *Against the velour* Cricket looks at me *The couch* I say *you look comfortable* Cricket looks at me her lips part the traffic blends with the room I want to be here forever

Did I ever tell you how time used to stop when I played sports No Cricket says the traffic is low and smooth a silky light blue ribbon through the room *Everything was in slow motion* I say *I felt so alive Like right now* Cricket says *Yes* I say I want to hold her these feelings this moment never let it leave go back to the chaos and confusion of my heart *I think I know what you mean* Cricket says the words flow through her lips like water *It's like being under water* I say imagine my hand reaching out slow motion touching the skin on the inside of her thigh *Yeah* she says looks at me *I know what you mean*

Let's go women Amanda comes out of her bedroom flicks on the kitchen light *gotta leave it on so the pimps think we're home* Cricket and I don't move the timelessness splits the traffic drowns out the birds *All right* Cricket suddenly stands up *C'mon* Amanda takes my hand *Babes in Toyland await I'll drive* Cricket says *Good* Amanda slaps her on the back as we walk out *I don't have a car*

An aristocrat without a car I say irritated that she barged in on us Amanda laughs *A former aristocrat* she locks the apartment jiggles the doorknob *an unwilling aristocrat* doubt it I think Cricket's boots kick down the stairs I want to finger each of her curls kiss the back of her neck instead I drag my fingertips over the piss colored plaster

First Avenue

Amanda yells *take a left lot on the right anyone want a toke* she inhales loudly *Don't mind if I do* Cricket turns into a spot takes a drag hands it to me I look in my rear view mirror for a cop the smoke curls against the windows like hair and I see the woman's hair splayed around her as he drags her to the car I did not help Patty or that woman what does that make me

Babes in Toyland

here we come Amanda slips her leg out from under the steering wheel nearly falls to the pavement catches herself on the door *You are stoned* I say point at Amanda laugh *you are so stoned* First Avenue is in front of us two stories high no windows black concrete with gray stars painted on the side *Look* Amanda points at one of the stars *The Wallets* she says and jumps on the balls of her feet hands flying *I saw them at a free concert in Loring Park I simply adore them* she says *I love them and I love you* she grabs our hands holds them together *I just love both of you* she pulls us onto the sidewalk *you two make the cutest couple* Cricket grins I look away as if I didn't see her grin stare at the Ziggy Stardust star

Three

Amanda stands so that her bare feet are under the turnstile the man big as a gorilla in black tank top black jeans paste colored skin can't see she doesn't have shoes *Twenty one* he runs his hand over his bald head Amanda kisses Cricket so gorilla man knows we're dykes I hold back a laugh don't want to piss him off and get busted for being high he doesn't seem to have noticed or care nods to me the way big men do they don't have to speak

Women everywhere Amanda flops into a chair overlooking the dance floor Cricket and I sit next to her *This a good high* I whisper across the table Cricket and Amanda watch the dance floor below they don't say anything suddenly my mood shifts and I'm embarrassed I don't belong with them I'm a freak loser loner they're best friends maybe I'm wrong about them not wanting to be lovers I breathe don't let it grab hold of my guts ruin my whole night

downstairs the drum player waves her sticks in the air the crowd yells offstage a throaty guitar screams the woman playing the guitar struts onstage her long black hair in an off center pig tail green black striped tank top with tight black pants *Hello Minneapolis* she growls the crowd screams the music takes me away spinning floating colors on the ceiling I am stoned at a concert with two hundred women! two hundred women!

Dance

Amanda jumps out of her chair runs downstairs to the main floor 200 women slamming arms in the air yelling music bashing out our brains *Cricket* I grab her arm *let's go* I slip my hand down to her wrist *now* I miss slamming in Madison before I got the flashbacks before I got the flashbacks! our fingers lock

Pinks shades of blue

melodies wrap me up then hit my body sweaty bare flesh against mine I watch my feet black shoes with big bumper toes then stare at the ceiling beams black lines my art! my art! it's good it matters it matters! I matter! a woman's voice growls over the microphone *let it loose ladies let it loose!*

bump slick skin bare arm hand don't know whose keep on dancing keep on dancing! a woman growling prowling on stage long stringy hair in her eyes she is beautiful I'm in love I'm in love! with her with women with myself the sweat on my arms I'm in love bare skin hand grabs mine whirlwind sound energy colors turn I kiss Cricket whirlwind dervish the lonely spirits scatter

Ready

Cricket says Amanda grins at me the band dismantles the instruments I danced to the very last song then danced to the music they put on the loudspeakers I couldn't stop it was like I was possessed *I suppose* I step on a burning cigarette want to dance stay free Cricket walks toward the door *C'mon* Amanda grabs my arm grins I don't know what to do or say it's like I'm a kid I kissed Cricket what if she is mad what if she is mad!

Last call a bartender yells two women scramble across the floor to the bar pretend to fight with each other for the only empty stool we follow Cricket's saggy jeans out the door *Gnight* Cricket says to gorrilla man he grunts doesn't nod this time

we hit the street Cricket's hands stuffed in her jean pockets Amanda yells *Babes are foxy* her arms in the air we climb in the truck Cricket looks at me *Put your seatbelt on Okay* I say unsure if she's mad she smiles at me less big and open and I realize she is shy Cricket's shy! Cricket's shy! and I realize how my self absorbtion and fear keeps me from understanding Cricket is nervous keeps me from interacting like a normal person *You look really nice tonight* Cricket says I look at her profile love her determined face love the softness of her curls and I feel it in my heart that I can heal *Oh c'mon you two love birds let's get some ice cream* Amanda says from the jump seat *I'm hungry*

Melted pistachio

ice cream spirals down Cricket's wrist she licks it off driving down 94 one handed we drive under a bridge no one says anything the moon on our right *Want the last bite* Cricket holds the tip of the sugar cone toward me as the street lights flash shadows in the truck I am moved by the beauty of her fingertips so round they curve down into her wrist like the beak of a bird and I want to remember it draw her hand holding the cone in one of my pictures a symbol that I belong somewhere with someone 200 slam dancing dykes *Hmm* Cricket twirls the bit of cone in the shadow between us *Thanks* I say take the cone from her fingertips put it on my tongue creamy sweet

Mmm Amanda says from the jump seat I lean back in the bucket seat riding shot gun pow pow I shoot holes in the moon I live in Wisconsin which makes me a stupid cheese head *I don't want to live in Wisconsin anymore* I say *Mmm hmm Madison Wisconsin* Cricket says pulling the a out like a piece of watermelon taffy *such a cow town Can we stop at a* convenience store I say *I want taffy Mmm* Amanda says from the jump seat *yes taffy and sunflower seeds and Gatorade More ice cream* Cricket pleads and I drag my hand in the air outside the truck *Yes* I say *oh most definitely more pistachio ice cream*

This taffy

is soo good Amanda drops a string of purple into her mouth the three of us lying on the pulled out sofa bed I work the watermelon taffy between my teeth lick my lips want every bit of the flavor *This is a long high* Cricket says *Lasts forever* I say *Long lasting* Cricket says we burst out laughing I jab her in the shoulder

headlights swing around the room from the street below *Wow* Amanda says *my neighbors are home* she stumbles off the sofa gets a glass of water from the faucet picks up the bottoms of her feet black as tar looks at them over her shoulder then walks into her bedroom *Gnight* Cricket says Amanda says nothing lost in the chewing of her taffy shuts the bedroom door Cricket and I are on the bed with watermelon kiwi flavored taffy

This is really good taffy I hold up a chunk of it *Really good* Cricket says emphasizes the *really* pulls the word out *uh huh really* I slide until my back is against the back of the couch one of Cricket's legs hangs off the bed her foot taps the floor *You know what they say* I can't believe how forward I am being *Huh* Cricket looks at me over the chunk of green taffy she's biting *who They* I say *just they some people* no one says anything I lick my lips for the taste of watermelon *I saw it on TV in a movie Saw what* Cricket snaps a piece of the taffy *They say* I start over *that the only safe way two people can sleep on a bed is if both people have one foot on the floor at all times* Cricket chews *Why* she says and I don't know if she's pretending to not understand what I'm saying or if she's still that stoned *Never mind* I say hoping she is too stoned

Cricket licks her fingers slowly one at a time *Kelly used to lick her fingers like that* I say *careful one at a time Who's Kelly* Cricket says rubs her fingers one at a time on her t shirt I pop the last chunk of taffy into my mouth think about her question how to explain Kelly *Who is she* Cricket says taps her foot on the floor *An old friend* I say *From* she leans up on one of her elbows so she can look at me *High school* I say the taffy balling up in my mouth instead of sticking to my teeth *Huh* she says traces something on the sheet *I didn't know you were out in high school* I clamp down on the ball of taffy stamp it with my teeth *I wasn't not really* I say my teeth stuck together *I knew but I didn't do anything Did you date boys* she says No oh no I laugh unstick my teeth suck on the taffy stare at the couch *Patty* I say *I was out to her*

Patty Cricket says like a question *Yeah* I toss the wrapper on the floor *I'm tired Me too* Cricket says tracing the sheet *why don't you sleep up here* she touches my forearm *with me*

We wake

at the same time my hand on Cricket's back her curls on her pillow *Good morning* she says her back to me I take my hand off her back *You can leave it there* she says I freeze I don't know what to do I don't know what to do! should I put my hand back if I do it'll be like saying I like her and then she'll know and she'll disappear and I'm not stoned now if I don't put my hand back I'll be saying I don't like her that my hand was there as a mistake that I didn't mean to kiss her last night it happened because I was fucked up

What to do what to do!
crazy girl can't decide!

I decide to touch her I decide to take a chance my fingertips touch her spine between her shoulder blades the sun hits the floor and wall in patches there's no curtain on the window but it's okay no one can see in there's a forest outside the window I run my fingertips to her shoulder blade protruding like the wing of a bird underneath she is vulnerable tender soft

and I realize she wants to be taken care of and I move across the sheet until the front of my body reaches the back of hers my breasts push into her shoulder blades my belly into the curve of her low back my thighs rest against the back of her legs and she lets go falls into me I touch my lips to her neck breathe in her skin

Hey sunshine

Amanda says from her bedroom her voice tied up and dragged behind a truck *up yet No* Cricket rolls over so she can look at me runs her hand across my cheek *another hour* she smiles at me whispers *at least another hour All right* Amanda says *I can use the beauty sleep* Cricket grabs my arm rolls over so she's face down on the bed pulls me with her until I'm on top of her *Hey* I whisper *sneaky*

my hips move into the curve of her back her body against mine feels so good so right I bend over push aside her curls lick the salt off her neck we ride each other slow motion time loses me in her hair softer than the cotton of the sheets her skin so salty her lips a green fresh fruit the ocean over us in us through us

Rise and shine

sunshine Amanda says her feet slap on the floor we roll off each other *the day's a wasting* Cricket and I giggle I flop over to my side of the bed throw my arm across my pillow close my eyes for a moment I want to remember this feeling make a painting of it in my heart and mind forever *Whatcha want to do today* Amanda says runs water in the kitchen skids a chair across the linoleum the sun plays on the wall nothing matters to me right now in the moment it's just sun chair Cricket my bare arm life is what it is

I forget I'm on welfare I forget I'm in my hometown a ten minute drive from mad dad sad mother disappeared Patty nothing matters because

Cricket's body has been under mine her body has been over mine her body has been next to mine the sweetness of her smile is changing my life making the bad things less important this is what love does this is what sex can do this is what sex can do! it doesn't have to hurt maim own destroy this is what sex can do!

I just made some lemonade Amanda says raises a pitcher in the air *real lemons* she sets it on the kitchen table *Thanks* Cricket waves her hand Amanda enters the bathroom shuts the door Cricket leans over puts her face in mine *I like you* she whispers *a lot* I smile she kisses me deep long slow and now I know kissing doesn't have time either only mismatched patches of morning light on the wall soft hair on an arm threadbare sheets across a back

* * *

My house

is just around the corner I point to the intersection Kelly used to drop me off at when we stayed out late *at the vacant lot there* I tap my finger against the inside of the windshield *take a left How're you feeling* Cricket stops for a yellow light *Good* I say don't tell her how scared I am a city bus rumbles west toward my house *California sun* I say under my breath tap my knuckle on the dashboard trying to keep all of me in my body

You sure you're okay Cricket says *Fine* I say I don't tell her that I'm afraid mad dad'll pull me out of her car drag me upstairs rape me keep me locked up in a room for the rest of my life like those girls you read about in the paper *I just don't want anyone to see me Okay* Cricket pulls one of her curls behind her ear *I just want to see the house and then go meet Amanda for lunch* I say watch a bird hop along the sidewalk the light turns green I sit back in my seat like I'm taking off in a rocket ship terrified to see the house or my parents in the yard terrified of the past what it looked like smelled like felt like

Cricket I say

as we turn the corner *I'm afraid I know* she says

We drive toward

the house I put everything inside on hold like I used to in the bedroom mad dad slamming downstairs everything on hold! no feelings no sense of being anywhere I disconnect my senses until I am watching a movie of a street that looks like the street I grew up on the house next door to the one that looks like the one I grew up in is white two stories high wood siding it's a dream an old home movie with the black specks and jerkiness of a 1960s hand held camera

Here we go I say not sure if I say it in my head or out my mouth

The last place I saw Patty I say not sure if I say it in my head or out my mouth

Did he kill her I say not sure if I say it in my head or out my mouth

I watch a movie film strip of a street like mine Patty Patty I miss you! there is a corner of my old house *They painted it green* I say out my mouth Cricket slows down the cedar bushes in the front almost cover the windows bright cut out wood ducks with clumsy orange feet in the yard *Ducks* I say what's going on my father would never allow those in his yard *Ducks* Cricket says tries to look but we're past the house lilacs wave their purple heads *Ducks* I say *fake ones with stick legs Gotcha* Cricket says *Like flamingos in Florida here they're ducks* and the movie is over my body is flesh and water instead of limitless space I look across the street at Patty's house trucks in the front yard a snowmobile to the side it's the same *Ducks* I say my head pressed into the head rest

All those bad things

happened right there I say *working class Americana flags up flagpoles pansies tulips in the flower boxes* we run into Lake Phalen *take a left* I say *we have to wind around it* I watch the bright patches of sunlight on the lake sparkle *who would guess it No one* Cricket looks to her left at the lake *it's important to talk about it* and I look at her profile amazed she thinks it's important to talk about things no one wants to hear she shifts into second I think I love her

Do you really

think your dad killed Patty Cricket says we are sitting on the fire escape outside Amanda's bedroom *What* I say shocked that Cricket would ask me that like she read my mind *I've never told anyone I thought that* I feel like I'm going to fall through the holes in the fire escape *You said it in the truck today* Cricket says a red VW pulls into the parking lot below us *What when* I am unnerved I didn't know I told her *In the truck* Cricket drinks her lemonade *when we drove by your house I did* I say and I know I must have because how else would she know the red VW parks Cricket clinks the ice in her lemonade

panic like heroin releases into my bloodstream how come I don't remember telling her a car door slams gravel kicks out from under the woman's feet as she walks across the lot I feel like I'm going to tear down this metal fire escape with my bare hands how come I don't remember *I'm sorry* Cricket says *I didn't mean to upset you* she stirs the lemonade with her finger and I want to smack the glass down into the lot crash it everywhere say how the fuck do you think it would make me feel I stare at the tree limbs hanging over us full of green pine cones half the size of my fist how come I don't remember and something releases overrides the panic I see the white house in my head just like a movie and I know that's when I said it and I remember not knowing if I said it out loud or just inside my head

a squirrel dashes across the lot then up a tree its tail whisks around the trunk I run my hand down the smooth black railing and an image of Dana on the steps of Bascom Hall pops into my head *2 4 6 8 who do we want to berate* and I'm there again the sun and excitement Dana her long hair and the triplets *Where are you* Cricket's voice cuts into the memory *Huh* I say *What are you thinking about* she says *Oh* I say *a long time ago a rally we did at the U Who's we* she coughs *The anti rape something I forget the name* Cricket moves her feet *I used to be in a group like that back in college* she says *Really* I say still back at the protest *Yep* she says *after college I worked at a rape crisis center Oh* I say embarassed *did you like the work Loved it* Cricket says and I want to know why she quit but I don't ask

A man

on a Harley drives into the lot *I'd love to have a bike like that* Cricket says *Uh huh* I say and I watch him but not really my eyes focused on the house I grew up in the ducks the tall cedars *Too close to the telephone lines* I say *What* Cricket says *The cedars* I tap the back of my hand *they're too close to the telephone lines I wonder if my father died Huh* Cricket says *I'm not following* the man on the bike walks across the parking lot his cowboy boots shoot gravel against the side of the building I wonder if my father's dead if that's why the cedars are so tall and the ducks are in the front yard I flash to the day we moved in mom and me in the living room the sunshine piling around the boxes on the floor *California sun* I say under my breath jump up out of the lawn chair *He didn't kill her* I say *she ran away hopped a truck California somewhere South Dakota North Dakota* I throw my arm toward the parking lot *west gone she left he didn't kill her* Cricket's eyes are big

I'll bet you a thousand dollars she hitched a ride with a trucker I say and Cricket sits in her chair her ass 6 inches off the fire escape deck *Patty ran away after my father raped her* I grab hold of the railing *will you take me back to the house* Cricket nods her mouth wide open her eyes shift from my face to my belly to my face

Drop

head in hand *You okay you okay Nooo nooo I'm not not at all* whistle while you work whistle while you work scrub lady scrub those knuckles clean *What's happening Nooo noo nothing at all happening Can I hold your hand Can you hold my hand hanzzzs I don't have any hanzzzs* face up floating at sea *lie down lie down here on the couch* push board down back on couch soft soft couch on back *So soft like at sea dead in a sea of throw up* Patty's face Patty's face! dead in a sea of throw up the corner of the bedroom Patty's face!

sweet Patty I watch her float I am above her sweet sweet Patty I have risen from the dead sweet sweet Patty does not float like I do she does not know these things her hair tangled in throw up reminds me of the oatmeal at oatmeal's house I have been here before dead died buried risen to the light sweet sweet Patty's face covered in oatmeal

Trip trap trip trap said the bridge *I'm going to kill this little bitch* said mad dad his shadow far below a hoary troll under a bridge kneels down over sweet sweet Patty carefully ever so carefully wraps his fingers one by one around sweet sweet Patty's neck *Patty! we wish there were something we could do! Patty we wish there were something we could do!* sweet sweet Patty's throat wrapped up in our bedroom never thought it would come to this sweet sweet Patty the love of our life we wish we'd never known you

so you would never have been hurt *Patty!* grab shirt *What what I'm here it's me Cricket Patty!* twist shirt *Patty! What's wrong what happened to Patty* mad dad's shadow down below thumbs press on the windpipe Patty's breathing is the sound of wood shavings off a rasp used to make a hole for a dowel in a stained rosewood two coats of polyurethane message board made in shop that mom hung on the kitchen wall next to the phone *Take a message mom yells from the basement I scribble call Marilyn about brownies on Wednesday 774 1289 call Marilyn!*

What who's Marilyn Cricket says soft soft couch on the back *Patty's neck choked I'm sorry I'm sorry she was hurt* I say from the ceiling above sweet sweet Patty her face tangled in oatmeal *oatmeal! Cricket what's going on is she okay* Amanda says *She's okay* Cricket says *Oatmeal!* I say from the ceiling *What* Amanda says *Nothing she's okay* Cricket says *Is she tripping* Amanda says *Oatmeal's house flying through the air with a lasso* I say *Man what is she on* Amanda says *Nothing just leave us alone* Cricket says *All right I'll be on the fire escape* Amanda clomp clomp clomps *if you need me*

rasping wood chips flying thumbs pressing tighter choking the breath out of sweet sweet Patty the troll devil man on his knees this is what I feared he would do to me sweet sweet Patty her face afloat in a sea of throw up that was at Oatmeal's house once upon a time in a land far far away Oatmeal's! Oatmeal's the judge judged me crazy! crazy girl! crazy girl! no one will believe you!

Patty Patty

down below dying in the northeast corner of my attic bedroom in a house that was supposed to have California sunshine no sun no shine no California just dirty truckers greasy jeans bald tires that split off litter the road like orange rinds headed to the Dakotas they split at 94 n 35W some go south some go north Patty! I see you now your bright lips faded to blue I see you now! he unwraps his fingers one by one slowly and carefully one by one mad dad troll man changes his mind he changes his mind! walks down the stairs lies in wait under the bridge mother mean mean mother cleans the wall while you lie there Patty Patty! mother is a monkey on a chain you mustn't hate her Patty! but I do! a monkey on a chain do you know what that feels like to be a monkey on a chain to mad dad troll man I must not hate her but I do! white knuckled mother monkey licks the walls clean with her wash cloth and bucket of Pine Sol Patty moves the Pine Sol wakes her she's alive she's a live! Patty comes back from the dead

You must think

I'm crazy I say *No* Cricket says smooths the cowlick on my temple the soft couch on my cheek *you're not crazy You must think so* I say can't believe I'm saying this to her wildly out of control animal fear flaring horse nostrils *I won't blame you if you want to leave get away from me send me back on a bus You're not crazy* she curls my fingers inside her hand *this is the way traumatic memories process* shut up I think just shut up don't say that say I'm crazy so I can leave

Can't see

blackness lights went out curtain pulled

You must hate me No no why would I hate you You must think I'm stupid No no why would I think you're stupid You must want to hurt me No no why would I want to hurt you You must hate me No no why would I hate you You must Do you know who you're talking to tears running down my face *Yes no I don't who are you My name's Cricket Cricket like the bug Yes* laughs can't see anything blinder than a bat my voice is above me below me I can't find it or my body *Why Why is my name Cricket Uh huh It's a childhood nickname Why Well when I was little probably about your age I guess I used to catch bugs and keep them in fish tanks so my grandpa started calling me Cricket and it stuck Oh why did you get the bugs I liked them I liked to watch them and feed them and take care of them Oh I see* can't see blackness lights went out curtain pulled listening to a little girl talk to Cricket

See Cricket

bounce her curls see Cricket turn her head see Cricket smile at us see Cricket smile at us!

see Cricket look at her hand see Cricket talk to us see Cricket talk to us!

see Cricket see us see Cricket see us!

Wow

well hey that was trippy I watch Cricket out the corner of my eye *I got to stop doing so many drugs You okay* she touchs my hand *Sure* I don't know what just happened why I couldn't see but could hear why I sounded like a little girl asking Cricket little girl questions in a little girl's voice

we sit next to each other on the couch *What just happened is okay* Cricket says I don't know what to say I am embarrassed birds chatter *I just love that painting* I point to the one near the window with the purple spikes Cricket looks at it doesn't say anything

we sit in silence I wonder if she heard me then she looks me in the eyes *It's lovely* she says and she is crying and I am uncomfortable because she should not cry for me she should not cry for me! and I think she is not talking about the painting but about me and I have no ability to understand why she would think I was lovely I have no ability to understand what she just said and I feel like my head is going to blow off *whoo whoo train whistle!* what is going on and then I realize I have no ability to understand what she just said because I hate myself

Two hours

before the big party Amanda flips her book shut sets it on the kitchen table *are you two hungry Nah* I say slouched into the armpit of the couch one of my legs across Cricket's knees Cricket opens one eye then the other her head resting against the back of the couch *I'm good* she murmurs *Okay then* Amanda stretches her arms above her head then bends at her waist like a hinge slaps the floor with her palms *I'm going running* she disappears into her bedroom and I am glad she is gone I want to be with Cricket process what happened not have Amanda run interference

Cricket closes her eyes Amanda springs out of her bedroom her running shoes have soles so thick she looks like Herman Munster *Hey* I say and I am uncomfortable talking with her since she saw me acting so weird *Hey* she says stands in front of me puts her hands on her hips *How long you going to run* I feel a pang of guilt because I want her to be gone for a long time *Oh 4 or 5 miles* she says her smile runs off her face *Oh that's good* I say *I mean it's a long way to run* now I feel like real shit because I don't mean it I am being sneaky change my mind I want go to my old house case it out

Amanda clomps out the front door *See ya* I say she says nothing and I feel a zing of satisfaction run up my spine knowing that I bugged her I lean over cup my hands around Cricket's cheeks *Let's go* I say *take me to my house What* she opens her eyes pulls me next to her *Take me to my house Are you serious* she says *Yeah* I say *we've got two hours before the party* Cricket pulls me closer puts one hand on the small of my back under my shirt *I want to spy on them come on it'll be fun* and I'm serious it will be fun but more importantly I need to know why those ducks are in the yard

Stop here

I say into the idea of sneaking up on my parents especially my father the way I used to spy on him in the kitchen sneaking around corners my back flat against the walls or hiding under the couch watching his heels move back and forth as he scratched them against each other

I slump until my head is just above the truck's dashboard look up and down the sidewalks *All right* I am a commando *turn it off follow me* I hop out of the truck Cricket kills the engine gets out slowly sometimes she moves like an old cowboy *Psst* I say from behind the truck *this way* I run next to a low concrete block building painted white years before when it was a garage when I was just a kid when grease monkeys in gray striped overalls smoked cigarettes between their forefingers and thumbs then dropped them let them burn out on their own *Isn't that dangerous* mother asked me waiting for an oil change I shrugged my shoulders was seven how would I have known

Cricket run!

I say we run behind the building past a boarded up window tufts of grass between the pavement cracks half a door cut off right above the handle lying flat on the pavement and I wonder if any of the butts are still there a stupid thought I tell myself but I want to stop and look anyway find something to tie me to my past to Patty to all I've lost

Everything!

we run past the boarded up garage we run faster than the speeding cars on the street we run like there is no tomorrow like today is it we run like we are Ahmad Rashad Fran Tarkenton Rod Carew rounding third base sliding in to beat the throw home we run through Teclaw's back yard jump over their row of drooping wine colored peonies we run like Bruce Jenner around a lopsided wading pool we squeeze between waist high bushes we run I feel my leg muscles stretching and squaring and pushing off and my arms pumping I am a scrawny seven year old straight out of a Barbara Beasley book my body shrinks my nose grows freckles my bangs cut straight across I am seven! Yo Adrian! I am seven! playing with Patty playing with Cricket run! feel your girlbody's strength run! me and Cricket run! we are Bruce Jenner! we are Martina Navratilova! we are Ahmad Rashad Fran Tarkington Muhammad Ali float like a butterfly sting like a bee fists above our head Rocky Balboa style I am Rocky! *Yo Adrian I love you!*

Cricket

I say stop in Jerozek's dark backyard shaded by a three story maple their TV hums through their porch door *watch out* Cricket is not as quick as me runs into my shoulder I grab her she is panting her curls tight from the heat *Cricket* I hold her by the shoulders look into her eyes and I am not afraid I am not afraid! *I have to find Patty* I shake her I am not here to find out about the ducks I am not here to find out about the father I am here for Patty I am here for Patty! *Okay* she says and I imagine she is impressed by how fast I am how agile I am how Muhammad Ali I am

I pull

her into the alley we stand underneath a basketball hoop its lopsided frame displaying a dirty red white and blue three stranded net *Maybe mad dad had an accident he's in a wheel chair he can't stop my mother from putting the ducks out arranging them largest to smallest all facing in one direction* the words slip sliding out my mouth confusing me I just decided I was here for Patty *maybe mad dad is dead got hit by a truck when he went out one morning to check the mail bam flattened* I smack my palms together Cricket is staring at me the lowest edge of the net inches above her head I am over the edge want to stop but can't

Maybe they got divorced yeah that's it mom divorced him finally after all these years she's taking classes at the U he's gone gone gone out I snap my fingers *of the picture* I say Cricket's mouth is round like a fish I think maybe she is part fish *I always wanted* I stop talking cry for a second then stop crying stand there like I've never shed a tear in my life she stares at me the nylon net over her head like a crown *you look funny* I say *like a fish* then wish I hadn't I sound rude but I didn't mean to be rude she looks like a fish! *c'mon let's go find Patty we got to find Patty* and I see a picture of her in my head lanky Patty hair in a pony like the day I first saw her from my bedroom window using a sword like a stick *she didn't deserve it* I say without meaning to speak and I feel a sympathy in my bones and it's for Patty and it's for me too a new feeling

I pull Cricket down the alley past the garbage cans and the remnants of a gutted bathroom vanity fake cream colored marble top an orange ringed toilet a stack of newspapers tied with twine to a gray garage the side door padlocked and then the alley ends

This is it I stop running stand stock still feel oddly proud I'm showing Cricket where I came from and there's no shame for a moment I have no shame take a deep breath say *this is it* again slowly *my home* I look past the alley at the yard sloping away from the house an overgrown yard covered with mole trails and rhubarb patches the size of a red VW parked under a tree

Patty's back yard

years ago another lifetime this was my home the swish of the ball as it rolled through the grass like a snake we cut criss crossed trails up and down her yard preparing for the day we would play in high school and then college be the stars listen to the fans roar the way they did when football players ran on to the field fists pumping in the air Martina Navratilova slamming a forehand down the line that's who we were going to be heroes adored victorious our dreams of glory spinning black and white through the tall grasses

Where are we going Cricket says *I can barely keep up with you* and I don't know if she means I run too fast or if it's my mood swings and I want to say try being me but I don't *To the river* I say *I want to hear it sing* we sit on the bank made steeper and more craggy by the lack of water the tan earth jutting into emptiness dried and cracking I shut my eyes my hand across my belly I can feel my heart throb

I imagine the rubber soccer ball mother bought for me at Target swish through the grass I can still see us standing in the aisle picking it out three soccer balls in red cardboard boxes one black one white one small and white next to the tennis rackets *Isn't it strange that your heart throbs in your belly* I say Cricket says nothing I can barely hear the water running downstream there is no singing I open my eyes lose the ball and the sound of the ball in the grass the sight of two farmer tanned girls on their toes *I'm sorry I'm so weird* I say Cricket picks up an egg shaped rock throws it into the water *What's weird that we live in a society where these kinds of atrocities happen to kids every third house out there* she says waves behind her *in the cities suburbs country every third house children are raped beaten so no not really* she throws a smaller rock *just depends on what you define as weird Okay* I say Cricket can be with me *And feeling our hearts beat in our bellies makes me think about survival we're animals we can't help but survive our bodies are built that way* she sits up skips a rock across the surface of the water lands in the middle of the island then falls off taking part of the dirt with it

The garage door

opens behind us I jump to my feet would recognize the screech then the rattle an old man coughing up his bones then the abrupt slide ending with a slam *C'mon* I say hold out my hand pull her to her feet my heart is beating so fast I hear it in my ears drowning out everything else Patty! Patty! I want to yell Patty's come home! but I keep my mouth shut listen to my heart pounding after all these years I still want Patty I want Patty! my best friend forever and ever! all these years my desire a puck trapped under the blade of a hockey stick

I pull Cricket up what am I thinking I am not thinking I am moving my heart is pushing pulling me toward what I want I grip Cricket's hand in mine I am afraid I am excited I never really lost hope is what I realize the pounding in my ears I never lost hope Patty would come back someday she will! she will! and I can't let go

Patty!

running up the hill to the garage two blue bearded irises tip over on their stems against the garage wall *Patty!* she is back Patty has come home! *Patty!* I am ten I am nine I am eight running to see my savior my teammate my best friend forever and ever the girl I kissed the girl named P for pee for *Patty!* takes me away from my parents mad dad devil man *Patty!* makes it okay makes it possible *Patty!*

Jimmy

stops dead a tall six foot five bony Jimmy faded jeans tank top stands in the garage *Jimmy* I gasp then take two steps through the back door into the shaded garage my house in the distance through the open garage door a motorcycle to my right a weed whacker garbage can cardboard boxes push lawn mower its wheels stained green mud or shit in the cracks *is that you* bag of sunflower seeds bag of Scott's weed killer bag of sand stack of pink Easter baskets tufts of synthetic green grass *Jimmy* I am not a little girl I am twenty five year old me short dykey me left five years ago me

he doesn't move black hair down to his shoulders left over platinum dye on the last two inches tattoos up and down one arm veins stick out up and down his forearms his mouth drops open *It's you* he says we stare memories flood cleaning his plate after dinner kicking him out of the basement during floor hockey curling his hair with a curling iron putting his mom's dried out make up on him orange clown cheeks *Jimmy* I gasp shocked at how much he has changed in my mind I still saw him as a little boy now he's a man I'm a woman our bodies grew and grew changed but I still live in the past as a girl a little girl a littler girl it is now not then I am here now not there inside I swirl

You came back he says his voice deeper stronger slower but still his sweet boy self wanting wanting wanting as much as Patty and I wanted he wanted as much as we did he needed as much as we did *Yes* I say Cricket scuffs her boot behind me I turn toward her shock etched across my face I don't know what to do or say *Ah* I sweep my arm through the air at nothing toward nothing everything lived in my head in my memory now it's real I can't escape it

Hey Cricket looks past me smiles wide leans forward and as she puts out her hand sun lights up her shoulder and neck I am struck by how much I like her *I'm Cricket* she says Jimmy steps forward reaches out shakes I watch in slow motion as two of my worlds collide *I'm Jimmy* he says the veins on his arm popping his voice hollow

My god

I say *it's good to see you* my head spins rusted steel pipes lying over the garage beams above me I can't figure out what they are *This is Cricket* I say then realize she just told him her name I don't know what to do Jimmy nods tucks one hand in his jean pocket *Um* what do you say after leaving for five years to the brother of your best friend who disappeared at ten after your father raped her he looks down at a grease spot on the floor covered with sand

What's that I point to the rusted pipes *Um* he says keeps his hand in his pocket *an old TV antennae Oh* I say feel stupid *I don't remember it* the three of us stand in the garage looking at the walls or floors or grease spots *Yeah* Jimmy says rubs the back of his neck *me neither*

My god I say again just to say something no one says anything *it's been a long time Jimmy* he nods his eyes red staring at the grease stain *you're all grown up* I say then can't believe I would say something so stupid so adult *You too* he says looks at me quickly *Not really* I say he reaches into his back pocket *Mind* he pulls out a red and white pack of Marlboros *Nah* I say look at Cricket she is in the door frame arms crossed shakes her head

Jimmy smokes

I never thought you'd come back he shakes his head *Me neither* I look past him at the house *can we go out back* I want to hear about Patty where she is what she's doing but I don't want my father to see me *Yeah* Jimmy says

I sit by the blue bearded irises he sits on the grass where the yard begins to slope toward the river turns his back to me runs his arm over his face Cricket is smelling a mound of violet lilacs Jimmy's shoulders jerk I look at Cricket to see if she has noticed Jimmy but she has moved to the other side of the lilac bush the only thing I can see is the toe of her boot and the knuckles of her left hand Jimmy spits in the grass runs his hand through his hair smashes out his cigarette in the grass

I want to ask about Patty maybe I can call her tonight maybe I can call her tonight! but Jimmy won't look at me picks at grass I pull the head of the iris toward me stare at the yellow streak that runs down its throat touch the hair on the lip *Jimmy* I say *are my parents still here* I release the iris its head snaps against the side of the garage *Nah* he says and shivers of excitement relief curiosity loss run up my back

It's over! it's over! Little Miss So And So won! we won! we won!

They're long gone he tries to sound like he's not crying just like he did when he was a boy *When* I say *A year ago* he says *Where* I say Cricket moves around the lilac bush looks at me raises her eyebrows I smile at her a huge weight drops off my body mad dad is not across the street *He got transferred or lost his job something like that* and the emphasis Jimmy puts on *he* makes me know Jimmy doesn't like my father either *Out of town out of state* I say Cricket moves next to me *Um* Jimmy says pulls his hair into a pony tail then drops it *I think they went to Colorado or maybe Montana Really* I say imagining my parents living in Montana with cowboys *He got some sort of job making leather stuff belts like that* and my stomach tightens *Perfect for him* I mumble *Yeah* Jimmy says kicks his toe into the ground *and um* he looks at me looks away *I don't know if I should tell you* glances at Cricket *but he came over here before he left told me to tell you if I ever see you that he got a job you know making belts* I feel sick *Gross* I say under my breath he got in one last punch Cricket sits down next to me kicks her boots straight out in front of her touches my hand

Cricket props

the heavy iris head against a stake but it thuds against the garage wall *What about your parents* I say I want to ask about Patty but something stops me *Same old same old* he hunches over his knees *Yeah I hear you* I say *Dan is on the JV soccer team Cool* I say have to think a second before I figure out Dan was their last baby *I guess he's taking after you* Jimmy says it is good to be around someone who knows me from before Jimmy missed me remembered I played soccer *How's school* I feel guilty because I never thought about him I don't remember how old he is don't know if I should ask if he's graduated or not *Fine* he says *I'm in tech school* he brushes at a fly on his face *to be a chef Great* I nod at the grass

it feels good to be here my parents are gone Jimmy is here Patty might be here I run my hand across Cricket's back I'm happy excited thinking about how things will be no more parents I can come back here be friends with Jimmy and Patty I'll have family maybe Cricket and I could move here I scratch my fingertips up and down her bumpy bumpy spine

Creepy crawly spider

walks up the spine one two three four *her back is degenerating at an alarming rate* I pull my hand away *the headboard did it the head board did it!* my head spins Jimmy's shoulder blades jerk a bird stabbing at seed *creepy creepy spider walks up the spine alarming degenerating rate* Jimmy sobs *What* I look from Cricket to Jimmy *what's wrong* I panic *where's Patty* I yell slide into my childhood a slippery steep slope and I am gone *I didn't do anything* I shout *I love her I want to see her right now* Jimmy wraps his arms around his head *You can't* he says *she's dead*

The headboard

did it the headboard did it! whish whish whish the head board did it! is all I hear see

think *head board head board head board the head bored head board!*

Rusted steel pipes

clatter to the floor break cement chunks lodged in the air this is the last of my past *What how when no no no* I hear myself say dams smashed bricks sod poles fly sobbing an ocean from his eyes joining the stream below

On the streets drug overdose always down on Lake Franklin never left Minneapolis came home a few times after you left stayed once for two weeks but always went back died in an alley tried to save her looked for her on my bike she hid had a boyfriend beat her up threatened mom and dad she asked about you the last time I saw her she said she was going to find you in Madison get it together go to school

No California sun

for Patty no California sun for Patty! no California sun for any of us California sun is a lie

*   *   *

Cricket says:

lie down, so I do
Cricket says: cry so I do
Cricket says: put your head on my shoulder so I do
Cricket says: let me wrap you in a blanket so I do
Cricket says: breathe so I do

Cricket's boots walk away talk to Amanda I creepy crawly into a coffin shut the lid pound in the last nail it is rusty and bent I see it sliver through the pine I hear the rust creak against the grain of the fresh wood Cricket's boots pick me up slide me in the truck bed shut the tail gate drive to Madison to Tara to Frida the whir whir of the road

Cricket delivers

me to the therapist

I am made of glass, I say

I am the underside of a hoof, I say
I am the broken wing of a crow so black it's blue, I say
I am the weathered eye of a cat, I say
I am the fray in the weave of a white bassinet, I say
I am the stainless steel tip of an orange handled scissors, I say

T*he point is* I say *I know the point* therapist says sips her mango tea *why do you talk in so many metaphors Metaphors* I say *keep me alive Uh huh I see* therapist says *Patty is dead* I say therapist does not see *I know* therapist says *you can't change that how are you going to stay alive I did not think therapists were supposed to be so brutal* I say *I am sorry about Patty* therapist says *deeply sorry but you are my concern right now Once upon a time* I say *there was a girl who was being tortured in a modest but adequate home with a TV and a driveway and running water and tulips along the front that bloomed in mid spring the girl was sent to a nurse and the nurse sent her to the police and the police sent her to a foster home and the foster home held her until a man in a suit took her to a judge and the judge judged her crazy and she was sent home to be further tortured on a street named Rose Avenue that unbelievably was one block off Payne Avenue life is certainly stranger than fiction Okay* therapist says *The point is* I say *I understand* therapist says *why should you trust me Good point* I say *my point exactly* therapist says nothing so I say *when you are tired of being a therapist you can go to school for English Well* therapist says *You are a smart therapist* I say *the only way I will stay alive if I am still alive you understand the coffin* and I point to the coffin therapist nods *are through the metaphors and similes and the pictures I see in my head then put down on paper I see* therapist says but I do not know if she does *I think* therapist says *you should come back tomorrow That will be fine* I say *because I can imagine lying in this coffin on top of the bed in the small room forever* and in that way I know I need to see the therapist whether or not she has big glasses and a pointy nose which she does not by the way have *Perhaps I can trust you* I say and sit up yoga style in the coffin *smells like fresh cut wood* I say *I know* therapist says *the scent is overtaking the room*

The therapist delivers

me to Cricket Cricket loads me into the truck bed drives me home places me in my coffin on the bed Tara is home but she does not make me chicken soup

I am guilty

I say *don't you see I should punish myself forever Just like your father would have you do* therapist says and I think she is smart but irritating *You don't understand* I say *Patty is dead it is my fault That is not logical* therapist says *You should be a lawyer* I say *you are logical and cold No* therapist says *I don't want to be a lawyer or an English student I want to be a therapist and right now I am wondering if you are going to be okay through the weekend I am glad* I say *I am like a fish in water* and I begin to sweep my arms out wide except I bump them into the pine boards *do you think I avoided a cliché by saying a fish is glad to be in water I don't know* therapist says *enough about the literary world to answer your question Some help you are* I say and turn my attention to conjuring pictures of my emotions in my head instead of devising dead metaphors

    I feel like I would like to die I say as a statement of fact *I can understand that* therapist says *let's talk about that What's there to talk about* I say *It is important to share your feelings with other people in that way you begin the process of* I shut my eyes breathe in the smell of the pine think about how long would it take before the fresh smell of the wood turned sour and musty in the earth *transference projection avoidance are all normal ways of dealing with trauma* colors list about in my mind *If I could figure out how to get all these pictures I see in my head onto canvas I would be rich Or another starving artist* therapist says *But wealthy inside* I say *both of which are dead clichés* I see nothing but black eyeballs and wonder if I would be self conscious if I were blind *Say* I say *in therapy school did they ever talk to you about the overuse of clichés it seems it would be an important consideration when dealing with matters of the soul* I sit up a little taller *I mean one does not want to have Hallmark therapy Did you hear what I was saying Not really* I say *I tuned you out* and I open my eyes but when I open my eyes there are children sitting around me like I am the second coming of Jesus Christ and I see the blue children's Bible I had in second grade religion class and there was Jesus with his wavy golden beard and pointy knees sticking through his robe and part of a brown leather sandal and I wonder if somehow this means I have been redeemed or if it is merely a cruel trick

The therapist

does not seem to notice the children so I look at them closely while the therapist talks about Alice Miller's books which I read three years ago and found to be trite for the most part anyway never in any book I have read has there been mention of children sitting on one's lap at one's knees on the floor couch and tables who upon closer inspection look just like me when I was their age *Patty is dead* I say and some begin to cry and others simply look sad two nod their heads *Yes* therapist says *Patty is dead* and I look at her she does not seem to see any of the me children I have clearly gone insane but perhaps it is not so bad perhaps it is more interesting than being sane

    I see I say clear my throat watch one me child of seven pick at a scab on her knee *We love Patty* she says and the rest nod their heads *but we don't want to die just because she did* and the rest nod or tuck their heads in their arms like small birds *I see* I say again *You see what* therapist says *I see little me's everywhere* I say why not tell her the truth at this point it is too late to pretend to be sane therapist holds her breath for a moment then says *Where*

Around me I say *they don't want me to die Do you know where they came from* therapist says *No* I say *although they seem like they've been here forever I feel like I just got into a warm bath loaded with Epsom salt* one who looks to be about five holds my hand places her forehead against my arm *Are you going to lock me up now* I say feeling surprisingly peaceful about my fate what I have been running from forever *No* therapist says leans forward her head cocked to the right she really wants to bond with me on this point *What's wrong with me* I say *Nothing* therapist says clasps her hands together *I think you have separate parts of yourself What* I say notice the coffin is gone *Your confusion over names now this I think you're multiple Oh* I say *as in personalities Yes* therapist says *I've heard that before* I say look at the me children who are looking at the ceiling touching the bent over end of a spider plant staring at their red keds sitting up straight arms crossed across the chest they look sweet I think I could love them *On second thought you should stick to therapy* I say *but Alice Miller is old hat*

Your grandma

the therapist says *What* I say *We need to talk about your grandma Why* I say *Well for one thing because you want to avoid talking about her so badly that is the first clue the second clue is that she was someone you loved and she loved you yet you no longer have any contact with her why Those are a lot of questions all at one time* therapist I say then add *I'm sorry I don't mean to be a smart ass sometimes people's words are like a room filled with flies they all look the same sound the same and I have to sort them out* therapist nods sips her coffee says *Ah hem* I hunch over she isn't giving in *My father told me she cut off her phone* I hang my head deeper into the day *because she didn't want anything to do with me* I can barely breathe *Oh* therapist says almost perky *that doesn't mean anything I know* I say *but I checked and she wasn't listed You need to find out for sure* therapist says *must you continue to deprive yourself of love No* I say stare at the tip of my thumb *no not really I don't*

I had a dream

I say therapist has a new outfit today lime green chenille v neck sweater with black stretch jeans and matching lime green earrings that look like someone's old fishing lures *Nice outfit by the way Thank you* she says curtly uninterested in my utterances about her fashion sense *You're welcome* I nod absently to my left amused by the five year old me scowling on the eggplant colored couch reserved for the family in family therapy sessions *Well we are sort of a family* I say to the five year old *Huh* therapist says *These children and I* I sweep my arms out *they've been following me since I saw you yesterday* I rest my chin on my hand therapist crosses her legs moves her foot up and down slowly like a bridge lifting for a sailboat I roll my eyes to the left narrow them shake my head slightly at the five year old who is thumping the back of her red ked tennis shoe against the couch *What's going on* therapist says *Nothing* I say *nothing at all I see* therapist says I notice she has a habit of saying I see when I don't see how she could possibly see given that I am speaking about me children she does not see

the therapist's lime green ankle stops *Tell me about the dream* she says *What dream* I say curtly imitating the attitude she took with me when I commented on her dangling fishing lures probably originally designed to snare northerns out of murky waters I have gone crazy I think privately to myself but the five year old vigorously shakes her head no apparently when I think to myself I think to her too she nods yes *The dream* therapist says *Oh* I say suddenly remembering *that dream* one of the four year olds starts to pick her nose *No no* I say shake my finger at her she drops her hand like a lead weight number ten was attached to it therapist blinks raises her perfectly plucked eyebrows at me *Never mind* I wave my hand see the murky cover to Nirvana's Nevermind CD in my head a white infant under water reaching for a soggy dollar bill I buckle down *In my dream I was walking toward the ocean located interestingly enough in Minneapolis not Saint Paul you know Minneapolis is considered the more upbeat modern city of the two they're not twins you know not at all in fact they're basically opposites anyway back to the ocean where I worked for some reason still unknown to me I was carrying like a briefcase a miniature Chinese man who was awake and alert I still can see his face he turned it about this way and that it was square and too large for his face sort of like a briefcase sized Asian Frankenstein*

What happened therapist says *Nothing happened* I say and give off a slight snort I am beginning to doubt her intelligence *What does it mean to you* she says *I don't know* I shrug *you're the therapist you figure it out* and I want to say that's why I pay you but can't since the state writes out the checks *Okay* therapist says *what is the significance of the man's race how does he relate to your past* Hmm I say and I am immediately transformed into a four year old me being read to by a white knuckled mother *snip snap trip trap this tale's told out* my foot thumping like a rabbit against the couch the shiny pages of the book smooth as glass mother reads *Five Chinese brothers went down to the ocean one crisp fall morning* and my eyes feel as if they will roll back my mind snaps like the necks of the moles we couldn't save caught in the traps behind Patty's house I am half here and half with my mother at four mother says *This Chinese man was very bad a very very bad man he killed his brothers it was all his fault* and I realize that something was not right with my mother from the very beginning what a strange thing to say to a child what a strange strange thing

Crazy

comes to me through a cardboard tube *Huh* the smooth cool surface of my stainless steel bracelet brings me to the room *When you refer to yourself as crazy you are abusing yourself* the therapist shifts her weight watches me rub the bracelet *On sale* I smile wave my wrist in the air *I see* she touches her fingertips together *Have you heard what I've been saying* Well I say I heard you say crazy *And you came to* she says snaps her fingers *I suppose* I say *Has it always been like this Well* I slip the bracelet off hide it beneath my leg don't like it that she knows my secret survival strategies *in some ways* I say *but it's worse when I'm in here* she sneezes *Excuse me* she says *makes sense* blinks a few times *what I was saying* she clears her throat *is that it is counterproductive for you to call yourself crazy the judge made you feel crazy your parents made you feel crazy even told you you were crazy and now you carry it on* she reaches for a kleenex *I don't think anyone should be called crazy* I blurt out like a nine year old *it's mean mean mean You're right* the therapist says wipes her nose *I agree you and others like you have tremendous survival skills some people even think people like you are geniuses the test scores usually indicate a high intelligence level There's others like me* a nine year old me blurts out and the therapist nods and then I lose my focus stare at the black and white photograph of a lake with a pill sized hazy sun yeah I think survival skills genius not crazy not crazy!

Truth

I choke on the word spit it out on the carpet it's much shinier than I expected I kick it under the couch *What about truth* therapist says tilts her head looks under the couch *Do I know what it is how could all these things have happened to me in one lifetime not even a liftetime a childtime it's supposed to be time to be a child what does that even mean when so many kids are fucked by adults bullshit* I say *it's bullshit all lies* I curl on the couch like paper to a flame therapist sits forward *What is true* I say orange flames leaping off my sleeves therapist reaches under the couch slides out truth sets it on the floor between us *Here is truth* she says *and there are you what is your relationship to it* and I think she must be stupid to be asking me such a loaded question while I'm on fire *That's a loaded question and I'm on fire* I say she nods *I can see that It's so shiny* I say the flames turn blue *Yes* therapist says *Shiny almost metallic* therapist nods spits on her sleeve shines the r in truth *It's the holy grail* I say *For some* therapist says *Truth my father told me I did not know it* and then he hit me said this is what truth is I pause as if I'm taking a vocabulary quiz *truth is a noun it is the state of being the case a fact the property of being in accord with fact or reality You looked it up Of course* I say *in high school for a term paper it's always effective to define words or terms in an introduction even if it's something as simple as truth lesser known meanings and associations can be spun out of dictionary definitions teachers like that* she blinks and I see child pointy psychologist and the suit man and the judge *case dismissed the girl must be crazy Oh* she says and the flames lap against the ceiling I watch them with one eye watch therapist with the other is she one of them was I right to trust her so quickly is she really just going to leave me hanging like the rest *Is it important to you What* the flames burst across the ceiling I hold my arms out charcoal flakes fall off *I'm on fire the ceiling's on fire the bumpy bumpy ceiling What* she says looks at the ceiling *Can I know true* I nearly yell aware that the sentence is worded incorrectly aware it's not what she asked *I'm not crazy I know what's real I know what's true right right* I plead with her the fire crawls along the ceiling burning holes into the floor above us *right* I beg see child pointy psychologist oatmeal lady suit man judge in his black robe *No* she says *you're not crazy My feelings are real but they are not always the truth I thought mad dad killed Patty killed her my imagination imagined it but he didn't kill her she ran away and all these years I thought maybe he killed her sometimes I believed but it wasn't true my feelings were real she was gone I blamed myself I feared I cried I missed I longed but he didn't actually kill her* the flames burn to embers *so what does that make me a non truth a liar a crazy one of them my parents who don't care about truth who don't want truth who want lies that serve their purposes* I kick truth topple it *what does it make me* therapist sets truth upright smiles concerned even touched not like child pointy psychologist suit man oatmeal judge *It makes you a little girl who did the best she could and And* I say *memory can be right on exact and sometimes it's a composite of events and sometimes it comes to you as symbols in a dream and sometimes it's about the emotional truth no pictures or specifics at all I was hurt so many times so many ways some of it I won't ever remember some of it I'll remember it like it happened just this second some of it won't be exact but that doesn't mean it's not true right people don't make this shit up right right Right* therapist nods sets truth on the table next to her *you could spend your whole life stuck on the past what exactly happened mine the battlefield or you can accept the truth of the totality of your childhood deal with the specific triggers when they occur heal your emotional responses and move forward* I reach over touch truth it is smooth and cold as steel *Sometimes when I think of truth I see a bowl of oatmeal nothing more than a bowl of oatmeal murky lumpy and all the same color I see it right in front of me steaming why* I say *why would I see a bowl of oatmeal does that make me crazy I feel crazy telling you I see literally see a bowl of steaming oatmeal when I think about truth about whether I'm crazy* therapist shrugs *Could be a symbol could be a memory your brain connected with truth when you were a child* I study truth on the table it is shiny and bright like metal *Metal doesn't burn* I say therapist nods *by extension then truth does not burn not in a normal fire I'm not following* therapist says *Truth* I say *there are two versions a shiny bright metallic truth a murky lumpy same color truth made of boiled oats Okay* therapist says I am testing her limits *It's your choice Is it* therapist says *Yes* I say *you can choose to believe what you want what role does perception play in truth are there many truths is there one bright and shiny is truth a bowl of oatmeal* and it pops into my head I see black words on bright white paper *I'm just saying the truth. Like oatmeal by Tim O'Brien* I say *What* therapist says *Do you think I'm crazy now* I say *I just saw the page of the book where once I don't remember when or where I read truth is a bowl of oatmeal* therapist nods her eyes wider than normal *And* I say I'm getting excited as I always do when I make sense of my shattered consciousness *there was the oatmeal lady she fed me oatmeal every morning when that judge judged me crazy* therapist nods *this is how I am this is how my brain works I see pictures Yes* therapist says shaking her Doc Martin foot *did you know that highly visual people have higher rates of PTSD than non visual people I see* I say excited to have cracked the code of truth and the mystery of the steaming bowl of oatmeal *thank you for telling me that I did not know that highly visual people have higher rates of PTSD but I am thinking that we have two paths to choose about truth but behind those choices behind our perceptions there is truth bright and shiny and metallic and that it exists no matter what our perceptions my father raped me repeatedly throughout my childhood and my mother did nothing to stop him that is the truth* therapist stands up places truth on the shelf above her chair *I agree now that that is settled I believe that Patty's death has brought on all this self doubt and distance between us* I nod the fire's out the ceiling is smooth and white again *And* therapist says settling into her overstuffed chair *your father did in some respects kill Patty I know I know I know* I say staring at truth it shimmers when the light outside changes *he didn't pull the trigger but he set the machinery in motion I know I know I know* I say *I know it's true a murky murky true* and I nod at the therapist and I am aware that I did not use the correct form of truth but I am half child half adult and I can live knowing truth is a murky bowl of oatmeal dependent on our perceptions and it exists all on its own in a museum somewhere solid and bright and shiny *Mettle* I say *m e t t l e What* therapist says picks up her coffee cup *The substance or material out of which a person is made see how helpful it is to be familiar with dictionary defintions truth is shiny and bright and cold like steel metal is mettle is substance see the associations* I say *see how my brain works* and I tap my temple *Aha* therapist says sips her coffee *I see but not like you*

Truth is real

I shout in a little kid's voice *Yes it is* the therapist says nodding her head and her foot at the same time *Mad dad is the liar* I shout *not me I agree* the therapist says *what is your name Mouth*! I shout *my name is Mouth and I like to talk and I don't like liars Neither do I Mouth you chose a most appropriate name didn't you Yes* Mouth crosses her arms and satisfied disappears into the recesses of my consciousness I return to fully inhabit my body no longer half grown up half child

* * *

How many

do you have Tara says licks all the ice cream off her spoon *I dunno* I say *three four ten maybe So far* Tara says *Whatreyou* I say *an expert on multiple personalities Maybe* Tara laughs her flirty laugh digs out a cherry *Hey* I say *don't take the last cherry There's a whole pint left* she says one of my kids whines she doesn't want to share I jab at a cherry *Things make so much more sense now* I say Tara laughs *I've been reading up on multiples Why* I say *because of me Partly Why else* I say dig the cherry out feel triumphant *oh Stephanie* I say Tara laughs *Maybe* she says grabs the pint of Cherry Garcia from me *Hey* I say *give it back* it's one of my kids and the song Isn't She Lovely by Stevie Wonder pops into my head yes I think to my selves you are you are all so lovely

* * *

I brush my teeth

spit into the sink *Pah! Pah! I did not run off to California! I stay right here right inside you!* I spit one more time *Pah!* hear the water run downstairs rinsing off the dishes *creepy crawly spider went up the back* and I feel like I am crazy shouldn't be around other people *creepy crawly spider one more spot and you're going to foster care again No!* I rack the toothbrush a light clicks off downstairs mad dad turning off the lights walking up to my room clunk clunk clunk the troll under the bridge the panic of the body knowing what is coming my mind split into a thousand pieces or more rolled in oatmeal and deep fried my god how many people do I have in here *Lots!* I hear someone say she doesn't sound concerned she sounds happy *No more comments from the peanut gallery* I hear someone say *We're not a peanut gallery* the one who said lots says *we're a chorus A chorus* someone says *laaaa!* and laughs *No not that kind of chorus a literary chorus a greek chorus a* and I stop listening how could you be happy going through life knowing you have other people living inside your head who can you tell beside a few people everyone will think you're crazy stay away from you *I never went to California* I look in the mirror see a round face raven black hair small red lips China Doll Girl!

I wake

make art vomit the sea creatures swim on canvas purple black ochre *Wow* say Cricket Tara the neighbor's cousin's son who helped Cricket carry a used washing machine to the basement *Wow*

China Doll Girl

never ran off to California I say *Mmm hmm* therapist says sporting a new haircut her bangs are gone swept off the to the left side of her face she looks strange *Who's China Doll Girl* therapist says sits back *Nice haircut* I say *and I like those running shoes you must be going walking over lunch* she knits her brow is hip to my attempts to distract her *Oh just you know my imagination* a four year old twists the therapist's gold door knob pulls the door open then shuts it *Does she have a connection to your dream What are you Freud or something* I think about lying down on her couch as a joke but decide not to *I suppose* I say *I had a doll with half a jelly bean stuck in its basket she was Chinese the doll* I add come sit here next to me I think to the four year old she lets go of the door knob hangs her head dutifully walks toward me *A jelly bean* therapist says her bangs begin to creep toward her forehead *Irrelevant* I say *just a detail to make it seem more real Was it real What The doll The jelly bean The doll Was the doll real* I say musing the four year old climbs into my lap I have never been the mothering type I feel the weight of her on my lap and smell her Johnson's baby shampoo hair the same kind I used when I was kid I feel her need to be taken care of *My god* I say *how could someone hurt a child* and I wrap my arms around her she wraps her fingers around my wrist *What's going on* therapist says *China Doll Girl* I say *was she real what is real are the voices in my head real are the children running around your office real or is it simply my imagination* and I know the question is so basic it's silly an elementary inquiry but I know the answer doesn't matter the agony of the four year old on my lap and her need to be acknowledged is what matters

Well the therapist says leans forward arms crossed eyes focused on the carpeting *Bad parents!* flies out my mouth in the Chinese accent I used in high school when I was drunk *very very bad parents Patty their responsibility not ours* therapist sits up *we did nothing wrong* and I slam the hand that the five year old is not holding into the couch's cushion China Doll Girl is back *I never leave* China Doll Girl says we all sit silently staring at one another *She used to harass my parents* I say to the therapist *she was very brave* and I see China Doll Girl her round face nodding eyes closed *everyone wants to be acknowledged* I say to the therapist *for their role in our survival* China Doll Girl nods vigorously her arms crossed over her chest therapist says *Yes* her bangs pushed to the side again the four year old nods her cheek against my arm *Everyone* I say under my breath *the jocks stoners kids drinkers readers artists everyone* and I think of Grace Paley and something enormous stirs inside

Stirring

oils Cricket bought for me making colors shapes life on hatched canvas in a basement in Madison Wisconsin where I live things formerly in my mind taking shape in the world I transfer them like those patches we ironed when we were kids dragons unicorns flowers melted onto denim across a thigh butt back I peel the layers of my mind inside out won't hold them anymore won't keep my parents' secrets won't drink their death

Days fly

by on broomsticks their tailcoats flitting behind them Cricket visits her family in New York Tara washes clothes in the basement worships Cricket for the machine I stir oils flash dry acrylics powder pastels paint a white clap board house tulips a garage door a big eared girl here is where I will tell the world what the girl with the biggest ears in all the world in all the world! what she I we know

Blue bells

I come to look at therapist for a clue she nods she says *I've been having an interesting conversation with a little one five or six*

Cricket's home

Look at all those paintings! she whistles through teeth *beautifious fantabulous you are remarkable* they fill the basement overflow up the stairs spill into the hall *Missed you babe* kisses *Missed you too*

Cricket clicks

pictures of my art lined up against the dining room wall *What are you doing* she adjusts the five foot by five foot portrait of a screaming face steps back kneels her curls flop over the lens she tucks them behind her ear snaps three shots *I'm going to get you a show* I grumble *I could never get an art show anywhere* still uncomfortable with people doing things for me

The sun

comes up the sun drops down I go to therapy paint paint paint go to Monty's Blue Plate Diner with Cricket and Tara drink a Cherry Coke eat a mushroom burger with salt licked fries paint paint paint sleep next to Cricket's silky skin slide my fingers through her curls the sun arches falls arches falls I go to therapy paint paint paint demons trolls abalone shells n pebbles n bottom feeding fish

You got

it Cricket shouts slams the front door bounces into the kitchen grinning *What* I say *A show at Gallery 36 in Minneapolis* Cricket waves an envelope I slow the flame under the broccoli say nothing think I heard what she said but act like I don't it must be a mistake *Did you hear me* Cricket says *Sure* I say keep the happiness and fear tight rip open a box of Annie's shell shaped macaroni and cheese my back to Cricket *Jesus* Cricket says *you can really be something else* I splatter the noodles in the pot she's mad wonder if what she said could be true set two spoons on the table *Shit woman* she says *you act like I told you the sewer backed up and it's all your fault* I nod *What happened* I say hoping what she said is true hoping it won't be taken from me *Amanda's doing an internship at a gallery so I sent her your pictures* she grabs my arms *you got a show a real bona fide solo art show at a real bona fide gallery Amy says it's unheard of for someone who's unknown to get a show there Uh huh* I say thrill jumps inside me like a small silver fish *Jesus* Cricket shakes her head *you've got to let something good in some time* I know she's right I wrap my arms around her whisper *Are you kidding me* squeeze her hope she'll forgive me

The noodles

boil over flipping cartwheels beneath the foam Cricket kisses me *You've got a show* she says flicks off the flame *I'm sorry I couldn't just be happy* I say *I'm sorry I'm so fucked up Just be happy* Cricket says *let's eat later Yes* I say make circles on her back with the palm of my hand

Art

is my only justice I say to Cricket over a plate of mac and cheese and broccoli between us on her bed *Mmm* Cricket nods gulps points her spoon at her plate *this is good I like it* she is being polite the food sucks the noodles are hard I play with one of her curls *Art's justice* she says *but not the only one* I wanted her to agree with my black and white statement Cricket spoons up the last of the mac on our plate *Thanks for dinner honey* she says and I say nothing surprised that she called me honey Cricket moves the plate slides next to me *What else could be justice* I kiss her chin *Well* she says *you said you're Indian Part* I say *How come you never talk about it I dunno* I rub her ear *no one really talked about it except for my gramma Except for her* Cricket says traces the curve of my thumb *is she alive Yes* I say *as far as I know* I swallow the sadness push too hard crack the walls *We'd better find her* Cricket says *so you can know who you are* she holds the back of my head brushes her lips on mine kisses me *I need a girlfriend who knows herself* she smiles my breathing snags *There's more than one kind of justice in the world* she adds all the grief and longing for my gramma swells *I have to go to the bathroom* I say I have to get away from Cricket from the emotions I yank the chain the light highlights my face leaves the edges of the bathroom a murky gray I kick the door shut with my foot grip the sides of the sink look into the mirror at a round faced thick lipped black haired woman and I understand why China Doll Girl exists but I don't see her right now I see my gramma and then I see me

Age 25 1/2 - Epilogue I

I'm looking

for Martha Wadena I say *None listed* the operator replies *None listed* I glance at Cricket tap the pencil against the pad of paper *Uh huh* I say to the operator who rambles on about the weather a small town talker I remember people like her from the visits to my gramma's *Not anywhere in the vicinity* I say *No honey there's no Martha Wadena or M Wadena in our service area Huh* I say stand the pencil on its head *What about anyone with the last name Wadena* Cricket whispers *Any Wadenas* I say *Let me check* the operator coughs *just a minute now the system is slower today there were some problems last night with one of the computers you know how that goes honey Uh huh* I say *sure* roll my eyes at Cricket *Why honey there is a Wadena a Raymond Wadena Really* I say Raymond is my father's name *Yes in Dilworth as a matter of fact now I live in Glynden right next door to Dilworth I don't know him though never heard of him do you want his number is he one of those ah Wadenas that are ah Indians* I ignore her question nervous about calling a possible relative with the same name as my father *Okay here it is area code 218 435 9670 how's that* she says *I hope it helps Good* I say *it's good thanks* I'm trying not to float away my therapist says I do it every time I feel overwhelmed which makes sense but after 25 years it's a hard habit to break I hang up the phone *What* Cricket says she is more excited than I am *They have a Raymond Wadena Any relation* Cricket says I shrug my shoulders *Call him* Cricket smiles big as a winning sunflower at the state fair *What if he knows my father and tells him where I am C'mon* Cricket says rubs my neck *you don't have to be afraid of him anymore call him find out where your grandma is plus* she leans close to my ear whispers *I'm here now I won't let anyone hurt you* I pretend like she didn't just say that

Hello

an old man's voice says with a thick up north accent like my gramma's *Ah hello* I say think about hanging up telling him I have the wrong number what if my gramma hates me for leaving what if she is dead *I hope I'm not bothering you* I say *Not so far* he says *Okay* I close my eyes get spinny open them fast focus on the telephone cord *I'm looking for Martha Wadena Martha* the man says *who's this I'm um her granddaughter holy man* he shouts *her granddaughter Yeah* I say *that's me Well* he says *I sure do know where she is saw her and Snoos the other night that's her husband she married again after all those years right about the time you went missing I suppose Anna when was that we saw Martha* he yells *hold on my girl* part of me melts he called me my girl like my gramma did those words come home to my soul I hear a woman's voice in the background *Anna thinks it must have been last Saturday over at Legion bingo didn't win anything not a damn thing not even a cent on the pull tabs can you believe that* I'm in shock part of me wants to slam the phone down run from the room from Cricket saying she'll protect me from being multiple from the abuse from my therapist from my gramma *My girl it's good to hear from you she's been worried just sick about you for years now better give her a call Anna do you have Martha's number* he yells into his house I hear shuffling papers a muffled voice *I remember you when you were just a baby* he says *your folks brought you up we had a big party for you just a big party! everyone came just right out of the woodwork yeah it was a good time I'm your uncle your grandma's big brother hold on* he says *holy man still can't believe it Anna found it here go* he says *got a pencil Yeah* I say barely breathing *701 669 3724 they're over in the Jamestown area now Jamestown* I say floating away *North Dakota* he says *just over the border not too far Oh* I say *Better repeat that number to me don't want to be responsible for talking to you then losing you again now make sure you visit soon real soon hear me my girl say where are you you visit real soon Uh huh* I say don't tell him where I live don't want him to go on about my father want to keep that nailed shut *Anyhow* he says *you're welcome here anytime you're family always will be always welcome here with us now repeat that number for me calm my conscience so I can sleep tonight 701 669 3724* I say *You'll call* he says *she's been worried something sick about you forever now I'll call* I say *thank you You bet* he says *you bet oh you just bet oh*

Crumple cry

not worried about saving or being saved or killing anyone with my feelings I never had that power it didn't matter what I did or didn't do he was going to do what he wanted I didn't kill Patty I didn't rape her I didn't make my mother do the things she did Cricket sits down next to me slides her big boots across the wood floor hugs me kisses my ear *Baby* she says holds me I cry my tears like a thunderstorm release the remaining bits of sea fishes crabs broken bottles rusted tin cans fish hooks lost wedding rings marbles shoe horns pieces of elastic pens pony tail holders crossword puzzles bracelets mood rings paper clips puffy hello kitty stickers red heart shoe laces oversized orange combs dog collars an arrowhead a plastic mountain lion watches shredded pictures of dad mom pointy glasses broken fingernails spiders roach clips silky umbro soccer shorts empty chapstick tubes the wound insides of a baseball broken picture frames pizza boxes toe nail clippers a leather bag a small red stuffed mouse soggy post it pads the crooked tip of a razor a feather headress keychain a bottle of bleach snails leeches tufts of gray carpeting pills in a fluted cup a faded ripped University of Alabama sweatshirt empty vodka bottles a pack of Winstons manila files rough orange curtains a bird feeder plastic wrap hand lotion a condom McDonalds hot apple pie wrapper eyelashes feathers rain toothbrush chalk drawing paper a ripped in half bed a red stuffed dog a pile of shit coated nickels I gag Cricket holds me Cricket holds me Cricket holds me *Call her* she whispers once I stop *find out*

Gramma
I say
no sound
Gramma
rush of air inhaled breath drawn brow
My girl half a question half a flat line
no sound
Gramma I say one second two seconds it's me
My girl she exhales
spider crawls up my back follows my spine until it reaches my head knock knock
one vertebrae
two vertebrae
three vertebrae
four
no sound
knock knock find a spot push it in creepy crawly nurse pointy nose child psychologist suit man oatmeal lady judge
no sound
they made it worse!
one vertebrae two vertebrae three vertebrae four knock knock who did it they did it! they did it!
if they hadn't done that I wouldn't have lost gramma! I wouldn't have lost gramma!
I want to blame them do blame them they made it worse
one vertebrae two vertebrae three vertebrae four
he was afraid she'd turn him in
Gramma
no sound
one vertebrae two vertebrae three vertebrae four
he didn't want me to have her love
one vertebrae two vertebrae three vertebrae four

he didn't want me to escape
one vertebrae two vertebrae three vertebrae four
he didn't want to get caught
Is that really you
It's me
All these years my prayers
no sound
You've come back to me you'll come home she says
I see her bent over the countertop from when I was a kid her face in her
hands back rounded like a question mark
Yes I say it's true it's true it's the truth

Age 26 - Epilogue II

Trip trap

   trip trap goes the bridge *Who's that* roars the troll who lives under the bridge his eyes as big as saucers and nose as long as a poker *It's me* says Rock River Woman *formerly of East Rose Avenue one block off Payne and now of my grandma's people who are my people as well Well I'm going to gobble you up as a midmorning snack* shouts the troll No Rock River Woman says *I know my name now and you do not frighten me*

About the Author

Where did you grow up?

I grew up in rural and suburban Minnesota. Even though there are aspects of Minnesota culture that I don't like, such as "Minnesota Nice" which generally translates as passive aggressive behavior and leads at least some folks to feel like they never really know what is going on when encountering it, I have a deep love for the area. I moved away as a young adult, but I moved back to Minnesota ten years later because of my connection with the land and for the genuine kindness that does exist here despite this Minnesota Nice business. I have lived in four states other than Minnesota as an adult, and I always felt like I was not home. I always felt pulled back to Minnesota.

Why you are uniquely qualified to write this book?

Nickels is a work of fiction; it is not my life. However, I did set the story in two places I have lived: Minnesota and Madison, Wisconsin. The character, Little Miss So And So, who eventually grows into Miss So And So, does some things I have done, such as play sports. We are also both lesbians and survivors of sexual violence. However, this is her story and other than those rather broad similarities her life is not my life. Another qualification I have regarding writing a book like *Nickels* is that I have heard many stories of sexual assault from those assaulted over the past twenty years, and wisps of those stories are woven throughout *Nickels*.

Why did you write this book?

First, I wanted to tell a good story. I have heard a lot of people say that all the stories have been told and I always thought, are you kidding me? I know many stories that haven't been told and so I endeavored to write one. Someone also once said to me, about Sapphire's *Push*, that it was the best portrayal of dissociation they have ever read. I agreed. However, I decided I wanted to write about dissociation in a much more immediate and centrally focused way than it appears in *Push*—one of my favorite books. Another reason I wrote *Nickels* is that lesbian life is not portrayed much in literature and the little bit that is written about very rarely deals with homophobia and sexual violence, which are often inseparable, or with these under-the-radar poor and working class lesbian and queer communities that exist all over our country.

What do you think readers will get out of it?

A good story, no matter who you are or what you have experienced, along with a new or perhaps deeper understanding of surviving trauma, particularly incest, and how the intersections of gender, sexual orientation, class, and biracial identity can be both burdensome as well as sources of great strength, belonging, and love. Despite suffering years of abuse and humiliation and isolation, Little Miss So And So frees herself by accepting herself and that's an awfully good template for all of us.

Another thing I think readers will find intriguing is the protagonist's voice, created to most immediately and authentically convey the protagonist's point-of-view, including a rich inner world she creates to live through her parents' denial of her physical sovereignty, her developing personhood.

And lastly, I want readers to consider "girlhood" differently than it is typically portrayed. What does it mean that we continuously discredit, sexualize, and put down girls (she throws like a girl, screams like a girl and so on) when one third of those considered to be the epitome of weakness in our society are surviving sexual violence by family members and others close to them? Little Miss So And So is an example of how a girl is severely harmed by these things, and she is an example of the resistance and resiliency of girls, and by extension, the capability of the human spirit to withstand what we like to call "unspeakable" and "unimaginable". Little Miss So And So has to speak in order to recover her life, and the only way healing will occur is if there is someone there to listen.

What will you do next in your life?

Currently I am finishing a memoir and co-authoring a major research project about sexual violence against Native American women in Minnesota. I have another novel, *Carnival Lights*, which I hope to finish editing. It's an historical novel set in Minnesota in the 1960s and very different from *Nickels*. I also teach writing at a university and a community college, so I'm quite busy during the school year grading papers in a variety of Minneapolis coffee houses.

Biography

Christine Stark is an award-winning writer and visual artist whose work has been published in numerous periodicals and anthologies, including *The Florida Review*; *Feminist Studies*; *Poetry Motel*; *Hawk and Handsaw: the Journal of Creative Sustainability*; *Birthed From Scorched Hearts*; *To Plead Our Own Cause: Narratives of Modern Slavery*; and *Primavera*. She is a co-editor (with Rebecca Whisnant) of *Not for Sale*, an international anthology on sexual violence and her poem, "Momma's Song," has been released as part of the double CD/manga *Deadly She-Wolf Assassin at Armageddon/ Momma's Song* in collaboration with musician Fred Ho. She is a 2009 Pushcart Prize nominee in fiction and a 2010 Loft Mentorship winner in creative non-fiction. She regularly shows and publishes her visual art in galleries and periodicals. She also speaks nationally and internationally on a variety of social justice issues at universities, conferences, and rallies. Christine teaches writing at Metropolitan State University and Normandale Community College. She lives in Minneapolis with her partner, April.

You can reach her through her site **www.ChristineStark.com**

The Reflections of America Series
From Modern History Press

Soul Clothes
by Regina D. Jemison

Tales of Addiction and Inspiration for Recovery:
Twenty True Stories from the Soul
by Barbara Sinor, PhD

Saffron Dreams
by Shaila Abdullah

Confessions of a Trauma Junkie: My Life as a Nurse Paramedic
by Sherry Jones Mayo

My Dirty Little Secrets—Steroids, Alcohol, and God
by Tony Mandarich

The Stories of Devil-Girl
by Anya Achtenberg

How to Write a Suicide Note: serial essays that saved a woman's life
by Sherry Quan Lee

Chinese Blackbird
by Sherry Quan Lee

Padman:
A Dad's Guide to Buying...Those and Other Tales
by Mark Elswick

Nickels: a tale of dissociation
by Christine Stark

"Literature that is not the breath of contemporary society, that dares not transmit the pains and fears of that society, that does not warn in time against threatening moral and social dangers--such literature does not deserve the name of literature; it is only a façade. Such literature loses the confidence of its own people, and its published works are used as wastepaper instead of being read."

-Aleksandr Solzhenitsyn (1918-2008)

CPSIA information can be obtained
at www.ICGtesting.com
Printed in the USA
LVHW031927210322
713999LV00004B/111

9 781615 990504